two story HOME

Two Story Home

by

Tracy Broemmer

Women's Fiction

Published by Tracy Broemmer

Edited by Lexie Broemmer

Cover by Vanilla Lily Designs

Copyright © 2013 First Edition, © 2024 Second Edition

ISBN#: 978-1-951637-91-0

PART I
1ST STORY

CHAPTER 1

KAMRYN

Every day was some sort of anniversary, right? Somewhere, in someone's life, every day meant something special. Wedding anniversary, an anniversary of time on the job, the anniversary of a loved one's death. Even birthdays were anniversaries. Mark never forgot their anniversary. Mark never forgot to send roses to celebrate their wedding anniversary. He never forgot to send her *two dozen* roses on the twins' birthdays, never forgot to send her a dozen on Ian's birthday. Up until a few years ago, he sent her flowers—always something different, always a surprise—on little anniversaries. Like the anniversary of their first kiss. Which was well over twenty years ago. The anniversary of their first date. Again, well over twenty years ago. The anniversary of the first time they made love, twenty years and counting. That particular date was in September; Kamryn had only to look at the bouquet of asters and the card with the standard 'M' to feel the rush of warmth he always brought to her. When they were younger, the flowers brought an intense heat that made her wish he'd delivered them himself. Now that the girls were older and now that they had Ian, and now that life had taken them by the horns and run away, the asters just warmed her heart and reminded her that Mark was always and would always be there.

Aside from being drop-dead gorgeous (still), Mark McHale was a stand-up family man. Kamryn had listened to countless girlfriends complain about their husbands—most of them madly in love but still always able to find something to complain about. But she'd never had much of anything negative to say about Mark. Sure, he left the cap off the toothpaste just about every morning, and he ate left-handed even though he was right-handed, and sometimes he was overprotective and a little bit old-fashioned. But those were things she could live with. Things she had lived with for twenty-three years. Things she hoped to live with for the next fifty years.

Kamryn sipped her coffee as she nudged the mouse on her desk.

"What're you doing?"

"Trying to find something to do for dinner tonight," she mumbled without looking up at Adrie Fuller. She clicked through three recipes before turning away from the screen to look at her friend and coworker.

"What's tonight?" Adrie asked. She backed up and perched her butt on the desk behind her.

"House."

Adrie grinned. "Oh yeah. The anniversary of moving into the house."

Kamryn ignored Adrie's teasing and looked back at the screen. "I'm thinking of seared tuna."

Adrie nodded when Kamryn looked back at her. "Your kids really eat stuff like that?"

"They really do."

"Sounds good, then." Adrie reached to her right and picked up a Twix bar. Kamryn watched her open it and take a bite. "What kind of wine?"

"Chardonnay, I think." Kamryn clicked back through the recipes and then off the internet.

"Here's what I wanna know."

Kamryn glanced through the big glass office window to see what her patient was doing. When she saw that Steve was still working on the last set of exercises she'd given him, she looked back at Adrie.

"What?" She took another drink of her coffee and watched her friend. In the ten years that they'd worked together, she and Adrie had become as close as she'd been to her college roommates years ago. God or Lady Luck or someone had put really good, caring people in Kamryn's life, and there wasn't a morning that went by that she didn't say a thank you.

"If you and Mark and the kids have a big celebration dinner for the anniversary of the day you moved into the house, what do you and Mark do to celebrate the first night you christened it?"

Kamryn chewed on her lower lip as she considered how to answer Adrie's snarky question. Finally, she grinned and stood up.

"Depends on which room you mean," she said with a wink. She set her mug down on her desktop and left Adrie alone shaking her head at her, and went to check on Steve Mixer.

The new house anniversary had always been her celebration. No flowers from Mark; though she loved the flowers, she always told him they could send the girls to college with what he spent on the bouquets. Every year, for the past seven, Kamryn fixed dinner (something a little fancier than the usual casserole or cheeseburger), served it on the china she and Mark had received as a wedding gift, and the five of them (no friends or boyfriends welcome) sat down together around the dining room table (as opposed to grabbing a plate at the kitchen bar as time and schedules permitted) and ate dinner. And talked. They shared the highs and lows of their days, talked about TV or music or politics. There were no rules, other than mandatory attendance.

Kamryn had never heard any complaints. In fact, if she had to guess, she would say the kids and Mark enjoyed the night as much as she did. Well, she knew Mark enjoyed it, because as much as he traveled, and as often as he was gone, he had made it a point to be home for dinner on New Home Night.

The house wasn't new anymore. She and Mark had bought the land nearly ten years ago, but they hadn't started construction for a couple of years. Though excited about building their dream home, they were patient and tried to sock a little more money away. The idea of *socking money away* was diametrically opposed to parenting—especially with soon to be seventeen-year-old twin girls in the house— but they'd managed to save a little.

Two stories, gray and white stone, with a deep, dark red front door, Kamryn loved the house more today than when they first moved in. They had plenty of room, without having too much. The girls had their own rooms. Ian's room was across the hall from Braelyn's, and the master suite was down the hall at the other end of the house. Decorated in shades of gray—dove, slate, and down pipe (the name always made her laugh; she'd even asked their builder why it wasn't just called charcoal or wet cement) and white woodwork and cabinets, the house was cool and calming.

Each room had its own splash of color and personality. The throw pillows on the black leather sofa in the living room were a mix of burgundy and red and white. The granite counter in the kitchen was Bordeaux, their everyday dishes were bright red Fiesta Dinnerware.

The master suite boasted muted blues, and Ian's room (he'd been an infant when they moved in, so he didn't choose) was decorated in blues. A Chicago Bears fan, his room was currently an NFL shrine, complete with a Bears bedspread and Edmonds and Fields posters on the walls. The girls had chosen their colors, and true to their night and day personalities, their rooms were completely different. Ashton's was more like the master suite, ranging from soft, muted blues to midnight blues and almost blacks. Braelyn's walls almost knocked you over when you stepped inside. Purple—not violet, but not lavender. Just a shade darker than Easter egg purple. White carpet. And a purple, white, and lime green comforter, with geometric designs.

Kamryn and Mark had christened every room in the house, except for the kids' rooms, at one time or another in the seven years they'd lived there. Not that she planned to tell Adrie that.

Tonight would be bittersweet, though, because Mark, a pharmaceutical sales rep, would leave tomorrow for a three-day business trip. Sure, Kamryn was used to him leaving, used to him being gone. So used to it, in fact, that sometimes (she'd probably never admit this to him), he got in the way when he was home. They'd all learned to live in his absence, even Ian, and it wasn't that they didn't want Mark home more. It was simply that Braelyn had somehow gotten used to sitting in Mark's seat for dinner, and Ashton made coffee in the mornings, and she generally used the Starbucks brew, not Peet's which Mark preferred.

Mark had rocked Ian to sleep most nights and put him in his crib when he was a baby. And Mark had helped with the twins, of course, when they were babies. But now Kamryn handled bedtime, and showers, and homework—the triumphs of the good grades and test scores, the melt downs (of which there were plenty) and everything in between. There were nights when the girls forgot to tell their dad goodnight when he was home.

It bothered Mark; Kamryn could tell. She had been reading him like a well-loved and well-worn book for too many years not to know. But he never said much. He would wait for a commercial if he was watching TV or he'd close whatever document he had open on his laptop and go upstairs and tell them goodnight.

Kamryn watched Steve Mixer now. Forty-something, rotator cuff tear. Surgery. He was doing well now, but he had a tough time in the beginning. Kamryn expected she would be releasing him soon. She liked the success stories.

"Did you watch that movie last night?" Will Cheney called to her. Kamryn turned and looked at him over her shoulder. "The Bill Bateman Story."

Kamryn grinned sheepishly. Of course she watched the movie. True crime stories were her guilty pleasure. Okay, *one* of her guilty pleasures.

"So did Rena," Will said. He rolled his eyes.

"Hope you have two TVs," Will's patient mumbled.

Will looked down at him and laughed. "Oh yeah. I watched the game."

Kamryn usually watched the games. Didn't matter who played, whether it was basketball or football, whether it was pro or college. She'd been a high school and college athlete, and up until two years ago, she had coached Pius the X's girls' varsity basketball team.

But true crime movies often took precedence over games. *Especially* if Mark wasn't home. *Especially* since it was Bill Bateman. The guy had been arrested for murdering his wife, sister-in-law, and mother-in-law just a few years ago. Kamryn had gone through her usual argument with herself last night. She didn't want to watch the movie, because she didn't want Bateman to end up with a dime made from the movie. And yet, she had to watch the movie, because she had a sick, obsessive curiosity about what made people like that tick.

Mark laughed at her obsession. If he had been home last night, they would have wrestled over the remote control and ended up rolling all over the floor—laughing uncontrollably —until one of their kids had caught them and run out of the room, traumatized at the sight of Mom and Dad rolling all over each other.

Except maybe Ian. He might have helped her win the remote. Of course, then she would have had another fight on her hands, because Ian would've wanted to watch *Phineas and Ferb*.

"Mizzou won," Will announced.

"I heard that." She nodded. "Steve, you're looking good."

"All the same, I don't think I'll be ready for spring training."

Kamryn grinned. She watched Steve stand and pull his coat on. He was using his right arm, and he didn't have that grimace of pain anymore.

"Same time next week?" he asked. She nodded and watched him walk to the front desk to make the appointment.

"Rena said to thank you for the recipe," Will called across the open treatment room.

"You don't even know what you're in for."

"Well, if it isn't meat and potatoes, I won't eat it."

Kamryn shook her head as she ducked back into the office space. Adrie was at her desk, phone at her ear. Kamryn bumped her mouse and clicked on the file folder marked Mixer. She had just enough time before her next appointment to update Steve's file. That way she would be ready to send a note with him to what would probably be his final follow-up with the surgeon.

"What's for dinner tonight?" Will asked from the door of the office. "It's New House night, right?"

"Asian seared tuna and green beans. Rice. Chardonnay. And cheesecake."

At the last, Will's eyebrows lifted. "Cheesecake? From Henrietta's?"

"Yep."

"And you're bringing the leftovers tomorrow, right?"

"Leftovers?" Kamryn lifted only her eyes to look at Will. In tan corduroys, brown loafers, and the button-up black and tan shirt he wore, he could have passed for one of the girls' friends. She didn't know how old he was. She figured he was at least as old as she was-—if not older—but he had a boyish face that only looked younger when he grinned the way he was right now. "Have you met my family, Will?"

CHAPTER 2

ASHTON

Braelyn didn't get it. Braelyn *never* got it. Ashton kind of thought the whole *twin thing*—you know, the whole spiritual connection between twins, how when one feels something, the other feels it, too—was a load of crap. She loved Brae, a lot really, but sometimes she felt like they were the opposite of twins.

Braelyn wore her honey-blond hair long and curly. She had big blue eyes, like Mom, and she had a big, bawdy laugh that made everyone else want to laugh with her. She was an inch, maybe an inch and a half, taller than Ashton, though she was younger by two minutes. She was bigger than Ashton, period. She looked bigger, and she lived bigger.

Which is why she just didn't get it. Ashton had studied for the ACT for months. By the time she had taken the stupid test, she felt like she'd had her head run over by some obscure piece of farm equipment and her brains had leaked all over the garage floor.

Maybe that's what happened, Ash. You left your brains on the garage floor the morning of the test.

Brae hadn't given the ACT much thought at all. Sure, she read as much as Ashton, and she did well in school. In a *hold-onto-your-ass, fly-by-the-seat-of-your-pants* kind of way. Braelyn never gave anything much thought, which gritted on Ashton's last nerve. Well, no, actually it didn't *grit*. It stomped the hell out of that last nerve and made Ashton want to scream.

They got their ACT results at school today. In eighth hour. Honors English. Unfortunately, Mrs. Spencer, like most teachers, lacked any imagination when it came to seating charts, so she and Brae sat next to each other. All the better for them to share their results. Ashton got a 27, which was two points higher than she scored on the practice test. Braelyn got a 27. A point less than she'd scored on her practice test.

The headache had come suddenly, like someone had smacked her in the face with a shovel. Which, really, Ashton thought, was the equivalent of Brae scoring the same as she did on the ACT. She'd spent the remainder of English class— over forty minutes, because Mrs. Spencer had been so excited about the results, she'd practically shoved them down their throats the second they walked into the room—with her head bowed and fingers rubbing—sometimes gently, sometimes viciously—at her temples.

Mrs. Spencer must have realized she had a headache, because she left her alone. Ashton liked Mrs. Spencer, but on a day like this—CRAPPY ACT RESULTS DAY—*thank you, Mom for having to name every other damned day on the calendar,* she didn't particularly like anyone. Ashton hadn't even listened when Mrs. Spencer assigned homework. She tried very hard to hear nothing and stare at the blank white wall she was envisioning in her mind.

Of course, after school she had to wait for Brae. Again, most days it didn't bother her that they rode to school together, that they shared a car. But with that heavy, sinking feeling in her gut—like someone had thrown a bowling ball at her stomach and it had just knocked the wind out of her—and the headache, she hadn't felt like waiting for Braelyn to talk to every other person they passed in the hallway.

She had barely lifted her head for Garret's kiss as he jogged past them through the halls in a hurry to get to basketball practice. He would call later; she knew that. But neither of them had said a word to each other when he kissed her.

"Do you ever get tired of kissing him?" Braelyn had asked her when they slid into the car their parents got them when they turned 16. It was Ashton's turn to drive, but Braelyn had known without Ashton saying so that she didn't want to drive. Maybe there *was* something to the twin thing? Or maybe Ashton looked as bad as she felt.

"No." Ashton stared straight ahead.

"Did I tell you Andrew kissed me yesterday?"

That was news. Ashton pulled herself together long enough to twist sideways in her seat and look at her twin. Andrew Carter had been moping after Braelyn for nearly a year. They were buddies, like Andrew was Braelyn's best girl friend, or Brae was one of the guys, or something. Mom had been telling Brae from day one that Andrew liked her, but Braelyn had rolled her eyes and mumbled *whatever* so often that Ashton believed her.

"Like *hey girlfriend, see ya later?*" Ashton asked. "Like a smooch?"

"Like seriously laid one on me."

"When?"

"Second hour. Remember? Dr. Roberts asked me to take that envelope to the main office?"

"Yeah."

They had three classes together. Second hour—world history —was one of them. Ashton loved world history and Annica Roberts, the new professor Pius the X had brought in from some prestigious college. Why a woman as sophisticated and smart as Annica Roberts would leave a prestigious college to teach at Pius was anyone's guess. Ashton thought maybe she was certifiably insane under the knowledge of world history.

"He was in the hall, too. At his locker. Grabbed me and pushed me up against the wall by the chapel door."

"And?"

Braelyn looked at Ashton and frowned. She had started the car, chosen a song from a playlist on her phone, and turned the heat on, and then she just looked at Ashton like she didn't know what they were talking about.

Typical Braelyn McHale. She had already forgotten that Andrew Carter kissed her, that she had just told Ashton about it.

When they were finally home, Ashton had rushed upstairs to her room and closed the door. The colors never failed to soothe her, and the headache had lessened in intensity. But she was still angry with herself. It wasn't that she wanted Brae to fail. It wasn't even that she wanted to do better than

Brae. Just that she had been shooting for a 30—36 was the highest score—and she had fallen short. Much too short.

She flopped backwards over her bed and took a deep breath.

Okay, and the fact that she'd been studying this crap since last year at this time, and Braelyn never bothered to study for anything pissed her off.

She tugged the corner of the dove gray bedspread over her legs and turned to her side. Too many late nights. She had been up past midnight studying for a chemistry test last night. Almost midnight the night before doing calculus homework. And one in the morning before that, putting the finishing touches on a three-page religion paper on the Assumption.

She had to write something tonight for English. Some kind of essay. She had heard Mrs. Spencer's words, but she hadn't really processed them. She had calculus, too. And Spanish, although she figured she could do that while she slept.

Maybe she would just skip dinner tonight. Sleep for a few hours and then eat something later, while she did her homework. She could eat the spaghetti left from last night.

There was a light knock at her door as she felt her body start to relax. She blinked hard and opened her eyes. Five minutes. She hadn't even had five minutes.

"Ash?"

Ashton pushed herself up on her elbow and looked at her little brother, framed in her doorway. He pushed his round glasses—she thought of them as *Harry Potter* glasses—up on his nose and stepped inside her room. Just a step.

"Hey, Ian," she said softly.

"Mom wants you to come downstairs."

Ashton took a deep breath and sat up. She didn't *want* to go downstairs. She didn't want to talk to Mom yet. She didn't want to *move*. But she only smiled at Ian.

"Tell her I'll be down in a while?"

"Dad's on his way home," Ian reminded her.

Ashton rolled her neck and closed her eyes. *Oh yeah.* It was New House night. Dad was coming home. And Dad would be gone tomorrow. They were having dinner together tonight and discussing anything and everything and of course Brae was going to tell their parents what her ACT results were, and then they'd want to know what Ashton's results were.

Great.

"I'm coming." She scooted to the edge of the bed and stood. "How was school?"

Ian answered with a shrug. "Okay."

Born a few weeks premature, Ian had always been scrawny. He didn't have a lot of health problems, unless you counted his allergies, and she didn't. He wore glasses and was pretty much blind as a bat without them. He picked up colds the way some people picked up milk at the grocery store. But he never had issues with his lungs or heart.

"Where's Moses?" she asked as she followed him out of her room. As if in answer when he heard his name, the miniature black dachshund trotted into the hallway from Ian's room. "Hey, buddy."

Moses licked her nose and her face when she picked him up to cuddle him. Ian watched her carefully. Though Moses had been under the Christmas tree a couple years back for all three of them, he had somehow become Ian's dog. Ashton didn't mind. In fact, she was glad Moses had attached himself to Ian. Brae felt the same way.

Brae was sprawled on the couch watching TV, but Mom was in the kitchen. Ashton slid onto a barstool, but she turned to see the TV. One of those stupid shoes on TLC, something about weddings and bride wars. She looked away as she felt the pounding pick up again in her head.

It wasn't even three-thirty yet. Dad wouldn't be home until after five, at least. Why did she have to sit down here and listen to the TV?

"Hey, Ash." Mom offered her a smile. "How was your day?"

"Okay," Ashton answered, because anything less than okay would invite questions and she didn't care to get into *any* details yet.

"Is something wrong?"

Hmm. So now okay *invites questions, too.* She should have stopped in the bathroom. Maybe she looked like something Moses hacked up now and then. Ian hadn't said anything, but then, Ian wouldn't.

Ian, who was now holding Moses, stood at the counter and took a big drink of his white milk. When he set his glass down, he looked up at her and grinned.

Ashton leaned over and wiped his milk mustache away and then looked back at Mom.

"Just have a headache."

"How come?" Mom frowned. Her hands, which had been slicing a cucumber, stopped as she waited for Ashton to answer her. "Are you coming down with something?"

Ashton resisted the urge to roll her eyes. Can't have a headache without being sick. Can't cut your finger without needing stitches. Some days, Mom made her nuts. It was nice when she was little, having a mom who was so involved in her life. But these days, she wished her mom would back off just a little.

"No, I'm just tired," she answered finally. Mom glanced at the clock.

"Why don't you go upstairs and lay down for a while? I'll have Ian come and get you when dinner's ready."

Ashton smiled and grabbed a slice of the cucumber. "Thanks, Mom."

CHAPTER 3

KAMRYN

DINNER HAD BEEN JUST a shade off perfect, but Kamryn *didn't do* perfect. Contrary to what her coworkers and maybe even some friends might say, Kamryn seldom had it all together. She scrambled just the same way millions of other working moms did. She didn't aspire to perfection; both because she knew she would never achieve it and because she didn't want it.

Perfection didn't allow for mistakes and improvement, and Kamryn believed in both. The food had been okay; she wasn't crazy about tuna, but it was something different. She got tired of the same old, same old every night, and she knew everyone else did, too. The conversation had been better than the food, except maybe for the cheesecake—there really wasn't much better than Henrietta's cheesecake—though Ashton had been too quiet. She had only chimed in when there had been a loll in conversation, like she wasn't listening but didn't want to be *caught* not listening.

Kamryn hated that Ash was so hard on herself. Ash's ACT score hit her hard in the heart, but only because she knew it bothered Ashton so much. She and Mark were proud of both girls.. Brae was thrilled with the 27, ready to run with it and find a college that would provide her with a fun learning environment.

Kamryn feared that even though Ash was above average intelligence, she didn't know the true meaning of the word *fun*. She could take a lesson in fun from Brae, but then again, Braelyn didn't seem to know the meaning of the word *serious*. Instead of twins, sometimes her girls seemed polar opposites.

"A piece of gold for your thoughts, milady."

Kamryn groaned and sank back into Mark's arms. She rested her soapy hands on the edge of the kitchen sink and the back of her head on his chest.

"Just one?" she mumbled.

"Inflation," he said softly, but Kamryn wasn't listening. Instead, she closed her eyes and let go of the day, the week, while Mark brushed his lips over the side of her face and her neck.

"I've missed you," Mark said as she twisted to look at him. To touch her lips to his.

"Me, too."

"Dad?"

Kamryn pressed her lips together and pulled away from Mark.

"Hmm?"

Mark had taken off his suit coat and tugged his tie from his shirt collar the minute he had come in the door. Kamryn watched him now as he unbuttoned his shirt cuffs and rolled them back from his forearms. His shirt was still crisp, and the crease was still in his tan trousers. She wondered how he managed to look brand new all day every day, whether he was in a plane, the car, or on sales calls.

He looked expectantly at Ian now as he ran a hand over the five o'clock shadow on his face. Mark wore his dark, sandy blond hair short with the front combed to the side and sexy 1950's sideburns. Trim and neat, nothing *Fat Elvis* about them. Thick eyelashes framed deep brown eyes, and his smile was just about perfect. White teeth, mostly straight, except for the one he used to field a ground ball when he was seventeen. The tooth had been chipped, though he still played the ball with a bloody lip and thrown the runner out. A week before his mom had scheduled his senior pictures.

Kamryn remembered kissing the split in his lip and telling him the chipped tooth was kind of cute. Added a boyish charm to his smile. It still did.

"Would you check my math?" Ian handed him a worksheet.

"Absolutely." Mark nodded. Kamryn smiled, warmed by Mark's tone and the grin on Ian's face. She watched Ian climb up to sit on a barstool next to him.

"I don't like story problems," Ian said as Mark reached for the Chardonnay bottle. He had already had two glasses, the same as Kamryn. Surprised that he would want more to drink when he had to roll out before five in the morning, Kamryn topped her glass off and then put the cork back in the bottle.

Mark sipped from his glass and winked at her as she put the bottle back in the refrigerator.

"Story problems are funny."

"Why are they funny?" Ian asked with a look of suspicion.

"Well, because who has five oranges and wants to add four apples and a banana? If it were you, wouldn't you rather deal in cookies?"

"Chocolate chip?" Ian considered Mark's suggestion.

Mark raised his eyebrows and looked up at Kamryn. "Is there any other kind?"

"Mom likes peanut butter," Ian whispered to Mark. Kamryn grinned and turned back to the kitchen sink.

"Yeah, but that's Mom." Mark spoke quietly, pretending he didn't want Kamryn to hear. "Doesn't *everyone else* like chocolate chip?"

"Well," Ian sighed, "yeah. I think so."

"Okay, so for the rest of these problems, we're dealing with chocolate chip cookies."

"What about this one?"

Kamryn looked over her shoulder and saw that Ian was pointing to the last question on the page.

"If Train A is at a train depot in Boston and Train B is..." Mark frowned and looked at Ian. "What grade are you in, dude? I thought this was at least fourth grade stuff."

Ian giggled. "Dad, I'm in first grade."

"Wow. Ian, I think we need cookies." When Ian didn't move from the barstool, Mark nudged him with his elbow. "I think we need cookies to figure this out. Don't you?"

Ian studied Mark for a moment and then looked at Kamryn. "Mom, can me and dad have a cookie?"

Mark shook his head slightly. Ian moved only his eyes to look at him and then looked back at Kamryn. Mark held up two fingers.

"Two cookies?" Ian whispered incredulously. "Really?"

"Try it," Mark said quietly. Kamryn snorted.

"Mom, can me and dad have two cookies?"

"Yes, you and Dad may have two cookies," Kamryn answered. She let the water out of the sink and then dried her hands. "But I don't have any homemade."

Mark groaned and let his body sag on the barstool. He rested his forehead on the bar. "I'm not sure I can deal with packaged cookies."

"Mom." Ian tried again. "Will you make me and Dad cookies?"

"Are you nuts?" She laughed. "It's after eight o'clock, child."

"Sorry, Dad." Ian leaned close to Mark. "I tried."

Mark sat up, wearing a huge grin. "You did try," he said with a nod. "Can't expect any more than that."

Kamryn got the package of Chips Ahoy! cookies from the pantry and set it on the counter in front of them. Mark took another sip of his wine as she poured Ian a glass of milk.

"Two cookies, mister," she told Ian. "No more."

"Thanks, Mom."

Ian's grin hit her just as hard in the heart as Ashton's ACT score had earlier, but in a good way. Motherhood was all about those direct hits. Thank God, some of them were good bullets, packed tight with love and kisses and grins.

"Hey, Ian," Mark said as he dug a cookie out of the package. Ian, now sitting on his folded legs, looked up at Mark with big eyes. Moses nudged Kamryn's leg, so she leaned over to scoop him up. "We'll make cookies this weekend. You and me."

Ian grinned and nodded.

"And no, I'm sorry, Moses," Mark continued. "No cookies for you."

Moses stretched toward the counter, clearly interested in the bright blue package and the cookies inside.

"Okay." Mark crunched down a cookie and then took a drink. "So, train A, which was full of Mom's homemade chocolate chip cookies…"

Kamryn snorted again, set Moses down, and went to check the load of towels she put in the washer before she had started cleaning the kitchen.

MARK WAS in the office when she went to bed. He had helped Ian with his homework and then sent him off to his shower. The girls had locked themselves away behind closed bedroom doors shortly after dinner. Kamryn assumed Brae was on her laptop and Ashton was doing homework. Mark had pulled her away from the sheets she was folding and started an impromptu make-out session, but they had reluctantly abandoned the heat and the need when they heard Ian coming downstairs.

Rather than pick up where they left off, Mark had turned his laptop on and disappeared into the office. Kamryn had read for a bit, but she was tired, and she didn't want to wait up for Mark. She went to bed after ten, sure she would be asleep the second her head hit the pillow, sure Mark would be waking her up when he came to bed later, to make love. And yet, with her mind jumping from worry over Ashton and her obsession with perfect grades and a perfect grade point average to Mark working himself too hard, being on the road so much, she tossed and turned for a good hour.

She felt the bed move when Mark joined her, but she didn't stir, and he didn't curl up with her and slide his hand up her side. Apparently, he was as tired as she was. When they were first married, they had been typical hungry newlyweds. And even after they had the girls, and then Ian, they still made love often, most especially when Mark was leaving for a business trip or just returning from a trip.

Anymore, even as much as she loved him, Kamryn felt like sex was just one more thing on her to-do list when Mark was home. She rolled over onto her back and stared at the ceiling, wondering now if Mark felt the same way.

CHAPTER 4

ASHTON

"Seriously? You're not going?"

Ashton finished reading the fashion article in the latest *Seventeen* and then looked up at Braelyn. She covered a big yawn with her fingertips and then grinned at Brae.

"What?"

"You guys aren't going?"

"Going where?" Ashton took a small drink from her water bottle. She leaned over to tie her shoe and stretch her legs out while she was hanging from the hips. It had been a little warmer around lunch time; she and Garret had walked outside for a while. They had eaten their hotdogs on the go—well, Garret ate a hotdog and Ashton had eaten a small bag of crackers—as they walked, huddled together, around campus. Too brisk to be out long, but it had been nice to get out and feel the sun on her face. Which was exactly why Ashton had decided to go for a run when she and Braelyn got home from school. She had run last night, but the treadmill in the exercise room didn't provide the best scenery, and since it wasn't painfully cold outside, she had put on her Under Armor and run outside today.

Her cheeks were still cold, and she knew without looking that they were ruddy and red. She stood up straight and pulled the lavender headband from her ears.

"Good," Braelyn sighed. "Maybe now you can hear me."

Ashton rolled her eyes and took another drink.

"Are you and Garret," Brae spoke slowly, "going to Mason's party tonight?"

"Mason Jones?"

Brae raised her eyebrows and shook her head. "Is there another Mason at Pius?"

Ashton laughed and drained her water bottle. "No. We're not going."

"Why not? It'll be fun, Ash—"

"Because I don't want to," Ashton answered. She tossed the empty bottle into the recycle bin.

"So, what're you guys doing? Mom and Dad are taking Ian out for dinner and to a movie. You don't even have to stay home to babysit."

"We're not staying home to babysit," Ashton told her. She headed upstairs to take a shower, but Braelyn was hot on her trail.

"Then what're you doing? You guys never go anywhere. You're like an old, married couple."

"We're going to a movie."

"Seriously? Why would you go to a movie when you could go to a party? Last time we were at Mason's house, we had a huge Rockband—"

"Contest," Ashton interrupted Braelyn. She nodded. "I know. But we're not going."

"Why? Go to the movie, and then come to Mason's."

"Maybe." Ashton toed her shoes off and yanked her closet door open. Braelyn crossed the room and sat on the edge of Ashton's bed.

"Maybe means no," Braelyn groaned. Ashton laughed and turned to look at her over her shoulder.

"Nuh-uh."

"It does. Just like when Mom says *we'll see*, she means *no*."

Ashton considered Braelyn's comment and eventually nodded to concede the point. "True." She stepped into the walk-in closet, set her running shoes on top of her shoe rack, and then studied her jeans. She plucked a pair from a hanger and then turned and tossed them at her bed. When they hit the side and slid to the floor, Brae leaned over and picked them up.

"So, you're saying no," Braelyn said, "just to clarify, you're saying you and Garret won't be at the party."

Ashton pulled a green blouse from a hanger and then found a gray tank top in her dresser drawer. "This look okay?"

"Yeah, it'll look great," Brae mumbled.

"I'm tired, Brae," Ashton sighed. "I'm beat. I've been up late every night for the past couple of weeks. Garret and I went to that party last weekend. I just wanna do nothing."

"The party last weekend was lame," Braelyn argued. "Mason's will be fun. You need to have some fun."

Ashton shrugged. "I don't know. Maybe. I really don't even wanna go to a movie. I wanna put my pjs on and lie on the couch and stare at the TV."

Braelyn flopped back on the bed and stacked her hands behind her head.

"Sure you're not still mad at me?"

Ashton paused on her way out her door and looked back at Braelyn. "When was I mad at you? *Why* was I mad at you?"

Green and yellow striped thong and solid green bra in her hands, Ashton leaned against the doorframe and watched Braelyn.

"Eww." Braelyn turned her nose up as she sat up on Ashton's bed again. "When did you get that?"

"Get what?"

"The butt floss."

Ashton glanced at her underwear. She didn't feel like telling Braelyn that Garret had bought the thong and two others for her. Or that most likely when it came off tonight, it would end up in his pocket and back at his house. No way she could let her mom wash it, and no way was she up for this conversation. Not now. Not ever, probably.

"I got it the other day." She shrugged again, hoping Braelyn would drop it.

"Yuck." Braelyn shivered. "I'd rather just go commando."

So would Ashton, but when she and Garret had been at the mall the other day, he had seen the model in the Victoria's Secret window, and she was wearing a thong like this one, so Garret decided he wanted to get her one. Sure, he liked sliding her jeans off and seeing and touching nothing but skin, but the thong would be *so* sexy, or so he'd said. Ashton couldn't care less; most of the time she was into whatever got it over with quickly so she could curl up in his arms and sleep.

"When was I mad at you?" Ashton asked again. Sometimes she and Braelyn could get into knock down drag outs. And they were both skilled with the silent treatment. Though, they were both usually quick with an apology. But Ashton didn't remember any drama between them lately.

"The whole ACT thing." Braelyn stood up.

"Oh." Ashton raised her eyebrows. "I wasn't really mad at you. More like mad at myself."

"Whatever," Braelyn mumbled. She squeezed past Ashton and down the hall a few steps where she slipped into her room and shut the door.

Ashton stood silently for a moment. Now Braelyn was upset with her. Because of the stupid party. She sighed and then continued down the hallway to their bathroom. Garret wanted to see some stupid action movie. And then he would want to go somewhere and have sex. And what better place than her house, since her parents, Ian, nor Brae would be home. Ever since she gave in, since that first night they had sex, he wanted it every time they were together, and it drove Ashton crazy. Throw in the English test Monday that she should start studying for tonight and Brae wanting her and

Garret to go to the party, and Ashton almost wished the weekend was over.

She turned the shower water on before she stripped out of her sweaty running clothes. Naked, clothes piled on the floor, she studied herself in the mirror, giving the water time to get hot. Braelyn had bigger boobs than she did, but Ashton didn't think hers were too bad. Garret liked them. She guessed that's what mattered. He liked to put his hands on them and roll her nipples with the tips of his fingers. The first time he did it, it had taken Ashton by surprise, and she'd gasped out loud at how good it felt. Now he seemed to think she was dying for it any time he was around.

When the steam began to roll up and out of the shower, she stepped inside. The hot water felt good on her shoulders and her back. Good enough that she almost forgot about Garret and what he expected tonight. He loved her. She really did believe that. They had been friends since eighth grade, and they started holding hands in ninth grade, and then that summer, he asked her out. They had been together since, and Ashton sort of figured everyone expected them to stay together and for Garret to give her a ring sometime after high school.

Funny. She guessed she loved him. But she had liked him a whole lot more before they started having sex.

As she lathered shampoo in her pixie cut dark blonde hair, she wondered about Braelyn. She and Andrew were friends. Kind of like it used to be with Ashton and Garret. But they had never dated. Ashton wondered if Brae had ever been with anyone. If she had ever hooked up at any of the parties she went to. If her twin disliked sex as much as she did.

She kind of hoped not. She hoped Braelyn hadn't taken that leap yet. It just wasn't worth it.

CHAPTER 5

KAMRYN

Because Ian was premature, none of them was prepared for his birth. Of course, Kamryn had given birth nine years before, so she knew what to expect. Even Mark knew what to expect since he'd been with Kamryn through everything the first time. But there had been no bag packed and ready for the moment they ran off to the hospital. No one lined up to watch the girls, although Kamryn had left them alone on a couple of occasions for just small amounts of time.

Ian's birth had been no small amount of time, though. Kamryn delivered the twins within a couple of hours. But Ian, once he made it known he was coming, took his sweet old time. After seven hours of hard labor, Kamryn pushed the scrawny, low birth-weight baby out and cried from sheer exhaustion.

Though he had never been particularly unhealthy, and was only small for his age, all of them were a little overprotective of Ian. Kamryn guessed she was a little overprotective of all her kids, and maybe Mark was, too. He hated the fact that Ashton had a steady boyfriend but was just as bothered by the fact that Braelyn was heading out to a party tonight with a friend. Kamryn figured Mark might be more concerned that Brae might find someone to hook up with at the party, and yes, even at their uncool age, they both knew what *hooking up* meant.

Both girls were overprotective of Ian, but for the most part, he allowed it. Now and then he put his foot down and let them all know he was completely capable of doing his own homework or tying his own shoes—which he'd actually figured out just before his fifth birthday—or telling the bullies at school to leave him alone. He came home once with a bruise on his cheek and scraped hands and knees. When he told them at dinner that Sam Dawson pushed him on the playground, they had all been angry at the bully and worried about Ian. Ian only shrugged and told them he later caught Sam unaware and popped him in the face with his skinny little fist.

Probably the fist hadn't hurt Sam, and yet, just the fact that Ian had hit him and been seen by a teacher and taken his punishment—he was sent to the principal's office— without saying a word in his own defense seemed to strike Sam as courage or strength, because mostly no one bothered Ian now.

Ian wasn't really her baby anymore, and yet, Kamryn wasn't about to let him slip away too fast. It already hurt her heart terribly that her girls were nearly finished with their junior year of high school. She still babied them when she could, though those moments were growing further and further apart.

Kamryn loved the nights she and Mark spent with Ian. Sure, she wished Ashton wasn't out with Garret—truthfully, she wished she could just shoo Garret out of the picture, maybe just erase him from the scene—and she wished Brae had come with them instead of going to Mason's party. On the other hand, she felt a little more at ease with Brae's plans for the night than she did with Ashton's plans.

They bothered her.

"What?" Mark asked when she suddenly sat up straighter and reached for her soda. Ian dipped the corner of a chip into the hot, spicy salsa Mark preferred and then crunched it down in two big bites. Kamryn figured Ian didn't like the spiciness, but he wanted to be like his dad.

"Nothing." Kamryn shook her head. It wasn't nothing; this sudden worry about Ashton, just another on a long list, was far from nothing. But she couldn't talk to Mark about it now.

"You sure?" Mark picked up his bottled beer, but he only held it while he waited for her to say something. "You look like lightning just hit you in the butt."

Ian giggled.

"I'm pretty sure I wouldn't look like this if lightning hit me in the butt," Kamryn said and shook her head. "For one thing, I think I'd be smokin'."

"You are smokin', babe. Smokin' hot." Mark grinned and took a long pull from the bottle.

"Eeewwwww." Ian shivered.

Kamryn laughed and rolled her eyes. Her girls had certainly taught their brother well.

"I'm hungry, Ian." Kamryn nudged him. "Go see what's taking that pizza so long, will you?"

"Whatever, Mom." This time Ian rolled his eyes, and Kamryn could have sworn she was talking to one of the girls.

"What kind of party was Brae going to?" Mark asked.

"Just a party at Mason Jones' house." Kamryn shrugged. She and Mark knew Mason's parents. They had all worked together on fundraisers, and Kamryn had coached Mason's older sister before she had given up coaching. She had no idea what kind of party it was. She didn't think Mason's parents wouldn't condone drinking, but she also knew kids had a way of sneaking around and getting themselves into trouble anyway.

The last time Brae had gone to a party at Mason's, she and Andrew had won the Rockband contest. That's really about all she knew about what the kids did at the Jones' house.

"I hate it that the girls are at that age," Mark mumbled. Kamryn glanced at Ian, but he was looking at the Nintendo Switch Santa had brought him for Christmas. They had given both girls iPads but decided Ian was too young for one. He used Mark's now and then, and of course, now they were using them at school. Kamryn figured they probably should've gone ahead and given Ian one, too. Then again, they were always missing the boat on technology. Didn't help that each time the boat pulled away from the dock, a new, bigger, fancier ship sailed in.

"I know," Kamryn agreed. "Me, too."

She was still more concerned about Ashton than Brae, but she still didn't want to talk about it in front of Ian. It was one thing to wonder if the girls attended parties where they had access to alcohol. Quite another to wonder aloud if their daughter was sleeping with her boyfriend.

"Do you think they drink?" Mark asked her suddenly.

Kamryn opened her mouth to say no. But she couldn't make the word come out. She didn't want to think their daughters drank; she didn't want to think they did anything wrong. But they were kids; of course they made bad decisions sometimes.

"I don't know, Mark," Kamryn finally answered him. She and Mark had partied when they were younger. In fact, the worst hangover she'd ever had was the morning she took her ACT. Pretty dumb of her to party the night before the test, and she had known it. She'd managed to score a 25 anyway, and she had told the girls her score, but the not the events surrounding the test.

She and Mark had lost a good friend in high school. Drunk driving accident. They never swore off alcohol, and yet, both had seen too much of the gritty, ugly world of blood and internal injuries and EMTs to ever get behind the wheel of a car if they'd had too much to drink. They had preached to the girls over and over about the dangers of alcohol, of drinking too much, of driving after drinking. They had told them about Eddie Ferris; Kamryn had shared pictures of him —he was a cute guy under the long, shaggy brown hair—and told the girls stories about him and the things they had all done together. Maybe she had poured it on a little thick, but Kamryn had wanted Ashton and Braelyn to feel like they knew him so they would feel like they had lost him, too. So, they would think twice.

Always think twice, Kamryn had told them quietly. Always think twice, and never hesitate to call home if they needed a ride somewhere.

"Guess we have to trust them, right?"

Kamryn stared at Mark, but she could only nod. What if they had trusted Ash too much? What if Ashton was at their house right now, taking her clothes off for that kid? What if Brae was playing drinking games at Mason's house right now? What if Brae wasn't drinking, but Andrew was? Would Braelyn call them for a ride home?

Again, Kamryn squirmed in her seat. The worries might be different, but the sudden overwhelming fear, panic, wasn't. She supposed it was just part of motherhood. No. Not motherhood. That sounded so impersonal. Being a *mom*. Now and then fear for her kids gripped her so tightly, it felt like someone had stuck a knife in her lungs. Like she wouldn't be able to take one more breath. *What if? What if she ever lost one of them?*

"Kam?" Mark arched his eyebrows. "Are you okay?"

Kamryn looked up as their waitress approached the table with their pizza. She cleared her throat and glanced at Ian. He would never rat either of the girls out. She knew that. No sense in poking around there to see if he knew anything about them that she didn't.

Nope. Best just to let it go. She and Mark had raised them right. Now it was time to trust that they would make the right decisions.

"Yeah," she said softly. "I'm gonna run to the bathroom."

Mark nodded, but he watched her closely as she got up and walked away from the table.

Get a grip, Kam.

In the bathroom, she stood at the sink and stared at her reflection in the warped, perpetually dirty mirror. The last year had added crows' feet to her face, and somewhere in the last few months, her eyes had acquired permanent red lines and dark circles and instead of forty-three, she looked fifty-three.

Mark, though a good dad, wouldn't get it. Maybe dads just didn't get it. Maybe dads were wired so differently that they just couldn't get this kind of fear. Sure, Mark worried about the kids. But she had never seen him *paralyzed* with fear for the kids.

She sighed, turned the cold-water faucet on, and leaned over to splash a little on her face.

Get a grip, she told herself again. Everything's fine.

Ian was giggling like a hyena when she returned to the table. Mark was trying, unsuccessfully, to hold the laughter in. She slid into the booth beside Ian and looked from him to Mark, wondering what was so funny.

Ian's Switch was turned off and sitting on top of her purse. All three drinks were upright, nothing spilled. Each of them had a piece of pizza on his plate. Kamryn looked around the pizzeria, still no clue what they were laughing about.

"What?" she finally asked.

Ian only cackled louder. Mark shook his head and tried to shush Ian, but his voice broke in a wave of laughter. His eyes were glassy with tears, and his grin lit up the room. God, she loved him. Maybe she was too hard on him sometimes. Of course Mark loved the kids every bit as much as she did.

Being a dad might mean he was wired differently. But it was no less intense than being a mom.

"Mm-kay," she mumbled as she raised her eyebrows. "You guys are loony. I'm gonna eat."

Mark coughed and wiped at his eyes.

"This girl," he started, but he broke up laughing again. Kamryn looked down at Ian. He held up a hand, as if to ask for a minute, but Kamryn just shook her head.

"Eat, men," she ordered. "We're gonna be late for the movie."

CHAPTER 6

ASHTON

They went out for Mexican food at a hole in the wall place called Amigos. Garret had rattled about basketball, and he talked so long that when he stopped and asked her something, he caught her completely zoned out. She liked basketball, and she liked watching him play. It was especially nice that he was talking tonight and not just rubbing her hand and trying to play footsy with her under the table. Like all he could think about was getting through his food so he could get her somewhere alone and take her clothes off her.

And yet, she was so tired, and he seemed happy to talk, so she zoned out, thinking yet again about the ACT and her chances of getting into a good pharmacy program. When he caught her daydreaming, he only grinned and asked her what she was thinking about. So, she told him, and they had a good conversation about college and their future plans. Garret wanted to study engineering. He would do well in engineering; he liked physics and math. She kind of hoped, though, that he would go to a different college than she did.

Preferably one that was kind of far away. Maybe someday, when they were done with college, they could find each other again. But for now, it was just too much. *Garret. Love. Sex. Dates.* It was all just too much for her to deal with, and she hated that she felt that way. She hated herself for how she was feeling about Garret because he was a good guy. She didn't want to hurt him.

When they left Amigos, they went back to her house. The thought of getting naked and letting him touch her and doing all that other stuff left her feeling a little worn and a little irritable. She told him to go on up to her bedroom, that she would be there in a minute. God only knows what he thought she was doing, something to enhance his experience probably. She stood at the kitchen counter for a minute, thinking. Wondering. She inspected the two open bottles of wine, trying to decide which bottle would go unnoticed if she nipped a bit from it. In her left hand, she held a bottle of Pinot Noir, and in her right, she held a bottle of Cabernet Sauvignon. She knew her parents enjoyed drinking wine, that they only bought what they thought was good. She hated all of it, including the Chardonnay she knew she would find in the fridge. But she had found that sometimes it helped to take the edge off.

She had taken a drink from her mom's glass once at a party about six months ago. It had been right after school started. Her mom had been upset with her for not going out for volleyball. She had already been assigned two papers, and she had an English quiz the following Monday. Garrett had just discovered that she sometimes went commando, and his hands seemed to always end up in her jeans.

She sometimes went commando just because she forgot to get her laundry down to the mud room. Or because she hadn't had time to throw her delicates into the washer. Or because the pants she wore—she had a pair of super skinny jeans—were so tight they showed every line and left nothing to the imagination. She had never gone commando with the intention of turning Garret on.

That night, the first time she took a drink of wine, she had been ready to explode. So angry and so desperate for an escape from life, she had spotted Mom's glass and Mom was nowhere to be seen, so she took a drink. And then another. The red wine was warm and sort of bitter, and it made her pucker up and even quiver in distaste. But then something magical happened.

She felt the heat slide down her throat and into her stomach. She actually felt the wine flow through her blood and coat her nerves, like a balm on sunburned skin. Ashton had been prepared to make excuses, to laugh off her mom's questions if she was caught. To say something fun like, "hey, Mom, it's a party! Come on!"

But no one had seen her. And on the occasions since then, when she found herself standing at the counter, studying the wine bottles and finally giving in and drinking as much as a glass at a time, she hadn't been caught.

She could hear Garret moving around upstairs. Probably taking his clothes off and getting into her bed. She wondered if he remembered to grab a towel from the bathroom. *Towels* she could throw in the wash when they were done, but her mom might wonder why she washed her sheets at odd times on the weekends.

A glance at the microwave clock—it was after eight—spurred her into action. She wiggled the cork out of the bottle of Pinot Noir and drank straight from the bottle. One swallow.

Two swallows. She was getting better about drinking, but she wasn't sure that was a good thing. It wasn't that she actually liked the taste of the wine, or the vodka either when she had tried that, but she didn't feel like she was twisted up and turned inside out now when she drank it.

One more big swallow, and she put the cork back in the bottle, put the bottle back on the counter next to the wine rack, and then hurried upstairs. She would have liked to stand there for a minute. To sip it slowly, so she could feel the warmth come on gradually. So, she could enjoy that numbing feeling. But she didn't have time for that. Not tonight.

She needed to make sure they were done and gone before Mom and Dad came home.

"What're you doing, Ash?" Garret called when she ducked into the bathroom.

"Be right there," she answered over her shoulder. She brushed her teeth quickly, but thoroughly, and then swished a mouthful of Scope. Unbuttoning her blouse, she hurried back to her bedroom. Garret was naked in her bed. For being a basketball star, he was actually pretty scrawny. Not that she would tell him that. He had hard little muscles in his arms, and his legs were all muscle. But his chest and shoulders were still skinny, and since it was the middle of January, he was pale like the underside of a fish.

Not that she was much to look at right now, she reminded herself. She was as pale as he was, and probably fat, too. She had only run three nights this week, instead of the usual six. And she had eaten the burrito tonight, not to mention three sodas this week.

Garret watched her pull her tank off over her head and then reach back and unhook her bra. But when she started to unbutton her jeans, he sat up and shook his head. Oh yeah, she reminded herself. The thong fantasy. So, she stepped closer to him and let him unbutton and unzip her jeans and push them slowly over her hips. Too slowly in her opinion. As he plastered his open mouth over her belly button and started to inch down, she turned and watched her open door.

They wouldn't be home for a while, and she would hear them when they did get home. But this still made her nervous. She pushed him back on the bed, after he slid his hands inside her jeans and over her butt and fingered the thong. Gracefully climbed on top of him, watched him roll the condom on and then took him inside her.

Graceful ended there, though, as Garret flipped her over and went at it hard and fast. The wine finally numbed her a bit, and she lay quietly, moving an inch here or there, until he was done. She listened to him gush about how good it was, how much he loved her, and then finally, she half sat up, kissed him like she was madly in love with him and what they just did, and stood up to get dressed.

As she figured, Garret stuffed the thong into his pocket and then dressed and followed her downstairs.

"Wanna watch a movie?" he asked her as she started a load of towels in the washer.

She looked at him, still so caught up in her thoughts about why she was doing all this that she was almost surprised to find he was still there. She didn't want to watch a movie. She didn't want to be alone with him.

Actually, she wanted to go to bed and cry. The first few times had been kind of new and fun, but now mostly she just wanted to cry when it was over.

"Wanna go to Mason's party?" she asked him. She wanted to be with Brae. She wanted to talk to Brae. To know if Brae had done this, if she liked this. Or if there was something wrong with her because she didn't.

And maybe since it was a party, she could score a beer or something. Surely if a little wine could calm her down about sex or studying or tests or whatever, a beer might make her stop thinking about any or all of the above, right?

"Really?" Garret raised his eyebrows. "You wanna go to Mason's?"

It was very unlike her; she knew that. And she didn't want to raise any flags to Garret that something might be wrong. While she did want to talk, and right at the moment, she wanted to talk about *IT*, she wanted to talk to Brae, not Garret.

"Yeah," she said with a smile. "I don't wanna stay here. I've been studying all week. Let's do something fun."

Garret nodded. "Okay."

As soon as she got out of Garret's Mustang, she could hear music. More than that, she could feel the bass pumping in her bones. Okay, maybe this was good. Maybe this was what she needed. A place to slip away from Garret for a while. They hurried up the driveway—Mason lived out past civilization; Ashton thought they should have a barn and chickens—and then Garret just opened the front door, and they walked in.

It was chaos, and most of the time, Ashton hated chaos. But not tonight. Tonight, chaos was perfect. Garret offered to get her a beer, and she nodded eagerly. Room to breathe while he was gone looking for the keg, and the hope of a beer when he did finally return. She slipped into a crowd of people in the family room as Garret disappeared.

But she quickly realized she was surrounded mostly by guys, and that they were watching some kind of porn on a big screen TV, and she certainly didn't need more of that tonight. She pushed through the other side of the crowd and found herself in the kitchen. Two girls from her Spanish class were snitching some chips and salsa. They said hi to her, and Ashton knew them well enough to stay with them. To have a conversation with them. But right now, she was looking for Brae.

Ashton followed the noise down the steps into the basement, where she finally found her twin playing air hockey with Andrew. A crowd was gathered around watching them. Brae had her hair pulled back in a ponytail, so Ashton knew she was in serious game mode. Brae hated to lose. Whether it was Monopoly or air hockey or volleyball, she hated to lose.

Ashton said hi to a few people, asked a guy from her ethics class who was winning the game, and nodded when he told her Braelyn was. Upstairs the music had been something hip-hoppy and most definitely headachy. Down here it was Jefferson Starship. Much better. She watched Brae score again, and she watched her flash Andrew a brilliant grin and she wondered again about her twin. Did she love Andrew? Did she drink? Of course, she had a beer or two at parties like this. Who didn't? But had Brae ever needed a drink just to get through a night of studying?

She wished she could talk to Braelyn. For a minute, the need to talk to Brae was so strong, tears burned her eyes.

"There you are." Garret's voice reached her just as she felt his breath on her neck and her ear. She smiled at him and took the beer he offered her.

"Ash!"

Ashton turned around to see Braelyn rushing toward her. She took a long swallow of the beer and grinned at Brae.

"You came!"

Ashton bit her lip before she could say anything that might require an explanation.

"Play me," Brae said with a nod to the air hockey table. Ashton took another drink and then nodded. *Why not?* She needed this. She needed time to just forget everything and have fun. Isn't that what Mom always told her? To relax now and then? To let go and have fun?

Okay, so Mom probably hadn't meant for her to get drunk, but then again, she wasn't *drunk*. And she wasn't driving, anyway.

"I'm on a roll," Brae told her. "I've won six games in a row."

"Oh, it's on now," Ashton said with a laugh. She tipped her plastic Solo cup, drained it, and handed it to Garret. He stood with Kyle Winters, his best friend, and watched her play. But after a while, and another beer that he brought her, she tuned him out and forgot he was there.

She laughed. She laughed often and hard, so hard she thought she might pee her pants. She and Brae laughed so hard, they cried. After the third beer, she knew she had to stop, that she was probably legally drunk. And she had to be able to walk into the house and act normal, just in case her parents were in the living room when she came home. Besides she didn't *want* to be drunk. She didn't want to feel like shit tomorrow. She had only wanted to take the edge off.

The edge was most definitely gone, she decided as Garret walked her up the steps, through the house, and back out to his car. Even the drive home was okay, with Garret holding her hand and rubbing his thumb over her wrist. And the good night kiss was actually pretty nice.

In fact, the kiss felt so nice that she kind of wanted it to go a little further. She kind of wanted to unbutton her blouse again. But then Garret had set her gently back in her seat and whispered that her dad would be out looking for her if she didn't get in the house.

He was right. Of course he was right. Her dad wouldn't hesitate to walk right up to Garret's car, open the door and haul her out by her ear, if he thought they were making out.

"Call me tomorrow?"

Garret nodded, kissed her on the cheek, and then helped her out of the car and to the door. Before she could unlock it, Andrew's black Chevy truck pulled into the driveway behind Garret, and he jumped out of the driver's seat. He called a greeting to them, as Braelyn got out of the truck, and they walked up to the door together.

"Are you gonna kiss her?" Ashton asked Andrew.

"Ashton!" Braelyn groaned and shook her head.

"Because I wanna see you kiss her," Ashton said. "She told me you kissed her the other day. And I'm thinking it's about time, so now I wanna see you—"

"Ash." Garret cupped her face in his hands and kissed the tip of her nose.

"Hmm?"

"Get in the house. Now."

Ashton took a deep breath, leaned forward and rested her head on his shoulder for a minute, and then straightened.

"Right." She nodded. "Night, Garret. See ya, Andrew."

Without another word or even a glance at Brae and Andrew, Ashton unlocked the front door and stepped inside. The TV was on; she could hear it down the entrance hall.

She wondered who was up. It wasn't quite midnight; she had time to spare. Or more importantly, Brae had time to spare. It would be nice if she had a chance to get upstairs and brush her teeth before she talked to either of her parents, but that wasn't likely to happen.

"Hey." Her mom looked up when she dropped her keys on the kitchen counter. Mom was dressed in sweats, wearing her reading glasses. Curled in the recliner, she had a book in her lap, but her eyes were bloodshot like she either wanted to sleep or she had been sleeping.

"Hi."

"Where'd you guys go?" Mom asked. "I thought you might be here when we got home."

"We went to Mason's party."

"Oh." Her mom sat up straighter, and Ashton silently pleaded that she wouldn't ask a ton of questions. "Was it fun?"

"Yeah."

"Lot of people there?"

Pretty much the whole junior class, but Ashton didn't say so.

"Yeah."

"Did you see Brae?"

"Yeah. She's outside. With Andrew."

Her mom grinned. "Really? Can we spy on her?"

Ashton laughed. "No, Mom. That's gross." Even though she'd just told Andrew she wanted to see him kiss Brae, not even five minutes ago.

"I'm kidding."

Her dad stretched on the couch. He must have been sleeping. The movie playing on the big screen TV most definitely seemed like something he would pick, but apparently, he had gone to sleep, so Mom had decided to read while they waited up for her and Brae.

"Do you think they've ever kissed?" Mom asked.

"Yeah, she told me the other day that he kissed her," Ashton answered. She took her coat off and then carried it upstairs, praying with every step that her mom wouldn't follow her.

CHAPTER 7

KAMRYN

Kamryn juggled the travel mug and her keys as she reached for the door. Adrie stood down the main corridor, just outside the office. She looked upset. Kamryn yanked on the door, only to nearly rip her arm off. She turned her wrist to look at her watch and spilled coffee on the pavement. Not quite seven. Will hadn't even unlocked the doors yet.

She flipped through her keys and took a drink of her coffee. Her purse strap slipped off her shoulder. She tugged it up with her right hand, losing the correct key in the process. Inside, Will hugged Adrie, and outside, Kamryn's heart skipped a beat. Something had happened. Something bad had happened, and she couldn't even get the damned door open to get to her friend.

She found the right key again, just as Rita Steinem, the receptionist, hurried to unlock the door for her from the inside. Kamryn smiled at Rita, said hello, and wondered to herself if this might be one of those Mondays from hell. Even though it was actually Tuesday.

Adrie stepped away from Will and wiped at her eyes, and Kamryn all but ran down the hall. She stopped short when Adrie turned to her.

"What happened?"

Adrie, at least a foot shorter than Kamryn and Kamryn certainly wasn't tall, ran her fingers through her long dark hair. Adrie was put together, as always, very attractive; though according to her, she needed to drop ten pounds off her thighs and another twenty off her butt. Her eyes filled, and Kamryn felt her heart slip a little into her stomach.

"They took Dad into the ER last night," Adrie told her. Her voice was strong, but she wiped at her eyes with her fingertips.

"Oh, Adrie," Kamryn said softly.

"He had a heart attack."

"I'm sorry."

"He's in ICU," Adrie continued.

"What are you doing here?" Kamryn asked. She reached around Adrie and dropped her stuff on the counter. Her travel mug tipped, and coffee spilled on the counter. Kamryn caught it before it touched anything important. She muttered a few choice words, but then reminded herself there were worse things in life than spilling coffee.

Like her best friend's dad having a heart attack.

"Mel's with him," Adrie sighed. Melanie was Adrie's younger sister. There was a whole slew of them, actually; Adrie had four sisters and three brothers. Maybe they would begin the whole *Taking-Turns-Taking-Care-of-Dad* thing now. Brother One would sit with him in the ICU, while Sister One cleaned his house, and Brother Two fixed his dinner. She and Mark had done this two years ago when his dad died.

Didn't matter if he was sixty-six or eighty-five. Old age didn't make death any easier to accept. Mark had been really close to his dad, and his death had hit him hard.

"Is there anything I can do?" Kamryn heard herself ask. Of course there wasn't anything she could do. She didn't know Adrie's dad, for one thing. Or the rest of her family, other than Melanie. Kamryn wasn't sure anyone ever accepted that particular offer, but everyone always extended it anyway.

She meant it sincerely, and she hoped Adrie knew that.

"Thanks." Adrie nodded. "Just praying right now that he pulls through."

Kamryn didn't know how old Adrie's dad was or if a bypass was in the picture. She should ask, but her first patient was due to be here in less than twenty minutes, and she needed to get to her computer to check her notes. Adrie needed to do the same. Unfortunately work meant work, and there was never enough time to catch up.

She and Adrie used to go out now and then after work to grab a quick dinner or once in a great while, a drink. But those nights had fallen off the calendar without Kamryn even noticing. When had she become so busy? It didn't really make sense to find herself so crazy busy when her girls were getting older. They had been driving for almost a year. Ashton hadn't even played volleyball last fall. Neither of them had a real job, although she and Mark had been pushing them both to find one. Ian wasn't involved in much outside of school. He had tried Cub Scouts, but he hadn't been too crazy about it. He played baseball, but that was Mark's deal. Kamryn went to his ballgames, but it wasn't like he played ninety games a season like the majors.

She quit coaching when the girls were freshmen. Things had been so damned nuts then, with Mark gone so often, and both girls involved in volleyball and English Club and Spanish Club. That had been the year Ian was in Scouts, and he had been taking piano lessons then, too.

Just thinking about it made her tired, and most of that insanity had ended. Then again, there was all this new insanity. The new worry. Ashton and her steady boyfriend. The grades and the testing scores and college visits and the parties and Ian. She *always* worried about Ian. Every day she dropped him off at before-school daycare, and she hated that she had to do that, but with Mark gone so much, it just seemed easier to do it that way. Maybe it was time to change her hours. But if she did that, she wouldn't be home with Ian after school.

"You okay?"

Kamryn looked up when Adrie nudged her. *Wow.* She had just timed out right there in the middle of the hall. For just a minute she thought about how good it would feel to dump all of this at her friend's feet. Not necessarily so Adrie could make it better. Just to say it and know someone was listening. Mark was a good listener, but like most men, he wanted to fix things when maybe there *wasn't* any fix for something. He didn't get that sometimes she just needed to talk, to say what was on her mind. That sometimes she cried, but it didn't mean anything.

"I'm fine," she told Adrie with a smile. "Obviously, I'm gonna have one of those days," she added, nodding at the coffee mug.

Adrie laughed.

KAMRYN PUT it all out of her mind—the whole nine yards—and poured heart and soul into patient care. She wrote a note for Steve Mixer's surgeon and wished him well when he left, note in hand. She worked with Eden Casey, one of the girls who had played for her when she coached the Pius basketball team. Eden, now playing basketball for the local college team, had torn her ACL for the third time in the holiday tournament. Kamryn and Mark had been at the game, and Kamryn knew the second Eden went down that she wasn't getting up anytime soon.

At six one, Eden towered over Kamryn. She was attending college on a scholarship; Kamryn thought she might be the best basketball player she had ever seen. She could see her playing in the WNBA one day, though she wouldn't encourage it. Why not go to college and have a real plan and get a serious career? Especially after the same injury took her down the third time.

"Kam?"

Eden, who had been telling Kamryn about a date the previous Friday, stopped talking, and Kamryn looked toward the office. Adrie was leaning out the door.

"Yeah?"

"Your cell phone is ringing."

"Excuse me," Kamryn said to Eden. She hurried to the office and grabbed her cell from her purse. "Hello?"

She hadn't bothered to look at the caller ID. No one called her at work unless it was serious. Had to be one of the kids.

"Mommy?"

She sucked in a deep breath and dropped to the first available seat. Will's. She looked around, eyes stopping on a picture of his wife.

"What's wrong?"

"I don't feel good," Ian told her.

"What doesn't feel good, buddy?"

"I threw up."

She squeezed her eyes shut. "You did?"

"Yeah. I didn't wanna eat that lunch, but I had to," he explained. "My tummy didn't feel good before the peas."

Kamryn laughed softly.

"Okay, buddy." She ran her fingers through her hair. "Hang on. Let me move some appointments around, and I'll be there."

"Thanks, Mommy."

Again, with the bullet in the heart. She hit end on her cell and dropped it back in her purse.

"I got it," Adrie told her. "Go get him."

Kamryn shook her head. "I'll just reschedule."

"Just go. I've got it."

"Adrie," Kamryn argued. "You don't have to—"

"I know, but Mel's with Dad. I'll go up after I leave here."

"I have four appointments."

"Okay, go."

Kamryn sighed. If it were one of the girls, she would tell her to go on home and get in bed. And she would go home after work and check on her. But Ian couldn't drive, obviously. Mark was gone again, of course, so she had to go get him. She couldn't leave him there to vomit again.

She nodded, grabbed her purse, and then went out to apologize to Eden. Adrie followed her out and assured Eden, tongue in cheek, that she could handle her care. Anxious to get to Ian, Kamryn left the two of them there talking, but she felt rotten for leaving Adrie when she had the true emergency.

All that guilt was gone, though, when she stepped into the school office and saw Ian sitting in the chair in the corner waiting on her. He sat all the way back in the chair, so his legs dangled. His cheeks were fire engine red, and his eyes were watery and dull behind his glasses. His hair was mussed, like he had sweat and run his fingers through it. Probably when he threw up.

"Hey, Ian." She reached out to him. "Let's go home, bud."

He stood up, put his coat on, and then pulled the straps of his backpack up over his shoulders. Kamryn signed him out and thanked Mrs. Miller for letting him call. As they walked, he slipped his hand into hers.

"So, you think it was the peas, huh?" she asked as she helped him climb up into the SUV.

"They were gross," he announced. "You were supposed to fix me cold lunch today."

Kamryn had buckled his seat belt, and she was backing away from the SUV to shut his door. But she stopped and stared at him.

"I was?"

"Mm-hmm."

"Oh, Ian, I'm sorry, honey." She leaned over and kissed his head. His hair was sweaty, and he was burning up right now.

"I hate peas."

"I know."

"And chicken fried steak."

"I forgot, Ian."

He nodded and rested his head on the seat. She waited for him to say something, but he only rolled his head against the seat and looked the other way.

Wow. It has been a shit day.

Ian was quiet on the drive home, so quiet she thought he had gone to sleep. But just as she pulled into the driveway, he moaned. She hit the button on the garage door opener and turned to look at him.

"Mom, I'm gonna—"

"Oh, no!" Kamryn looked around frantically for something to give him. Nine times out of ten, she could find an empty grocery bag or a box or something in her SUV, but not today.

Ian leaned forward and threw up again. Kamryn took a deep breath. It didn't last long, and really, there wasn't that much.

But it was in the car. She pressed her lips together when Ian flopped back in his car seat and stared at her.

"You okay?" she asked softly.

He nodded. She pulled into the garage, careful to make sure she was out of the way of the twins' car. She had no idea who drove today; she had long since lost track of their driving schedule.

She got out of the SUV and hurried around to the passenger side. Ian let her help him out of the booster seat and then he climbed down. Kamryn picked up his backpack— thank God he missed that—and herded him into the house. She left the car door open but closed the overhead garage door.

Ian brushed his teeth while Kamryn pulled his comforter back on his bed and laid a blanket out on the floor. She put his garbage can next to his bed and then helped him strip out of his school clothes and into pjs. He crawled into bed, and she hurried down to the kitchen to get him something to drink.

While she was downstairs, she took Moses outside and hooked him up to the stake in the yard. Back inside, she put ice in a glass and poured Ian some ginger ale.

"You sure you don't wanna be in the living room?" she asked him. Normally she put a sick kid on the couch, so she was close by if he or she needed her. But Ian shook his head no.

"This is fine," he told her.

"Do you want a movie on?"

He nodded. "*Cars.*"

She set his glass on the nightstand and then squatted down to find the *Cars* DVD on his shelf. The phone rang as she stood up, but she didn't run for it. No one knew she was home, so she figured she didn't need to talk to whoever was calling. And if she did, she could call back.

She put the DVD in Ian's TV/DVD player and then handed him the remote.

"Are you still mad at me, Ian?" She stood at the foot of his bed, deliberately blocking his view of the TV. It wasn't often he got mad at her, and maybe it was silly, but it bothered her when he did.

"Kinda."

"Honey, you have the flu," she told him. "It wouldn't matter if you had eaten ravioli or peas."

"How do you know I have the flu?"

"Because peas don't normally make you throw up."

"I don't eat peas," he corrected her.

She sighed and nodded and tried again. "You have a fever."

"What's my temperature?"

"I don't know. But I can tell just from touching you that you have a fever."

"How can you tell?"

Kamryn's thoughts flashed to the vomit in her car, the vomit that at this very moment was settling into the black carpet. Making the SUV stink.

"I just can," she answered patiently. "I'm a mom. Moms know these things."

"I want you to take my temperature," he told her. He said it calmly, but she knew there was a threat involved. If she didn't take his temperature and prove to him that he had a fever, and therefore had the stomach flu, he would blame her. He would be angry with her for making him eat peas.

"Okay." She smiled. "I will."

She stepped out of his room.

"Where are you going?" he called.

"To get the thermometer, Ian," she answered.

The bathroom was looking a bit like a disaster zone. There was a small pile of dirty clothes in front of the sink, even though there was a hamper not two feet away. Kamryn sighed and picked up the clothes. She dumped them in the hamper and then reached down to pick up a price tag from the floor. Small, oval shaped and pink. *Victoria's Secret. Hmm.* Which one of the girls was spending money there, she wondered.

She tossed it in the garbage can, noticing something shiny at the top of the pile.

"Mom!"

Kamryn opened her mouth, thought better of it and closed it again, and then counted silently to ten.

"Coming, Ian." She grabbed the thermometer from the top drawer and hurried back down the hall to his room. She perched on the side of his bed and put the thermometer in his ear. He shivered, as usual, because his ears were ticklish.

"What's it say?" he asked when it beeped, and she pulled it away from Ian's ear.

"One hundred and three."

"Does that mean I have a fever?"

"Yes, you have a fever."

"And the peas didn't cause it?"

"I swear to you the peas did not cause the fever."

"Promise?"

"Promise."

"Okay," Ian said quietly. He turned to his side.

"So, you aren't mad at me anymore?"

"I guess not."

"I'm sorry I forgot your lunch."

"I know. But Ash forgot, too."

"What?"

"Whenever you forget, Ashton makes it for me."

Kamryn started to answer him, but she couldn't. She had nothing to say. Instead, she stood up and walked toward the door. Once there, she turned back to look at him.

"Do I forget your lunch a lot?"

Ian shrugged. "Sometimes."

Kamryn raised her eyebrows and took his word as a punch in the gut. She told him to holler if he needed her, and then she went downstairs. She grabbed the carpet cleaner and a couple of rags and went out to the garage.

As she let Moses back into the house, she remembered the phone had rung when she was dealing with Ian, so she went back inside to check the caller ID. Adrie's cell. She knew without talking to her why she'd called.

So today hadn't been just one of those days. An epic fail. Kamryn glanced at the wine bottles lined up on the counter. Thought about a glass. A bubble bath. Candlelight. She didn't want any wine, though. And she didn't want candles or a bath. She wanted Mark.

CHAPTER 8

ASHTON

Funny how the better she did in school, the better grades she got, the more pressure she put on herself to do better. To achieve more. She justified it to herself by promising that it would end. That she wouldn't drive herself this way forever. And yet, she knew she would. She had another year of high school, and four years of undergrad studies and another four years of school to get her doctorate in pharmacy. Yeah, so, see? Another nine years and she could back off.

If she wasn't dead by then.

She aced her last Chemistry test, and she got a ninety-seven on her English exam, and she got an A—Dr. Roberts didn't show them percentages, just letter grades—on the two-page history paper she turned in last week. Brae had done as well, but that didn't matter to her. Of course it would have if Brae had received *better* grades.

"What're you working on?" Ashton asked. She stood in the doorway of Brae's room. Brae was sitting on her bed, legs drawn up like a pretzel. She had a sketchbook open in her lap, and her hand and charcoal pencil flew across the paper.

Braelyn jumped, and for a second, Ashton thought she looked guilty. Like she had been busted doing something bad. *As if.* Their parents never seemed to catch on to anything either of them ever did. Not that Braelyn ever seemed to do any wrong, except for those Solo cups of beer she managed to milk all night, so people at parties thought she was drinking a lot.

"Nothing."

"What is it?" Ashton stepped further into the room. "What are you drawing?"

"Nothing." Braelyn tried to close the sketchbook, but Ashton sat on the edge of her bed and reached out to stop her. Braelyn had drawn Andrew. Just his face in profile, but Ashton could tell with one look that it was Andrew.

"Wow." She brushed her fingers over the page and looked up at Braelyn, whose face now appeared to be on fire. She looked like Ian, who was holed up in his room with a fever. "That's really good."

"Thanks." Braelyn nodded, but she closed the sketchbook. "How come you're not studying?"

Ashton snorted. "Believe it or not, I have nothing to study for tonight. And I finished math. And I read those English poems last night."

"Ashton McHale has the night off?"

"Awesome, huh?"

Brae grinned.

"So," Ashton nodded to the sketchbook. "Do you like him?"

"Sure."

"No, I mean *like him*, like him."

Braelyn started to answer her, but she stopped. She was quiet for a long time and finally she shrugged. "I don't know."

Ashton wondered how far she could push before Brae figured out there was something *specific* on her mind. Since she wasn't in the mood to talk about *what* was on her mind, she knew she would have to tread lightly with her sister.

"That kinda looks like you like him," Ashton said with another nod at the sketchbook.

"I do," Braelyn admitted. She grinned at Ashton. "And I don't."

"So, it's like the brother thing?" Ashton asked. She moved from the edge of Brae's bed to sit in her lime green bean bag chair. "You like him like a best friend? Big brother?"

"No." Brae tossed the sketchbook down to the floor and avoided Ashton's eyes. "No, not really. I like him. I just…"

Ashton cocked her head and waited silently for Brae to finish her sentence.

"I'm not ready for that," Brae admitted. "For what you and Garret have."

Ashton's heart punched in her chest. She was glad Braelyn wasn't looking at her, because she was pretty sure *her face* was in flames right now. Then again, this was kind of the opening she had been hoping for. Could she talk to Brae about Garret?

Before she could decide what to say, Braelyn continued.

"It's just that he's always there." She shrugged and raised her eyebrows. "Like...sometimes you don't have your own life. You're with him more than Mom and Dad are together."

Ashton laid her head back and closed her eyes. Braelyn was right.

"Well, then again, Dad might as well live on another planet as often as we seem him," Ashton mumbled.

Eyes closed, she didn't see Braelyn nod in agreement.

"I just wonder who you would be, sometimes, without Garret Jackson around."

Head still back on the bean bag chair, Ashton opened her eyes to find Braelyn watching her cautiously.

"Me too," she whispered.

"Do you love him?"

"I do," Ashton said with a nod. "But maybe not enough."

"What do you mean?" Brae leaned forward and stretched out on her stomach. She stacked her arms and rested her right cheek on them.

Ashton shrugged. "There's a lot going on out there," she said softly. "Sometimes I feel like..."

Okay, so she couldn't do it. She couldn't say it out loud. If she couldn't say it to Brae, how the hell was she ever going to be able to say it to Garret?

"He's holding you back."

Ashton studied the walls in Brae's room, the bulletin board with pictures tacked on it, the *Ed Sheeran* poster, the bright

colors—she felt alive in Brae's room. Alive and almost happy.
Like a kid.

The hell of it was she knew in her heart she was still a kid.
Suddenly she was in a pretty grown-up role with Garret, and
she didn't want it.

She finally met Brae's eyes and nodded.

"I was so surprised when you guys showed up at Mason's."

"I don't even mean the parties we don't go to." Ashton shook
her head.

"I know what you mean," Brae assured her. "You're not you.
You're not free. Everything you do, everything you think,
you have to filter it through the Garret process. *What will
Garret think? What will Garret want?*"

Ashton tilted her head as a small acknowledgement that Brae
was right.

"Which is exactly what I don't want with Andrew."

The phone rang. Ashton glanced at Brae's alarm clock. It was
just after six. Dad wouldn't be calling this early. It continued
to ring, but just as Brae sat up to pick up the extension in her
room, it quit.

"Mom looks pretty strung out tonight." Brae turned her head
to her door. Ashton wondered if Mom got the call and who it
was and what was bothering her.

"Yeah, well, wouldn't you be if Ian puked in our car?"

Brae laughed softly. "Poor kid."

"He's still mad at Mom for not fixing his lunch."

"How come he's not mad at you?" Brae scooted back to lean on her headboard. "You forgot, too."

"But I guess I'm just that charming that he can't be mad at me," Ashton answered with a shrug.

"Full of shit, too."

"Maybe Mom's getting sick, too."

"Oh God, I hope not." Brae shuddered. "I don't wanna get sick."

Ashton's stomach growled. She grinned. "Me neither. Wonder what we're doing for dinner."

"I don't know, but I feel like we shouldn't ask Mom."

"Ask Mom what?"

Ashton felt her heartbeat quicken yet again. She looked up at Mom, who had appeared in Brae's room so suddenly it was like magic, like *Harry Potter* or *Bewitched* or something. What if Ashton had decided to confess to Brae that she was having sex with Garret and Mom had appeared out of the blue like she just did?

"Who was on the phone?" Braelyn asked.

Mom frowned at her and told her it had been a consumer survey. "Why would you feel like you shouldn't ask me who was on the phone?"

"What's for dinner," Ashton told her. "That's what we were talking about."

"Oh." Mom stepped the rest of the way into Brae's room and sat on the end of her bed. "Hamburger Helper."

Brae turned her nose up. "No anniversary to celebrate tonight?"

"I needed something easy tonight." Mom reached out and laid her hand on Brae's leg.

"I like Hamburger Helper." Ashton put her foot on the edge of Brae's bed. She stretched her leg and then turned sideways to pop her back.

"Ugh, quit." Mom groaned.

"What's wrong? Did something happen today?"

Mom looked at Brae, seemingly surprised by the question.

"Adrie's dad had a heart attack last night," she said quietly. "He passed away this afternoon."

"Oh." Brae glanced at Ashton. Mom and Adrie had been good friends for years; Adrie was a little like an aunt and a little like a really cool *older* friend.

"Just after I walked out and left her with my four appointments."

"It's not your fault—"

"I know," Mom interrupted Brae. "I know." She nodded. "But still." She shrugged. Ashton scooted around and crawled forward when she saw Mom's eyes fill with tears.

"I feel bad for Adrie," Mom said softly. "And it reminded me of losing Poppy."

Ashton rested her chin in Mom's lap, while Brae leaned her head on Mom's shoulder. Their dad's dad had been a jokester, and sometimes a playmate and sometimes a typical grandpa, but mostly he had been well-loved and well-liked. And losing him had changed Dad.

Another thing Ashton had never brought up to Braelyn. Had she noticed the way Dad's smiles just never quite reached his eyes since Poppy died? Oh sure, there were times when everything was the way it used to be. Dad was still Dad, and Ashton knew they were blessed—she knew enough kids whose parents were divorced or whose dads or moms just weren't around because of jobs or because there was a corner bar that was more important to them than family-—but something fundamental about Dad had changed. Kind of like coloring a picture and one tiny little stroke went the wrong way.

Mom ran her fingers through Ashton's hair.

"I haven't had a chance to talk to Dad yet," she told them, and then she took a deep breath, and Ashton knew that was the end of it. Mom didn't break down often, not around them anyway, and if she did, it never lasted long. "Let's go eat."

Mom pulled Ashton up from the floor, and she and Brae followed her out the door. Ian's TV was on; Ashton could hear *Kung Fu Panda* playing.

"Is he sleeping?" she asked Mom.

"You didn't fix peas, did you?"

"Don't make me smack you, Braelyn McHale!" Mom called as she chased Brae down the steps.

CHAPTER 9

KAMRYN

Ian threw up again after dinner. Kamryn had gotten him to eat a few spoons of chicken noodle soup and a small bowl of cherry Jell-O. He'd been okay when she checked on him before bringing the girls downstairs for dinner. He had been sprawled back against his headboard, propped up on pillows, watching the second *Kung Fu Panda* movie.

He threw up when Kamryn had taken just two bites of her dinner. When he hollered for her, the twins watched her with raised eyebrows, curious as to how she would react. Apparently, she was looking a little worse for the wear tonight. First, they had been afraid to ask about dinner, then Brae had asked her what was wrong, and then they had acted like she might come unglued when Ian had yelled at her

She simply put her fork down, took one last drink of tea, flashed the girls both a smile, and hurried upstairs. Ian had thrown up, but thankfully, he hit the trash can so there was no mess to clean up. She waited with him in the bathroom while he rinsed his mouth and then brushed his teeth again. His cheeks were the same cherry red as his Jell-O, so she took his temperature again, not surprised to find it was 102.

"Did he get sick?" Brae asked when she went back downstairs to get him Tylenol.

She nodded as she poured out the correct dose of children's Tylenol.

Ashton groaned, and Braelyn asked if he made it to the bathroom.

"No."

"Oh, man!" Brae squealed.

Kamryn laughed. "He hit the garbage can in his room. It's fine."

"You're mean," Braelyn told her.

Kamryn looked at them over her shoulder. "So Ian says. Stupid peas." Brae and Ashton were still eating. Kamryn noticed Braelyn had given herself another small scoop of the hamburger and noodle concoction, but not Ashton. The girl rarely ate anything; she was always so concerned with her weight. Kamryn figured a little weight would do her good, give her a little color and boost her energy. Between her late-night study hours, the pressure she put on herself, and her fear of getting fat, Ashton always looked a little bit pale and rail thin.

"I'll be right back." Kamryn grabbed the small plastic cup of Tylenol and another plastic cup of water to wash the medicine down. Ian felt about medicine the same way he felt about peas.

"Yeah." Ashton snorted. "Good luck with that."

"I'm hungry!" Kamryn laughed as she hurried back up the steps to Ian. She still wished he had just crashed on the couch, would have been much easier to take care of him. Then again, *she* could use the exercise of running up and down the steps a million times a day.

Ian had told her he was over having to eat peas for lunch, but she could tell he was still upset with her. Unusual for him. Ian was always her buddy. Since when did kids actually eat what was on their lunch trays, anyway? When she was in school, if you didn't want to eat your peas or corn or whatever, you chugged your milk and then scooped the gross stuff into the empty carton and folded it all up so the lunchroom Moms and teachers wouldn't know.

He was sluggish and sleepy, and his eyes were glassy again. Kamryn was shocked when he took the little medicine cup from her and downed it in one swallow. She decided he must feel pretty rotten.

"C'mon," she said as he took a drink of water. She picked up the stuffed dinosaur he slept with. Mark had brought it home from one of his business trips when Ian was a baby. Ian had been sleeping with it since.

"C'mon what?" he mumbled. He put his head back down on his pillow and closed his eyes.

"Come get in my bed," she said, and she tugged on his comforter.

"No." He screwed his face up into a mean frown.

"Ian."

"What? Ash and Brae don't sleep with you when they're sick."

"They used to."

"Well, I don't need to anymore, either."

"What if you get sick? Through the night?"

He shrugged and rolled away from her. She leaned over to see that his eyes were closed.

"So, the peas today. Did they make my buddy grow up? You don't need Mommy anymore?"

"I just don't need to sleep with you," he growled.

Kamryn sighed. She waited a few more minutes to see if he changed his mind or if he asked for anything else. When he didn't move, she took the two cups and left his room. *Nice.* Her first grader had grown up within school hours today, and he was still pissed that he had to eat peas.

"Is he okay?" Ash asked her when she returned to the kitchen and dropped the cups in the sink.

"Yeah." Kamryn nodded. She started running dish water and then yanked the door of the dishwasher open. They used the dishwasher on a regular basis, but she often did the pots and pans and skillets in the sink.

"Mom, you haven't eaten," Braelyn told her. "Ash and I'll do the dishes."

"It's okay." Kamryn shrugged. "I'm not really hungry anymore. Why don't you guys do your homework?"

"Done."

Kamryn frowned and looked at Ashton over her shoulder. "You? You're done with your homework? And it's not even midnight?"

Ashton grinned.

"Don't you have a paper due next year or something? Shouldn't you start on that?"

"Mom!" Ashton laughed. "I'm not that bad."

"Sit down." Braelyn put her arm around her shoulders and turned her back toward the kitchen bar. "Eat."

Kamryn sat down while Ashton put her plate in the microwave to warm her dinner, and Braelyn started washing the pots and pans.

"Have you talked to Adrie?" Ashton asked her.

"No. She called earlier, but I was busy with Ian." Kamryn yawned and ran her fingers through her hair. "She left a message. I need to call her back. I need to call Grandma, too."

"For Ian?" Braelyn asked without looking at her.

"Yeah. I need someone home with him tomorrow."

"I'll stay home and take care of him," Braelyn offered with a grin.

"Yeah, and then I'll have double the make-up homework duty. No thanks."

Ashton put her plate back in front of her.

"Thanks, hon."

She watched Ashton take a wineglass from the cabinet, choose the bottle of Pinot Noir, and pour a glass.

"What are you doing?"

"Thought you might want some wine," Ashton answered as she set the glass in front of her.

"Did you guys wreck the car or something? Do you need gas money?"

The girls giggled. "No, Mom. You just look a little tired."

"A little tired," Kamryn repeated.

"Can we watch a movie tonight?" Braelyn asked suddenly. "A chick flick, since Dad's not here, and Ian's upstairs."

"Sure." Kamryn sipped the wine and toyed with her fork. She didn't really want the wine, she wasn't hungry, and she had no idea how she would stay awake for a movie.

"Ash?" Braelyn asked as she scrubbed the skillet.

"Yeah, why not? Whose turn to choose?"

"Mine." Braelyn nodded her head back and forth, considering their movie options. "How about *My Sister's Keeper*?"

"How about not?" Kamryn answered immediately. Braelyn glanced at her. "Not tonight, Brae. I can't handle that."

"How about *27 Dresses*?" Ashton raised her eyebrows and watched Kamryn, waiting for a reaction.

"That works." Kamryn nodded.

It wouldn't have mattered if they watched *My Sister's Keeper*, because Kamryn was asleep twenty minutes into the movie. She had called her mom and asked her to watch Ian tomorrow. Then she called Adrie, and this time she had talked to her for just a few minutes. It sucked, having left Adrie at work with her appointments and then missing Adrie's call and leaving a message apologizing for missing the call and offering condolences and then calling back and saying *I'm sorry for your loss* over the phone. That didn't cut it.

Not for a polite acquaintance and certainly not for your dearest friend.

Kamryn had cried before she got off the phone. She was okay until Adrie's voice broke, and then they cried together. Kamryn had offered Adrie the standard line again: *if there's anything I can do*. But this time, she felt the words being dragged up from the bottom of her heart. She sincerely wanted to help, and yet, she was unprepared at the moment to do anything for her friend.

She had seen *27 Dresses* three or four times, so when her eyelids grew heavy as she sat curled in the recliner, she let go. Ashton and Braelyn were flopped at opposite ends of the couch. Kamryn had felt a moment's peace, seeing the two of them together, the same as she felt earlier when she had found Ashton sacked out on the bean bag chair in Brae's room.

"Mom?"

She stretched and turned her head away from the voice. From the nagging poking at her left shoulder.

"Mommy?"

At this, she squeezed her eyes shut and then blinked and tried to focus. The girls were asleep on the couch, and the DVD was stuck on the screen with the options and the movie trailer constantly playing. Ian stood by the recliner, cheeks still flaming red.

"My tummy hurts," he whispered.

"I know, buddy."

"I threw up again."

"Okay." She stretched her arms up over her head and yawned. "Let's go rinse your mouth out."

"On my bed."

Kamryn pushed the recliner's footrest down and sighed. *Great. Another mess to clean up.* She sighed and then rubbed her face with her fingertips.

"I was sleeping," Ian told her. "I didn't mean..."

"It's okay." She offered him a tiny, tired smile. "It's okay. I'll change your sheets."

She stood up, surprised when he slipped his hand into hers.

"Mommy?"

"Hmm?"

"Can I sleep in your bed?"

Kamryn looked down at her son and studied his face. The anger was gone. The peas were forgotten, and her little boy was back. That kind of made the job ahead of her a little less daunting, anyway.

"Sure." She nodded. "Let's get some more medicine in you, though. You're burnin' up, dude."

As Ian worked to get the medicine down, Kamryn woke the girls.

"Why don't you guys get ready for bed?" she suggested.

Ashton was the first to move. But she only squinted at the lamplight and then she threw her arm up to cover her eyes.

"Is the movie over?" Braelyn grumbled from the other end of the couch.

"Yeah."

"What time is it?" Ashton asked from her hiding place under her arm.

Kamryn looked at her watch. She was surprised to see it was just ten o'clock. It felt like midnight.

"Ten. It would be good for you to get to bed early, Ash."

Ashton groaned and then nodded. "Garret's gonna call."

Kamryn rolled her eyes, no danger of Ashton seeing her since her wrist was still over her eyes.

"Okay. But you can go ahead and get ready for bed." Kamryn looked up as Ian started gagging. "Garbage can, Ian," she called across the room.

"Ewwww!" Ashton jumped up and rounded the couch at the end furthest away from Ian. "Gross. Why's he down here?"

"I've never seen you move so fast." Kamryn grinned. Ian spit into the garbage can. It was just medicine this time. The poor kid couldn't have much left to throw up. "Braelyn!"

"Hmm?" Braelyn blinked hard and then struggled to sit up.

"Go to bed."

Brae looked around, obviously disoriented. "Oh, man."

"What's wrong?" Ashton asked her.

"I was dreaming."

"About what?"

Braelyn stood up and stumbled around the end of the couch. Kamryn watched the girls as they headed for the steps.

"Andrew. That kiss the other day."

Kamryn glanced at Ian. She wished she could follow the girls upstairs, to hear the details of Brae's kiss. Either the real one or the dream one. She didn't even know if it was Brae's first kiss or not.

Moms didn't need to know every detail; Kamryn knew those details might break her. But she was curious about Brae and Andrew.

Curious about Brae and Andrew and worried about Ash and Garret. She sighed again and then turned her attention to Ian.

"Ready?"

He nodded and followed her upstairs. After he brushed his teeth and rinsed his mouth yet again, she examined his pjs, and when she found them clean, she tucked him in on Mark's side of their bed. She grabbed a blanket from their closet, spread it out on the floor by Ian and then took the garbage can from the master bathroom and set it where Ian could reach it.

"Where're you going, Mom?"

Kamryn stopped at the doorway and looked back at Ian.

"To put your sheets in the washer."

"But I'm sleeping in here."

"I know, hon, but I still need to wash your sheets." She smiled. "I'll come to bed soon."

He thought about that for a moment and then nodded.

"Mom?"

Kamryn stopped, two steps into the hallway.

"Hmm?"

"Would you bring Darrell?"

Darrell the Dinosaur.

"I will."

"Okay."

CHAPTER 10

KAMRYN

Kamryn held her breath while she used a wet rag to wipe up the mess on Ian's bed. She was surprised at how much Ian had thrown up, since he hadn't eaten much for dinner. There had been times through the years when she got sick cleaning up after the kids after they had vomited. She was much better with bloody accidents, though she wouldn't wish them on her kids just to make her life easier.

She gagged and wondered why she was thinking vomit versus blood. Darrell the Dinosaur had something sticky and wet plastered down his right side, so she set him aside to throw in the wash with the sheets. The girls were getting ready for bed, so she had to wait for Ashton to move away from the sink before she could rinse the rag out.

"Mom, that's so gross." Ashton shuddered.

"What do you want me to do with it, Ash?" Kamryn gestured with the rag. "Throw it away?"

"Yeah, that'd be good."

"Why don't you invent disposable sheets and towels? So, moms don't have to clean things up?"

"Pharmacists don't invent things," she answered as she stepped around Kamryn.

"Invent a drug to stop the stomach flu," Kamryn suggested.

"Don't I wish," Ashton grumbled as she walked out of the room. Kamryn rinsed the rag out and then tossed it on the floor in the hall. She went back to Ian's room and tugged the sheets from his bed. She tossed Darrell and the soiled sheets out into the hall and then went to work remaking Ian's bed.

"Why's Darrell—"

"Don't touch that!"

"Oh yuck! Mo-om!"

Kamryn peeked out Ian's door to see Brae, white as a sheet, hurry to the bathroom. She chuckled, but she hoped like hell Brae didn't get sick now. When his bed was made, she stepped into the hallway and glanced into Ashton's room. She wanted to say something to her, to thank her for taking care of her tonight. But Ashton was burrowed under the covers, with her cell at her ear. Talking to Garret.

Kamryn had liked Garret in the beginning. When he and Ashton had been friends. Before the hand holding and the dating and the beginning of the exclusive part of their relationship. It wasn't really that she didn't like him now. She just hated how serious they were. They were both too young for such a serious relationship.

She kissed the top of Ashton's head, careful not to touch anything with her hands. Even if she'd scrubbed the skin off her hands with a wire brush, Ashton and Braelyn, too, would be scared to death of picking up Ian's germs.

"Night, Mom," Ashton said softly.

"Night." She headed back to the hall, planning to say goodnight to Brae.

"Garret says night, Mom," Ashton called. Kamryn fought back the urge to snap at Ashton and remind her that she was not Garret's mom. They were nowhere near that sort of commitment. Instead, she took a deep breath and said, with no feeling, "Night, Garret."

She found Braelyn curled up on her side, with a book open.

"You ever gonna tell me about that kiss?" She leaned on the wall at the head of Braelyn's bed.

"It was just a dream," Braelyn said quickly.

"Ash said he really kissed you. A couple of weeks ago."

"Thanks a lot, Ashton!" Braelyn yelled. "It was just a kiss, Mom."

"Good kiss or bad kiss?"

Kamryn wondered why she was pushing this. She was concerned about her other daughter and how seriously she might be involved with her boyfriend, and yet, here she was encouraging this one to kiss a boy that followed her around much the same way Garret had followed Ashton around forever.

"Good." Braelyn blushed and buried her face in her pillow.

Kamryn smiled. This is why she was pushing it. Ashton had had a steady boyfriend for over a year. Brae had never had a boyfriend and had been out on only a couple of dates. Kamryn didn't want Braelyn attached to someone the way Ashton was; if she could help it, Ashton wouldn't be involved with anyone. But Kamryn didn't want Ash to leave Brae completely behind, either.

"Hmm." Kamryn stood up straight and then leaned over to kiss Braelyn goodnight. "Whatcha reading?"

"Another vampire book."

Kamryn rolled her eyes again. "Just what the world needs. More vampire books."

Braelyn laughed into her pillow.

"Goodnight, Mom."

"Night."

In the hall, Kamryn squatted down to pick up the pile of sheets. Moses, who had been in Braelyn's room, followed her out and stuck his nose up against her leg.

"You gotta go potty, doncha?"

Moses backed away and wagged his tail in answer.

"I know. Hang on a minute, buddy."

She picked up the sheets and Darrell the Dinosaur and hurried to the steps.

"Mom!"

Kamryn counted to ten. She thought about Mark, and she thought about how much she wished he was home, and how it would be nice if he were around for these kinds of nights. She pressed her lips together until she was calm.

"What, Ian?"

"Where's Darrell?"

"I need to put him in the wash, hon," she answered. "You got him when you got sick."

"Nuh-uh!"

"Well, then he crawled into it when you came downstairs," she mumbled.

"I want Darrell!"

"Ian, I'm sorry," she answered. He started to yell again, but she went downstairs. There was only so much she could take and only so much she could do. Moses followed her downstairs, so she hooked his leash on him and took him outside. Arms folded over her chest, she huddled into her sweatshirt wishing she would have put a coat on. Moses tended to take his time, especially when it was cold.

Her mind wandered while she waited. Adrie. Poor Adrie. She wondered how Adrie's daughters were doing. Mia was eleven, and Lucy would be turning six in a few weeks. Both had been crazy about Adrie's dad. Mia might understand things a little better than Lucy, but it would be hard for both of them and hard for Adrie to see them hurting when she was hurting, too.

The phone rang. Moses was still sniffing around, as if it was seventy-five and sunny outside. Kamryn waited to see if one of the girls would answer it. It quit ringing, so she assumed Brae had picked it up. Good, she could talk to Mark.

"Moses, come on," she groaned. She curled her toes in her flip-flops, glad to at least have socks on.

The front door opened, and Ian stepped out onto the porch.

"Ian! What are you doing?"

He stood shivering in his thin PJs. Kamryn sighed yet again as he reached to hand her the cordless phone. *Really, Mark? You can't wait five minutes?*

She took the phone from him and then turned him around and directed him back inside.

"I want Darrell." He stood just inside the door, hands on his hips and a pouty look on his face.

"I'm sorry, but Darrell needs a bath."

"Then wash him—"

"Do not use that tone with me, young man. Get upstairs and get in bed."

Ian stomped his foot and then whirled around and hurried away from the door. Moses was finally taking care of business. Teeth chattering, Kamryn raised the phone to her ear.

"Hello?" She intended to tell Mark she would call him back in a few minutes.

"Kam? What's Ian doing up? It's after ten. Why didn't you get the phone?"

She heard music and voices in the background.

"Ian is awake because he's sick. He just vomited in his bed, so I just got him put in our bed. I didn't get the phone because I'm outside with Moses, and I assumed that one of your daughters could have grabbed it."

Her outburst was met with immediate silence, but she could still hear the background noise. Mark said something quietly; she knew he was talking to a colleague.

"Well. Why don't you call me back when you have time?"

Unbelievable. He attacked her for Ian being awake after ten, and then he had the nerve to act offended because she snapped at him?

"Sure. I will."

Before she could say anything else, the phone went dead in her hand. It would feel good to scream right about now. No, actually, it would feel *great* to scream right now, but she was still outside, and a scream would wake the neighborhood. She didn't need an audience. A few more hands and a stiff drink, maybe, but no audience.

Moses hopped up on the front porch step and looked up at her.

"Finished already?" she mumbled, but the sarcasm was lost on the dog. Back inside, she put Moses' leash away and then tossed the pile of sheets and Darrell into the washer, added detergent, and set the washer to run.

Ian yelled from upstairs. She hurried up the steps to his room, grabbed a stuffed animal from the pile in the corner, and took it to him.

"I don't want that one." He shook his head. Kamryn squeezed the turtle around the neck, but she smiled at Ian.

"It's this one or nothing, Ian. I'm done. I need to finish a few things downstairs and go to bed."

"You're mean."

She nodded. "Yep, that's what I hear."

He snatched the stuffed turtle from her hands and rolled over, putting his back to her.

"Goodnight."

Back downstairs, she picked up the cordless from the kitchen counter and stared at it. She wanted to talk to Mark, but not now. Not after that two-minute phone call. She hadn't gone off on Mark. He had told her before how he hated when he was on the road and called home, and she went off on a rant about how terrible her day was. He missed her and wanted to talk to her. Not catch hell from her.

Now and then, she did blow up on the phone, and yes, tonight was most likely a night when she would blow up. But still, she was pissed. He had questioned her. Mark had taken the offensive, as if accusing her of being negligent because Ian was still awake.

He had made it sound like she was lounging in a hot bath while Ian was dragged from a deep sleep to answer the phone.

And yet, if she didn't call him back, she would feel awful. She would lay awake, feeling guilty that she hadn't called him. Missing him. Missing his voice. He had a deep, gravelly voice that turned her on more often than not. It wouldn't tonight.

She wondered what he would think. If she didn't call him back. Would he care?

Would he notice?

She checked the kitchen, satisfied that the girls had done a good job on clean up, and then she found herself in the office. She sank into the chair behind the desk as she dialed Mark's number.

"Mark McHale."

Seriously? He answered the phone to her like that? He knew it was her; their home number flashed on the screen of his cell when she called.

"Hey."

"Oh, hey," he said as if he really didn't expect it to be her. "It's dark in here. Couldn't see my phone."

Dark. Music in the background. Nice. Mark was kicking back at a bar while she was at home working her ass off.

"Where ya at?" she asked, because she knew he expected her to and because anything else that came out of her mouth might be explosive and dangerous.

"Some blues bar," he answered. "Just had dinner at a seafood place. Had some shrimp scampi."

"Mm. Sounds good," she said softly. Her stomach growled. Super. She couldn't have eaten another bite at dinner, and now it was nearly eleven, and she was hungry.

"Bad day?" he asked. She took a deep breath, because she wanted very much to dump her bad day at his feet. Not because she was angry. Because she just needed to talk. But she knew he wouldn't see it that way. He would think she was pissed at him, and that she was throwing it in his face just so he would feel bad, too. He would think she was trying to ruin his night at the bar.

"Busy," she hedged. "Ian called me to get him just after lunch. He's been throwing up all day."

"Poor kid."

"It's not the flu, though." She laughed quietly. "It's the peas."

Mark said something again, obviously to whoever he was with. She wondered who it was, but she wasn't going to ask. She didn't know most of the people he knew through work. She didn't know the other pharmaceutical salespeople, and she didn't know the doctors or nurses that he did. That was his world, and mostly she didn't want to intrude. Either that or she didn't care. She had enough on her plate.

"What'd you say?" he said now.

"Nothing." She shook her head. Her head was pounding suddenly, and she felt empty. Not hungry. But empty. She missed Mark.

"I'll call you in the morning—"

"Mark," she interrupted him. Part of her didn't want to tell him this. Part of her kind of wanted to keep it to herself. Sort of because she wanted him to find out from the girls and feel bad about being a dick to her over the phone. And sort of because once she said it and he said he was sorry, he was still going to go back to his beer or his wine or whatever the hell he was drinking, and she was going to go upstairs and go to bed only to lay awake thinking about it and feeling bad.

"What?"

He was irritated that she cut him off. She could hear it in his voice. He still thought she was going to rail on him about something.

Nice.

She waited a moment and thought about not telling him. Either way, she was screwed because she was going to feel like shit and Mark, though sorry, would continue his night as if nothing had happened.

"Adie's dad died today."

"Oh, Kam."

She closed her eyes and let the tears go. He did care. Right now, right at this moment, of course he cared. But he wasn't here, and he couldn't hold her. And once this call ended, he would be removed from how bad she felt right now.

"I'm sorry, babe."

"I just feel so bad for her," she said quietly. She wiped at her nose and continued. "I left her with my appointments, and then she called, and I couldn't even get to the phone because Ian had gotten sick—"

He was talking again, and again, from the way he was talking quietly and kind of aside from her talking, she knew he was talking to someone he was with.

She wondered then. Again. Who was Mark with when she needed him here at home? With her.

"What happened to him?" he asked.

Kamryn reached for a tissue from the box on the corner of the desk.

"Heart attack," she answered. "Look, I'll let you go."

She wanted him to say *no*, that it was *okay*. That he knew she needed to talk. Sometimes, if he was out for dinner or something, he would excuse himself and walk outside to talk to her. He didn't tonight, which made her wonder yet again who was with him at the bar.

"I'll call you tomorrow," he told her.

She licked her lips and nodded and imagined Mark in his shirt sleeves, the cuffs rolled back. The five o'clock shadow on his face. The smile that announced to the world that he might be damned near perfect-looking, but he was still a friendly guy. Everybody's friend.

"Yeah. I'll talk to you tomorrow."

"Love you."

Kamryn breathed deeply. "Love you, too."

CHAPTER 11

KAMRYN

"You need to stop beating yourself up about it."

Kamryn looked away from her computer, picked up her cup of coffee, and turned to Will. He stepped into the office and sat on the edge of his desk. Kamryn, who hadn't said much to anyone all day, stared at him expectantly.

"Beating myself up about what?" she finally asked when she realized he wasn't going to elaborate.

"Adrie," he said simply.

"How do you know I'm beating myself up about it?"

He shrugged. "You look like you think you kicked someone's dog down the block."

She snorted and took a drink of her coffee. "Never heard that one before."

"Adrie was fine. And when she got the call, the rest of us took your clients, so she could get outta here."

"Uh-huh." Kamryn nodded. "Now I feel like I kicked everyone's dogs down the block."

Will laughed and shook his head. "I didn't mean that the way it sounded."

"I know."

"You did what you had to do."

"Motherhood and careers don't mix well," she mumbled as she set her coffee mug on her desk. She rested her elbows on her knees and ran her fingers through her hair. "It's okay. I've heard it all before."

"Mark?"

"No, no, he's never said that. But enough people do, don't they? Why have kids if you're just gonna shuttle them off to a sitter or school and work all day and never see them?"

"Sounds like you're having some guilt issues. Bigger than just Adrie."

"Yeah," Kamryn said as she stood up. "Guilt. Something like that." She glanced at her watch, wondering where her next patient was.

"I'm not very good at this, am I?"

"No, Will, you suck." This time she laughed. "You're making me feel worse."

He acted like he zipped his lips together and tossed an imaginary key over his shoulder.

"That is awesome." She grinned. "If only it worked."

"What?" Will followed her out of the office. "You don't think I can be quiet?"

Kamryn looked at him pointedly, but he only grinned.

"Are you going to the funeral?" Her abrupt question killed the tiny, good vibe Will had ushered into the office.

"No. Rena and I are gonna go to the visitation, but…" He shrugged, clearly uncomfortable with the subject.

Kamryn nodded. She wished Mark would be home to go with her. He would be home in two days, the day of the funeral.

"Is Mark gone?"

"Yeah. Two more days."

"And you have Ian at home?"

She nodded. "My mom's with him."

Will seemed to consider something as she looked down the hall to the front desk. Apparently her ten o'clock was a no-show.

"Do you wanna go with Rena and me tonight?"

Surprised by the question, Kamryn turned back to him.

"Thank you," she said with a smile. "But no. I'll be fine."

Will gave her a nod and then shrugged a shoulder. "Let me know if you change your mind."

She left work just after three, called her mom to tell her she was going by Adrie's house, and then steeled herself to see her best friend. To offer comfort.

Adrie answered the door. Dressed in baggy sweats and a faded St. Louis Blues t-shirt, she looked cute and small and worn out. Kamryn stepped inside and wrapped her arms around her friend.

"I'm so sorry, Adrie," she said sincerely.

"Thanks."

Kamryn didn't even know how to ask. Had Adrie had a chance to see him before he died? Or had she been stuck at work, caring for Kamryn's patients because Kamryn had dumped them on her and run home?

"Did you get to see him? Before—?"

"Yeah. Mel called." Adrie sunk her teeth into her lower lip. "It was very peaceful, I think. He wasn't breathing very well, but he didn't seem to be in a lot of pain."

Kamryn felt a small sliver of relief break open inside her. She still felt bad for dumping her patients on Adrie, and apparently on the rest of her colleagues when Adrie left. But she had been so afraid that Adrie hadn't seen her dad before he passed away.

"I'm sorry," Kamryn started, "to run out on you yesterday. And then to miss your call."

"It's okay." Adrie appeared to be her usual, calm self. She'd been crying, and Kamryn guessed from the puffiness around her eyes that she hadn't slept much. But she was still Adrie, still Kamryn's best friend. "How's Ian?"

Kamryn groaned and laughed. "Threw up in the SUV on the way home. Threw up a few times once we were home. He's become very demanding."

"Poor little guy."

Kamryn reached out and rested her hand on the doorknob. She couldn't stay long. She needed to get home to Ian, to relieve her mom. And she needed to get out of Adrie's house, because she didn't want to open her mouth and have yesterday come rushing out. After all, Kamryn had had a bad day, but Adrie's father had died. No comparison. Kamryn's brain knew that, but her heart or her gut or the rest of the stuff in her head that was pounding again didn't seem to get it.

"He refuses to believe he has the flu," she told Adrie, knowing it would give her a much-needed laugh.

"What does he think he has?" Adrie asked. She pulled her hair back into a loose ponytail and moved an elastic band from around her wrist to hold it in place.

"I guess he thinks he's been poisoned by the school lunch. Peas."

Despite her loss and her grief, Adrie laughed loud and hard. She wiped at her eyes.

"Forget to make his lunch, did ya?"

"I did."

"Hang in there," Adrie said with a smile.

"You hang in there." Kamryn shook her head. Adrie nodded. "Is there anything I can do? Anything you need?"

"No." Adrie crossed her arms over her chest. "But thanks."

"Please call me," Kamryn said as she turned the doorknob and pulled it open. "Anything at all, just call me."

"Thanks, Kam." Adrie nodded and stepped closer to the door. She put her hand on it as Kamryn stepped back out into the brisk cold February day. "Thanks for coming by."

Kamryn started to say something, but she thought better of it. What was there to say? This was a family day for Adrie, and sticking around and being in the way of that family day just because she felt guilty for not being around yesterday was not a good plan.

Besides Ian needed her. Or actually, she thought as she made her way back to her SUV, her mom might need her. If Ian was being as surly and grumpy to her mom as he had been to her yesterday, she might have to do some serious damage control to get her mom to watch him tomorrow if he wasn't ready to go back to school.

Her mom said all the right things, even offered to take Ian home with her for the night and the next day. Apparently, Ian didn't blame Grandma for the pea incident. Kamryn thanked her mom, but she couldn't just send Ian away. She was tired, yes, and she could use a night of staring at the TV, but she was Ian's mother and that meant something to her. Ian was her responsibility. She hated it that she had to leave him on these kinds of days to go to work. Besides that, she would miss him.

"You would miss me?" Ian asked her. Her mom had talked him into sacking out on the couch. The TV was on, but of course, he was paying more attention to Kamryn and her mom than *Phineas and Ferb*.

"Yes, I'd miss you," Kamryn answered. She glanced at him and smiled, hoping the crankiness from the previous night was really gone. "Even if you are a crabcake."

"I'm not a crabcake!" He grinned at her. It was good to see him smiling, but he was still pale, and according to her mom he had thrown up again today after eating a piece of toast and then again after some chicken noodle soup.

"You were last night," she told him and then she turned her attention back to her mom. "Was he okay today? He was really mad at me last night because I forgot to make his lunch yesterday."

Kamryn's mom laughed and nodded. "He told me that you and Ashton both forgot to make his lunch. And that he had to eat peas, and that the peas had given him the flu. I told him peas don't give you the flu."

"I told him that, too," Kamryn mumbled.

"Grandma knows more than you," Ian hollered from the couch.

"Thanks, Ian."

She looked at her mom and rolled her eyes. "Another fun night ahead, ya think?"

"When does Mark get home?"

"Two days."

"How's Adrie?"

Kamryn shrugged as she yanked the refrigerator door open. She grabbed a can of soda, popped the top, and took a big drink. Maybe a little caffeine would give her a jolt of energy. While she stood there, she eyed the contents of the fridge, wondering what to fix for dinner for herself and the girls.

"She's okay, I guess."

"Did you tell Mark?"

Kamryn looked back over her shoulder at her mom. "Yeah. Why?"

"Just wondered if he's still a little tender about his dad."

Kamryn considered that and then nodded. "He is, but it didn't come up when we were on the phone." She didn't tell her mom that Mark had been out with colleagues and too distracted to really have a conversation with her. No need to have her mom upset with Mark.

The back door opened, and chatter instantly filled the kitchen. Kamryn gave up on dinner options and shut the refrigerator door. Braelyn was on her cell, yakking away to someone. She saw Kamryn and her mom in the kitchen and flashed them a grin. Rather than say anything, she held up a finger to signal she would be finished in a minute and made her way through the kitchen and family room to the office.

Kamryn heard the back door close and then, finally, a subdued Ashton appeared in the kitchen. Her mouth was drawn in a tight line. When she saw her grandma in the kitchen, she offered her a small smile.

"Hi, Grandma," she said quietly. "Hi, Mom."

"Hi." Kamryn watched her swing her backpack off her shoulder and drop it on the counter. It was bulging at the seams; Kamryn figured Ashton had a long night of homework ahead of her. "How was your day?"

"Fine."

Kamryn watched Ashton pull the refrigerator door open. She glanced at her mom, as Ashton took the gallon of milk from the fridge.

"Well." Her mom sighed. "I should go. I'm having dinner with Sandy Reed at five."

"What's Dad doing?"

"Baching it, of course," her mom said with a wink. "He came by for lunch. Hung out with Ian for a bit. He'll probably eat a TV dinner and watch the game tonight."

Kamryn didn't even ask what game. Her dad would watch any game, as long as it wasn't chess or table tennis. He even got wrapped up in the Little League World Series when it was on ESPN.

"Grandpa came to see me today," Ian, obviously still listening, yelled from the couch.

"Great," Ashton mumbled. "Now Grandma and Grandpa will get sick, too."

Kamryn's mom picked up her keys and drew her purse strap up over her shoulder.

"Say goodbye to Brae," Kamryn reminded her.

"Yeah." Ashton had taken the Chips Ahoy! Cookies from the cabinet. Now she dunked one in her glass of milk. Interesting. She went through phases when she wouldn't eat a piece of lettuce because she might gain an ounce. But now and then, she ate cookies or occasionally, even a candy bar. Kamryn didn't care that she treated herself to a cookie or a candy bar now and then. But it did make her worry a little bit. What if Ashton ate another cookie, gulped down the rest of her milk, and then went upstairs to throw it all up?

She had never suspected Ashton of anything like that before. She never worried that either of her girls had an eating disorder. Really, she didn't believe it now. But there was something about Ashton that was really worrying her lately. If only she could put her finger on it.

"Tell her to get off the stupid phone."

Kamryn's mom raised her eyebrows and looked from Ashton to Kamryn.

"Why can't she be on the phone?" Kamryn asked as Ashton dunked another cookie.

"It's Andrew. He called her, like the second we walked out of school. They've been on the phone since. They just saw each other at school."

Kamryn leaned against the counter and folded her arms over chest.

"You talk to Garret that much," she reminded Ashton.

"Well, you should hear her. She's all giggly, and she's acting like a ditz."

"Maybe she's having fun."

"Since when do you have to change who you are to have fun?" Ashton picked up her glass, drained it, and then rinsed it out. She set it in the dishwasher, put the cookie package away, and then wiped the counter off.

"Brae laughs a lot." Kamryn studied Ashton. "What's wrong with her laughing on the phone with Andrew?"

"Because it's the way she's doing it," Ashton snapped. "She's talking all soft and high-pitched, like she's trying to be one of those stupid girls who just follows the boys around. Like she's just doing it for Andrew's attention."

Kamryn met her mom's eyes over Ashton's bent head. Her mom raised her eyebrows, and Kamryn shrugged.

"I'll see you later," her mom said as she put her arm around Ashton's shoulders and gave her a squeeze.

"Bye, Grandma." Ashton kissed her cheek. Kamryn said goodbye to her mom and thanked her for watching Ian.

"So, what's wrong?" Kamryn asked Ashton when they were alone in the kitchen. Her mom was bent over the couch talking to Ian, so she hoped Ashton felt they could talk privately.

Ashton rolled her eyes and shook her head. "Nothing is wrong. God, can't I have an opinion? I just hate to see Brae acting like a ditz for Andrew. She's better than that."

Kamryn sighed. She ducked her head and rubbed the back of her neck as Ashton yanked her backpack across the counter, tossed it over her shoulder, and marched out of the kitchen and upstairs.

Nothing's wrong. Beat a hasty retreat, march out of the kitchen after snapping at me. Complain about your sister talking on the phone to a boy. But nothing's wrong.

Kamryn chugged the rest of her soda and tossed the can into the recycle bin. Most likely, all would be right in the world when Mark came back home. Ian would feel better. Brae would have a date with Andrew over the weekend, and whatever burr was up Ashton's butt would be gone. And even though Kamryn had dealt with all the shit all week, she would be expected to roll with the punches, let it all go, and welcome Mark with open arms.

Somedays she hated Mark's job. Resentment had no place in a happy marriage. But there it was, staring her in the face.

"Hey, Mom."

She looked up and offered Brae a smile.

"What's for supper?"

"Pizza. Call and order it, will you?"

CHAPTER 12

ASHTON

Two tests and two quizzes tomorrow. Mr. King had given them a calculus quiz last Friday, and they got them back today. Ashton was pissed. She got a B. Brae was in a different calc class, and then she had been on the damned phone the whole drive home, so Ashton had no idea how she had done on the quiz. A B was for someone who settled. Ashton McHale didn't settle. She had calc to do tonight for homework, a religion quiz and an ethics quiz tomorrow, and a history and a Spanish test tomorrow.

At least her Spanish teacher always offered extra credit. Her Spanish grade had dropped to a ninety-eight. That was unforgiveable, so she needed the extra credit.

Ashton's stomach cramped for a second. She rested her head on the open calc book on her desk. *Great.* Just what she needed. Ian's bug. She couldn't afford to be sick. Even if it would give her a few days rest from Garret. Had he really said he needed to see her tonight? Really? Hadn't they just had sex in this very room just a few nights ago? Seriously, though, she didn't have time to be sick.

Even Grandma and Grandpa would probably get it now, after being around Ian. Moses had been curled at Ian's feet. Did dogs get the stomach flu? Moses puked often enough, but Ashton didn't think he really got the flu.

She sighed and sat up straight again. The calc wasn't going to finish itself. The house phone rang. Ashton almost jumped up to answer it, but she stopped herself on the third ring. It could be Dad. She wouldn't mind talking to him, but she really didn't have time. Maybe later. Somewhere between translating that chapter in that Spanish story her class was reading and studying for the quizzes and tests tomorrow. It could be Andrew calling to talk to Brae because they had been on their cells so long Brae's battery had died.

Seriously. What the hell was up with that? Just last night Brae had said she didn't want to get involved with Andrew because she didn't want to end up tied down like Ashton was. That had pissed Ashton off a little at first. Who made Brae her judge, anyway? And how did Braelyn know just how close she and Garret were? The fact that they were really close, and that Ashton often thought of Garret as a weight around her neck, dragging her down really pissed her off. Why did Brae have to be right? Why hadn't Ashton kept her pants on that first time? Why hadn't she just said no? Maybe Garret would have found someone else.

A different girlfriend.

Ashton winced when her stomach cramped again. Okay, so she didn't like the thought of Garret with another girl. In fact, she hated the thought of Garret with someone else. But she still wished they didn't have to spend every waking minute together with their hands in each other's pants.

And okay, yeah, what was up with Brae telling her last night that she didn't want to be tied down with Andrew and then being on the phone with him and being all giggly and breathless and ditzy while Ashton kept turning the music up in the car so she wouldn't have to hear it? Each time Ashton turned it up, Brae turned it down, until finally Brae had smacked Ashton's hand away from the volume knob.

So then Ashton had heard more than enough. For the last few blocks on the way home she'd had to listen to Brae gush to Andrew about how sweet he was and yeah, she wanted to go out with him over the weekend. *What was Brae? Schizophrenic?*

She hadn't spoken to her since they got home. Well, okay, she hadn't spoken to her since they left the school building because Lover Boy had called, and that was that.

Ashton rolled her eyes now. Don't do it, Brae, she thought. Don't go out with him.

She remembered the way her stomach would feel full of butterflies, though. The way her knees would go weak when she saw Garret. The way her heart kind of skipped when he first kissed her. The clean fresh scent of his cologne when he put his arms around her. The way he laughed at her snide comments about school or teachers or whatever TV show they were watching.

She missed *that*. She understood that Brae would like *that*. But she wasn't sure how Brae felt about sex, about sex *now*, with Andrew. She really wished she could talk Brae out of it, but how would that go over? Brae would get bristly with Ashton for mothering her, and she would demand to know how the hell Ash knew anything about it. While Ashton really wanted Brae to wait, she didn't really want to tell her *why*. To tell her the way things changed *after*. Right now, no one knew but her and Garret.

Or did someone else know? Had Garret told anyone? Had he told Andrew? Was that why Andrew was pouring it on so thick with Braelyn right now? Had he told anyone else? What if he had told the basketball team? What if she was the hot topic of the locker room?

Why hadn't she thought of that before?

She jumped when she heard the knock at her closed bedroom door.

"What?" she called.

The door opened, and her mom stepped inside her room.

"Time to eat."

"I'm not hungry," she answered automatically. Except she was. She was starved, because she had skipped lunch after she had seen two senior girls staring at her at her locker earlier in the morning. She figured they were talking about how fat her sweater made her look. Now she wondered if they were talking about her and Garret and the things they did behind closed doors.

"You have to eat," her mom insisted.

She had eaten those cookies, and she shouldn't have. On the other hand, her mom wasn't going to go away. She could at least go downstairs and pretend to eat something. That had worked last night with the hamburger helper. Then again, Mom had been pretty distracted last night.

With a sigh of frustration, Ashton tossed her pencil down on her open book and stood up. She could use a drink. Some Cabernet Sauvignon. She liked it better than the white stuff, the Chardonnay. Maybe later. Maybe once her mom and Brae went to bed, she could sneak down and have a glass of wine or something. That might help her get through all of the homework and the studying.

Or she could pour some vodka in a glass and bring it upstairs and just sit it on her desk. As long as Mom didn't get close enough, she'd never know it was vodka. She'd think it was just water. Or she could mix it with something.

Feeling a little more at ease as she considered her options, she followed Mom down the steps.

"What are we having?"

"Pizza."

Brae was at the counter, pulling the delivery box open.

"I want some!" Ian hollered from the couch.

"No way," Mom answered quickly. "Definitely not cleaning that up."

"Yuck." Ashton groaned. She took the plate with the triangular slice, thick-crusted sausage and mushroom pizza from Brae and then glanced at the wine rack. No way could she get by with it right now.

Later. Her mom would probably go to bed early tonight because she was wiped out from last night. Ashton would get her fix later.

She ate slowly, giving that one piece of pizza time to fill her up. Moses sat at her feet, waiting to see if she might drop something. When he decided she wasn't going to, he moved on to Brae. Ian sat on the couch, watching silently as they ate their pizza. Mom had fixed him macaroni and cheese, and now they were all waiting for him to lose it.

Mom looked like she could face plant in her food. Ashton felt kind of bad for her. She had dealt with a lot of shit last night. Hardly seemed fair that Mom did the seven to three job and then had to come home at night and work the three-thirty to bedtime shift. Dad just kind of wandered in and out, as if the house was just another hotel with the added benefit of a warm body to sleep beside.

Ashton swallowed wrong and started coughing. Her mom jumped up and hurried to stand by her, ready to shove a glass of water at her or pound her on the back, the way she had always done for her and Brae when they were little. The way she still did for Ian if he got choked on something.

"I'm fine," she mumbled, taking a sip of her water. *Dad. Sleeping alone. In those hotels. What if he wasn't? What if there were nights when he slept with other women? He wouldn't do that, would he?*

Did Mom ever wonder about that? Because, man, that would suck, to spend half your marriage wondering what your spouse was doing. If he or she was sleeping with someone else.

Why did they call it sleeping together? There wasn't much sleeping about it, was there? Well, okay, after. Garret would probably flop backwards and sleep all night in her bed if she let him.

"What're you thinking about?" Mom asked her now. She was still hovering. God, Ashton wanted to throw something. To scream.

Leave me alone.

"Nothing."

"How'd you do on that calc quiz last week?" Brae asked.

Here we go, Ashton thought. She wished she could just disappear.

"Got a B."

Brae nodded thoughtfully, but she didn't say anything. Which Ashton knew meant Brae had done better than she had.

"What'd you get?" Mom asked.

"Oh." Brae looked up and raised her eyebrows, but at least she didn't look at Ashton. "Got an A."

Ashton studied her pizza really carefully, so she didn't have to see her mom watching her. The worry in her eyes. God, what did Mom think, anyway? That she was some jacked-up, tightly wound freak who needed to be on meds? What the hell was she always so worried about? It wasn't like she was going to go postal tomorrow and take a handgun in to school and blow away a handful of students and teachers. So she was driven. If she wasn't, her parents would be on her ass about letting her grades slide.

"Can one of you guys watch Ian tomorrow night?" Mom asked. Surprised by the change in subject, Ashton looked up at Mom. "I want to go to Adrie's dad's visitation."

"Oh." Brae nodded.

"I'll be home," Ashton told her, and then Brae nodded again and said she would be home, too. Ashton just hoped Ian was done with the puking by then, because as much as she loved him, there was no way in hell she was going to do any clean up duty.

"Ashton, finish your pizza," Mom ordered her. "I'm gonna go make a phone call, and then I'm gonna go for a run."

"Outside?" Brae asked quickly.

Ashton thought it had been warmer earlier, probably would've been a good day to run outside. But the later into the afternoon, early evening it got, the colder and darker it was outside. It would be dark before Mom got home.

"Treadmill," Mom answered.

"Who do you have to call?" Ashton asked. Mom didn't usually have to do much business from home. She talked on the phone to Adrie, but Ashton doubted she was going to call her now. She'd just talked to Grandma, so who would she need to call?

Ashton sighed and rubbed her eyes. Why was she thinking like this? Why was she flipping out suddenly? Every time she blinked her eyes, she was thinking some other, new ridiculous thought. She felt like she had been drugged, only not with something to slow her down or render her defenseless. Something to rev her up and make her push harder and harder until she just blew up.

"I gotta call Dad," Mom said now. "He called earlier, and it went to voicemail. I was at Adrie's."

Of course she was at Adrie's, checking on her. Adrie was Mom's best friend. And of course she would call Dad back. They had been married over twenty years. Why would something change now?

"Can we talk to Dad?" Ian piped up from the couch.

"Not right now. He'll call later. Before you go to bed. He's probably still in meetings."

Ashton glanced at the clock. It was almost five-thirty. What doctor stayed in his office this late? Nope. Whatever he was doing, Ashton was pretty sure Dad wasn't at a clinic right now, talking up the latest prescription drug.

CHAPTER 13

KAMRYN

The funeral left Kamryn feeling blue. She tried to put it in perspective; obviously Adrie felt worse than she did. But the cessation of life—just boom, it's done, you're gone, nothing remains—that had always left her chilled down to the bone. The older she got, and she knew being in the forty-something crowd didn't automatically make her old—even though she joked that it did—the more she considered her own mortality. When she and Mark were twenty, she thought they would live forever. They were just starting out, and they had houses to buy and build and love to make and babies to have, and death hadn't really ever been on the horizon. Now they were in their forties, and they were chipping away at a big mortgage, and they didn't often make love as much as they had sex, and their babies...Well, their babies weren't babies anymore. In fact, two of their babies were seriously talking about college. Her father-in-law had passed away. Her mother-in-law was diabetic. Her own dad had dealt with prostate cancer, and now Adrie's dad was dead and buried.

Life moved too fast. No matter how badly she wanted to put her foot out and drag her toes on the ground to stop it or at least slow it down, she couldn't do it. Life was running away for her and Mark, and half the time she didn't feel like they were on the same page, watching it pass them by.

Her head pounded through the rest of her day at work. She had kept mostly to herself, making small talk with her patients. Will had tried and failed to engage her in conversation. She just wasn't in the mood to make light of things, and her brain was moving at half-speed so she couldn't imagine trying to have a serious conversation about anything with Will or anyone else for that matter. He had finally given her shoulder a hard squeeze and left her alone in the office. She liked him, but when he finally left her alone, she slumped down in her chair, relieved that he had given up.

She had sent Ian to school this morning, and she worried about him, that he wasn't feeling well enough to go back. Those worries had slipped to the back of her mind, however, when the funeral started. She thought about him, now, though, on the way over to school to get him. Would she find her sweet, happy little boy or the sullen little monster that had taken over their home the past few days?

Kamryn found him just inside the door where the teachers released the kids by grade. She checked the clock on the dashboard before climbing out of the SUV and hurrying over the parking lot to the door. She wasn't late, but she still felt guilty. Ian was bundled up against the cold outside, and right now, his cheeks were bright red, and he looked wilted and sweaty. Kamryn looked at him and raised her eyebrows in askance, wondering how his day had gone. More to the point, wondering how he was going to greet her.

He grinned, but he reached up to tug at the zipper of his coat.

"I'm hot," he announced. It was warm in the hallway now, though Kamryn figured two minutes ago, the door had been opened and closed zillions of times and a steady, cold draft had barreled down through the hall.

"I bet you are," she answered with a smile. "Let's go home."

He reached a hand up to hers as they walked. Kamryn breathed a sigh of relief, though she still wasn't sure she was completely out of the doghouse.

"How was school?" she asked as she helped him climb up into the SUV.

"Okay."

"Got lots of work to catch up on?"

"Some." Ian sat back and closed his eyes. "I did some at school."

"Okay."

"I'm tired," he mumbled. He did look pale around those bright red circles on his cheeks. Kamryn wondered if he was truly over the bug. She laid the back of her hand on his forehead. He didn't feel warm. Then again, they had just walked across the parking lot, and it was only twenty-eight degrees today.

"How about we get you home and you lie down on the couch and take a nap?"

"I'm not sick."

"But you're tired," she answered. She clicked the buckle on his car seat, shut the door, and hurried around to her side of the SUV.

"Tired and sick," Ian said quietly as she settled into the driver's seat and buckled her own seatbelt.

"Sick and tired," she corrected him. He smiled, but he laid his head back again and closed his eyes. They weren't out of the woods yet. She had heard there was a nasty stomach bug going around, but it was pretty rare for anyone in the family to get it. They all passed around sore throats and sniffles like they were sharing popcorn at a movie, but the stomach stuff was rare.

Once at home, Kamryn ordered Ian upstairs to change clothes. She held her breath, wondering if he would argue and announce that he wasn't coming back downstairs or that he didn't need to change clothes. But he went willingly. Kamryn took Moses outside and stood shivering, waiting for him to finish his business. Two neighbors drove by, and she waved and felt the icy wind cut through her silk blouse.

As she and Moses turned to go back inside, the girls' car flew up to the driveway and then stopped on a dime. Kamryn cut the slack in Moses' leash and watched Braelyn ease the car into the garage by her SUV. Ashton got out of the car first, slung her backpack over her shoulder, and walked around the back of the car.

She glanced at Kamryn and then got down on her hands and knees.

"You're such a freak," Braelyn groaned as she got out of the car.

Ashton bent her head and kissed the garage floor. "She drove, like, ninety all the way home."

"Brae?" Kamryn frowned. "You know better than that. Do I need to take your key?"

"No, because I could just steal Ashton's." Braelyn bumped the car door with a hip to close it. "I didn't drive ninety. I drove, like, forty—"

"Even through school zones," Ashton added as she climbed gracefully to her feet.

"I have to pee." Braelyn rolled her eyes and turned her back to them.

"She doesn't have to pee," Ashton muttered. "Andrew's gonna call her. I told her I'd drive, but she was all *no, I'll drive. He can call me later.*"

"Braelyn!" Kamryn called.

"Gotta pee," she answered as she stepped into the house and shut the door behind her.

"Maybe she has to pee," Kamryn suggested.

"No, she doesn't."

"Is this one of those twin things? You know when she has to pee?"

"Mom."

"How was your day?"

"Long." Ashton leaned over and scooped Moses up in her arms. "Hey, buddy."

Moses leaned in and licked her face.

"Where's Garret's ring?" Kamryn asked when she saw that Ashton's fingers were bare.

"Huh?"

"You're not wearing Garret's ring."

"Oh." Ashton glanced absently at her hands as they made their way through the garage to the door.

"Why? Did you guys—"

"No. The stone felt a little loose." Ashton squatted down and let Moses walk out of her arms. "I wanted you to check it. Maybe I should take it to the jewelry store."

"Maybe Garret should take it to the jewelry store."

"Mom." Ashton rolled her eyes. Kamryn followed her into the kitchen. She saw that Ian, dressed in a pair of navy sweats and a white t-shirt, was sprawled upside on the couch watching *Phineas and Ferb*.

Wow. So far, so good.

Ashton dropped her backpack on the floor, missing her foot by an inch.

"Careful."

"Man, that would hurt!" Ashton laughed.

"It would, and I don't wanna pay for an x-ray for someone to tell me you broke a toe."

"Mom!"

"They can't do anything for a broken toe, anyway."

"Who has a broken toe?" Brae appeared in the kitchen with them. Her pants were unbuttoned and unzipped; she held them up with her hands.

"Nobody," Kamryn answered rather than try to explain what she and Ashton were talking about.

"Put some pants on." Ashton ordered Braelyn.

"I have pants on." Braelyn grinned. "See?" She let go of the waistband and danced around the kitchen with her arms in the air.

"Nice underwear." Ashton giggled. Braelyn looked down at the hot pink material and laughed.

"Shut up, Ashton."

Ashton stepped toward her and poked her finger in the waistband of Braelyn's underwear. The lace around the waistband had ripped.

Kamryn took a turn to roll her eyes, though none of her kids saw it. She guessed sometimes you just had to do it. With a sigh, she tugged the freezer door open. She hadn't planned this week's dinners, and by now she was tired of standing here each night wondering just what the hell to fix.

"Mom, I need new underwear," Braelyn told her. Kamryn looked over her shoulder as Brae zipped and buttoned her pants.

"Speaking of underwear, what's with the neon butt floss in your drawer, Ash?"

Kamryn leaned into the freezer and rooted around. She finally found a package of tilapia filets and pulled it out. When she realized Ashton still hadn't answered her, she turned around to look at the girls.

Ashton giggled. "I liked them," she answered with a shrug. Kamryn watched the flash of red flood Ashton's face. She felt the question niggling at the back of her mind, but she didn't want to acknowledge it. She didn't want to *think* it.

Was it that Ashton liked the thong? Or had Garret *suggested she get one? Had Garret picked it out for her? Had Garret bought it for her?*

"You like having something in your butt?" Brae asked.

Ashton took a swing at Brae, but she jumped away from her and grabbed her backpack from the floor.

"Hey, today isn't something, is it?" Braelyn stopped at the foot of the steps and looked back at Kamryn.

"What?"

"Dinner. Tonight. Nothing special, right?"

Kamryn glanced at the tilapia filets in her hand and looked back at Braelyn.

"Is tonight an anniversary? You know? The night Dad first cut his toenails in front of you or something?"

Ashton was joking, but Kamryn couldn't help but feel the sting of her words. Their anniversary nights, their special dinners, meant so much to her. She had never heard the kids complain; she thought they enjoyed them as much as she did.

"Nothing special," she answered quietly.

"'kay." Braelyn offered her a smile. "I'm gonna do some homework."

Ashton coughed into her hand and said *bullshit*. Kamryn watched Braelyn disappear and then turned back to Ashton.

"Bullshit?"

"Andrew's calling."

Kamryn nodded. "You know I could call you pot?"

"Huh?"

"You could be pot, calling the kettle," Kamryn nodded at the steps, "black."

"Mom, Garret and I aren't like they are."

"You are, Ashton. You most definitely are. If anything, you're worse."

"Oh. I was gonna show you his ring." Ashton reached for her bag and set it on the counter. It was bulging at the seams, as if Ashton had brought home every book in her locker. Which she often did. Braelyn's had appeared heavy, but not quite like this.

Ashton unzipped an inner pocket and then removed Garret's class ring. She handed it to Kamryn.

"What do you think?"

Kamryn touched the red stone in the center of the round, yellow gold ring. It was definitely loose, and yes, someone needed to take the ring to the jeweler, but Kamryn wasn't thinking about the ring. She was thinking about the thong in Ashton's drawer.

"Give it back to Garret and let him take care of it."

"Two people asked me today if we broke up," Ashton mumbled. "Not including you."

"You don't need a ring to show a commitment to someone," Kamryn told her. She wanted to ask Ashton about Garret, about how serious they were. But she was afraid to. Afraid of the argument that would surely follow. Afraid Ashton would sense her disapproval and clam up and lie about him. Even more afraid Ashton would tell her the truth.

"You and Dad wear rings."

"That's different."

"How?"

"Because we've been married twenty-two years." Kamryn ducked around Ashton and took a plate from the cabinet. She set the plate and the individually wrapped fish filets in the microwave and then set the microwave to defrost.

"Can I ask you something?" Ashton asked quietly.

Kamryn felt a rush of fear in her chest, like a volcano had gone off inside her. She wanted to be strong enough to be the mom who answered any question her kids had. But she was so afraid of the question right now, she couldn't find her voice. Instead, she just nodded.

"Would you trust Dad? If he didn't wear a wedding ring?"

Kamryn opened her mouth to answer Ashton, but it took a moment for the words to come.

"Of course I trust Dad, Ashton," she said with a frown. "Marriage is built on trust. It's not just love. It's faith and trust and passion."

Ashton held up a hand to stop her. "I was just looking for a yes or no."

"And besides," Kamryn continued, "people cheat with or without their rings, Ash."

Ashton nodded. She picked up her backpack and pulled the strap over her shoulder.

"Is it Garret?"

"What?" Ashton looked back at Kamryn.

"Don't you trust him?"

Ashton looked at her hands. "Mom, he's still got my ring."

Kamryn could have done without that reminder. She and Mark had both been angry when Ashton had handed her brand new four-hundred-dollar class ring over to Garret Jackson.

She might have asked Ashton if maybe Garret didn't trust her. Or if maybe Ashton didn't trust herself. But in that moment of hesitation, in the quiet that hung between them, Ashton hustled out of the kitchen, and Ian asked her for a snack, and life came rushing back at her.

CHAPTER 14

KAMRYN

After dinner, which true to her promise, had been nothing special, Kamryn kissed Mark again—she'd already laid one on him the second he stepped inside the house to welcome him home—and excused herself. She carried a book to the master bathroom, ran a tub full of hot water, and turned on the jets in the tub. She had started the book nearly two weeks ago, and though she considered herself an avid reader, she hadn't picked it up in days. Kamryn couldn't say what she did every day that made her so busy, and yet, there never seemed to be time enough in a day to relax. To watch TV. To read a book. In fact, she hadn't even taken the time to run last night or tonight. She supposed she could have gone downstairs to hit the treadmill now, instead of soaking in the tub. But the water was already running, and she was already anticipating the hot water and the jets pulsing on her legs and feet. She should have poured herself a glass of wine. That would have been a nice addition. But not needed enough to go back downstairs and risk being drawn back into something: Conversation. Cleaning the kitchen.

She unbuttoned her blouse and then dropped it on the floor. Seconds later, she dropped her bra next to it, and then she unzipped her slacks and let them slide to the floor. As she eased her panties down over her hips and stepped out of them, someone knocked on the bathroom door and pushed it open.

"Just a half hour," she groaned.

"Just me."

Mark closed the door behind him. He carried a glass of red wine, which he took a sip from and then handed to her. He bent his knees and dipped low in front of her to press his open mouth to her breast as she took a drink of the wine.

She moaned softly.

"The kids—"

Mark shook his head and then took a few steps backwards. He reached out behind him and pressed the lock. Kamryn watched him tug his tie out of his shirt collar. He looped it around her neck and drew her to him.

The kiss was slow and wet. Somewhere in there, while his tongue was dancing with hers, his hands began to roam. Kamryn, glass still in hand, moaned again as his fingers stroked and pressed, until finally her knees turned to jelly, and she sunk into him. Arms over his shoulders, she held him against her as the aftershocks radiated from her center to the tips of her fingers.

The resentment that had been building all week melted away. Mark slid his hands over her hips and held her there, his lips pressed to her neck.

"I missed you." That voice. Deep and gravelly and sexy, it stirred Kamryn inside.

"Me, too."

"Love you."

"Me, too."

"What're you thinking about?" he asked. She finally lifted her head from his shoulder and met his eyes.

"That I wanna dance with you," she said simply.

"No music."

"We've never needed music."

"What else?"

His hands moved up from her hips to knead the muscles in her shoulders. Kamryn groaned loudly this time.

"Ashton."

"And?"

"Garret."

"And?"

"The wine."

"And?"

"Ian."

"And?"

"Adrie."

"And?"

She rolled her head back and around her shoulders. Mark kissed the corner of her mouth and then nibbled at her lips.

"Do I have to fight all of those people to get into bed with you tonight?"

"No." She stood with her eyes closed, the glass still in her hand.

"Good." He kissed her forehead. "I miss my wife."

She opened her eyes to find him watching her intensely. His brown eyes studied her face so intimately she almost turned away. Half of her wanted to reach out and unbutton his dress shirt. To undress him and welcome him home, just the way he had just told her he missed her. But the other half was much too aware of what time it was and the fact the kids were all still up and that at any minute, at least one of them would need something, and that she was worried about Ashton, and she really wanted to talk to Mark about her concerns.

"Relax for a while," he said softly. She took another drink and handed the glass back to him.

"The girls made fun of me tonight," she told him as she stepped into the tub.

"About what?" he asked as he took his dress shirt off.

She sighed as she sank down into the hot water. He was sexy with just a white undershirt and his perfectly creased trousers.

"The anniversary thing."

She leaned back and closed her eyes.

"You didn't tell them, did you?"

"Tell them what?"

"What today is?"

She thought for a moment, but she was lost. He was watching her when she opened her eyes.

"What's today, Mark?"

"The first time we slept together."

"What? Nuh-uh. That was in September."

"The first time we *slept* together. Remember? We were juniors. It was cold outside, and we went for a walk. Came back home and sat by the space heater in my parent's basement. You were lying with your head in my lap, and you fell asleep, and I was leaning against the recliner, and I fell asleep. When we woke up, it was after midnight."

Kamryn grinned.

"And when we told our friends the reason why I was grounded for two weeks, they all started calling me Little Suzy."

Mark nodded and started singing "Wake Up Little Suzy." He squatted down beside the tub and reached for her hand.

"I didn't tell them."

"Good." He pulled her hand to his lips and kissed her knuckles. "I like having some secrets with you."

He stood up and vanished into the closet. Kamryn glanced at her book, but she had no energy for reading now. In fact, she was ready to climb into bed, and she was pretty sure she could sleep from now until noon tomorrow.

Except that she really didn't want to sleep.

Mark came back through the bathroom, dressed now in jeans and a t-shirt. He smiled at her but said nothing as he took the now empty glass and left her alone to relax.

DESPITE HER DETERMINATION TO stay awake until Mark came to bed, despite everything on her mind—not the least of which was Ashton—Kamryn fell asleep. Mark woke her when he came to bed; she didn't even glance at the clock. She simply turned in his arms and melted into him. Everything fell away as they moved together, touching, stroking, holding.

Ashton's words never crossed her mind—Ashton never crossed her mind—as she straddled Mark and moved over him. Fingers entwined, eyes locked, Kamryn knew only Mark and the love they had through the years. But when Mark was done, when it was over and she lay curled on top of him, her lips pressed to his collarbone, she heard Ashton's voice again. Asking if Kamryn trusted Mark.

The strangest part of it was that Kamryn did trust him. One hundred, no, one thousand percent. But every now and then, some ugly little insecurity inside her would rear its head and ask her if she wasn't being just a little naïve to trust him so blindly. And of course, the sane, rational part of her would argue back that she wasn't trusting blindly. She had known Mark over half her life, and he had never given her any reason to doubt him.

"What're you thinking?" Mark asked. Her stroked her back with his fingertips and kissed the top of her head.

"Wondering what I'd do without you." She didn't raise her head to look at him.

"Why would you wonder that? Are you planning to send me packing?"

"You could stop loving me."

"I won't."

"But you could." She lifted her chin, finally, and met his gaze. "You could be having a great time on the road, and you might realize how much you hate to come home to me. And you could get tired of how I didn't wash the dishes or how I forget to pick up your dry cleaning now and then, or you could hate it that I work, and I'm not home with the kids."

Mark frowned.

"Why would you think that? Kam, I live for you and the kids."

Kamryn pressed her lips together and raised her eyebrows. "Happens in books I read all the time. Just poof." She shrugged. "I don't love you anymore."

"So, now we're a novel? A badly written novel, where I just decide to leave you?"

"I know I'm not perfect, Mark," she whispered. "I wish I could be perfect for you. For the kids."

Mark shook his head. "Nobody wants perfect, Kam. I love you just the way you are."

She stretched just enough to touch her lips to his and then settled back against him.

"I love you, too. I guess it just hits me now and then how many nights we spend apart."

"I don't like those nights any more than you do."

She nodded, but she didn't answer him.

"You're still thinking."

She laughed softly.

"Do I need to throw you back on the bed and have my way with you again? Make you quit thinking for a while?"

"Could you?" She traced her fingers down his chest to his thighs.

"What about Ashton? You said earlier you were thinking about Ash. Something going on?"

Kamryn sighed. "I wish I knew, Mark. I'm worried about her."

"Why?"

"Well, for starters, she doesn't eat. Did you look at her tonight? She looks like she's lost weight."

"She pushes herself too hard."

"I know. I'm a little concerned about her and Garret, too."

"I'd like to see Garret out of the picture."

"Can I ask you something? Without starting an argument?"

Mark groaned and rubbed his forehead. He ran his hands back through his hair and then sighed. "Sure."

"What? What was that all about?" Kamryn climbed up to sit next to him on the bed. "That was like a drama king thing."

"Well, usually when someone wants to ask something without starting an argument, it means it's gonna start an argument."

"I don't wanna argue, Mark. I'm just concerned about something."

"Okay. Shoot."

Kamryn studied his face for a moment. She traced his lips with her thumb.

"When you're gone, do you drink a lot?"

"What?"

"When you're out of town. Do you drink a lot?"

"I thought we already covered this. I have never been unfaithful to you—"

Kamryn shook her head and touched her thumb to his lips again.

"I'm not asking that. I'm asking if you drink more when you're gone than you do when you're at home."

Mark stared at her, the beginnings of anger creasing the skin around his eyes. "I don't think so. Some nights, I have a few beers. Sometimes, if I'm with a doctor or someone in administration or someone from my company, we might have a bottle of wine."

Kamryn nodded and sighed. She rubbed her eyes and then started to get out of bed.

"Where are you going? Why did you ask that?"

"I don't know. I guess I'm just a little worried."

"About me? What? You think I'm drinking too much? Like I have a drinking problem?"

"No." She shook her head. "No. It's just…"

"What?"

"We've gone through a lot of alcohol here lately. At the house."

"Are you keeping track of how much I drink?" Mark sat up.

"No!" Kamryn stood up. "No. I'm just saying we—you and I—have gone through several bottles of wine in the last month. I don't get it."

"So, while I'm gone, you're at home inventorying our alcohol." Mark climbed out of bed. "That's great, Kam. What else? Would you like me to have a GPS chip installed so you always know where I am? Do you not believe me when I tell you where I am? You think I'm kicking back in a hot tub with a bunch of women in bikinis?"

"No." Kamryn reached for her panties and stepped into them quickly. "No, no, no. That's not what I'm saying, Mark. Dammit, listen to me."

"I think I've heard enough."

Kamryn stared after him as he stormed through the bedroom and slammed the bathroom door shut behind him. She sank down to the edge of the bed. She hadn't meant to accuse Mark of anything. He was an adult, and he had no more of a drinking problem than she did. But the fact remained that there were too many empty bottles in the recycle bin and the bottle of Silver Oak Cabernet Sauvignon—the high dollar 2006 Silver Oak Cab Sav that Mark's boss had given them for their anniversary—was nearly empty. They had only opened it two weeks ago, if that, and Kamryn knew that she only had one glass.

She hadn't meant to accuse her husband of anything. She needed to talk to the father of her children about her concerns. One thing about Mark being gone so much—it meant that Kamryn shouldered the everyday concerns, and this latest one had the potential to become a bit too heavy.

CHAPTER 15

Ashton

Ashton's headache started before she even got out of bed. Nothing to do with too much sleep or too little sleep or worrying about a test or school. She had heard Dad slam the back door and leave before five. She didn't think he was supposed to be leaving right away, and yet, he was gone, and he hadn't told her goodbye. He always told them all goodbye before he left town; it was something Mom had always insisted on. You always told Dad goodbye, you always told Dad you loved him before he left, because what if he never came home? What if his plane went down? What if he was in accident on the way to the airport? Okay, Mom didn't go into detailed scenarios, but she did insist on *goodbyes* and *I love yous*, because you never knew what could happen.

Ashton crawled out of bed. It was still early, but she wasn't going to go back to sleep. Not now. She thought about taking a shower, but her growling stomach sent her downstairs. Maybe Dad had made something for breakfast before he left?

Sometimes he did that. Sometimes he did sausage or bacon and left some for them.

Not that she needed to eat. Really, she should just skip breakfast, like she did most mornings. Mom thought she ate each morning; she thought she ate least ate a slice of toast. But Ashton rarely ate breakfast. She carried a slice of toast outside most mornings and tossed it piece by piece out the window on the way to school. Not really littering, she told herself, because animals would eat it.

She *was* hungry, though, and if she didn't eat, she would get the shakes. No breakfast. In fact, the lights were off in the kitchen, and the house was cold and quiet. She wondered absently where Dad had gone, trying to remember if he had another trip scheduled this soon.

Blank. Nothing. Ashton was so caught up in thinking about Garret—or rather imagining life without Garret—that she hadn't really paid much attention to her parents last night. Sometimes she watched them. Looking for that deep, unfaltering love that long-married couples are supposed to have. Sometimes she watched them looking for the cracks. The imperfections. She didn't get that. She didn't get the need to find imperfections in her parents' marriage. Was it that she needed to see that nothing was ever *one hundred percent okay*, but things could always be *okay enough*? Or did she have some deep-seated fear that her parents could be like other parents? That one day she could wake up to find that her parents had decided they wanted a divorce?

She tugged the fridge door open, took out the gallon of milk, and poured herself a glass. Of course that wasn't going to do anything for the hunger, so she rummaged through the cabinets until she found a box of Pop-Tarts. Frosted cherry.

Ian's favorite. She preferred strawberry, but since she ate one a year—if that—her favorite didn't matter.

"What're you doing up?"

Ashton jumped and dropped the box on the floor. She looked over her shoulder to see Mom leaning her elbows on the counter. She was dressed for work, but she looked like hell. Like she hadn't slept all night. Ashton knew the look well. Not because she saw it on Mom too often, but because there were a lot of nights that she didn't sleep, and she looked like shit the next day.

"Heard Dad leave," Ashton answered. "Thought I was hungry, but now I'm not."

Was that true? Was she *really* not hungry? Did her stomach kind of hurt now because she had put the pieces together and figured something out? Dad left before five, and Mom looked like hell and obviously, they had fought, and Mom hadn't slept.

Or *was* she still hungry? She had been caught with Pop-Tarts, *of all things*, in her hands. She didn't even want to think about the calories she had almost eaten.

Mom moved around the kitchen and picked the box up. Ashton watched her take a Pop-Tart from the box and drop it in the toaster. She flipped the light on and then took a plate from the cabinet. Ashton perched on the edge of a barstool and watched as Mom went through the motions to make coffee.

"What's wrong?" Ashton finally asked.

But Mom only shook her head. "Nothing."

"Did Dad go out of town?"

"No. He had a breakfast meeting this morning."

At five? Ashton caught herself from voicing the question. It was obvious that her parents had had a rough night. It would be stupid, not to mention insensitive, to poke at Mom just because she was nosey.

When the Pop-Tart popped up, Mom grabbed it and dropped it on the plate. She set it in front of Ashton.

"Eat. Please."

Ashton's stomach growled again. Mom raised her eyebrows, as if to say *See. You are hungry.*

"Mom?"

"What?"

"Do you think Brae should date Andrew?"

Mom leaned back against the counter and folded her arms over her chest. She hunched her shoulders like she was cold. Ashton kind of wanted to go to her and put her arm around her. But maybe daughters weren't supposed to comfort Moms after fights, any more than they were supposed to acknowledge fights between parents.

"Why?"

"What?"

"Why would you ask me that? Do you know something about Andrew that the rest of us don't?"

"No." Ashton took a big drink of her milk and set her glass down carefully. "No. He's a nice guy. I just…"

"You just what, Ash?"

"Garret was a nice guy, too."

"What does that mean?" Mom asked. She appeared exhausted. The whites of her eyes were lined with red, and the hollows under her eyes were dark, almost bruised. No puffiness, so maybe that meant she hadn't cried? But she hadn't slept. Mom looked beat, and she wasn't smiling, and Ashton knew something was really wrong.

What if Dad left? *Left, left*? What if he had walked out of here with a suitcase packed, and he wasn't leaving for a trip? He was just leaving? What if Mom lied to her? To all of them?

"Ashton, what does that mean? Garret's not a nice guy now?"

"No." Ashton shook her head quickly. "It's not that he's not a nice guy. It's just…"

"You're too young," Mom said quietly. "You're too young to be tied down with one boy. And you know that, Ashton."

Ashton avoided Mom's eyes.

"I don't want him to be with anyone else."

"There are plenty of boys out there." Mom turned away from her and took a coffee cup from the cabinet. "You don't need to fall head over heels with the first one you date."

"I do love him." Ashton hadn't meant to say anything, but then she heard her voice telling Mom that she loved Garret. The thing is, *she didn't know if she loved him*. She really didn't think she did. Not the kind of love Mom and Dad had. She couldn't close her eyes and imagine life with Garret. She didn't *want* to close her eyes and imagine life with anyone. Not right now.

But then, she was having sex with Garret, so that meant she loved him. And he loved her. *Right*?

Did she want Mom to question her? To push her? To make her admit that she *didn't* love Garret? That she was just playing a role? A role that she had sort of taken because she kind of felt backed into a corner? Did she want Mom to figure out she and Garret were having sex so Mom would step in and forbid her to see him?

She didn't know. That was the absolute hell of it, too. Once upon a time, not all that long ago, Ashton had known exactly what she wanted. In every facet of her life, Ashton had been in charge and determined to get exactly what she wanted. Now, she had no idea what that was.

Except that a glass of orange juice with a little shot of vodka seemed like a good idea right now. She rubbed her forehead and then moved her hands and dug her fingers into the back of her neck. Garret rubbed her neck and shoulders for her sometimes, and it felt great. But she wasn't sure it was worth it anymore, because he had come to expect a blowjob every time he gave her a massage. Again, she wondered why she ever did it in the first place. That first time, she had thought it would be quick, and she wasn't in the mood to take her clothes off and have him paw her and ride her until he came. It had been kind of okay the first time, exploring him like that, but it had gotten old fast.

"Ashton?"

"Huh?" Her cheeks burned. What the hell was she doing thinking about blowjobs and Garret when she was sitting here talking to her mother? Had she said something? Out loud? About Garret?

"What about Andrew? Why did you ask me if I wanted Brae to date Andrew?"

"I dunno," Ashton lied. "I guess I would worry about her if I were you. She's not very responsible. What if she got serious and ended up getting pregnant?"

Wow. Way to throw your sister under the bus, Ash.

Mom opened her mouth to answer her, but nothing came out. Ashton knew she had just floored her, and she felt bad about it. She felt bad for upsetting Mom that way, and she felt bad about what she said about Brae. Especially after Braelyn had told her she didn't want to get seriously involved with anyone.

Then again, no one said you had to be seriously dating anyone to start having sex. Brae went to a lot of parties; it was totally possible that she might have hooked up with someone at a party. Sisters, twins, didn't tell each other everything. Aston knew that for a fact.

"You're seriously involved with Garret," Mom said calmly. "What if you end up pregnant?"

Ashton took Mom's words like a jolt in the heart. Mom raised her eyebrows, poured herself a cup of coffee, and then turned to stand right in front of Ashton. She took a deep breath and then shoved her hands under her legs, so Mom wouldn't see that she was shaking.

Why had she said that? Did she know something? Or was she just fishing? She wasn't even smiling. She wasn't joking. Mom was dead serious.

"Milk mustache." Mom rubbed her thumb over Ashton's top lip. Ashton swallowed hard, prayed that she didn't look as guilty as she felt at the moment, and sat completely still, as if any movement might send the truth exploding out of her mouth.

She waited until Mom was gone—she heard her climb the stairs—and then she got up and put her glass and plate in the dishwasher. Hands still trembling, she went to the bottom of the steps and peered up. Mom was out of sight. Ashton hurried to the cabinet, got another glass out, and then poured herself some orange juice. She listened for a few seconds to make sure Mom wasn't coming back downstairs, and then she grabbed the bottle of vodka from the cabinet under the sink and poured a healthy drop into her juice.

She took a sip before she went upstairs. Waited for the calm to hit. For the nerves to quiet and her hands to stop shaking. When she finally felt the warmth of the liquor douse her nerves, she went upstairs to shower, her glass of juice still in hand.

CHAPTER 16

KAMRYN

It used to be that the fighting was temporary, and the *make-up* phase lasted forever and then the *everything's okay* phase settled in and lasted another forever. Now, sometimes, Kamryn felt like the make-up phase was temporary and the fights drug on and on, easily buried and yet easily dug back up and resumed. Kamryn had intended to sleep on the couch the night before. Well, okay, not really, because she knew she wouldn't sleep. So, she had intended to lie down on the couch and watch TV. Or stare blankly at the TV. But Mark had stormed out of the bathroom and then the bedroom and claimed the couch. She been just a half a second away from giving him hell for that. For taking the couch and the TV from her, when she knew she wouldn't sleep. Somehow, she had managed to keep her mouth shut.

It had been a horribly long night, and by three in the morning, her back and shoulders ached from lying in bed. Funny how nothing ached when she was asleep, but give her an hour awake, tossing and turning in bed, and every joint and bone and muscle in her body hurt.

She was furious with Mark for jumping the gun, for thinking she would accuse him of drinking too much. For dismissing her concern before she could ever talk to him about it. She was shocked that he had come so undone even when she hadn't come right out and called him an alcoholic. That he had jumped that quickly to accuse her of accusing him of something so dumb. What did that mean, anyway? Was he being defensive? *Too defensive?*

How unreal that she was staring at the ceiling at three twenty, thinking about Shakespeare and Lady MacBeth and protesting too much. And what the hell? What was the comment about the hot tub? Had Mark just pulled that out of thin air? Or was it an old memory he wished he could relive? Was soaking in a hot tub with sexy women something he wanted to do? Why had he thrown that in her face? Just to hurt her? To make her wonder?

And what the hell *was* the deal with the wine? Okay, yes, kids drank. Kamryn didn't live in a bubble; she hadn't lived the past twenty-five years with her head in the sand. Kids drank. Kids got drunk. Kids drove drunk. Kids killed kids. Kids killed themselves.

At parties.

Was it normal for kids to experiment with Mom and Dad's alcohol stash?

And *which* kid was it? Ashton? Kamryn couldn't wrap her head around that thought. *Ashton.* Super uptight, overachiever, damned determined to graduate at the top of her class. *Straight as an arrow Ashton.* Ashton and Garret?

Playing grown-up? Trying to create romance at their age? Nope. Kamryn didn't buy it.

But, Braelyn? Really? She couldn't believe that either. Sure, Brae was the partier. Brae was wild and had a little sparkle in her eyes that Kamryn read as trouble when she got a little older. Kamryn fully expected Brae to party so much her first semester away at college that she might come skulking home with barely passing grades. But not now. While Brae had the potential to be a wild card, Kamryn didn't see it *now*. She still had the little grin she wore when she was just a little girl. She still had a touch of baby fat in her cheeks. She still called Kamryn *Mommy* now and then. She still slept with stuffed animals.

Kamryn sighed and smiled at Eden as the girl desperately tried to straighten her leg. Eden was as determined to recover as anyone Kamryn had ever seen, but she was really struggling with her knee.

"Hey."

Kamryn looked up at Will. He was bent over a weight machine, setting his patient up with a new exercise.

"Did you watch *Dateline* last night?"

"No." Kamryn blinked a few times, as she realized she had been in a fog for the past—what?—fifteen? twenty? minutes? She didn't even know *Dateline* was still on. Seemed like it was on every night of the week for a while, and then suddenly it was sort of hit and, miss and then she had just forgotten all about the show.

"There was a woman on who was charged with setting her house on fire. With her husband and kids still inside. Rena watched it."

Kamryn raised her eyebrows. The TV had been on last night when she finished dinner and went to soak in the tub. Just before Mark had come in and erased all the previous week's tension with just a touch.

She had no idea what the kids had been watching.

"Mark got home last night," she finally told Will. "Dinner... Lots of conversation. Everyone talking at once. I didn't watch TV."

He nodded. "They let her off. Said she was crazy."

Kamryn wondered. Did you have to be crazy to kill your family? She and Mark fought, and God knows there were times when she was overcome with so much anger and hate for him that she could scream. But she could never hurt him. She could never hurt her husband and most certainly not her kids.

Did Mark ever hate her? Sure, he did. Only married couples could understand that kind of hate. The kind that burned so damned hot one second and then vanished in the next and turned into that fierce, possessive, protective love.

But did Mark ever hate her while he was gone? When he was surrounded by other women? Younger, sexier women who dressed in skirts and heels? Women who would offer a night of fun, of release, no strings attached?

"Kam?"

"Hmm?" She looked up, surprised to see Adrie standing in front of her.

"You okay? You seem distracted today."

Kamryn was embarrassed, falling into this haze at work when Adrie was back just a few days after she had buried her dad. Granted, Adrie was sad, more than sad, and yet she was functioning. She hadn't talked to her much since the funeral. Maybe before her dad had died, Kamryn might have sat down and told Adrie what was going on. Her worries about the kids. About the fight with Mark.

Not now, though. She wouldn't burden Adrie with the everyday stuff going on.

"I'm fine." She smiled.

Kamryn tried to stay tuned in then, because she hated being called out by coworkers. She wasn't one to share much about her private life, only with Adrie. And right now, it just felt wrong. Even if Adrie wasn't grieving for her dad, it kind of felt wrong to Kamryn to think about telling her. She was sitting on something that could go *really wrong*, this concern about the girls. It didn't seem fair to either of them for Kamryn to discuss it with someone, especially when she hadn't confronted them with her suspicions.

Confront. Apparently, that's how Mark had taken her approach last night.

"Hey."

She snapped out of it yet again. Will handed her a candy bar.

"What's this for?" she asked, eyeing the Snickers bar.

"Wake up." He winked at her. "It's chocolate. Chocolate makes everybody smile."

Kamryn laughed quietly and thanked him. She moved Eden on to her next exercise and opened the candy bar.

MARK WAS HOME BEFORE FOUR. Kamryn was used to fixing dinner around six, so she was sitting in the recliner reading an online article about stroke victims. She had seen four patients that day who were stroke victims, and although only one of them was *her* patient, it left her feeling stark and a little blue, to see the elderly fighting to recover. Or not fighting to recover.

Feeling guilty for not having dinner ready, she jumped from the recliner and set her laptop aside. Mark tugged at his tie as he flipped through the mail. The girls were both in their rooms, either doing homework or talking on the phone. The trouble with that assumption was that it was always Ashton pouring over her textbooks and always Ashton talking to Garret on the phone.

What did that leave for Braelyn? What child was Braelyn if not the studious one? Or the one with a boyfriend?

Kamryn took the wok from the island cabinet and put it on the stove. She felt Mark's eyes on her, but she didn't turn to him. She had a million things to say to him, and *I'm sorry* wasn't one of them. In fact, she kind of thought maybe he owed her an apology for the way he had stormed out on her last night.

"Where's Ian?" he asked. His gruff voice touched her in ways she didn't want it to.

"Basement."

"Playing?"

She bit her tongue. What the hell else would Ian be doing in the basement? Cleaning the furnace filter?

"Legos," she finally answered.

"Look, I'm sorry," he mumbled. "About last night."

She nodded, but she said nothing. She was too tired to do this tonight. Too tired to say it was okay, that it was a misunderstanding. They needed to talk, and they needed to get to the heart of the matter, and doing this *feelings* game wasn't going to get them anywhere.

"What? Are you gonna give me the silent treatment?" he asked after a few minutes.

"No, Mark, I'm not giving you the silent treatment," she snapped. "I'm fixing dinner."

"I didn't see any empties in the garage." He grabbed a bottle of water from the refrigerator.

"Then you didn't look very hard."

"They're hidden?"

"No, but they aren't in the recycle bin. There are three bottles right outside the door."

He frowned and went to look as if he didn't believe her.

"You and I drank this one," he told her, coming back into the kitchen with an empty Chardonnay bottle in hand.

"That one," she answered with a nod.

"So, what're you thinking? One of the kids is drinking?"

"That's kind of what I'm thinking, yeah."

"Kids drink at parties, Kam. Kids drink canned light beer or whatever's cheap. Kids drink from a keg, from plastic cups."

Kamryn took a knife to the bell peppers that she'd taken from the refrigerator earlier. She glanced up at Mark as she chopped.

"Kids don't drink expensive wine."

She agreed with him. *She did.* But then where the hell was the wine going? Did he think maybe she was drinking so much that she was blacking out? Passing out and forgetting that she was the one who had emptied all the bottles?

"Mark, someone drank that wine. And it wasn't me."

"So, are you saying I need to quit drinking? Because I'm setting a bad example?"

"No. That's not at all what I'm saying." She rolled her eyes. "I'm saying we have a problem. One of the kids is drinking here at home, and we have a problem."

"I think you're making too big a deal out of it."

"What?" Kamryn tossed the knife down on the counter. "What? I'm making too big a deal out of it?"

"You do this, Kam. You get all worried about stuff, and it's always for nothing. Everything's fine—"

"So, it's okay, until Braelyn's at a party, and she has a few beers in a plastic cup, and then she gets in her car and drives home and gets a DUI? Or worse? What if she drives her car over the line and hits someone?"

"Do you think it's Braelyn?"

"I don't know!"

"Ashton wouldn't do this."

Kamryn drew back, as if Mark had hit her.

"What?"

How dare he act as if he knew the girls better than she? How dare he act as if Ashton was better than Braelyn? As if

Braelyn would drink and Ashton wouldn't consider it.

"Ashton is going into pharmacy. She wouldn't drink. How do you think a DUI would look to the college of her choice? She'll have to sign a contract stating that she won't drink, because she'll be handling pharmaceuticals, Kam."

"And so that means it's Braelyn?"

"Ashton knows better."

"So does Braelyn!" Kamryn shouted. "Fuck your pharmaceuticals, Mark! That contract doesn't mean a goddamned thing, and she hasn't even signed it yet! We have a problem—"

"She's too responsible to do something like that. They don't even let doctors get their hands on that stuff."

"I know that! Doesn't that worry you? What if she *is* drinking now? What if she's drinking to get through school? To deal with the pressure? Doesn't it worry you that she'll have access to narcotics?"

Mark took a deep breath and laughed.

"So now we've gone from one of our kids drinking for recreation to having an addictive personality and maybe even developing a drug problem sometime in the future?"

"Why do you have to be such a dick about this? You wanna let them drink? You wanna take those chances with our kids' lives? What the hell is wrong with you?"

"I just think you're blowing things out of proportion."

Kamryn nodded. "Great. That's great, Mark. I'm glad I can talk to you about this stuff."

He walked out of the room, and Kamryn went back to chopping the peppers. She carried the cutting board to the stove, scraped the peppers into the wok and then started on the onion.

"Hey, Mom!"

Kamryn looked up as Ashton bounded into the room.

"What?"

"Look what I got on my world history paper!"

Ashton, whose skin had become so pale lately that it was almost translucent, was grinning from ear to ear. Her cheeks were flushed pink, and her eyes were shining.

"Mom!"

Kamryn wiped her hands on a kitchen towel, took Ashton's paper from her, and looked over Ashton's shoulder as Braelyn hurried to stand behind Ashton.

"What?"

"Andrew asked me out! He asked me to go to a movie on Friday!"

Kamryn stared at the beautiful, beaming faces in front of her and wondered if maybe Mark was right. Was she making too big of a deal over this? Maybe Ashton and Garret decided to sneak a glass of wine one night while she and Mark were out?

And so what if after sneaking that glass of wine, they started kissing and ended up making out on the living room floor?

Wasn't that what kids did? Isn't that what she and Mark used to do?

CHAPTER 17

KAMRYN

Even if Mark was right—that there was no need to worry about the girls (she hadn't even mentioned how worried she was about Ashton and Garret)—and she wasn't entirely convinced that he was right, she was still pissed-off about the whole deal. Or as Mark put it after dinner, while he was loading the dishwasher and she was helping Ian with his reading homework, she was in a mood. He knew that had only pissed her off again, and he had probably said it on purpose.

At dinner, Ashton had alternated between watching Kamryn and Mark closely, like she was doing research on marital disagreements, and gushing about the A she got on her world history paper. Kamryn was thrilled for her; she had slaved over that eight-page paper, and then she had typed a few more words and ended up with eight and a quarter pages and worried for the following week that Dr. Roberts would dock her grade for that extra quarter.

But Kamryn hated being under a magnifying glass, especially when it was one of her kids doing the scrutinizing. Especially when she was irritable anyway.

Braelyn had rattled all through dinner about Andrew asking her out and about movies, and then she and Mark had started a conversation about which *Star Wars* movie was the best. Thankfully that conversation drew Ian in, so Kamryn only had to pretend for Ashton. Pretending everything was peachy for one kid was hard enough.

Especially when that kid was one of the biggest causes for worry. When worry over that kid had launched the latest argument. Kamryn found herself tuning the movie conversation out—*Return of the Jedi* was by far the best *Star Wars* movie, she saw no need to debate that—and wondering again about Ashton and Garret. Why was Ashton so worried about Brae dating Andrew?

She really wished she hadn't taken the laundry upstairs the other day and opened Ashton's drawer and seen the thong. If she had any flame of worry before that, it was now a raging fire. She and the girls often went to *Victoria's Secret*, and she bought the girls boy cut underwear and bikinis and sexy, lacy stuff. But never with the thought that anyone would actually *see* it, other than an occasional sleepover moment when the girls were changing from clothes to pjs.

Why would Ashton have a thong in her drawer? Had she bought it? Neither of the girls had a job, and yes, she agreed with Mark that they both needed to get a job. They both needed the responsibility, as well as their own spending money. But Kamryn couldn't help but wonder if Garret had bought the thong for her.

If he'd intended for Ashton to model it for him.

Was she stupid to obsess over it? Was she supposed to just ignore it? Because kids were kids, and they were going to experiment whether she liked it or not? Maybe if Ashton was eighteen, though she doubted that she could help worrying even then.

Kamryn wondered about Andrew, too. Had Ashton heard something about Andrew? Surely it wasn't just a case of sibling rivalry. The girls were competitive, but mostly about school and grades. Really, *Braelyn* wasn't competitive; it was Ashton. But Kamryn didn't believe that Ashton didn't want Brae to have a boyfriend.

Her thoughts were caught in a circular path, and the constant thinking and worrying was giving her a headache. She could use a little dose of Mark's magic hands right now, a little squeeze here and a little stroke there. Except she was still mad at him, and he was a huge part of the headache.

When Ian finished his homework, Kamryn challenged him to a game of Checkers. They crashed on the living room floor; Kamryn sprawled out on her belly with her chin in her hand as she studied the board and Ian, sitting like a pretzel, studying the board intensely. He often beat her, and she figured he probably would tonight. The red and black squares on the board were enough to clear her mind of everything, but not enough to really make her think about the game.

At eight-thirty, she followed Ian upstairs and supervised his getting ready for bed. He bathed himself, but she often spot-checked places like his ears and his toes, to make sure he wasn't skipping anything. Once bathed and in his pjs, she read him two picture books and then a chapter from a *Magic Tree House* book. While she zoned out as she read *Dinosaurs Before Dark*—Ian's favorite *Magic Tree House* book—she had to pay attention to the actual words on the page. Her brain didn't process the story itself, but she often got tongue-tied with the constant speech tags.

She kissed Ian goodnight and promised him that she would have Dad come up and tell him goodnight, too.

"Mom?"

Kamryn stopped just outside Ian's door.

"What?"

"What do you think?"

She stepped back into his room and leaned on the wall.

"I think it's a good thing we cleaned your ears out, or you wouldn't be able to hear tomorrow in school."

"That's not what I meant."

"Oh." She chuckled to herself. "What did you mean?"

"Which *Star Wars* movie is the best?"

"*Return of the Jedi.*"

"Really? Dad thinks the first one is. The very first one. The old one, from when you guys were kids."

Kamryn sat on the edge of Ian's bed.

"Well. Sometimes the first one of anything is the best. Because it's new to you. Like the first *Harry Potter* movie."

"But you don't think the first *Star Wars* is the best?"

"Nope."

"I like the one where *Anakin* becomes *Darth Vader.*"

Kamryn couldn't deny that it was very dramatic, and yes, she liked that movie. But it was just another sore subject, because she had asked Mark not to let Ian see it yet. She thought he was too young, and that the scene with the fire and *Anakin* being injured and becoming *Darth Vader* was too much for him. Mark had rolled his eyes and let Ian watch it anyway.

Ian had had nightmares three nights in a row after watching the movie with Mark. Of course, those three nights happened to be when Mark was out of town, so it was Kamryn who got up with Ian each night and talked to him, soothed him back to sleep.

"Kind of yucky," she told Ian now.

"But it's sad, too. *Anakin* really wasn't a bad guy, Mom. I mean, you see that in the movie you like. When *Luke* takes *Darth Vader's* mask off."

"Ian, it's after nine. You have school tomorrow. We're not going to discuss whether *Anakin*, AKA *Darth Vader*, is a good guy or bad guy right now."

"What does AKA mean?" Ian asked as she stood up.

"*Also known as.*" She kissed his forehead again, told him goodnight, and walked out of his room.

"Mom?"

"Yes, Ian?" she called from the hallway.

"So, are you like, Kamryn McHale, AKA, Mom?"

Kamryn thought about a glass of wine. She quickly pushed the thought away, because with all the suspicions right now, the last thing she needed to do was drink to relax. Maybe instead, she would go downstairs and hammer her head against the office wall.

"Goodnight, Ian."

She heard him sigh. "Night, Mom."

Mark was sitting on the edge of the couch watching an NCAA basketball game when she went back downstairs. Illinois versus Ohio. On another night, she might have sat with him to watch the game. Or sat down by herself to watch the game. But she still had the mad on, and she didn't really want to be in the same room with Mark.

Instead, she went to the office, picked up the book she had taken with her to read in the tub last night, and sat in the wingback chair in the corner. She even opened the book and found the right page. But after reading the same paragraph three times and having no idea what she read, she closed the book and leaned her head back.

She didn't know how much time had passed when the office door opened. Angered by the interruption, she watched Mark through slitted eyes as he closed the door behind him.

"What are you doing? Why don't you come watch the game with me?"

"I don't want to."

"How long are you gonna stay pissed, Kam? I leave Monday."

"Story of your life, Mark."

He muttered something; she caught the word *job*, but she let it go. She didn't really care what he said. She really just wanted him to leave her alone.

"What're you doing?" she asked him when he knelt in front of her. Instead of answering her, he reached for the fly of his jeans. "Mark? What're you doing?"

The corner of his lips twitched up. She rolled her eyes and shook her head.

"This doesn't count."

"What?"

"Angry sex is better, I know that."

"Okay, so we're fighting, let's make up." He wiggled his eyebrows at her.

"That ship sailed. I was pissed before dinner."

"What was I supposed to do? Jump you on the kitchen counter?"

"You have before."

"Not after the girls were old enough to wander around the house."

She laughed as he reached out to her and slid his hands under her top.

"For the record," he said as he leaned forward and pressed his lips to her neck. "Angry sex isn't always better. Last night was pretty incredible."

"Yeah, before the angry part."

"We could just make this a quickie."

"You better, because there's no lock on that door."

It was fast, but Kamryn heard someone on the stairs before they were done. Ankles crossed behind Mark's back, she hoped whoever was coming downstairs would detour to the kitchen.

"I'll go see," Mark whispered. She nodded as she stood and fixed her clothing and Mark tucked and zipped everything in. She opened her book to the bookmark, slipped it into the back of her book, and then laughed at herself. Why did she have to make it look like she had been reading? She and Mark were the adults, but apparently some things never changed.

Mark was back on the couch. Ashton was at the kitchen sink drinking a glass of water. Kamryn glanced at the clock on the kitchen wall. Quarter after ten.

"Done with your homework?" she asked Ashton.

Ashton snorted. "I wish."

"What do you have left?"

"Calc and chemistry."

"Ouch. What've you been working on?"

"Studying for a religion test." Ashton rinsed her glass out and set it in the sink. "And Garret called."

Kamryn glanced at the clock again. Ashton must have been on the phone with him for a long time.

"Did you tell him about his ring?"

"Yeah. Told him I'd give it to him tomorrow. He's freakin' out."

"Why?"

"Because I won't have his ring until it's fixed."

"He doesn't trust you?"

Ashton shrugged.

"You don't care?"

For a second, Kamryn thought Ashton was going to break. To talk. There was a moment, just a moment, when all the fear and pressure she was under shined in her eyes, but she blinked and looked away, and when she looked back Kamryn saw only the big brown eyes Mark had given her.

"Night, Mom."

Kamryn stood as her daughter rushed past her and hurried up the steps.

"Goodnight, Ashton."

CHAPTER 18

ASHTON

She usually closed her eyes when they did it. Not because she was caught up in the moment, but because she didn't want to chance looking at Garret. Meeting his eyes while he was scrambling over her, all caught up in his own moment. Tonight, though, she had her eyes open. She was watching the light from Garret's bedside lamp catch the tiny diamond on her ring finger. Garret's mom had taken his class ring to the jeweler, and he had spent two days having a heart attack, thinking that someone might think they broke up and move in on Ashton. Apparently, he didn't trust her to say *no*, that she was still dating him, and she wasn't interested in anyone else. Instead of trusting her, he bought her a tiny sliver of a diamond and called it a promise ring and slid it on her finger with one hand while the other started undressing her. Neither move had impressed her too much.

What the hell had she gotten herself into? A promise ring? Seriously? She didn't want it. To be honest, she kind of liked the last two days, not wearing any rings on her fingers. She hadn't flirted with anyone; she hadn't had any wild thoughts about calling another boy or kissing another boy. But each time she had seen her ringless fingers, she kind of felt a jolt of happiness inside.

She would never tell Garret that. But then, if she never told him how she really felt, she wasn't going to get too many moments of that pure, simple happiness, was she?

He dragged his open mouth up the side of her neck and then his lips were over hers. She closed her eyes then and kissed him back. It wasn't that having sex with him was awful; in fact, sometimes it felt kind of good. She was just bored with the routine. The nightly phone calls. The texts through the school days. The fact that every night they went out, it had to end with this.

His body shook when he came, and as usual, Ashton prayed that the rubber wouldn't break. What the hell would she do if she got pregnant? There was no way she could go to her mom and dad and tell them she was pregnant. She didn't have time for that. She wasn't all that sure she ever wanted kids, much less while she was still in high school.

They were in his bed tonight; his parents were at a party across town, and Garret swore they wouldn't be home until well after midnight. So here it was only eight o'clock, and he had already rushed her through a pizza and half a movie, before he dragged her up to his room and done the ring trick. Probably he thought they could do it more than once tonight, which is something they had never done, because they had never had quite so much time.

Ashton was relieved when he flopped over on his back, but the relief was short-lived. He pulled her toward him, not satisfied until she was lying with her head on his chest, his arm around her, his fingertips grazing the side of her breast.

"I love you so much." He was looking at her now, waiting for her to say it back. Her mouth felt dry; there was just no way she could lie her way through this tonight.

"Mm." She offered him a small smile. "Me, too."

Garret kept talking, but he switched to talking about basketball. The regional tournament started soon, and he was psyched about it. Ashton understood his excitement, even if she didn't really feel it herself. So, while he talked about basketball, she let her mind wander. She thought about school, about the tests she had taken, and the papers she had due within the next week or two. She had an ethics paper she had started on, but she hadn't gotten much beyond the first paragraph. She also had a Spanish translation that was due next Wednesday. And a religion project.

Her eyelids were getting heavy. She slipped into sleep wishing she had something to sip on. Though she had hit the vodka a few times the past week, right now a glass of wine sounded good.

A SMALL, shrill beep woke her. She knew, even in her sleep, that it was her cell phone. If she didn't pick it up soon, Braelyn would knock on her bedroom wall with her fist or even barge in and tell her to check her damn phone. Something that apparently didn't work with the twin thing: Ashton could sleep through the phone ringing and the doorbell ringing and maybe even a three-ring circus in her room, once she was asleep. Braelyn slept lightly most of the time, and even in her room when both their doors were closed, she could hear Ashton's phone. In fact, sometimes, she claimed she could hear the vibration of it against Ashton's desk when the sound was turned off. Ashton doubted that.

She stretched now and reached a hand toward her nightstand. Instead, she got a handful of pillow and pillowcase. She tried to scoot a bit so she could reach the nightstand. Her skin stuck to skin. She was naked. Shit. She was naked, in Garret's bed, and he was probably still naked. How long had they been sleeping?

"Garret!"

She pushed herself up on her elbows and looked around the room. The lamp was still on, and she looked first at her left hand, where the diamond promise ring still glittered, and then she turned to the alarm clock on the table by Garret's bed. It was almost midnight. She had exactly seventeen minutes to get dressed, wake Garret, make him get dressed, and for him to drive her home.

"Garret!" She shoved at him and rolled the other way out of bed. Far out of his reach. He stretched and rubbed his eyes and then lay still and watched her shimmy into her jeans and sweatshirt. He blinked hard and sat half-way up, eyes stuck on her left shoulder, which was bare. She had thought the sweatshirt was cute when she got it—Mom had bought it after Christmas, one for her and one for Brae—but now she hated it. She hated the way Garret always skimmed his fingers over her bare skin, and if he couldn't reach her, like now, he would stare at it, like maybe he was getting off looking at her bra strap.

"Garret, we gotta go. It's almost midnight."

"Mmm." He sat up and stretched. Ashton looked away, disgusted by the sight of him. He was still skinny and still pasty and pale, and she hated looking at *it*. "We fell asleep?"

"Yes! Your parents could come home any minute, and I need to get home."

"You wouldn't get in trouble." Garret shook his head.

"What?" Ashton shot him a look of disbelief. "What do you mean I wouldn't get in trouble?"

"Your parents wouldn't get mad if I brought you home late. They like me."

Ashton raised her eyebrows. He had no idea how much her mom seemed to dislike him these days. Rather than answer him, she snatched her phone off the nightstand and dodged his hands when he reached for her.

"Get dressed." She backed away from him and then turned to walk out of his room.

Her stomach kind of lurched, and she caught her breath when she saw her phone screen. She had four texts and three missed calls, all between eight thirty and twenty minutes ago. *Oh God. What if something was wrong? What if Mom had tried to get a hold of her for some reason?*

She touched the recent button to go to her missed phone calls. All from Brae, starting at ten-thirty. The texts were from Brae, too, each one sounding a bit more frenzied than the last.

Cme 2 Andrew's. Watching mvies. At 8:42.

Andrew made me a mixed drink. Can't c strat. 9:57.

Ash? Can u n G gmme rid hme? 11:18.

Andrw drunkkk. Plz cme get me. 11:27

Oh boy. What if Andrew was really drunk, and he was driving Braelyn home right now? What if? What if he was too drunk to drive? What if he got pulled over, and Brae was in the car, too? If Braelyn had been drinking, and clearly, she'd had more than she was used to, she would get in trouble, too. Worse, Andrew could get in an accident.

Shit. Ashton shouldn't have gone to sleep. She shouldn't have let Garret do this. She shouldn't have come over here tonight.

She had the presence of mind to move slowly and quietly down the hall, just in case Garret's parents had come home while she and Garret were sleeping. Not Garret, though. After a few moments, he bounded down the hall after her, cracking his elbow on the frame of the bathroom door. He muttered something Ashton didn't quite catch and then flipped the kitchen light on.

"What're you doing?" she asked when he opened the refrigerator.

"I need a drink of water."

She took a deep breath and glanced at her phone again. Her thumbs worked as she texted a message to Braelyn.

Do u still need a ride?

"Who are you texting?" Garret asked her as he popped the top on a can of Pepsi.

"Brae. She texted me a while ago and said Andrew was drunk. She asked me for a ride home."

"Andrew's not drunk." Garret rolled his eyes. "No way."

"Since when did you become such an authority on everyone else's business, Garret?"

Her words surprised her, just the fact that she had *said* them, but the irritation she heard in her own voice *really* surprised her. She guessed it shouldn't. It had been building inside for far too long.

"Huh?" He picked up his keys, oblivious to her mood. "C'mon. Let's go."

Ashton groaned, but she followed him without a word. Sucked to be spoiling for a fight and not get one. She could push it. She could repeat herself. But she didn't. It wasn't worth it. Instead, she huddled deep into her black coat and leaned on the door, eyes closed. Garret probably thought she was tired, but she wasn't. In fact, she was wide awake. She could probably go home and finish that ethics paper, no sweat. But she would let him think she was tired.

She checked her phone every few seconds on the drive from Garret's house to hers. Brae didn't answer her. Ashton worried about the silence. It could mean anything, and she knew that. Most likely, Brae was already at home and just pissed at Ashton for not answering, let alone not coming to get her and bring her home safely.

But it could mean other things, too. It could mean Andrew had an accident. Drunk-driving accidents were never pretty. Weird how you never heard of a drunk driver just grazing a parked car or bumping into a utility pole as he eased out of a space in a lot. No fender benders. Nope. Drunk-driving accidents were all about head-on collisions or someone getting T-boned and blood and someone always seemed to end up dead.

Dead.

Maybe she was tired, because with her eyes closed and no conversation going on between her and Garret, Ashton pictured a scene where Andrew's truck was wrapped around a tree or crunched up like an aluminum can, crushing some smaller car. Andrew's head was on the steering wheel, blood gushing everywhere. Brae's head was against the passenger window, and there was blood, and Brae wasn't breathing.

Ashton half-screamed and came fully awake and looked around the front seat of Garret's car. Garret studied her with concern and then reached for her hand. Five minutes ago, she sort of thought she hated him, but now she needed comfort.

She slid her fingers through his and then sat straight up, with her eyes wide open, for the rest of the ride. Garret was singing with the radio, but Ashton was praying.

Just let Braelyn be home safe. She didn't care if Brae was pissed; she didn't care how pissed she might be. She just hoped to God that Brae was safe at home.

CHAPTER 19

KAMRYN

Mark was pissed. Well, Kamryn was pissed, too, but for different reasons. Or for the same reason and others, too. Mark was pissed because she had been proven right. Not even an hour ago, Braelyn had called. Thankfully, Mark had answered the phone, so he couldn't later accuse Kamryn of making something up, of making a mountain out of a molehill. God, she hated that expression, especially when her husband used it on her.

They had been watching a movie, or rather, Mark had been watching a movie, and she was reading. Mark was still dressed, anyway, but Kamryn already had her pjs on and her makeup off. She was tired, but too wired to sleep, so she had stayed up to read rather than go to bed. Ian was fast asleep, had been so for a few hours by then.

Moses stirred in Kamryn's lap when the phone rang, and Mark got up to answer it. Kamryn watched him closely, because they didn't often get nearly midnight phone calls.

She worried that it might be bad news. It could be anything, but most often, her mind jumped to her parents and Mark's mom.

Well, most often, on a weekend, if the phone rang near midnight, she thought of the girls, both out and about. And though they didn't get many late-night calls, when they did, it was usually one of the girls asking permission to stay at a friend's house or reporting in before they left to come home.

Tonight, though, Kamryn sensed the phone call was different, because Mark looked confused. Confused, at first, and then angry. He fished a pen out of their junk drawer and asked in a tight, too-controlled voice, "Where are you?" and then he jotted something down.

"What's going on?" Kamryn asked him when he hung up.

"Brae needs a ride."

"Really?" She frowned. "How come? Isn't she with Andrew?"

"Yep." Mark shoved his feet into the loafers he had kicked off behind the couch when he came home from work. "She's with Andrew. But Andrew's drunk, and under all the crying, it sounded like Braelyn was pretty damned close to drunk."

Though they had had that argument just the other night, Kamryn was shocked. First, she had hoped it wasn't true. That maybe someone had snuck a drink of her and Mark's wine, and they hadn't liked it, and it had been a dumb, little experiment, and it was over. She hadn't considered the possibility that one of their daughters was out partying and drinking and would consume enough alcohol to need to call for a ride home.

Yeah, thank God Brae *had* called for a ride. But still. She had no idea there was this much drinking going on.

Really, though, she was shocked that it was Brae. Kamryn would have put money on Ashton being the drinker.

"Wait'll she gets home," Mark muttered as he snatched his car keys from the counter.

Kamryn sighed and flopped back in the recliner. Moses seemed to sense her distress, because he stretched and then eased away from her, until he was close enough to the edge of the recliner to jump down. She closed her eyes and listened to him lap water from his bowl.

Braelyn.

They were back home just after midnight, and though Kamryn was angry with Brae, she also noticed that Ashton was late. Only by four minutes at the moment, but late, nonetheless. Brae staggered into the kitchen, and maybe by adult standards, she was tipsy not bombed. But it didn't matter. Sixteen-year-olds being tipsy was the equivalent of grown-ups being drunk, and it looked wrong, and it looked stupid, and it looked dangerous.

Kamryn, who had gotten up minutes after Mark left, was standing at the kitchen counter, drinking a bottle of water. She folded her arms over her chest and raised her eyebrows, waiting for Brae to speak or Mark to join them.

"What do you have to say for yourself?" she finally asked when seconds had ticked by, and Mark hadn't appeared in the kitchen.

Braelyn, whose eyes were bloodshot, and eyelids were heavy, reached to pull the elastic from her ponytail.

"I'm sorry, Mom," she whispered.

Kamryn shook her head. Sorry wasn't enough. Sure, there was the fact that she had called for a ride, rather than getting into the truck with Andrew, since he had been drinking, too.

But Kamryn didn't know where to start. She felt about this drinking thing—this drinking thing and Braelyn—the same as she did about Ashton and Garret and wondering if they were having sex. Though she was the mom, she was afraid to ask.

Because she was afraid of the truth. That line from that old Tom Cruise movie popped into her head. *No*, she *couldn't* handle the truth.

"Brae, I'm glad you called," she said quietly. "I *am* glad you called—"

"I know, I know," Braelyn wailed. "Daddy already said all of this. I called, and that's good, but I've been drinking, and I'm not of age—"

"Not of age?" Kamryn repeated. "Honey, you're sixteen. You're not of age by five years."

"I'm almost seventeen." Brae licked her lips, but she had the sense not to meet Kamryn's eyes.

"Did you really just say that to me?" Kamryn asked. She leaned forward and ducked her head, trying to catch Brae's eyes. "Really? Like it's gonna be okay to drink when you're seventeen? The legal drinking age is twenty-one, Braelyn. You'll still be short by four years."

Brae sighed and sniffled and still avoided Kamryn's eyes.

"When did this start?" Kamryn asked quietly. She wondered again where Mark was. Had he been so pissed that he had gone on to bed? He was pissed at Braelyn, but Kamryn knew he was pissed at her, too. Because she had been right. Because apparently, they did have a problem here, and Kamryn had called it.

What the hell did he expect? She lived with the girls day in and day out. Mark dropped in like a traveling uncle, one who just happened to sleep with the mom, but still.

Brae lifted her shoulder in a shrug, but before either of them could say anything else, the front door opened and there was a scuffle and raised voices. Kamryn shot Braelyn a look meant to freeze her in place and walked out to the entrance hall to see for herself what was going on.

"Say goodnight, Ashton," Mark said firmly. He had his fingers wrapped around her upper left arm. Kamryn thought it looked like he had pulled her away from Garret. The two of them, Garret and Ashton, looked like they had just woke up. In fact, there was a line across Ashton's cheek, like she had slept on a creased sheet or something. A sheet. In a bed.

But their cheeks were flaming red, and no one was making eye contact, and finally Kamryn heard Ashton mumble goodnight to Garret. She saw the daggers Mark stared at the kid, too, before Garret all but ran out the door and Mark shut it solidly behind him.

"Get upstairs. Now."

Ashton looked up at Mark.

"Daddy, you're hurting me."

She yanked her arm from his grasp, turned, and ignored Kamryn as she raced up the stairs to her room.

"Is it a full moon or what?" Mark mumbled. He toed off his shoes and this time picked them up. "One daughter comes home drunk, and I find the other one making out on the front porch with Boy Wonder. Judging from the ring on her finger, I thought maybe they ran off and eloped, and that kid was about to carry her over the threshold and start his wedding night."

"Excuse me?" Kamryn asked quietly. The headache that had begun to brew earlier, when she didn't go to bed because she was wired but probably should have gone to bed because she was wired and would soon hit the wall, exploded now. Behind her eyes. At the base of her neck. She pinched the bridge of her nose and then rubbed her jawbones, desperate for relief.

"Maybe you oughta go see for yourself," Mark suggested as he looked up at her. "Maybe she can explain to you how she plans to go to college and pharmacy school and wear this ring—"

"Daddy, it's just a promise ring!" Ashton called down the steps. "It doesn't mean anything."

Kamryn opened her mouth to argue, but her mind was spinning so fast, she had no idea what to say. What part of the past ten minutes should she comment on? What the hell could she possibly say to any of the three of them right now that might make sense?

"Promises don't mean anything?" she mumbled more to herself than anyone else.

"Mom!" Ashton rushed down the stairs, two at a time. "It's just a promise ring. It's because his mom had to leave his class ring at the jewelry store."

Kamryn stared blankly at Ashton. She glanced at Mark and then turned to look back at the kitchen. Was Brae still standing there?

Finally, she pulled herself together and reached for Ashton's hand. There was a ring on Ashton's left ring finger. It *might* have been a sliver of a diamond; as it was it was so tiny, Kamryn couldn't tell if there was truly a stone in it or not. She hoped Garret hadn't spent much money on it, because Ashton sure as hell wouldn't be wearing it. Maybe he could return it.

"Take it off. Now."

Lips pressed together, anger painted across her pretty face, Ashton tugged the ring off and dropped it into Kamryn's open hand.

"You're sixteen. This is—"

"I'm almost—"

"Yes, I know. You're almost seventeen. And like your almost seventeen-year-old sister, you've shown poor judgment tonight, and Dad and I are disappointed in you both."

"It's just a ring!"

"A promise ring clearly implies it's more than just a ring, Ashton. And if a promise means that little to you, I'm not sure who you are. However, living in this house as a sixteen, almost seventeen-year-old, means you abide by our rules, and you will not wear a promise ring from a boy. This is ridiculous."

"He loves me."

Even with a stomach and head full of rage, Kamryn heard her. Kamryn heard Ashton say that Garret loves her. And she heard what Ashton didn't say.

"Why are you late?" she asked. She took a deep breath, grateful for the calm it brought.

"What? I was like, five minutes late."

"Five minutes." Kamryn nodded. "What did you do tonight that had to make you five minutes late?"

"What?" A dark blush climbed her cheeks. Kamryn felt her heart sink.

"Go to bed." She turned away from Ashton and tried to mentally change gears so she could go back to talk to Braelyn.

"But Mom—"

"Go to bed. Now."

Brae was still in the kitchen, but she was on a barstool, slumped over the counter now. Her eyes were closed, her messy, tangled hair spilled over the bar.

"Braelyn?" Kamryn nudged her. "Wake up."

"I'm so tired."

"What did you drink?"

"I don't know," Braelyn answered, eyes still closed.

"You don't know?"

"Nuh-uh. Something Andrew mixed and gave me."

"You drank something that Andrew mixed. But you have no idea what it was?"

"Hmm."

Kamryn sighed. She could use Mark's help right about now. It would do no good to question Braelyn further. To give her hell right now. To punish her now. That would have to wait until morning. Kamryn glanced at the clock on the microwave. Twenty after twelve. Okay, Kamryn amended her thoughts; it would wait until *later* in the morning.

For now, she needed to get Braelyn upstairs to bed. Obviously, Mark had left her to it.

"Let's go, Braelyn," she said, and for just a moment, just in those three words, she heard her own mother. That cross, tired voice. Sure, she had been in trouble her share of times when she was younger, but Kamryn had never come home drunk at sixteen.

Braelyn sat up and yawned. She rubbed her eyes, leaving her face looking like a raccoon or a circus clown. Makeup smeared around her eyes, and when Brae wiped at her mouth to dry the slobber that had gathered in the corner of her lips, she even streaked a little mascara across her lips. Kamryn had half a mind to snap a picture, so she could show both the girls how glamorous it was to be drunk.

Instead, she followed a very slow-moving Braelyn upstairs and watched her fall into bed. She didn't insist that Brae wash her face or brush her teeth. Let Braelyn wake up to the mess tomorrow.

Kamryn turned in the hallway, glad to finally be going to bed. She nearly tripped over Moses. She scooped him up and carried him back down to the kitchen. Mark stood at the kitchen sink eating a cookie.

"I'll take him out."

Kamryn bit her lip. She had been about to rag on him. How in the hell could he eat now? How could he eat a cookie when one daughter came home drunk and the other came home with a damned promise ring?

How in the hell could Mark eat? She felt like she could probably go upstairs and throw up the lasagna she had eaten for dinner.

Rather than say a word, she simply smiled, handed Moses over to Mark, and hurried up to the bedroom. She wished she could be sound asleep when Mark came up to bed, because she was in no mood for sex and who the hell knew what Mark was thinking these days.

CHAPTER 20

KAMRYN

She didn't sleep. She tried for a while, forcing her eyes closed, making them stay closed even when they wanted to open. Even when in her mind she was seeing a drunken Braelyn at the kitchen counter, that deep angry blush on Ashton's face when Kamryn had asked her what she and Garret had done that made them run late.

At four, Kamryn gave up trying to sleep and lay awake staring at the ceiling. When she was a little girl and she spent the night at her grandparents' house, she would count the little squares in the ceiling. They lived in an old house with threadbare carpeting, an ancient mustard gold wall phone with a rotary dial, and two rooms—the living room and the bedroom the grandkids slept in when they stayed over—finished in dark faux-wooden paneling.

Forty-seven. Kamryn frowned now, wondering if that was right. Forty-seven squares on the ceiling? She would get close to the last corner, and something would distract her, and she had to start all over.

Like it mattered. What she knew for certain was that at the age of ten or twelve or twenty, she had never given a thought to what her kids might do as they grew up. She had never once worried about her teenaged daughters partying. Probably nobody did. Be kind of weird, wouldn't it? Being sixteen or eighteen and thinking twenty years or more into the future and worrying about your kids? Kamryn wasn't sure she had ever thought about *having* kids at that age, much less what they would be like.

At five, the headache and the lower backache drove her out of bed. The headache was still stress and the fact that she had probably slept a total of seventeen minutes the night before. The lower backache? She hoped it was from lying awake and tossing and turning and not the official notice that she was starting her period. She showered slowly, hoping the hot water would soothe her and push the headache away. Her back still hurt, though, as she washed her hair and then lathered her body with shower gel and finally shaved her legs. When she shut off the water, toweled herself dry, and dressed in running pants and a Boston Celtics t-shirt, she dried her hair and gave half her mind to styling it and let the other half roam.

It seemed like forever since she had talked to Adrie. She wondered how she was doing and thought about calling her today. Even suggesting lunch or shopping or something. She needed to get out of the house. Away from Mark—how ironic was that?—and away from the girls. Just for a while.

But she wouldn't call Adrie. She knew she wouldn't. Because as soon as they sat down to lunch or started walking the mall or God knows what, Kamryn would start talking, and she wouldn't stop until that awful pressure in her chest let up, and it stopped feeling like she was carrying around an anvil strapped to her back.

Adrie didn't deserve that. No friend deserved that, especially not when she was grieving for her father.

Kamryn skipped the makeup and then plucked her birth control pills from the medicine cabinet. She was down to the last one, which meant she *was* due for a period. How had the week gotten away from her?

She sighed and then slipped out of the bathroom, through the bedroom without waking Mark, and then downstairs. Five-thirty on a Saturday morning. She rolled her neck as she went through the motions of making coffee; Mark's brand today, if for no other reason than she was disgusted with Ashton and didn't want her to waltz in and pour herself a cup of Starbucks brew and then sit down and sip it and enjoy herself.

Kamryn knew she was being petty, but she didn't care. She was the mom, after all, and she and Mark had taught both of their girls better than this. Or so she thought.

March had dropped on them this past week, and the forecast called for sunny skies. Kamryn wondered if it was warm, if she should have gone for a run outside before showering. When the coffee was done, she pulled Mark's jacket from the hall closet and slipped it on, poured herself a cup, and went out to the deck.

Chilly, but bearable. Actually, the brisk morning air felt good. She leaned a hip against the deck rail, wrapped her hands around the mug, and took a sip. She dropped her chin to her chest and inhaled Mark's clean, woodsy scent. The tip of her right ring finger rubbed over her wedding ring. She loved him. She loved him even more now than the day she married him. But there was so much more to her and Mark now, and so often all that other stuff came between them.

It scared her sometimes. Not the traveling. The fact that she slept alone more nights than she slept with him. She trusted him. Now and then she might feel a pang of jealousy, of fear, but she trusted him. Mark McHale was a stand-up guy, always had been. Always would be.

Probably.

She took another drink of coffee and sighed. *Probably?*

Where the hell had that come from? Mark had vowed to be faithful, the same as she had. She had never been tempted to cheat. Why should she ever believe Mark would?

Because of all that other stuff. The everyday worries. The bills. The chores—the stuff that needed to be done around the house and never seemed to get done. The new faucet Mark had been meaning to install in the basement shower. The windows that needed to be washed. The double college tuition they would be paying in less than two years.

The fact that one of their daughters was drinking. Maybe if Kamryn hadn't noticed that someone had been hitting the wine bottles, last night's incident with Braelyn wouldn't be that big of a deal. Bad judgment for drinking, yes. The fact that Brae didn't even *know* what she drank really bothered Kamryn. Maybe it could have just been a lecture: bad decision to drink but good decision to call for a ride. Punishment. Probably Kamryn would have taken Brae's phone. For a day or two. Case closed.

But Kamryn *had* noticed that someone was drinking the wine. And that felt like the incident last night was a much bigger problem, and she and Mark were not even in the same book, much less on the same page on this.

She was cold now, but it didn't bother her that much. In fact, she would have sat down, but Mark had taken all the deck furniture into the garage to protect it from winter weather. She paced the length of the rail as she drank the rest of her coffee.

The grass was still winter brown, and the trees were still bare. It was barely March, after all. But breathing the fresh air deep into her lungs and holding it there as long as she could still brought her a tiny wisp of energy. And hope.

Kids make stupid choices, Kam. Stupid choices are learning opportunities.

She considered the girls she used to coach, how often she had caught bits and pieces of conversations. The talk about the parties. The senior she had benched after the girl was arrested for DUI. The girls who shared sex stories on the bus rides for out-of-town games. Even then, she had never considered she would be standing here on a morning after what she and Mark had seen last night.

Things were different now. Life for her girls was faster and older than it was for her. Kamryn understood that. But that didn't mean parenting should be laxer. She had set behavior expectations for her kids, and by God, she meant to hold each of the three to those expectations.

She didn't want to go inside. It was so quiet outside, and it was growing lighter, and Kamryn prized the solitude at the moment. But her mug was empty, and she wanted more coffee.

The house was still and quiet when she went back in. She breathed a sigh of relief, poured herself another cup, and then sat to put her shoes on. Moses, who had most likely slept curled on the end of Ian's bed, trotted through the kitchen to greet her as she took his leash from the hook by the door.

"Gotta potty?" she asked him.

He barked, but she laughed and shushed him. Still in Mark's jacket, she hooked Moses' leash to his collar, grabbed her coffee, and punched in the code to disarm the house alarm.

Moses tugged eagerly at the leash as they made their way through the garage. He darted across the driveway to the grass before he lifted a leg to pee. Kamryn waited patiently, staring at the coffee cup, but thinking about the girls.

When Moses was ready, he trotted down the driveway. Kamryn followed, still thinking, but enjoying the brisk morning. She glanced back at the house as they walked. It was one of the biggest on the block, though she and Mark hadn't set out to best anyone. She glanced at each house on the street as Moses led her along. Wondered what kind of drama played out behind each front door, because probably, no matter if it was brick or adobe, single story or two story, red door or white door, life inside each home ran along the same chapters.

IT WASN'T QUITE seven when she pushed the back door open and stepped inside the house. Moses hopped the step and sat at her feet, waiting patiently for Kamryn to give him a treat. She listened as she put his leash back on the hook and then took his treat jar from the cabinet. Didn't sound like anyone else was up yet, but she couldn't be sure.

Moses stood on his back paws, begging for the peanut butter flavored treat in her hand. She held her hand out for him to take it and chuckled when he snatched it and darted from the room. She heard the TV as she stepped into the kitchen. *Spongebob*. Ian must be up.

She rinsed her empty coffee mug and set it in the sink. When she turned, she was surprised to see Braelyn lying on the couch. Still assuming Ian was up—Braelyn up at seven on a Saturday to watch *Spongebob*?—Kamryn looked around for him.

"Is Ian up?" she finally asked Braelyn.

"No."

"Why are you up?"

Even flopped out on the couch as she was, Kamryn recognized the lazy shrug of her shoulders.

"Couldn't sleep anymore. My head hurts."

"Really?" Kamryn couldn't stop the eyeroll, but Brae's eyes were still on *Spongebob*, so she missed it.

"Can I take some Advil?"

Kamryn watched Braelyn push herself to a sitting position on the couch. The kid looked like hell. She was hungover.

"C'mere a minute," Kamryn said. She walked by Braelyn, took her hand, and pulled her from the couch. She walked down the hall, past the office to the bathroom, and tugged Braelyn into the small room with her. "Take a look." Kamryn flipped the light on. Braelyn looked around the room and then back at Kamryn.

"What?" She frowned. Her face was twisted in a mask of confusion and maybe a hint of irritation. Kamryn figured she was desperate for the Advil, and probably some kind of greasy breakfast, although Braelyn wouldn't realize that.

Or would she? Was she a seasoned enough drinker to know that big, greasy breakfast or sandwich would help to soak it up? God, Kamryn hoped not.

Kamryn gave Brae a gentle shove toward the sink.

"Look up."

Braelyn studied the sink for a moment before looking up into the mirror. She met Kamryn's eyes and shrugged her shoulders.

"What, Mom?" she snapped. "You keep saying look. What? What am I looking at?"

Kamryn reached from behind her and cupped her face in her hands. "Look at this. Look at this beautiful face."

Braelyn turned her nose up and tried to turn away.

"Look, Braelyn McHale."

Braelyn, finally understanding Kamryn's motives, sniffled, and tried again to turn away from the mirror.

"Don't make me…"

"Look at your eyes, Brae. The makeup all over your face. Look how puffy that skin under your eyes is."

Braelyn closed her eyes. Kamryn watched a single tear roll down her daughter's face.

"Pretty glamorous, huh?"

"Mom, you and Dad drink."

"Yeah, we do," Kamryn agreed. "We don't drink enough to need to call for a ride home, usually. If one of us does, the other drives."

Kamryn backed away and let Braelyn come out of the bathroom. "Dad and I are also adults, Brae."

"I called for a ride," Braelyn whined. She followed Kamryn to the kitchen and watched her take the carton of eggs and a package of bacon from the refrigerator.

"Thank God you did." Kamryn nodded.

"You and Daddy always said if we needed a ride to call."

"Yes. We do always say that."

"No questions asked. No one gets in trouble."

Kamryn shook her head as she laid strips of bacon in the skillet on the stove top.

"Nope. Neither of us ever said that." She looked up at Braelyn, but she continued to arrange the bacon in the skillet. "You made a bad choice, and now we have to talk about it."

"I don't wanna talk about it," Braelyn groaned. "Can't you just ground me? Send me back to bed?"

"And then what do you take away from that? That it's okay to drink, as long as you call home for a ride and accept your punishment?"

Braelyn pushed her hair out of her face.

"That smells awful," she mumbled.

"Trust me, you'll want to eat it."

"Did Ashton get in trouble for being late?"

"I'm talking to you right now, Braelyn."

"Look, I messed up. I know that. I'm sorry."

"You told me last night you didn't even know what you drank."

Braelyn frowned as she stared down at her hands. Kamryn noticed her class ring on her right hand and thought about Garret wearing Ashton's class ring. About the promise ring on Ashton's finger last night. The one that didn't mean anything.

Kamryn took the Advil bottle from the cabinet by the window and handed it to Braelyn.

"I don't know," Braelyn finally answered. She shrugged yet again. "Andrew mixed something. It tasted fruity."

Kamryn nodded. "Who was at Andrew's house?"

"Me and Andrew. Scott Tullock and Amy Eddy. Robbie Mast was there for a while, I think."

"How well do you know those guys?"

Braelyn squinted up at her and then shook her head. "I've been going to school with them forever. You know that."

"What if one of them would have slipped something in your drink?"

"What?"

"It happens, Braelyn—"

"Mom, Andrew mixed my drink. God, what are you so freaked out about? *Andrew* did it. You *know* Andrew."

"I know I know Andrew," Kamryn said with a nod. "That's why it's called date rape, Brae."

Braelyn sank back against the barstool and stared at Kamryn in shock.

"Seriously? You're gonna worry that Andrew's gonna try—"

"And besides the fact that you don't even know what you drank, have you ever heard of alcohol poisoning, Braelyn?"

"I didn't drink that much."

"You don't know that. You don't know what your body can tolerate."

Or did she?

"I'm fine, Mom," Braelyn said flatly.

"This time."

"Yeah, because I get bombed every weekend."

No way Kamryn could have missed the sarcasm in Braelyn's words, but she ignored it.

"Do you?"

"No!"

"When did this start, Brae?"

"What?"

Kamryn and Braelyn both glanced up as Mark walked into the kitchen.

"When did it start?" Kamryn repeated. "When did the drinking start?"

CHAPTER 21

ASHTON

Since Mom was on the warpath, Ashton kept to herself all morning. First, she cleaned her room. Not the bare bones kind of cleaning Brae did. No shoving things under her bed or throwing stuff on the closet floor, closing the door, and pretending the room was done. Ashton hung up the few items of clothing she had tossed around through the week, straightened both of her shoe racks in the closet, and made her bed. She dusted her furniture, ignored a call from Garret, pulled her furniture out from the wall as far as she could, and dusted behind it and then ventured out to the hallway for the vacuum cleaner from the closet at the opposite end of the hall.

The closet just outside Mom and Dad's closed bedroom door. Since she turned twelve, she cringed anytime she saw their bedroom door closed. Nothing creeped her out like that did. Now, though, she could hear them arguing. She didn't stick around long enough to hear what they were arguing about, but she could hear heated words zipping back and forth.

Knowing it was a risk—but then, that was kind of half the fun, right?—she hurried downstairs and grabbed a soda from the refrigerator. She filled a glass with ice and then poured the soda over it. She stood for a moment and watched Ian to make sure he was really into *Phineas and Ferb*, and then she grabbed the vodka bottle from under the sink and splashed a bit into the glass.

Ian never glanced her way, and Mom and Dad's door was still closed when she went back upstairs. She pushed the vacuum from where she had left it in the hall into her room and then tapped on Braelyn's closed door.

"What?"

Ashton pushed the door open just enough to peek her head in.

"You okay?"

"Peachy," Braelyn mumbled.

"Did she ground you?"

"Yep."

"How long?"

"Two weeks with no phone."

"Damn."

Ashton took a drink. The vodka and soda tasted gross, but she really liked the burn as it made its way down her throat. Maybe if she mixed it with something different.

"How much did you drink?" Ashton asked.

Braelyn, lying on her bed, with her hands holding a book open, shrugged.

"I dunno. I think just two drinks, but I dunno what Andrew put in them."

Ashton raised her eyebrows.

"Yeah. Got that lecture, too. He could have drugged me and raped me."

Ashton wondered how that would compare to drinking herself numb and having sex with Garret. She didn't share her thoughts with Brae.

She winced and shook her head.

"I'm sorry," she started to say, but Braelyn jumped up off the bed with lightning speed.

"Thanks, though, Ash!" She grabbed the door and yanked it all the way open. Ashton almost lost her balance, and righted her glass before anything spilled.

"Brae, I didn't get your—"

"Didn't get my texts." Braelyn nodded. "Because you were busy. Right? Busy with Garret? That's okay. Whatever, right?"

"Braelyn, really. I'm sorry. We fell asleep."

Braelyn laughed sarcastically. "Whatever."

Ashton watched her turn and walk away from her, retreating further into her room.

"At least now I know."

"Know what?"

"Can't have my back if you're on your back, right?"

"What?" Ashton stepped into Braelyn's room. "What did you say?"

Braelyn, amused look on her face, watched her close the door.

"You heard me," Braelyn said with a cold smile. "But don't worry about *them*. They didn't hear me, because they're too busy fighting about me and my drinking problem and the possibility that I might get date raped."

Ashton raised her eyebrows. If that was truly the case, she would like to invite her English teacher into their home to observe a case of real-life irony. If it wasn't, and Braelyn was just jacking with her, she had to wonder just exactly what Brae knew and *how* she found out.

"Maybe next time you shouldn't let Andrew mix your drink."

Ashton saw the anger in Brae's eyes, but she quickly left her room so she wouldn't hear her parting comment.

What the hell was that all about? She pushed the vacuum into her room and closed her door. Did Braelyn really know something, or was she just guessing at what Ashton and Garret were doing when she texted? It could be that Braelyn just took a wild stab, but then again, what if Garret had told Andrew? Andrew might tell Brae. He might use her and Garret as an example of why Brae should have sex with him.

Ashton chewed nervously on her thumbnail. She set her drink on her desk and stared at the stack of textbooks there. She should quit. Everything. She should quit the drinking. For one thing, Brae coming home drunk last night would be sure to put Mom and Dad on the alert, and they would be watching the household stash.

Wouldn't they? Then again, just because teenagers drank at parties didn't mean they really had a problem and they drank at home, when no one was around.

Ashton dropped to sit on the desk chair for a moment. Drinking alone was sometimes a symptom of a drinking problem, wasn't it?

She fidgeted for a minute with the corner of her chemistry notebook. No. She didn't have a drinking problem. Of course she had to drink *alone* at home. *Hello?* Wasn't like she could have a cocktail or a glass of wine with her parents, was it? She drank alone just because it was the only way she could have a glass of wine now and then.

She could get through a day without a drink. Hell, she could get through a week without a drink. If she wanted to. So what if she snuck a few drinks now and then? Brae probably did, too.

Okay, but she could quit if she wanted to. And maybe she should. There was that contract she would have to sign when she went into pharmacy school. The one where she swore not to drink or use drugs. But maybe drinking the way she did, just to take the edge off, just to help her get through the homework headaches and just to numb herself so she could do it with Garret, maybe drinking like that *now* would create a problem for her in the future.

That's ridiculous, she told herself. She stood up and took a drink. Cringed again from the taste. She took another big gulp, set her glass down, and then turned back to the vacuum cleaner.

Garret. Okay, she could definitely quit him. She was almost sort of glad her mom had taken the ring last night. God, she wasn't quite seventeen and Garret wanted her to promise herself to him? Well, he had already seen and touched everything about her, so that had to mean she was promising him marriage, right? *No way.* No way was she even thinking about marriage when she still had a year of high school to go before she even started college.

Maybe she should use this time to break up with him. His class ring was at the jeweler's being fixed. Her mom had taken the promise ring; no doubt she would return it to Garret's mom. Maybe this was the perfect excuse to end it.

Ashton took a deep breath. This time it was relief that pounded through her body. Freedom. No more Garret. No more every day and every night phone calls and texts and no more hands all over her. No more anything.

Funny. She didn't want to give up the alcohol, but she decided she would gladly give Garret away.

Except what if he told someone about her? Not that she drank sometimes, but that they had been together for a few months now? What if he told the guys on the basketball team that she was easy?

The things she had done with Garret knotted together in the pit of her stomach. She took a deep breath, but this time there was no relief. Only fear. She didn't want that reputation. She didn't want her friends to look at her and think about the things she had done with Garret. She didn't want teachers and coaches and counselors to know she did that stuff.

Why hadn't she thought about all this stuff before?

Ashton jumped when she heard the loud thump on her door, but it opened before she could move.

"What're you doing?"

She looked over her shoulder at her mom. "Cleaning my room."

Mom nodded. She tilted her head and studied Ashton long enough to make her uncomfortable.

"What's wrong?"

Ashton shook her head.

"You look a little green. What's wrong?"

"My stomach's bothering me a little," Ashton answered.

"Garret called. Said he thought maybe your cell was dead because you aren't answering."

Ashton shrugged. "Don't really wanna talk to him right now."

Mom nodded. She folded her arms across her chest and leaned back against the doorframe.

"Do you love him, Ash?"

"God, Mom, I don't wanna talk about this now."

"I think maybe this is something we need to talk about. You came home wearing a promise ring last night, Ashton. I need to know what's going on with you two."

"It's nothing—"

"It's something. A promise ring is something. And you're only a junior. What about college? What about pharmacy? You don't have time for a relationship like that. Is that what you want? To be tied down all the time? You wanna be tied down when you leave for school?"

"No! No, I don't, okay?" Ashton ran her fingers through her hair and sighed with frustration. "I don't want any of that. We're just dating, Mom."

"Really? Is that it?"

"What are you saying?"

"You're not ready, Ashton."

"Ready for—"

Mom stepped out and pulled her door shut behind her. Ashton reached a shaking hand to the vacuum cleaner and turned it on. Did Mom know? Because it sounded like Mom knew she was having sex with Garret. Did Brae tell her? But how did Brae know for sure? Would Brae tell her? Ashton didn't think so. Not even if she was mad at her, she didn't think Brae would tell Mom what she was doing.

Then again, how many times lately had she been willing to sacrifice Brae just to get out of a lecture or an uncomfortable conversation?

CHAPTER 22

KAMRYN

Kamryn pushed her salad away as Will entered the break room. Completely out of smiles, she raised her eyebrows to acknowledge him and then went back to studying the word search book someone had left on the table. She hated puzzles, but she didn't mind crosswords and word searches. Right now, she would do anything to not think about things at home, so rather than eat lunch—her stomach was pretty iffy today—she was looking for words that related to deep-sea diving.

"Adrie's snorting," Will announced as he pulled a leftover container from the refrigerator.

"I'm sorry?" Kamryn looked up. She watched him take the lid from the plate and then stick the plate in the microwave.

"Adrie's out there snorting."

"Okay."

"Bob Hayworth just told that joke again."

Kamryn couldn't help but laugh and roll her eyes. "It wasn't that funny the first time."

Will nodded and leaned back against the counter. He crossed his arms over his chest and cocked his head to the side.

"Yeah, it kinda was."

Kamryn pursed her lips and considered Adrie's quiet, seemingly no-nonsense stroke patient. "Yeah, okay, it was."

"And anything's funny with Adrie laughing."

Again, she had to agree with Will. She should have been out there; it would have been good to hear Adrie laugh.

"What is that?" Kamryn asked when Will took his plate from the microwave. He set it on the table and then grabbed a bottle of water from the refrigerator.

"Swedish meatballs and sour cream and chive noodles," he answered as he sat down across the table.

"Smells good." She raised her hands above her head and stretched.

"Mm-hmm." He nodded as he hefted a forkful of noodles to his mouth. "Because you're obviously so hungry."

Kamryn glanced at her salad. She wasn't hungry. She felt like she had a brick in her stomach. Looking at the salad only made it worse. Mark had left again this morning. He had almost kissed her goodbye, but his lips had sort of missed and just kind of touched the corner of her mouth and then he was gone, and she was still standing at the counter, chopping up the green pepper for her salad.

She raised her eyes to look at him and grinned.

"No, I'm not hungry."

"You're not dieting, are you? Because if you lose a pound, the next big wind is gonna blow you away. And March is all about wind, ya know?"

"Not dieting," she said quietly. "But you're full of shit."

"I can see it now. First spring thunderstorm we get, funnel cloud's gonna suck you right up and drop you in, like, Ohio or something."

She pressed her lips together and finally shook her head. "If I'm gonna blow away, I should get to pick my destination."

"Okay," he agreed. She watched him chug half the water. "So where will you go?"

"Rena make that?"

"Yep."

"Cool."

"Where ya goin'?"

"Beach," she answered. "Of course. Nothing commercial. Just somewhere quiet."

"Mm-hmm." He nodded. "Okay. Nudist beach?"

She laughed and rolled her eyes. "I don't wanna hurt anybody, Will. I could just use some time to myself."

He grinned.

"You wanna try a bite?" he asked. Kamryn giggled, busted for eyeballing his lunch yet again.

"Really? I can?"

"Sure." He forked the other half of his meatball and reached across the table with it. Kamryn meant to take the fork from him, but he didn't let go, so she ended up just covering his hand with hers.

"Mm!" She smiled and nodded. "Very good."

"Hungry now?"

Another glance at the salad and the feeling of a ghost kiss barely brushing the corner of her lips.

"No."

"Want the recipe?"

She almost said yes. The meatball was good, and it was always good to have something new to fix. But she had a slew of new recipes in her little white binder in the kitchen. Didn't matter. Nothing was working these days. Nothing in the kitchen or bedroom or anywhere else for that matter. She and Mark were barely speaking; the girls were both flirting with trouble; and Ian had turned into Jeckell and Hyde. He had taken her head off this morning on the way to school when she told him she'd packed him Oreos today instead of Chips Ahoy!

"No, thanks," she said simply.

"No?"

"Maybe it's time I admit I'm not good in the kitchen."

Will's turn to raise his eyebrows.

"I find that hard to believe."

Kamryn heard the teasing in his words. She fought the blush, but naturally, it won.

"What's going on?" Will asked after a few moments of silence.

"Nothing." She closed the word search book and reached for her salad. She put the lid back on the Tupperware container and put it back in the fridge. *Try it again tomorrow.*

"Kam," Will said quietly. "I can see something's wrong. Something's been wrong for a while now."

Kamryn stared at him silently.

"I know Adrie's your best friend." He polished off the last meatball and wiped his mouth with a napkin. "And I know you haven't talked to her about whatever you're dealing with, because you don't wanna burden her."

She broke the eye contact first and looked down at her hands in her lap. Her diamond caught the overhead light and winked at her. It made her think about Ashton. And Garret.

"Thank you, Will," she told him as she stood up. "I appreciate your concern."

"Not gonna tell me."

She shrugged. "No."

He nodded. Kamryn put her Tupperware container in the refrigerator and tossed her water bottle in the recycle bin.

"Kam?"

She paused at the door but said nothing.

"I'm a good listener."

He might have been looking, but she wasn't sure. She only nodded and then left the break room. She glanced at her watch. Just after twelve. And she had another nine appointments before she could leave.

And then what? Rush home to her kids? Eenie meenie minie moe...which one did she even want to talk to today? None of them, really. She was kind of tired of getting her head bitten off. She and Mark had fought the rest of the weekend over what to do with Braelyn. Even though he had initially been angry with Brae, the intensity had faded, and he was now telling Kamryn that kids will be kids.

Kamryn had talked herself blue in the face and hands and feet, trying to get Mark to see how serious this could be. He hadn't wanted to listen. They had ended up arguing over the mortgage payment, which Mark accused her of paying late and the SUV, which Mark had accused her of parking too close to another car, as there was another scratch on the driver's door. He had retreated to the office and his laptop last night, and she had gone after him, rather than let it go.

She knew better. He had already pulled the cool, polite business persona back on, and he hammered away at his laptop while Kamryn complained about his job and the fact that he was never home when things got bad, and she needed him. Naturally, he pointed out that he was home last weekend when things had gotten bad with both girls, and he picked at her because she hadn't even called Garret's mom yet about the promise ring.

Kamryn had gone to bed angry with him. Mark had come to bed hours later and turned to his side, giving her his back. The sort of kiss this morning had only served to bring back all the wondering she had kind of been doing lately.

She hated the way they had left things. She hated that she was suddenly consumed with thoughts of Mark around other women. Professional women. Professional women with dazzling smiles, perfect nails, and heels. Professional women who could offer him no-strings-attached sex. No talk of the twins or Ian or mortgages or cars or alcohol.

Will had touched on a nerve. She did want to talk. But she couldn't. She certainly wasn't going to drop all of this on Adrie, and she couldn't imagine talking to anyone else. Not Will. She appreciated his concern, but she couldn't imagine talking to him. Not about this stuff.

She had five minutes left of her lunch hour. No time like the present, she decided, and she stepped outside the front door and slipped her cell phone from her pocket. Hopefully Garret's mom would be at work, so there would be no long, drawn out conversation.

Kamryn sagged in relief when she got her voicemail.

"Hi Mary," she said into the phone. She leaned against the brick wall at her back, surprised that she sounded calm and in control. "It's Kamryn McHale. I'm not sure if you're aware of this, but Garret gave Ashton a promise ring over the weekend. I'm calling because Mark and I don't approve of their relationship being so serious when they're so young. I asked Ashton to please give the ring back to Garret today. Give me a call if you wanna talk about this. Thanks."

She ended the call and then considered texting Mark to tell him she had called Mary Jackson. But it was noon, and most likely, Mark was wining and dining someone for lunch, and the thought irritated her enough to skip the text and slip the phone back into her pocket.

CHAPTER 23

ASHTON

"Where's Mom?"

Ashton jumped and turned around to look at Brae.

"She called a few minutes ago. Said she was taking Ian shopping. Something about his school pants being too short for him."

Braelyn laughed quietly. "Poor Ian gets to go through the next ten years doing all that fun stuff with Mom."

Ashton stared at her soda, okay her *spiked* soda, and considered what Brae said.

"Do you remember when Mom used to take us for ice cream after school?"

Braelyn smiled. "Fridays. If we were good all week." Braelyn slid onto a barstool.

"Guess that's why we don't get ice cream days anymore, huh?" Ashton laughed softly. She took a drink from her glass and thought about how close Brae had been to catching her splashing vodka into her glass. Her hands still tingled with the near catch, but at least she wasn't actually shaking.

"Are they still fighting?" Brae asked quietly. Ashton glanced at her, but Braelyn was picking at her fingernails.

"I dunno."

"Pretty shitty weekend."

"Mm."

"Can I ask you something?" Braelyn finally looked up and met Ashton's eyes.

"No."

"Did you break up with Garret today?"

"I said no." Ashton didn't want to talk. Not about school. Not about Garret. Not about vodka. Not at all. Not with her mom. Not with her twin.

"Did you?"

Moses trotted into the kitchen, probably looking for Ian. He settled for Ashton. She ran her foot over his back when he sat down by her.

"You're so rotten." She rolled her eyes when Moses slowly rolled onto his back. "I don't wanna rub your belly."

She wished Braelyn would go away. Not like, forever. Just upstairs. To her room. Away from her.

"No."

"No?" Brae sat back like Ashton had shocked her.

"No. I didn't." Ash took a drink, careful not to flinch at the taste. Shouldn't she be used to that flat, watery taste by now? "Why? Are people saying I did?"

Braelyn raised her eyebrows. "Yeah. Some are."

"What else?"

"Can I have a drink?"

"No."

Braelyn rolled her eyes and then jumped off the barstool. Ashton watched her take a soda from the refrigerator and pop the top. Did Braelyn ever wonder why she always drank from a glass?

"They're saying how you gave his class ring back last week. And now today that you gave him his promise ring back. I heard you were flirting with Trevor Fenton at lunch."

"I don't even know Trevor Fenton."

"He's pretty hot."

Ashton shrugged. "I know that, but I don't *know* him."

"Ashton, do you love him?"

"Trevor Fenton?"

Braelyn stared at her, unfazed by her sarcasm.

"Do you love him?"

Ashton sighed. Why not tell the truth? Just once?

"No."

Braelyn sat down again on the barstool and stared at Ashton for a few moments.

"Did you ever?"

"Do you know what love is?"

"Spare me the lecture, Ashton. I don't consider you an authority in this area."

"I don't either. That's my point. Do you know what it feels like to be in love with someone? Because I don't. I really don't."

"You always look like you've got your shit together. Like you have everything figured out."

Ashton shook her head. "My shit is most certainly not together, and I have nothing figured out. And I don't really know how I feel about Garret."

"Then why do you keep going out with him?"

"Because I'm afraid of what he might say about me if I break up with him."

"So, it's true?"

Ashton chewed on her lip, afraid to answer Braelyn.

"You and Garret?"

She nodded and looked away. "How did you find out?"

"I didn't," Braelyn answered simply. "Just kind of figured you were doing it."

"What? Just because we've been dating you figured we were having sex?"

"He bought you a thong."

"Three, actually," Ashton mumbled. "Are you sure?"

"Sure about what?"

"You're sure you didn't hear it somewhere? Andrew didn't tell you, did he?"

"You think Garret's already talking?"

Ashton shrugged. "I don't know. Couldn't he?"

"Sure, but you could, too. You never even told me."

"I hate it."

"Then why do you do it?"

Ashton folded in; her shoulders slumped, and she dropped her chin to her chest. So simple, really, and so like Braelyn to hit the heart of the matter so instinctively.

Why did she do it?

"I don't know how to stop," she whispered.

"Tell him no."

"I'm afraid to."

Braelyn took a deep breath. She rolled her head on her neck and then closed her eyes. "This is what I meant. When I said I didn't want to get involved with Andrew. I don't want this stuff happening."

Ashton licked her lips. "Then don't do it."

"I think he wanted to last night."

"Last night? You're grounded, Brae. You mean Friday?"

"No, I mean last night. I snuck out after Mom and Dad went to bed."

"What? You—"

"You are not going to wear those pants anymore! I don't care what you say!" Mom's sharp tone carried into the kitchen as the door opened. "They're two inches too short, Ian."

"I hate the new ones," he grumbled.

"Sorry. You'll be back in shorts in no time."

"I hate shorts."

Ashton watched Braelyn, wanting to know more about last night. Since when did Braelyn sneak out? Hell, *she'd* never snuck out. When had Brae started doing that? Braelyn was looking at Mom, who looked like she could bite a nail in two. Peachy. Another night of Mom ragging at them about anything and everything.

Ashton took one more long drink and then dumped the ice in the sink. She rinsed the glass out and then dumped it in the sink, to rinse it out, too.

"Can I watch cartoons?" Ian asked. Ashton figured Mom would say yes, just to get Ian out of her hair for a little bit.

"No."

"No?" Ian exploded with a fresh tantrum. Ashton wondered where his behavior was coming from. It wasn't like him to act like this. He had been on and off like this since he got sick. Poor Mom. Ian was starting to get on Ashton's nerves. How bad could it be for Mom to listen to it constantly?

"No," Mom repeated. "You can go sit on your bed for fifteen minutes. I'm tired of the attitude, Mr. McHale."

"I'm not doing time out."

"Twenty minutes."

Mom hadn't even acknowledged her and Braelyn in the kitchen. Ashton decided it probably wasn't a good time to ask what was for dinner.

"I wish Dad was home," Ian mumbled as he shoved past Mom and then hurried up the steps.

"Yeah, that would solve everything, wouldn't it?" Mom muttered. She looked up at Ashton and Braelyn, but she didn't say anything.

"It's hard when Dad's gone, isn't it?" Brae asked her.

Suck up.

"No, Brae, it's hard when Dad's here and then gone and then here and then gone."

Braelyn nodded, but she didn't say anything else. Ashton caught Brae's eye and nodded toward the steps.

"Did you do that calc assignment yet?" Braelyn asked. She stood up and started toward the steps.

"Started it."

"Girls, I don't even know what we're doing for supper. I'll let you know when it's ready."

Ashton glanced back at Mom. She stood with her elbows on the counter and her head in her hands. Eyes closed, she rubbed her forehead like she was trying to get rid of a headache.

"I feel bad for her," Ashton said softly.

"Yeah, she didn't ground you," Braelyn answered. Ashton waited for Braelyn to grab her backpack so they could work on their homework together in her room.

"Why's Mom so grouchy?" Ian hollered at them.

"Because she's tired, Ian," Ashton answered. She stuck her head in his doorway, not surprised to see Moses flopped on his side, his head close to Ian's leg.

"She's always tired."

"Take it easy on her," Ashton told him. "Why are you always so grouchy these days?"

"I'm not!"

"Okay." Ashton nodded and backed out of his room.

"So, did you love him? I mean, is that why you did it?" Braelyn pushed Ashton's door closed behind her. Ashton picked her bag up from the floor and then sat down on her bed. Braelyn dropped her bag by Ashton's desk.

"Wait a minute." Ashton shook her head. "We were talking about you. You can't just tell me you snuck out and leave it at that."

Braelyn rolled her eyes. "Not that big of a deal."

"Yeah, it kind of is."

"It's not like I took the car or anything. Andrew meets me outside. On the patio."

"*Meets*? He *meets* you outside? You do this a lot?"

Braelyn shrugged. "Sometimes."

"So whadda you do? You sneak outside and make out?"

"No. Well, last night, but no. That was the first time."

"Do you sneak out and drink with him or something?"

"No. We just talk."

Ashton leaned back against her headboard. "Wow. What's that like?"

"Pretty cool. He's pretty cool. I just don't wanna get stuck. Like you are."

Ashton sat up again and unzipped her backpack.

"Then don't."

"Did you? Love him?"

Ashton watched Brae take her calculus book from her backpack and thumb through it, looking for the right page. She was still staring at Braelyn, when she found the page, set the book on Ashton's desk, and looked at her, waiting for an answer.

"Sort of. But. I don't know." Ashton picked at her thumbnail and avoided Brae's eyes.

"Did it hurt?"

"Kind of."

"You don't like it at all? Because I hear so many girls talking about it and…"

"Sometimes it's okay, but I hate how…"

"Hate how what?"

"It's all he wants to do now. I mean, we never just watch a movie now. We watch a movie and then go to his room or my room and do it. We never just talk. If we do, it's always about him and basketball. I'm just…I don't like it that much. And it feels like that's all he likes now."

"I told Andrew last night that I wanna do pre-med at school. He thought that was cool."

"Really? Pre-med?"

"Yeah. Why not?"

"No reason." Ashton shrugged. "You've just never said anything. I didn't know you had even thought about it."

"You think I'm a blow-off. Just like everyone else thinks I am."

Busted, Ashton only laughed.

"That's why it was so bad that Mom and Dad saw me drunk last weekend. I think they've always just assumed that I would do that. Or that I do it a lot. Now I've proven to be the problem child."

"I'm sorry about that," Ashton said sincerely.

Braelyn shrugged and gave Ashton a hint of a smile.

"Do you worry about getting pregnant?"

"No." Ashton shook her head. "We're careful."

"Ash?"

"Hmm?" Ashton, pencil in hand, looked up at Braelyn.

"Do you think Mom and Dad still love each other?"

Ashton didn't know. She didn't know how to answer Braelyn. Mom and Dad had always been so perfect together, so perfect that she and Braelyn thought they were gross. But lately, nothing was perfect, most especially Mom and Dad.

Brae was watching her expectantly. There was something on her face that Ashton didn't immediately recognize. And then it hit her. She couldn't be honest now, not with that raw, innocent hope on Brae's face.

"Yeah. I do, Brae."

Ashton figured Braelyn couldn't be honest either. Because instead of arguing with her, instead of reminding Ashton of all the fighting lately, she simply nodded, mumbled *me too,* and turned her attention back to her calculus book.

CHAPTER 24

KAMRYN

"You're not telling me everything." Adrie sounded a bit hurt and a bit pissed. "So you and Mark got in a fight. That's not a big deal. That's not a big deal to you. Any other time you guys fight, I hear about it, and then I hear about the makeup sex, and that's that."

"You're the one who gives details on makeup sex," Kamryn answered, not bothering to look away from her computer screen.

"Look, I'm doing okay," Adrie announced. Kamryn looked over her shoulder and met Adrie's eyes.

"I know you are. I'm glad."

"You can talk to me."

Kamryn nodded. "Thanks, Adrie. I just really…I don't wanna talk about it."

So that was a lie. But then again, not really. She wanted to talk about it. She just didn't know how. It was different, really, to talk to Adrie if she and Mark were fighting over something dumb. But this time it wasn't dumb; it was the girls, or Braelyn, at least, and Kamryn felt funny sharing that information with anyone, even Adrie.

"Okay." Adrie backed out of the office slowly, as if she expected Kamryn to change her mind. Kamryn turned back to her computer screen. The words of the article on screen were blurry suddenly. *Not here.* Kamryn took a deep breath and blinked.

She laid her head down on her desk and closed her eyes. *Get a grip. Get angry again.* At least when she was pissed at Mark, there was no room for sappy, teary crap. And really, she still had every reason to be pissed, because Mark was still gone, and she was still worried about both girls, and Mark hadn't even bothered to call her last night. She called him once. True, it had just been the obligatory phone call. She hadn't exactly wanted to talk to him, because she'd known it would be more of the same. More of her just talking to fill up the silence between them. Telling him about Ian's temper tantrums. Which he would take as Kamryn complaining to him.

He hadn't answered, though. The call had gone to voicemail. And when he called this morning, he had sounded about two degrees away from dead. He had apologized for not calling, for missing her call, and then admitted to a splitting headache. Massive hangover. He told her he and three other guys had killed a fifth of Maker's Mark after three buckets of beer.

Kamryn had been stunned at first. How in the hell could Mark go out and drink that way after all the talking, all the shit, that happened this past weekend? She had gone from stunned to pissed. Mark, probably perfectly dressed and sexy as hell even with a hangover, had pretended not to notice that she was pissed.

And then, of course, after they hung up, Kamryn had wondered. If it had been three guys with Mark last night. If anyone else had been around to entertain him.

"Hey."

Kamryn took a deep breath before she sat up. She kept her eyes closed.

"Hey."

She dared to open them, afraid that Will would be right there. Too close. Will had been nice. But she had dreamt of him last night, and now she knew he had been *too* nice, and she wasn't sure she could look at him.

Not *that* kind of dream, but still. It didn't feel right to Kamryn to dream about another man, even if he was fully clothed in the dream. Even if he was working with a patient and talking to Kamryn about a made-for-TV movie.

He wasn't close, though, and he wasn't looking at her. He was leaning over an open binder, studying something intensely. Kamryn felt the tension in her shoulders break. She hadn't realized how much the dream had upset her until she had come to work and seen Will talking to his first patient.

"Damn." He closed the binder and then drummed his fingers on the desk.

"What's wrong?"

"Insurance," he mumbled. He glanced at her, raised his eyebrows, and then hurried back out to his patient.

Kamryn told herself it was okay. It was better than okay that he just walked out without paying any special attention to her. She shouldn't feel slighted, because she shouldn't want or need any special attention from Will Cheney.

Suck it up. Two days. Mark would be home in two days, and they would fix it. They would fix everything.

THINGS GO WRONG. If Kamryn were a yoga instructor, her mantra would be *things go wrong.* Which didn't have to mean things can't be fixed. She reminded herself often that she and Mark could fix things. Really, there wasn't that much to fix; they just needed to get on the same page with the girls. They had to work together with the girls, because the girls were smart enough to know if they didn't see eye to eye on something.

Kamryn hated to think the girls might push that, like pouring salt in a wound. But then Kamryn never would have thought Braelyn would come home drunk, either.

The *possibility* of your kid coming home drunk wasn't the same as *your kid coming home drunk.* It still bothered her that Brae didn't even know what she drank. She liked Andrew, and she doubted he would do anything to hurt Braelyn, but then how did she know? How did anyone ever really *know* anyone?

She tugged her purse strap over her shoulder and headed for her car. What kind of mood would Ian be in today? Maybe she should set up a meeting with his teacher to see if she had noticed any changes in his attitude or behavior. Maybe someone was bullying him again. And yet, he handled that so well the last time. What if it was the way things were at home? Could Ian sense the tension at home? Did she want to chance *that* coming up in a meeting with his teacher?

"McHale."

She looked up when she heard someone call to her.

Will was hurrying across the parking lot toward her.

"What?"

"You forgot your phone." He stopped when he was toe-to-toe with her. Their eyes met, and though it had been an innocent, boring dream, Kamryn thought of it again, of how she'd dreamt of Will, and her heart fluttered a bit in her chest. She looked down at his outstretched hand, which did indeed have her cell phone in it.

"Thank you."

She looked up again and met his eyes. Brown, like Mark's. Except not really. Mark had that fifties rocker look going, and when he flashed a smile, Kamryn felt it down to her core. Heat and excitement and passion and love.

Love.

Will had kind eyes. Long lashes.

And maybe a little bit of heat. She would never admit it to anyone, not even Adrie, but right now, she felt a tiny little fire inside her.

But not love.

"I might be out of line when I say this."

She couldn't hear it. She *wouldn't* hear it, and it didn't matter. She shook her head and reached to touch his lips with her finger.

"Then don't say it."

Will sighed. He wanted to say something. Kamryn couldn't guess what he was thinking, but she figured it couldn't be appropriate.

Because there was Rena.

And there was Mark.

She took her phone, thanked him again, and then turned her back on him and walked on trembling legs to the SUV. She didn't dare look to see if he was still standing there. If he had gone back inside. Her hands shook so hard she couldn't get the key in the ignition.

Instead, she closed her eyes and leaned back in her seat. Her eyes burned with tears, but she couldn't let them go. She had to pick up Ian. She couldn't let him see her if she cried. She couldn't let his teacher or any other teacher at school see that she had been crying.

What the hell? Nothing had happened. Will had run her phone out to her. He was a friend who had seen she forgot her phone, and he had run it out to her before she could leave. No more. No less.

It was a crossroads, though. However weak the moment was—
—didn't she at least deserve a little flair? Something a little sexier? A scandalous kiss in the supply closet? A long, hot kiss that would leave her wanting—it had been a crossroads, and she could easily have taken the other road. The wrong turn.

She hadn't, though. Her attraction to Will wasn't real. Yeah, he was nice-looking, and he seemed to care about her. Okay, maybe not. Wasn't that how any affair started? *My husband doesn't get me, but you do?* No love. *No thanks.*

Kamryn took a deep breath. She wanted Mark. God, how she wished Mark would be home tonight.

What would he have done? Just now. In her shoes.

What would Mark have done?

CHAPTER 25

The bass pumped in her breastbone. She didn't even know the song; some kind of hip hop mix, she thought. She wended her way through the milling crowd of kids gathered around the keg in the garage. She wondered whose house this was; Garret had suggested they go to a party, and she had jumped at the chance to get out of his house. She knew he thought they would do something here at the party. That she would at least do blow him. But she had no intention of touching him.

In fact, she had been considering breaking up with him. She'd thought about it all through first and second hour and then again after lunch and then right after school, he had called her and told her he had his class ring back, and he would give it to her later, after the party. And she had thought just maybe she wouldn't take it back.

Trevor Fenton was manning the keg. Ashton watched him, wondering if this was his house. Where his parents were.

What was up with so many parents not having a clue about what their kids did, anyway? Okay, so maybe Mom and Dad were a little slow to catch on to what she and Brae did. But no way could they have a party like this and keep it from their parents.

Trevor handed Ashton a full cup as Garret handed over a couple of fives. It kind of irked her that he always paid her way. Maybe some girls liked that. But what if Ashton wanted to flirt with Trevor? Kind of hard when her boyfriend was walking around behind her, paying her cover charge.

She didn't, though. She didn't want to flirt with Trevor. She didn't want to flirt with anyone. She just wanted to have a few drinks and then go home. Or, she thought, as she stepped up inside the house and the music changed to rock, dance. She wanted to dance. With her girlfriends. Not Garret.

"What're you doing here?"

She had to yell to make Braelyn hear her.

"Talked Dad into letting me go out!"

"Seriously?" Ashton raised her eyebrows. "Does Mom know?"

"Who cares?" Brae shrugged. "At least I'm out of the house!"

Ashton wanted to ask her if it didn't bother her, pitting Dad against Mom like that. But the music was so loud, and Brae was dancing with their friends, and Garret had his arm around her.

"Go do something," she said as she turned to look at him.

"What?" He leaned closer to her so he could hear her.

"Go play or something."

"I'm fine." He shook his head and squeezed her side.

"No, really, Garret. Go away for a while, okay?"

"Oh." He looked at her, wide-eyed like a little kid and then nodded. "Okay. I'll find you later."

She looked at Braelyn as he walked away. Braelyn knuckled her. Ashton took a drink of her beer, wished it was something a little stronger, and decided to dance. Might as well enjoy the freedom.

Though she had vowed to enjoy herself, Ashton found herself keeping tabs on Braelyn. Still, it beat having Garret hovering around her constantly. Besides, she still danced. In fact, she had fun dancing with her twin and the rest of the girls. And Brae wasn't drinking much. She had the ever-present plastic cup, but Ashton hadn't seen it refilled since she had first seen Brae.

It wasn't that she didn't want Brae to have fun. She just didn't want her sister getting bombed again. Because then it would fall to her to get her home and sneak her up to her room before Mom and Dad saw her and figured out what was going on. Ashton didn't want any more parental scrutiny with the alcohol. Not that big of a deal if Mom or Dad really figured it out. She could quit. If she wanted to, she could just quit sneaking the drinks. But she didn't want to. It wasn't like it was doing anyone any harm.

They danced to Billy Idol and Whitesnake and REM; Ashton was aware that it was their parents' music, but she liked it. Brae seemed to like it, too. When they were hot and worn out from dancing, Ashton and Brae followed their friends outside to the garage. Ashton noticed that Brae passed on another beer and fished a bottle of water from a well-stocked camouflage cooler.

Drinks refreshed, the girls walked out to the backyard and sat in empty patio chairs. There were other kids back here, in fact, so many that no one noticed them walk back and sit down.

"Where's Garret?"

Ashton opened her mouth to answer Sydni Ross, but she hesitated. She had been tempted to tell Sydni, who had been a good friend since they started high school, that she and Garret broke up. But she couldn't. Yes, Syd was a good friend, but she would still tell someone and then that someone would tell someone and so it would go, until someone told Garret. Maybe she was ready to break up, but he deserved better than *that*. He deserved to hear it from her.

And it wasn't just that she was afraid of what he might say about her. She really didn't want to hurt him.

"He's around here somewhere," she finally answered.

"How come Andrew's not here?"

"He went out of town with his parents. Visiting his grandparents and then on Monday, he's doing a campus tour at SIU."

"Carbondale?" Sydni asked. Braelyn nodded.

Ashton leaned back in her chair, drew her legs up, and hugged her arms around them. She tuned the conversation out and closed her eyes. It was chilly, but not so bad for early March. She was glad she had grabbed her fleece jacket before she left the house, but it was kind of nice just sitting out here. She could smell smoke, but she knew they wouldn't be welcome by the bonfire. Only seniors or people dating seniors were allowed close to the bonfire at any party. That was something Pius the X students learned their freshman year.

It would be nice, though. To be sitting by a fire and watching the flames lick up the pile of wood. Watch the way the wood ever so slowly turned to ash.

She could have fallen asleep there. So many late nights and so much homework and so much worry over all the stupid stuff. Okay, some of it not so stupid. The homework. The tests she studied for. The Ethics quiz she got a B on.

Ashton had no idea how long she had been sitting there when Brae and Sydni stood up. Brae bumped her, and she opened her eyes.

"Seriously not cool to fall asleep at a party."

"God, I know," she answered. She stretched and then lowered her legs so she could stand. "My legs are stiff," she said with a giggle.

"We're gonna go shoot a game of pool."

"Okay."

"You coming?" Brae asked her.

"Of course."

Feeling a little out of it, Ashton followed Sydni and Brae back around the side of the garage, through the garage, and back into the kitchen.

The basement looked like a game room. Again, Ashton wondered whose house this was. There was a pool table and an air hockey table. Four arcade games lined one wall. An old-fashioned jukebox sat in the far corner. Music played, but the lights on the jukebox were dead, so Ashton assumed the music came from somewhere else.

She stood with Brae and Sydni while two other girls finished a game of pool. Just as the two girls finished, Ashton felt an arm slide around her shoulders. She gritted her teeth when Garret pulled her to him and kissed her cheek.

"Hey. Where ya been?"

She glanced at him and looked away quickly. "Outside."

"Wanna go back out? Take a walk?"

Ashton glanced at Brae and Sydni. She would rather just stay here and watch them play. Maybe even shoot a time or two herself, even though she sucked. It would be fun, though.

But she needed to walk with Garret. She needed to talk to him, and she needed to stop putting it off.

"Sure."

Garret waited while she stepped closer to Brae to tell her she was going back outside. And then he slipped his fingers through hers and led her back upstairs, through the kitchen, and back outside. Ashton thought she might be walking that route in her sleep.

Garret led her away from the crowd. They walked for a while, hand in hand, but then Garret stopped. They were several houses down, standing in front of someone's mailbox. She was grateful for the dark; it gave her a place to hide.

"Oh." Garret let go of her hand and reached into his jacket pocket. Ashton felt her heart quicken, but not because she wanted what he was going to give her. Because she didn't want it, and she had to tell him that. She had to figure out a way to tell Garret she didn't want to see him anymore.

"Almost forgot."

Even in the darkness, she could see the smile on his face. It was the old smile. The cute one, with the dimple and the slightly crooked front tooth. That was stupid; she knew that. He had the same smile since she had known him. It just quit being cute to her when their friendship changed into something so much more complicated.

She looked down. His class ring sat on the palm of his left hand. She couldn't make out the details, because it was dark. But she could see it in her mind. Yellow gold. Red stone. The basketball on one side. Garret's name. She couldn't see her ring either, but she knew it was there. On Garret's pinky finger. So much the same as his. Yellow gold and red stone. The symbol for academic achievement. Her name.

Normal stuff. Boy and girl stuff. Should she do this? Should she break up with him? Was there really anything wrong with how they were now? With what they did? Wasn't that what was supposed to happen?

"What's the matter?" Garret asked her.

She opened and closed her mouth and then opened it and closed it again. So many things in her head, but she had no idea which thing to say to him. She could just take the ring. Keep pretending.

And end up hating him. She had kind of hated him already a few times, hadn't she? She thought about taking his ring back. Going back to his house or her house and making out. Texting a million times tomorrow.

She took a deep breath. The thought of keeping everything the same suffocated her.

"Garret, I can't." It hurt to swallow over the lump in her throat. "I can't do this anymore."

"Do what?"

"Us. I can't do us anymore." She dragged her fingers back through her hair and turned her back to him. "I need a break."

"You're breaking up with me?"

She nodded, but she knew that wasn't good enough. That was being a chicken shit and besides that, he couldn't see her anyway.

"Yes."

"Forever? You're just breaking up with me?"

"Yes," she whispered.

"But."

She turned back to him. He was still holding his class ring.

"I'm sorry."

"Is it—" He cleared his throat and started again. "Do you wanna date someone else?"

"No." She was glad she could be honest about that. It had nothing to do with anyone else. "No. It's just me."

"Oh. So it's not me, it's you? Is that it?"

"No." She wiped at her eyes, wishing she didn't have to cry. She needed to sound in control, so there was no question in Garret's mind that she was serious. "No, Garret, it's you."

"What?"

"It's too intense. It's too much for me right now," she said quietly.

"I'm too intense? Is that it? Just because I love you?"

"Do you love me?" she asked quickly. Her voice shook. "We're sixteen. How can you know you love me? How can you know?"

"You don't love me?"

"I don't know. I don't think I can, yet. I don't want to right now. There's too much other stuff—"

"Stuff? You're breaking up with me because of stuff?"

"Look. I need a break. I study all the time, Garret. You know that. And when I'm not studying, I'm with you. And I need a break. I need me."

"You need some you time," he said sarcastically.

"There's just so much going on right now. In my house...with my parents..."

"Yeah, your mom called my mom the other day. About the promise ring."

"I didn't mean for Mom and Dad to see that, Garret," she said quickly.

"Whatever."

He moved, and Ashton figured he was putting his ring back in his pocket. He pulled her ring off his finger and stood there holding it.

"How long has this," he threw his hands out as if to show her what *this* was, "been too much for you?"

"For a while."

"Like what? For a week? For a month?"

"For a while," she repeated.

Garret sighed. He laughed softly, but Ashton could hear the edge in the laughter. He was upset. Pissed, maybe. Hurt. She wasn't sure, and she wasn't going to ask.

"So. Is this just a break, Ash? Or are we done?"

"I wanna be friends, Garret. You've always been—"

"Yeah, whatever." He reached for her and pushed her ring into her hands. Why was she crying when she was the one breaking up with him?

"Garret?"

"See ya."

"Garret."

He walked away and left her standing in the dark. She curled her fingers around her ring, but she didn't put it on. Not yet. She watched him walk away, just a dark figure in the dark night, until he was too far away to see even that.

She caught her breath when she thought she saw him stop walking.

Please don't come back, she thought. Please. Let this be it.

"Ash, you got a ride home?"

She sighed with relief.

"Yeah."

Ashton pushed her ring down in the pocket of her jeans. She couldn't let anyone see it. Not yet. Maybe Garret would go tearing through the house, letting everyone know they broke up. Maybe not. She didn't want to talk about it. With anyone. Sure as hell not with half the student body of Pius the X.

Maybe she should be upset. But she wasn't. Not really. If anything, she felt at home. Right there. Alone. In the dark.

CHAPTER 26

KAMRYN

Kamryn was stretched out on the couch, watching a movie on Lifetime TV when the girls got home. She glanced at the clock, and when she saw that it wasn't quite eleven, she didn't move. No need to meet them at the door. They would feel like she was testing them, maybe checking to see if she smelled alcohol. If Brae suspected that and then said anything to Mark, he would give her hell and their fight would rage on. At least at the moment, it was stalled.

Then again, right now, everything felt stalled.

"Where's Dad?" Ashton asked when Kamryn looked up and met her eyes. Brae was carrying a McDonald's bag. She sat down at the counter and opened the bag. Kamryn watched her snitch a fry and stick it in her mouth.

"Downstairs with Ian."

"Playing games?"

"I dunno." Kamryn shrugged. She sat up and watched Ashton get herself and Brae a glass of water.

"French fries?"

Brae grinned at her. Thank God, Braelyn hadn't stayed mad at her for long. Then again, if she knew her dad would undo any punishments Kamryn delivered, what was there to be mad about?

"I'm hungry," Brae said with a laugh.

The fries smelled good, but Kamryn didn't want any. She and Mark had taken Ian out for dinner; and she was still stuffed. In fact, miserably so.

"Where did you guys go tonight?" She hoped she didn't sound parental. She was just curious where the girls had gone. And hungry for conversation. Mark and Ian had kept a running dialogue through dinner. But Kamryn had nothing to add to the conversation about kung fu, nor did she have the energy to make stuff up as she went, the way Mark did, so she had stayed quiet and simply listened.

"Trevor Fenton's house," Brae answered.

"Really? That was his house?" Ashton leaned against the counter.

"You didn't know that?"

"No. Garret just asked if I wanted to go to a party."

Kamryn looked at the clock again. She glanced around the kitchen and then stepped out to look down the entrance hall.

"Where is Garret?"

"I came home with Brae." Ashton avoided her eyes and shot Brae a look. Kamryn wondered what that was about.

"Oh." She climbed up on a barstool and reached for one of Brae's fries. "Don't make me eat these. I'm stuffed."

"No, really, I insist," Brae said with a giggle.

"How come?" Kamryn asked, but she looked at Ashton now.

Ashton shrugged. "Just because. Andrew's out of town. Just wanted to hang out with Brae tonight."

Kamryn nodded. "Mm-kay. Well." She stood up and stretched. "I'm going to bed."

"Night."

She kissed each of the girls and then climbed the steps to her room without telling Mark goodnight. It had been that way last night, too. Polite conversation. No less. No more.

The girls were home early, though, and that was good. She decided, as she brushed her teeth, to concentrate on that. Concentrate on the good. The girls were home. Neither of them appeared to have been drinking. She hadn't smelled any alcohol on either of them, though she had been a kid once, too, and she knew all about sucking on pennies and chewing gum to try and hide your beer breath.

She hadn't gotten close enough to either of them to be certain. But maybe Mark was right. Maybe she was wound too tight about this, and it was better just to let it go. Assume that last weekend was the last of it.

Even if it meant she had to go to Mark and apologize. She would rather it be this way. She would rather be wrong. Rather last weekend be the end of it.

She climbed into bed and considered the possibility. Thought about apologizing to Mark. Making up with Mark.

Things had really unraveled the past several weeks, and Kamryn needed to pull the loose threads and set things back to right. Maybe admitting she was wrong was the first step in getting her family back on track.

She closed her eyes, already feeling the relief swoop in and ease the burdens. Her shoulders felt a little looser, though she wouldn't turn down a good back rub if Mark suddenly appeared and offered.

He wouldn't. And that was okay. He was having a good time with Ian, and that was as important for Mark as it was for Ian.

Maybe she should talk to Adrie, too. Maybe not everything. She didn't have to go into details, both because she still didn't want to just throw everything at Adrie's feet when she was still working through grief, and because she still felt a little protective of the girls and their secrets. Adrie was her best friend, and Kamryn knew Adrie never repeated anything she told her in confidence. And yet, there was still a little wall inside her, built up around the heart of her worries—the drinking and the intensity of Ashton and Garret's relationship. Kamryn just couldn't blurt the whole thing out.

She had shared some of that with Mark, with her husband for God's sake, and look where that got her. But, she decided, come Monday she would update Adrie. After all, she guessed truth be told, she would be hurt if Adrie had something so huge going on and kept it from Kamryn. She might be protecting Adrie from her world right now, but maybe Adrie didn't see it that way. Maybe Adrie felt like Kamryn had shut her out.

Kamryn thought about reading, trying to stay awake until Mark came to bed. But she was so tired, and she just felt so much better now, from thinking through everything. She turned to her side, pulled the sheets and quilt up over her shoulder, and let herself drift.

SATURDAY MORNINGS VARIED in their house. Some were all hustle and bustle, especially back when Kamryn was coaching the girls' basketball team, and the girls were playing volleyball. Mark always seemed to have somewhere to be, some sort of project to work on. But now and then, Saturdays started slow and smooth.

Kamryn lay with her eyes closed, unsure which sort of Saturday she wanted today to be. It would be nice if Mark was already up and going, attending to something around the house or running errands. It would be nice to see Mark doing something for them, for the family, and not his job. She didn't want to walk out to the kitchen and see him on his laptop.

Then again, it would be nice if he was still in bed. Lying here beside her, waiting for her to open her eyes. Kamryn didn't crave the sex so much as the intimacy it brought. She needed a few moments with him, just the two of them, to break the hold the last few weeks had over them. She needed to lie against him, her head on his chest, his arm around her and say she was sorry. That he was right, and she had let her worries get the best of her. And she needed, *God, but she needed* him to get that worrying about the kids was more a part of her than her heart. That she lived and breathed her kids, their happiness, and their well-being.

Moms were hard-wired that way. And sometimes they got a little crazy, Kamryn included. She needed Mark to say he understood that and that he was okay with it, that everything was fine.

Hard-wired to worry, to care. Kamryn realized she wasn't alone in her bed. She also knew, without opening her eyes, that it wasn't Mark beside her. Not Ian, either, because whenever he slept with her, he had to have something touching her. A foot in the middle of her back or his hand tossed carelessly over her shoulder or her wrist. As if he had to anchor himself to her, just in case he might float away in the dark.

Besides, she could smell perfume. If she wasn't mistaken, it was the Ed Hardy stuff she and Mark had given Ashton for Christmas. Braelyn wore something by Escada. Kamryn, eyes still closed, felt her lips twitch. Not only could she *see* the difference in her twin girls—even when they were younger and dressed alike and wore their hair the same—she could scent the difference. Bizarre.

She rolled her head to the side and opened her eyes. Ashton lay on her stomach, face buried in Mark's pillow, her arms up underneath it. Kamryn stared for a moment, studying Ashton's lean, muscular arms. Her sleek cap of dark blond hair.

Kamryn didn't look away when Ashton opened her right eye and stared back.

"Hey."

Ashton, brown eyes so much like Mark's, blinked and then continued to stare. Moments passed before she finally stretched, pushed herself up on her elbows, and mumbled something back to Kamryn.

"What's up?" Kamryn asked. She lifted her head just enough to see the alarm clock on the dresser. It was almost nine. Wow. Long time since she had slept so late. She wondered for a minute where Mark was, but she could hear faint noises from somewhere else in the house. She assumed it was him.

Ashton flopped back down on her belly and shoved her arms up under Mark's pillow again. All the better to hide from Kamryn.

Despite her decision to accept that the party last weekend was a fluke and the promise ring and all the other craziness going on in their house, to apologize to Mark for worrying over nothing and making him crazy, too, Kamryn felt her stomach twist.

Just a little.

"Garret and I broke up last night." Ashton's gruff voice barely carried to Kamryn.

Kamryn took a deep breath and wondered how she was supposed to respond. Maybe relief was inappropriate, but there it was. She couldn't tell Ashton that, though. Concern. Okay, she didn't have to fake that. Even though she was glad the two of them broke up, she didn't want Ashton to be hurt. Sad.

"I broke up with him." This time she whispered.

Saying the wrong thing right now would be really bad. Ashton had come to her to talk and saying the wrong thing— that it was for the best, that Ashton and Garret were too young to be so serious—would start an argument that would most likely end with Ashton storming out of the bedroom, yelling at Kamryn.

Kamryn wasn't necessarily afraid of Ashton's yelling, but she didn't want to say anything to alienate her.

"You okay?" she finally asked. Maybe asking why wasn't the most important thing to start with.

"I don't know." Ashton sighed. She raised herself up on her elbows, but she still didn't look at Kamryn. Instead, she let her head hang forward into Mark's pillow. "I thought I was. I mean....last night. It felt right."

Kamryn turned over to her side and reached out to stroke her fingers through Ashton's hair. "And now you're having second thoughts?"

Ashton lifted her head and looked at Kamryn. "No. It's not that."

Kamryn raised her eyebrows but said nothing.

"I like him, Mom, but things just got so complicated. I don't wanna deal with all of that anymore."

"Okay." Kamryn nodded. "You don't have to deal with it. You don't have to date anyone, Ash. Not if you don't want to."

Ashton's mouth worked, as if she wanted to say more, as if she was talking, but she shook her head and looked away again.

"I'm scared."

Kamryn breathed deeply, afraid of what Ashton would say next.

"What are you afraid of?" she asked gently. She hated to think Ashton was afraid of something. When the girls were little and they were afraid of the dark, it was so easy to cuddle with them and make them feel safe enough to close their eyes and sleep. Kamryn felt the electric tingle of nerves trace down her arms and into her hands and fingers. Ashton's fears as a teenager wouldn't be so easily dismissed. Within eighteen months, Ashton and Braelyn would leave for college, and Kamryn and Mark wouldn't be there to protect them or comfort them.

Kamryn's stomach dropped a bit. She hated the thought of her girls leaving for college. She was excited for their futures, yes, but she hated that she was so close to the beginning of losing them to their real, grown-up lives.

"What he's gonna say about me."

Kamryn said a silent *oh*. She felt her lips move in that perfect round shape, but she couldn't find her voice. Apparently, her biggest fear for Ashton had come true. She wished Mark was here right now, at her side, to comfort her. To protect her from the rest of this conversation.

And yet, if he was, Ashton wouldn't be. Ashton wouldn't have this discussion with him.

"Why didn't I think of that before?"

Kamryn pursed her lips and then sighed. "I guess sometimes it's hard to think when you're...in that situation."

Ashton nodded. She swiped at her eyes with her right hand, and then looking very much like the scared, little, brown-eyed blonde she had been so many years ago after a bad dream, she dragged herself closer to Kamryn and put her head on her pillow, eyes closed, tears on her face. Kamryn put her arm around her and drew her closer.

"I'm sorry, Mom," Ashton whispered. Kamryn snuggled her close. She didn't know if the tears on her face were Ashton's or her own. "I know you're disappointed in me."

Kamryn sighed. She didn't say anything. What could she say? Yes, she was terribly disappointed for Ashton maybe in Ashton, but saying those words out loud would only make Ash feel worse. They certainly wouldn't do either one of them any good. Not right now.

"Did you love him?" she asked when she finally felt her voice wouldn't fail her.

"I thought I did," Ashton mumbled into her pillow. "I do. But I liked him more...before."

"Did he love you?"

Ashton shrugged, still curled tight against Kamryn. "He said he did."

"Then maybe he won't tell anyone."

"I think he was pretty mad last night."

"Of course he was, Ash. That's natural."

"I just don't want people to know. It was between us."

Kamryn cringed at the thought of her sixteen-year-old daughter lying in bed with Garret.

"Ash, did you use—"

"Yes."

The relief was short-lived. It hurt to lie there with Ashton in her arms and remember the way she used to sing along with *Dora the Explorer* and how she loved to jump rope and ride her bike with no hands. The way she had been jealous because Braelyn had started her period first, completely unfair because Ashton was older than Brae.

"Mom?"

"Hmm?"

"Don't tell Daddy. Please?"

"Oh, Ash." Kamryn squeezed her eyes shut. "I don't like keeping stuff from Dad."

"Are you guys gonna get divorced?"

Kamryn opened her eyes to find Ashton staring at her.

"Why would you ask me that?"

"Because you fight so much. You've never been like this and now, it's like you guys can't have one normal conversation without yelling at each other."

"We're not getting divorced, Ashton. Please don't worry about that."

"I hate it when you guys fight."

"I do, too."

"Are you mad at me?" Ashton's bravado drained from her words. Kamryn read her lips more than she heard her voice.

"I'm sad at you, Ash," Kamryn answered after a long moment of silence. "I'm really sad that things happened this way. You deserved more than this."

"No, I didn't." Ashton shook her head. "I made this mistake, Mom. It's my fault. Why does that mean I deserved better?"

"Hey, are you people staying in bed all day or what?" Mark's voice exploded into the room and then there he was, standing in the doorway. Kamryn stared at him, hungry to touch him. To kiss him. To claim him. *Divorce?* Had Mark ever said anything about a divorce? Had he considered it? Or was that question just natural from a child who wasn't used to hearing her parents fight?

"Did I interrupt something?" he asked quietly.

Kamryn felt a pang of guilt. She couldn't keep this from him. She couldn't lie to him, not even by omission. But she couldn't break Ashton's confidence, either.

Ashton wiggled away from her and sat up.

"Daddy, will you fix pancakes?"

Kamryn saw the look of surprise cross Mark's face. Ashton, the calorie counter, hadn't eaten a pancake since she turned fourteen.

"Really?"

"And bacon?" she asked. Mark watched her as she sidled up to him, stood on her tiptoes, and kissed his cheek. "Please?"

His eyes met Kamryn's over Ashton's shoulder. Kamryn sat up in bed, praying that he could read it in her eyes. That somehow, looking into her eyes, he would understand what Ashton had just confessed to her. Because Kamryn needed him to know, but she needed to keep her promise to Ashton.

"Sure." Mark tousled Ashton's hair and watched her hurry out of the bedroom. Kamryn sighed and dragged her fingers back through her hair. Mark leaned back on the doorframe and studied her. "I don't wanna know. Do I?"

Lips pressed tightly together, Kamryn simply shook her head.

CHAPTER 27

ASHTON

Even though she was a little bit worried that her mom might tell her dad what they talked about, and even though the worrying made her stomach hurt, Ashton ate three pancakes and two slices of bacon. On top of that, she washed it all down with a glass of milk.

Thank God no one made a big deal about it. If anyone had, she probably would have gotten up and walked out of the kitchen. She might have even gagged herself and thrown it all back up, not that she had ever done that before. She knew girls who did, but the thought made her sick. Much easier to just not eat.

Braelyn had been three quarters of the way through her two pancakes when her cell rang, and she asked to be excused. Ian had eaten while being turned completely backwards in his chair. God help him if he missed an episode of *Phineas and Ferb*. As if he hadn't seen every one of them three hundred times.

"I've watched this show, like three times, and I've seen the same episode every time." Ashton stabbed a three-layer deep bite of pancake.

"Well, pay attention, because there's going to be a quiz on it later," her dad told her. She glanced at him, relieved to see that he was grinning. Maybe Mom hadn't told him? God, she hoped not. She could see him going over to Garret's house and ripping him a new one. As much as she loved her dad for wanting to protect her and her *virtue*, she couldn't forget that she was as much to blame as Garret.

"Don't even say that word to me," she muttered. "I am so sick of quizzes."

"Here." Ian snapped. She looked up, to see his arm stretched toward her, the syrup bottle in his hand.

"What?"

"You asked for the syrup." He turned his head to look at her for a second. Ashton laughed at the look of exasperation on his face.

"No, I didn't. I didn't say a word to you."

"Ashton!" He shoved the bottle at her again.

"Ian, she didn't say anything about syrup," Mom said with a small laugh. "I think you're a little too tuned into the TV."

"Can I spend the night with Grandma and Grandpa tonight?"

Mom opened the dishwasher door and started loading the dirty dishes inside.

"I don't care," she answered Ian as she worked. "You have to call and ask them."

"Cool!" Ian jumped down from his barstool. Moses, who had been sitting beside the stool, hopped up, ready to follow Ian. "Where's the phone? Mom, I need a cell phone! I want one like Ash and Brae's."

Mom looked at Dad with big, wide eyes. Ashton figured she was thinking something along the lines of *can you believe this kid?*

"Because that's fair. We got our first phones when we were thirteen, munchkin."

"Don't call me that," Ian told her as he continued to look for the phone.

"Wash your hands, Ian," Dad said.

"They're not dirty."

"You have syrup all over your hands." Mom stood up straight and looked closely at Ian. "And all over your pj top, too."

"Nuh-uh."

"Yes-huh." Dad nodded. He stood up and carried his plate to the kitchen sink. "Go wash your hands and get dressed. Then you can call Grandma."

Ian sighed in disgust. "It'll be, like, five o'clock then, and they won't even be home."

Ashton giggled again.

"Mom, make her quit laughing at me."

"Ian, you have turned into a grump." Mom turned to the sink and turned on the water.

"Have not."

Ashton watched Mom sort of deflate and fold in on herself. Dad squeezed her shoulder.

"Ian, upstairs. Now."

"Fine."

Ashton finished her breakfast and carried her plate to Mom.

"Thanks, Daddy."

"You're welcome." Dad snagged his arm around her shoulders and pulled her toward him. "Got homework?"

"Do dogs poop in the yard?" Ashton raised her eyebrows.

"Well, ours doesn't," Dad answered seriously. "He seems to like the driveway better."

Mom laughed softly. They heard Moses bark from upstairs, no doubt Ian's room, waiting for him to get dressed and go back downstairs.

"See? Something about the driveway." Dad shrugged. "Probably does it just hoping that I'll drive over it and my car will stink."

Ashton rolled her eyes. "Yes."

"Yes?"

"I do have homework. I'm gonna go work on it."

"Already?" Mom glanced back over her shoulder. "It's kind of nice outside. Why don't you go out for a bit? Go for a run or something?"

"Maybe later."

"Fresh air would be good for you."

Ashton nodded. "I know. But I have a paper to write. And two tests to study for."

"I don't ever remember having so much homework." Dad shook his head.

"That's because you never did your homework," Mom reminded him.

"That's right. You did it, in return for favors." Dad grinned at Mom.

"Yuuuck," Ashton groaned. "That's disgusting."

"What?" Dad looked at Ashton. "I paid for her gas and stuff."

"And stuff?" Ashton repeated.

"Yeah, I—"

"Don't wanna know!" Ashton shook her head and hurried up the steps. She lingered at the top, though. Not to see if any more was said about that, not to see if Mom and Dad flirted or anything. But to see if they said anything about her.

It was quiet, though, and Ashton imagined that they were kissing. Better than fighting, she guessed. But she still didn't want to think about it. Or hear it.

Ashton was almost ready to walk away, to go to her room to study, but she heard her dad say something. And she was pretty sure she heard her name.

She took a small step back to the top of the steps and strained to hear. They had to be talking about her, because they were talking in low voices.

"She broke up with Garret last night."

Ashton winced when she heard her mom's voice. *Please don't tell, Mom. Please don't tell Daddy what I did.* It had been hard enough to talk to Mom about it. And yet, she hadn't slept all night, because she was scared. What if Garret told someone? What if he told just one person? Like what if he told Andrew some of the stuff they had done? That they'd had sex, like, a million times in her bed and his? That she had given him blow jobs? What if he told Andrew that it wasn't good? That she didn't know how to do it or that she was too skinny, and her boobs were too little?

"How come?"

Ashton leaned even further over the top step to hear her mom's answer.

"I don't know. I guess it was just getting too serious for her."

Ashton sighed in relief.

"Maybe that promise ring really scared her," her dad suggested.

"Yeah. I'm sure that's a big part of it."

"What else would it be?"

"She's sixteen, Mark. She's got things to do. She probably misses her friends."

Ashton closed her eyes. That one hurt. She did miss her friends. She missed hanging out with *Braelyn*, and they lived in the *same house*.

"So," her dad said quietly. "If Ian goes to your mom's house, how about you and I go out for dinner?"

"Okay."

"Maybe it's time we talk some of this stuff out."

Ashton felt a stab of fear low in her belly. *Stuff? Talk some of this stuff out?* What did that mean? She was torn between wanting to eavesdrop and scared to death of what she might overhear.

She heard water running in the upstairs bathroom and remembered that Ian was up here changing clothes. She didn't want to be caught listening to Mom and Dad, so she went on down the hall to her bedroom.

Still in her pjs even after eleven in the morning, she lay back down on her bed and reached for her backpack. She had dropped it on the floor beside the bed yesterday after school. She unzipped the bag with one hand and then fished around for a notebook. She wanted her Spanish notebook. It would be her easiest test on Monday; she figured she would just go over her notes and be done with it for the weekend.

Ashton's fingers closed on a notebook, and she tugged it free of the bag. When she saw that it was her chemistry notebook, she sighed in disgust and tossed it to the floor. The second try produced the Spanish notebook, but once she had it on the bed with her, she didn't open it anyway.

She and Garret had done it the first time here in her bed. She remembered now how good it felt, how hot she was when he touched her. His hands all over her stomach and her boobs— was she supposed to think of them as boobs or breasts when she thought about this stuff?—His fingertips rolling her nipples and then his breath and his tongue hot and wet over them.

It hurt. When they did it the first time, it hurt. She couldn't really say anything about that felt good. Not the first time. Sometimes it had been okay, but not worth all the drama.

Okay, so she liked Garret. And sometimes that stuff had been nice. But why did he have to make it so important? Why did he have to make it seem like that was all he wanted?

She wasn't sorry, really. She didn't regret breaking up with him. She just regretted being with him. Like *that*. Ashton would give anything to call him up now and go play tennis or go for a run. Anything. Just to get back to that friendship they used to have.

The day ticked by so damned slowly that Ashton wondered how she would ever get to Monday, to see how it was going to be. She thought about checking online, on her Facebook page. To see if Garret had said anything mean about her. To see if anyone else had said anything about her. But she told herself Brae was probably online, probably had been all day. And if she had seen something mean about her, she would have told her, right?

Really, she was just afraid. Much too afraid to look.

At four o'clock, Braelyn knocked and asked her to help her pick out an outfit for her date tonight. Brae was decked out in sweats and an old, faded U of I t-shirt. Even though dates and boys were the last thing Ashton wanted to think about, she decided Brae needed some fashion help.

"You okay?" Braelyn asked her when they were standing in front of Braelyn's closet.

"Hmm?" Ashton raised her eyebrows. "Yeah, I'm fine." She yawned. A glass of wine would be nice right about now. Not that she could just go waltz downstairs and pour one. Even if no one was around, she couldn't walk around with a glass of wine.

She could grab a vodka soda, though.

"So what do you think?" Brae asked. She reached for a hanger. Ashton tried to focus on the yellow and white checked Abercrombie & Fitch blouse. It would be cute, yes, with jeans and Sperry's. Or Toms.

But now that she had thought about having a drink, she couldn't think about anything else.

"Where are you guys going?" she asked to buy herself time. Had Braelyn shown her anything else? Had she really zoned out, or was Braelyn just expecting her to reach into her closet and *shazam*, pull out the perfect outfit, magically?

"Dinner and a movie."

Ashton caught herself. How many times had she heard that? *Ash, wanna do dinner and a movie tonight?* Garret might as well have said *Ash, do you wanna do me tonight?* How many times had she told her parents she and Garret were going to do dinner and a movie?

"What movie?"

"Why does that matter?" Braelyn asked. She yanked the elastic hairband from her messy ponytail and shook her hair out.

"It just does," Ashton answered impatiently.

"Well, I don't know yet."

Ashton nodded and pressed her lips together. "I'm gonna go get a soda. You want one?"

"No." Braelyn plopped back on her bed. "But you can bring me a glass of juice."

"Orange juice?"

"Sounds good."

"Okay. Be right back."

Apparently, Ian was already gone, because the TV was off, and he was nowhere to be seen. Her parents' bedroom door was open, but she didn't see them either. She grabbed a can of soda from the refrigerator and poured it over ice in a glass. Then she took a good look around to make sure she was alone and grabbed the vodka bottle from under the sink. Her hands started to sweat a bit when she saw that she had really made a dent in it. It was a big bottle, one of those tall ones, with the rounded top. When she had started sneaking it in her soda, it had been nearly full. Now there was only a fourth of a bottle left.

She wasn't necessarily worried about what would happen when it was empty, and her parents wondered where it went. The thought that it might cause another argument made her stomach pinch for just a minute. But she splashed a liberal amount in her soda anyway and then hurriedly screwed the cap back on and set the bottle back in the cabinet.

What she was worried about was what the hell could she drink when the vodka was gone? Sure, she preferred wine, but vodka was so easy to hide.

The back door opened, and Mom walked in as she poured Brae a glass of orange juice.

"What are you doing?" Mom asked.

"Helping Brae decide what to wear on her date tonight."

"What are they doing?"

Ashton shrugged. "Dinner and a movie."

She felt her cheeks burn as she said it. How many times had she used that lie with her parents? How many dinner-and-a-movie dates had turned into get naked and do it nights?

"What're you gonna do tonight?" Mom asked as Ashton picked up both glasses and headed to the stairs.

Ashton, hands still sweating, though now it was nerves—if Mom had been a minute earlier walking into the kitchen, she would have caught her—looked back at Mom.

"I guess I'll just stay home. I should work on that paper, anyway."

"What class is it for?"

Ashton watched Mom wash her hands and then open the refrigerator and reach for something.

"Ethics."

"Mmm." Mom nodded. "That's probably kind of good you're taking that, huh? With all the pharm stuff you're planning to do. Have you had that talk yet, about how ethical it would be for a poor man to break into a pharmacy and steal medicine his dying wife needs but he can't afford?"

"No." Ashton shook her head. She wondered if her mom was just making conversation or if she was onto her. If she suspected Ashton was drinking.

Mom rubbed the apple she had taken from the refrigerator with the dish towel. Ashton watched her take a bite.

"You could go with us," she suggested. "Go out for dinner with me and Dad."

"No, thanks." Ashton shook her head. Dad wanted to be alone with Mom tonight. *To talk about stuff.* Ashton had overheard that conversation. No way she was going to tag along, whether they had that talk about stuff in front of her or not. "I'll be fine."

"Okay. Going back outside."

"What're you guys doing?" Ashton took a drink of her soda. She took a deep breath as the vodka burned its way down her throat.

"Cleaning out the garage. Wanna help?"

"No way."

She hurried back upstairs. The bathroom door was closed, and she could hear the shower going. Without knocking, she opened the door and stepped inside.

"Here's your juice."

"What took you so long?" Braelyn called.

"Talking to Mom. She wants me to go out with her and dad tonight."

"Eww."

"Exactly."

"I still don't know what to wear."

"I'll go find you something."

"Thanks, Ash."

Ashton couldn't escape the bathroom fast enough. Braelyn must have been boiling herself, because steam rolled up the walls and engulfed the whole room. She took another drink, this time a long one. The warmth of the drink loosened the knot inside her, the one that had been there since last night. Since she had told Garret she wanted to break up.

Brae's room was so different from her own. At first, Ashton thought it was childish, compared to hers. Now, she wondered if it was simply fun, while hers was boring.

She studied the yellow Abercrombie shirt but decided against it. Instead, she paired a sleeveless blue silk blouse with a silver leather jacket and jeans. She snagged a pair of silver flats from the floor of the closet and set them at the foot of the bed. Something caught her eye as she did, something in Brae's closet. She sat down in front of the open door and took another big swallow.

"What're you doing?"

Ashton grinned, but she didn't bother to look at Brae. She smelled flowery and fresh. Ashton reached for the *Easy Bake Oven* and pulled it out of the closet.

"How did you save this from the garage sale Nazis?"

Braelyn laughed. Towel wrapped around her chest, she stepped into a pair of boy cut Victoria's Secret underwear.

"I hid it."

"Where?"

"Under a pile of clothes."

"Remember when we had that bake sale? We made brownies and cakes."

"And no one bought anything."

They had sat in their front yard, at a card table, hoping to sell their baked goods to the neighbors.

"Daddy did," Braelyn answered. She pulled a bra from her drawer. "He bought everything."

Ashton smiled. She didn't tell Braelyn that she had found the remains of their baked goods in the garbage can. Dad had eaten one of the brownies but tossed the rest.

"Not that one." Ashton shook her head and climbed to her feet, careful not to spill her drink. Braelyn dropped the towel. "Geez, Brae, really?"

"They're boobs, Ash, you have them, too."

"You got the boob gene, Brae," Ashton mumbled as she dug through Braelyn's underwear drawer. "Here. Wear this one."

"Really?" Braelyn eyeballed the bright orange push-up bra Ashton handed her.

"Yes, really. They'll push 'em up." Ashton shook her head. "Put it on. I don't wanna look at your boobs."

"Is this boob envy?"

"I have bumps, not boobs."

"Ash?" Brae hooked the bra, twisted it around, and pulled the straps up. "Can I ask you something?"

"What?"

"What should I do? If he wants to...you know..."

"Say no, Braelyn." Ashton thought again of the *Easy Bake Oven* in the closet. Of how much she wished she could go back and tell Garret no. "Tell him no."

CHAPTER 28

Ashton's words had stayed with her all day. *Divorce*. God, it was such a harsh word. It sounded so different from *leaving* or *please don't leave me*. None of it was pleasant to think about, but *divorce*. Where had Ashton gotten the idea that she and Mark might divorce? Did she know something Kamryn didn't? Had she overheard Mark talking to someone else?

Or was it simply that suddenly she and Mark were fighting too much, and it had affected one of their kids? Or maybe all their kids, and they just didn't know the full extent of it yet. Kamryn didn't know. It was all new to her, the whole concept of divorce and loss. Her parents had been married for forty-seven years. Mark's parents had been married for forty-nine when his dad passed away. Divorce had never applied to anything in her life, and now she didn't know how to deal with the echo of Ashton's words.

Kamryn watched Mark as he studied the menu. She had insisted that Ashton come with them to dinner. Mark had wanted it to be just the two of them but not for romance. Tonight wasn't remotely about romance. It was practical, if anything. Practical discussion about their kids and the worry about Brae's drinking and probably, Kamryn should tell him about Ashton. And yet, Kamryn couldn't just leave Ashton sitting at home, feeling sad. Mark had pretended to get it when she told him Ashton was coming with them.

Well, actually that was harsh. Mark was happy to have Ashton join them, even without knowing the whole sordid story about the break-up. But he was frustrated, too, because he wanted to figure out where they were with things and then, if they weren't in the right place, he wanted to get there. Kamryn did, too. But they could talk after they got home. Ashton would retreat to her room, and she and Mark would have plenty of time to talk.

Mark's needing to fix things had nothing to do with divorce. Right?

"What do you want?"

Kamryn bit her lip and looked away when Mark caught her staring at him. Ashton was looking at her phone, most likely on Facebook, probably trolling to make sure her reputation was still intact. Kamryn had mixed feelings about everything Ashton had confided this morning. Of course she was relieved that Ashton had finally come to her to talk. And she was relieved that Ashton had ended the relationship. But she was disappointed in Ashton for being with Garret, and yes, she was worried about what Garret might say about her now.

"What?"

"What do you want?"

Kamryn sighed. The edge in Mark's voice wasn't sexy tonight. He was frustrated. Tired.

She rolled her neck on her shoulders and then ran her fingers through her hair. Really, she wasn't hungry, and she didn't want anything. But she didn't want to go home and sit and stare at the walls, as much as she did love the house.

These days, her house, their home, didn't provide much comfort. Not the emotional kind, anyway. Kamryn had found there really wasn't anywhere that felt safe right now.

She met Mark's eyes and pressed her lips together. What kind of words might spill out if she wasn't careful? *How did we get here? This isn't us.*

It was irrational, but she was afraid to say anything of the kind right now. What if that's all it took? What if Mark was thinking of leaving her? Would those words—*this isn't us*—would that just invite him to speak his mind? Would he say there wasn't any *us* left, and maybe they both needed space?

She didn't need space. She needed honesty.

Kamryn blinked and looked at Ashton again. She needed honesty, but mostly, she and Mark needed honesty from their kids. Most of the fights lately were about their kids.

She knew she was lying to herself, even as she thought it. Most of their fights lately were about parenting. Kamryn was seeing problems, little fires flaring up, and Mark was looking at their home through rose-colored glasses and not seeing anything.

Did he really not see what she did? Was he really not concerned about Brae? Or was he running away from them so he *wouldn't have to see* what she did?

And if that was the case, didn't that mean there really were bigger problems? Problems between them that had nothing to do with the kids?

Divorce.

"Kam."

"What?"

"What do you want?"

She shook her head and focused on Mark again. He took a drink of his beer and then set the empty bottle near the edge of the table.

"I don't care."

Kamryn took a small drink of her own beer and listened while Mark asked Ashton what she wanted on her pizza.

"Pepperoni and green peppers."

"Whatever," Mark mumbled. He closed his menu and looked up as their waitress approached the table. He ordered a large meat trio—which is what he always ordered if no one else chimed in—and another beer. Why did he even bother to ask? Kamryn wondered.

Again, she told herself to back off. If she had said she wanted something else, he would have ordered what she wanted. He had ignored Ashton, but that was because she might eat one piece, and he didn't eat green peppers.

"So." Mark leaned backwards and stretched his arms just a bit over his head. Kamryn's gaze dragged down over his chest and his abs, not quite a six-pack, but not bad for a guy in his forties, either. "How come you're with us instead of Garret?"

"We broke up."

Mark glanced at Kamryn. She had told him that much, but she hadn't given him any details. She didn't want to keep it from him, but she didn't want to break Ashton's trust. She told herself she just needed to think about it a little longer before she truly decided if she was going to tell him or keep it from him.

"Why?"

Ashton, eyes still on her phone, shrugged.

"I don't wanna be tied down. I don't like it."

"You broke up with him?" Mark asked, clearly surprised.

Ashton spared him a glance and nodded, as if it couldn't have happened any other way.

"I guess that surprises me," Mark said quietly. He looked at Kamryn again.

"Why? I never have time to myself. It feels like..." Ashton sighed and shook her head.

"Feels like what?" Mark prodded. "What were you going to say?"

"Nothing."

Ashton looked at Kamryn across the table. Her eyes were puffy, as if she had spent part of the afternoon crying. Kamryn wondered where the tears were coming from: sadness that she broke up with him or regret over what happened before she broke up with him?

"It just feels like..." Ashton's voice shrunk smaller and smaller, "everyone wants a piece of me. Everybody wants something from me, and it's making me crazy."

"What did Garret want from you?" Mark asked with a frown. Kamryn felt his eyes on her, but she studied the wood grain of the table between them.

"Dad!" Ashton rolled her eyes. "I don't mean that. He just… smothered me. He always wanted to be together, and I always had to study, and then when I was done, he was always there. I just got tired of it."

From the corner of her eye, Kamryn saw Mark nod.

"So are you upset? You're sad that you aren't dating now?"

"Kind of."

"He wasn't the one, Ash," Mark said softly.

"I know, Dad," Ashton mumbled. Kamryn could hear the eyeroll in her voice. "That's kinda the point."

Mark chuckled. Kamryn felt a rush of love for him as he scooted closer to Ashton and put his arm around her shoulders.

"Don't be sad." He leaned in and kissed her cheek.

"Dad!" Ashton scooted over and shoved him away at the same time.

"You'll always have your dad." He kissed her check again.

"Dad, we're in a public place," Kamryn said with a laugh. Ashton looked up at her, eyes bright with tears. Tears that Kamryn could have read from a mile away. Ashton and Braelyn were Daddy's girls, and now Ashton felt disconnected from that time and place. From the little girl who used to adore her daddy.

From the little girl her daddy used to adore.

Mark was on his third beer and Kamryn her second when the pizza finally came. Ashton asked for a refill on her glass of water and nibbled on a piece of pizza.

"So what was your sister doing tonight?"

Kamryn wondered at how Mark was directing all conversation at Ashton and not her. Was he just including Ashton so she wouldn't think about Garret and feel bad? Or was it just easier for him to look at Ashton and talk to her?

"She went out with Andrew."

"But what were they doing? Did they get pizza? Go bowling?"

Ashton looked at Kamryn and then Mark.

"Really, Dad? Bowling?"

"Dinner and a movie," Kamryn answered him. She wanted to be a part of this conversation. She wanted to help console Ashton, yes, but she also wanted Mark to talk to her.

Ashton swallowed hard and then coughed. She took a sip of water, still coughing. Mark slapped her back a couple times.

"You okay?"

"Mm-hmm." Ashton, red splotches on her cheeks, nodded but kept her eyes on her pizza.

Dinner and a movie. Kamryn cringed. Ash and Garret always did dinner and a movie. Or so they'd said.

She took a deep breath and then took a big drink of her beer. Maybe that was one of the benefits of bringing your almost seventeen-year-old daughter out for dinner. You could have a couple of beers, and she could drive you home.

Braelyn? Braelyn, too? Kamryn wondered how long Ashton's relationship with Garret lasted. How long had they been sexually active? Because it kind of seemed like the odds might stack up against them, if they had two sexually active teenage daughters out there. Were they gambling with a possible teenage pregnancy?

Yeah, let's throw in a grandchild and see what that does to the marriage, Kam. Two bright, college-bound girls with the world in their hands. Mark would come unglued if something like that happened.

Kamryn reached for her beer and drained the bottle this time. Mark flagged their waitress down and ordered another for each of them.

"What's wrong?" he asked Kamryn. She raised her eyebrows but shook her head. She wasn't ready to have this conversation with him, and she definitely wasn't going to open this can of worms when Ashton was sitting with them.

Instead, she looked at Ashton. "I think you're driving home."

Ashton gave her a funny look, something that looked a little like guilt, and then glanced at Mark's beer bottle.

"I'm fine." Mark shook his head.

"Four beers fine?" Kamryn asked. "What's a DUI gonna look like for a pharm sales rep?"

"I'm not gonna get a DUI, Kam." He rolled his eyes. "God, you are on some sado-masochistic worry bender lately. Chill, would you?"

"Chill?" Kamryn repeated. She glanced at Ashton and caught herself. The words were right there on her tongue. She almost said *what about Ashton sleeping with Garret? What about*

Brae out with Andrew? What if he's undressing her right now? What if Brae's at a party right now? What if Andrew has too much to drink and then drives her home? What if Brae and Andrew have an accident on the way home?

What if one of their daughters ended up pregnant? What if she and Mark suddenly had a baby to raise? What if one of their girls wanted an abortion?

"Yeah, chill." Mark nodded. "You're wound so tight, you're gonna explode."

"Mark."

"You need a good—"

"Mark!" Kamryn snapped. "Stop it! I'm a mom. Everything worries me. I can't help it, and I can't change it."

"You're gonna have a heart attack before you're forty-five-years old."

"I'm sorry," she mumbled. "I can't be all laid back like you."

Mark frowned. "Laid back? First, we aren't even talking about the kids. You're accusing me, yet again, of drinking too much, and goddammit, Kam, I'm tired of it. I don't have a problem. Maybe you're turning into some born-again Jesus person who thinks alcohol is a sin, but I don't have a problem. I can drive us home right now no problem. And goddamn you, I'm tired of you acting like I don't care about the kids."

Kamryn stared at him in silence.

Ashton rested her elbows on the table and buried her face in her hands.

"Bravo," Kamryn said quietly. "That was great."

"I'm not drunk."

"I don't remember saying you are drunk. I said that Ashton could drive home. We've both had a few, and since we have and since Ash is with us, she could drive us home. It doesn't take drunk driving to get pulled over, Mark."

"I'm not even buzzed."

"Why are you being so ridiculous about this? We've always watched the other; you drink a few, I drive. I drink a few, you drive. Why shouldn't Ash drive home?"

"I don't even know who you are anymore." Mark tossed his napkin down on the table.

"What?" Kamryn leaned forward. "What? What the hell does that mean?"

Mark got their waitress' attention again. Kamryn silently fumed while he asked her to box the rest of the pizza and bring the ticket.

"I'll tell you who I am, Mark," Kamryn said as the waitress walked away with what was left of their pizza. "I'm the one who's home with the kids while you're gone."

"It's my job."

"You're gone."

Mark sighed. "Shit."

"I'm the one home. I'm the one noticing the little things."

"What? That someone emptied a bottle of wine? Big goddamned deal. Who is doing this to you? Are you seeing a shrink or something? Someone putting this crazy shit in your head? There must be, because this isn't you."

Ashton dragged her fingers back through her hair. Kamryn noticed the tears sliding off her face.

"You're right about that," Kamryn whispered. "This…" She gestured back and forth between the two of them. "This isn't us, Mark."

"Oh, that's priceless." He climbed out of the booth. "Now not only do we have an alcoholic daughter who sneaks booze, and not only am I suddenly a drunk, now we have marital problems? Is that what you're saying?"

Kamryn stood up. She dug in her purse for her keys and handed them to Ashton as they walked out of the restaurant. Mark stopped at the front to pay the ticket, but Kamryn walked on outside. Ashton, clearly torn, waited a few steps behind her.

How had things gotten so out of hand? Not just tonight. The past couple of months had just kind of gone from bad to worse, the whole family kind of careening down a slippery slope with nothing to stop them.

Kamryn turned her back on Ashton and walked across the parking lot to the girls' Kia. Mark had offered to drive it tonight to fill the tank for them; Ashton had simply nodded and climbed into the backseat.

So, if they had both had a few drinks and they were in the girls' car anyway, what did it hurt for Ashton to drive? Was it just a matter of pride? Good God, was Mark hung up on pride after twenty plus years in this relationship? It wasn't like him; none of this was like him, and this constant bickering wasn't like *them*, and Kamryn's head was pounding by the time Mark and Ashton started across the lot.

Maybe Kamryn should have been happy to see them walking close, Mark with his arm around Ashton. She needed Mark to be close to the kids. The kids needed Mark. But right now, it made her angry. Why was she the parent that had to actually *parent* the kids? She was the one who worried about everything; she was the one who did everything at home for the kids or with the kids. She was the one at home with the kids, while Mark was on the road.

Nice that Mark could sweep in and play super-hero dad, roll his eyes at Kamryn, and then fly out again come Monday.

Ashton climbed into the backseat, but Kamryn stood and stared at Mark over the top of the car.

"I can't keep doing this."

He folded his arms on top of the car and rested his chin on them. "What are you saying, Kam? Do you want me to leave?"

"No." She sighed, frustrated all over again. When had they started talking at each other instead of to each other? "No, I don't want that, Mark. I love you. I love you more now than when we were kids. But something has to change. We can't keep doing this."

"And by doing this, do you mean fighting? Drinking? Because I really, honest-to-God, don't believe anyone in our house has a drinking problem, and I think you're getting way bent out of shape over nothing."

"I meant fighting," she said quietly. "Arguing. You questioning me. Telling me I'm worrying over nothing. I'm at home, Mark, with the kids, and I know what I'm seeing."

Mark threw his head back and groaned. "Jesus. This again."

"What again?" She jumped on his words. "What, Mark? What did I do now?"

"Is it hammer-Mark-about-his-job time? Have we moved on to Mark's-a-shitty-dad-because-he's-never-around-for-the-kids time?"

Kamryn wondered how long this had been building inside him. Maybe for a long time, because if she was honest, she would have to admit that her resentment over him being gone so much had been brewing for a long time.

"I don't think I ever said that."

"How about I quit my job and flip burgers at McDonald's? We'd have to move, though. Can't afford that fancy house we built if I'm bringin' home burger bucks."

Kamryn pressed her lips together and shook her head. "This isn't the time for this. Let's go home."

"Can I drive? Do you wanna do a sobriety test on me?"

"Actually, I would rather Ashton drive. Maybe you're fine, Mark, although I don't think so. Because I've never heard a sober Mark McHale act like such a dick." Kamryn yanked her car door open. "But it would be nice if you could just let Ashton drive and set a good example for her."

Mark tugged his door open, but he still didn't get in. Instead, he slammed it shut again. Ashton had to be upset, but Kamryn didn't look at her. She leaned her elbow on the door and pressed her forehead into her hand.

If she and Mark couldn't do a better job of communicating than this, then maybe they were headed toward a split.

"Ash?" Mark pulled Ashton's door open. "Do you think I'm okay to drive?"

"Mark," Kamryn rested her head against the seat and closed her eyes. "Jesus. Just someone get in the goddamned driver's seat and take us home. This is ridiculous."

One thing Kamryn did know. If she and Mark had reached some irreconcilable difference, there was more to it. Something was going on with him, because she had never seen him act this way. Something was eating him, and she was terrified to know what it was. There was no way around it; if they wanted to fix this and be who they used to be, they had to push right through the center of this and blow it wide open.

Mark would probably tell her she was getting all bent out of shape over nothing. Maybe if she was willing to sit back and turn her head and not think about Brae drinking and Ashton sleeping with Garret and how she and Mark could technically become grandparents now and whether Mark was unfaithful when he was on the road, maybe if she ignored all of that, they could be happy again.

PART II
2ND STORY

CHAPTER 29

MARK

"Kam? Kam? Kam!" Mark couldn't breathe. He shoved at something that felt sticky and wet and heavy. "Kamryn!"

He threw the bedspread off and sat up all in one motion. His body shook with a near electric tremor that shot from his heart to the tips of his toes.

That dream again. Dammit all. His head hurt. Not that pounding kind of headache that always seemed to get him when he hadn't had enough sleep. No, this was worse. This was so bad, a tiny, sharp little pain like someone was working an ice pick deep into his brain.

He wished whoever it was would just shove it in. Rip his brain to shreds, because this was goddamned unbearable. Nothing they had given him worked. Not Advil. Not the heavy-duty dose. Not the heavy-hitting crap; all that did was knock him out and drag him through this whole fucked up process over and over again.

Kamryn.

Mark took a deep breath and turned his head. She always slept on her back, with her right arm thrown up over her head. He used to tease her about it, ask her if she did it just so he had an easy route to touch her. To slide his hand up under her nightshirt and feel the heat of her skin. The curve of her breast.

Her side of the bed was empty. As it had been for the past— God, who the hell even knew??—days. The horror of the dream rushed back at him, and then the after-dream stuff, and he reached out and laid his hand on her pillow.

Kamryn. Oh God.

The dream was simple, really, but it was unsettling, and he was always sick in the mornings when he awoke and took the time to think about it. Sick even if he didn't think about it.

She was walking. In the dream, she was walking. Away from him. And he was calling to her back. *Kam? Kam. Kamryn?*

She never turned to look at him. Was she punishing him? God knows, he deserved it, but damn, he desperately needed to see her smile. In real time. Not in a photograph. He needed to see that smile light up her face, her eyes. He ran in the dream. He ran, chasing her, but he never caught her.

He would never touch her again. Apparently, not even in his dreams.

That was all there was. To the dream. Kamryn walking away from him with her back to him. Maybe some people would say God or someone was sparing him the memory. But he knew better. The dream was simple. It was what came next that tortured him. That tore through him every time he woke up. Shattered him all over again.

She was walking away, and he was calling for her, and then he was awake and gasping for air and reaching for her pillow and then came the hell.

Then came the memory. The way the car whipped out of control and crashed into the old faded red Bronco. The sound of metal screeching on metal. The glass breaking and the smell of gasoline and blood. Ashton and Kamryn both bloodied and unconscious.

The dream was simple. Waking up was hell, because when he was awake and he was seeing it over and over again, he couldn't get away. He couldn't force the images away, because his eyes were already open.

"Kam."

He scrubbed his fingers down over his face. He hadn't shaved since before. Since the accident. The beard growth on his face itched. He should shave it off. He wouldn't.

Instead, he flopped backwards on the bed and stared at the ceiling. Walking away. Why did this vivid dream have to be her walking away? Why wouldn't she turn around?

Well, he knew why, but who the hell wanted to face that?

Man up, motherfucker. If you'd stepped up a month ago, your wife wouldn't be dead, would she?

Mark rolled to his side and pulled Kamryn's pillow close to him. He could smell her, still. The mix of her shampoo and her perfume and sweat. The scent was so strong, it brought tears to his eyes. *Kamryn.*

Would she have left him? Where would they be right now if that night had ended differently?

Why had he been such an ass to her? Jesus, she was concerned about her kids. *Their kids.* What was the harm in that? Isn't that what she was supposed to do? Mother them? Protect them? Guide them? And he had given her so much shit for doing just exactly what she was made to do.

For what? Because he was pissed that she sensed he was drinking too much? Because he was jealous of her knowing their daughters better than he did? What the hell kind of man took that out on his wife? Jesus, he had a job to do, and why couldn't he have just kept his insecurities to himself and praised her for the job she was doing?

"Oh God, Kam." His throat was tight with pent-up emotion. He buried his face in her pillow and breathed deeply. "God, I'm so sorry."

He heard someone coming down the hallway. Brae or Ian. *God, please, don't let them need me. Not now.*

When he heard footsteps on the stairs, he breathed a sigh of relief. He couldn't look at either of them right now. Hadn't for days, actually. Hell, who knew? Weeks, maybe? Not that they wanted to look at him. Brae hated him. She had made that damned obvious from day one. Moment one. Ground zero. In the ER.

I hate you, Daddy. I hate you. You killed Mom.

Ian. Hell, Mark wasn't sure Ian *got* it. Old enough to get the concept of death, sure. But then again, this was his mom. His mother. *Gone.* Did Ian get that? That Kam couldn't ever come back to him? Did Ian know that it wasn't Kam's choice? That she would never have left him or the girls? Never in a million years would Kamryn have chosen to leave her kids.

Mark threw the blankets off again and climbed hurriedly out of bed. He had to talk to Ian. He had to make Ian understand that.

Too fast. Too much, too fast. Dizzy, Mark put a hand out, searching for the wall. He needed to lean. He needed someone to hold him up.

He needed Kamryn.

"Fuck."

Kam. He turned and sank to the edge of the bed. Squeezed his eyes shut and felt the tears slide. He had never been much of a crying man. A few tears when his dad had died. The sadness had stayed with him, and Kamryn had suggested that maybe it would feel better to let loose and cry.

But he couldn't.

He wondered now if he had been saving them up for this. For *this* loss. As much as he had loved his dad, this was so much more. This was his *wife*. *The love of his life*, and she was way too young to be gone like this.

The doctors had told him that she didn't suffer. That she didn't feel it. That she had been unconscious and gone far too quickly to know what was happening. Mark wondered how the fuck they knew that, since most likely none of them had died in a car accident and come back to talk about it. To assure the survivors that their loved ones died instantly.

Ian. Okay, he had to talk to Ian. Had to make sure Ian understood that Kam didn't want to leave him.

He stood again, slowly this time, and made his way to the foot of the bed. His body hurt. His right arm, broken, lay against his chest, cradled in a sling. His left leg hurt, and his knee was swollen and black and blue. But the doctors had seen nothing broken. He stood for just a moment to steady himself and then walked across the room to the bathroom.

For a moment, he expected Kam to be in the shower. To walk into the bathroom and be engulfed in steam and the scent of her shampoo and soap. His heart pinched a little when he found the bathroom empty.

How long would it last, this constant forgetting that Kamryn was gone? How many times would he have to lose her before he felt it in his bones, before he would stop looking for her in every room and listening for her voice, for her laugh?

It hadn't been long. He had no idea what today was. Not the day of the week or the day of the month. He thought it was April; he didn't care enough to look. The funeral had been on a Wednesday, he thought, but he had no idea how many days had gone by since then.

There was no more blood in his urine. Seemed like that had cleared up a while ago. The doctors had been concerned about it, and they had told him to watch it, and he had laughed his ass off, because what the hell else does a man do when he takes a piss but watch it?

He flushed and put the seat down and heard Kam's voice giving him shit about leaving the seat up. He studied the cut on his forehead as he washed his hands. Nine stitches? Nine? Or seven? Didn't matter. It was gross, and it made him think of Frankenstein, only he didn't give a damn what he looked like now anyway. Except that he had seen how Ian had eyeballed the jagged line of stitches. He had tried to be brave, but he puckered up and cried and run to Brae.

Mark rested his good hand on the counter and hung his head.

Widowed at forty-four. His wife was gone. His wife was gone, and he hadn't had time to say he loved her.

He hadn't had time to say he was sorry.

How? He raised his head and looked at his image in the mirror. The beard growth almost repulsed him. He had never worn a beard or a moustache, and his hair needed a trim, and his eyes were bloodshot, and his cheeks were hollowed. His cheekbones, always prominent, now stood out like the rest of his face had been sucked away.

He supposed it had.

How? How would he ever live without her?

Ian was on the couch. Mark glanced at the TV, expecting to see cartoons. Ian liked cartoons. Sometimes Mark watched them with him.

"Why aren't you watching cartoons?" he asked. His voice was gruff. True, it had been weeks since the accident, but there hadn't been much conversation. Enough to take care of the funeral plans. Enough to make his mother think he was getting by okay with the kids. The times he called out for Kam in his sleep.

In his dream. When he was begging her. *Come back.*

Ian shrugged. He stared, glassy-eyed, at the fireplace across the room. Mark shivered. It was cold in the house. He wondered, just for a moment, what it was like outside.

"Want me to turn some on?" he asked. He cleared his throat. *"Handy Manny?"*

"Phineas and Ferb, Dad."

Brae's voice pricked the guilt in his stomach. Of course, Ian's favorite cartoon was *Phineas and Ferb*. He knew that. He watched it with him. But he'd forgotten. Jesus, his brain wasn't fully functioning right now. He was allowed to forget things, wasn't he?

Brae wouldn't see it that way, though. She would accuse him of never knowing them the way Mom did. Of not knowing Ian's favorite cartoon.

Mark raised his eyebrows. "Want me to turn it on?" he asked Ian.

"No." Ian scooted down the couch to the opposite end, jumped up, and ran for the stairs.

"Great going, Dad," Brae snapped. He turned to see her standing with her hands on her hips. "It took me almost an hour to talk him into coming downstairs."

Brae was making breakfast. Mark could smell something in the oven. Cinnamon rolls or something. His eyes took in the kitchen, tidy, even though Brae was working. The carton of eggs set close to the edge of the counter. He considered pointing that out to Brae. Telling her to be careful, because they were fragile and if they fell, they would break.

"You're fixing breakfast?" he asked instead.

"Ian needs to eat," she answered, turning away from him. "You didn't feed him last night."

"What?"

"You passed out on the couch, Dad." Brae glanced at him over her shoulder. "It's okay. I made him some mac & cheese."

"I didn't pass out." Anger rose inside him. Oh yes, he *wanted* a drink. He desperately wanted a drink. He wanted a bottle. Or two. He wanted to drink the last three months away. He craved the way the alcohol could make him numb. If he couldn't bring Kam back, then by God, he would love to go away, too.

But he hadn't had a drink. He hadn't had a drink since the accident.

Too little, too late, he knew. But. Still.

"You were out cold."

"I fell asleep."

"Whatever."

"Braelyn McHale, do not use that tone with me."

"Dad," Brae said quietly. "I lost all respect for you when you killed my mom. I'll say what I want. How I want."

Mark swallowed hard. "Brae, it was an accident."

"That could have been avoided."

"You don't know that."

"You swerved over the center line."

Mark sighed. He ran his fingers through his hair and turned away from her. It occurred to him that he should just go back to bed. Nighttime was a little easier, because it was dark, and it was easier to slink around in the dark. But daytime meant facing the demons. Facing the kids. Facing Kamryn's kids.

The guilt haunted him in daylight.

"You're going today, right?" Brae's voice followed him up the steps.

He stopped halfway up and turned back to look at her. That ice pick boring into his brain hurt like a bitch right now. Brae looked uncertain. She had just ripped him a new asshole, with all the calm and cool her mother had shown through the years, but just now, she looked vulnerable. Scared.

"Going?" he asked quietly.

"Ohmygod," she sobbed. Mark heard the rainbow of emotions. The anger. The sadness. The fear. "Daddy, Ash comes home today. Don't you even remember?"

Ashton.

Of course he remembered.

"Yeah. I do." He frowned. Could he do it? Could he walk into that hospital again? Past the ER? Past the last place Kam had been alive? That wasn't true, though. She had flat-lined at the scene. The cops had tried to hold him back, and they were questioning him on what had happened, but he had pushed them away, and he had made his way to Kam's side, and he had seen the paramedics trying.

He'd seen them trying to resuscitate her.

He had seen her eyes, wide open, glassy blue. And dead.

"Never mind," Brae said now. "I'll go. I'll ask Grandma—"

"No," Mark snapped. He didn't want his mom involved in this, and by God, he didn't want to see Kam's mom. If his kids hated him, his in-laws wished him dead.

Why couldn't it have been him?

"No," he repeated. "I'm gonna shower."

"You're supposed to put a bag on your arm. Don't get the cast wet."

"Yeah, I know, Braelyn."

She shrugged then, and she rolled her eyes, and Mark wanted so badly to say something. To attack her for the attitude. For the disrespect.

But he didn't. Instead, he turned and made his way back to the bathroom, to the shower.

He stood under the hot spray for a long time, eyes closed, thinking about Kam. About the way they had gotten lost and fought so hard the past few months. About making love to her here in the shower. About the first night she had told him she was pregnant. And the day of her ultrasound, when he went with her, and they learned their baby was actually twins.

What kind of idiot gambles with that kind of love?

CHAPTER 30

MARK

The girls' car had been totaled, and now there was an empty bay beside Kam's SUV. He stood, frozen, in the doorway for what felt like years. Like maybe he shouldn't have to look up at Brae and see the resentment in her eyes, because maybe he had been standing there long enough that she was gone, away at college.

He hung on to the doorframe, as if Brae might come at him and grab him and try to yank him through the door. With his left hand, he hung on tight, and he swayed there in the doorway, looking at the empty spot in the garage.

Why had he ordered the last beer? Why had he ordered the one before that? Why had he kept ordering for Kamryn? Had he been trying to goad her?

"Dad."

Mark glanced at Braelyn, who stood by the SUV, by *Kam's* SUV, waiting for him. She glanced at her watch. He had only been out of the house a hand full of times since the accident. For the trip to the funeral home. To meet with their priest, who had reminded Mark that his door was always open if he wanted to talk. Mark translated that as the door was always open if he cared to come in and confess to killing his wife. Maybe if he confessed, God would leave him to rot in purgatory instead of sending him straight to Hell.

He didn't want to be saved. He didn't deserve it.

Mark took a deep breath and stepped down. He wondered if there would be an echo if he yelled. The garage felt way too big now.

He glanced to his right, to the other garage, where he kept his company car. Where he had parked his company car for years, since they had moved in here. Wasn't his. Not anymore. Not his car. Not his company.

Employers tended to frown upon drunk driving. Well, no, they frowned upon DUI citations. They fired you for DWI arrests. He took another step down and looked down at his loafers on the cement garage floor.

"Dad, let's go."

He looked up at Brae. He was moving like an elderly man; he knew that. But it wasn't pain. It wasn't that he couldn't go any faster, physically. He dreaded getting in a vehicle and riding and ending up at the hospital.

He dreaded the way the memories were going to suffocate him the second he buckled his seatbelt. The way he would smell the beer and Kam's perfume and the gasoline and the blood. He dreaded the sound he would hear. That Brae would have to turn the damned radio up in the SUV and that even though music would be blaring, he would still be hearing that god-awful metal on metal screech and the bone-crunching crash as the car came to rest, smashed up against that parked car.

The ice pick zeroed in again on that spot above his ear. No concussion. No head injuries for him, other than the cut on his forehead. Maybe that had been fate's way of making sure he was branded. Like a scarlet letter, only his was a D. D for drunk. D for dumbass, dickhead, drunk driver.

His eyes burning, he looked up again at Brae. She looked away quickly and then pulled the driver's door open. He hadn't driven. Not since that night.

When he pulled the door open, it hit him. He gasped out loud and regretted it when Brae turned to look at him. Kam drove this car most of the time. He breathed in the scent of her perfume, her hand lotion, her coffee. There was still a travel mug in the cup holder of the center console.

Jesus. Weeks had gone by, and his wife was dead and buried, and here was a travel coffee mug, and Mark had to fight the ridiculous sudden urge to pick it up and drink from it. To touch his lips to the same spot she had put hers to drink.

Ian watched him from the backseat.

Get a grip, McHale.

He climbed into the seat and then leaned out to pull the door shut with his left hand. Brae turned the key in the ignition, and he struggled with his seatbelt. He bumped the cast twice and sent a rocket of pain up through his arm. Kept his mouth shut and his face stone-cold and finally managed to buckle.

Braelyn reached over and with a quick punch turned the radio off. That shocked him, but he was secretly pleased. No music. He didn't want to hear music. Mostly because it would remind him of Kam, but also because of this damned headache. He thought he might throw up.

She backed out of the garage slowly, closed the door, and then put the car in drive. Mark couldn't watch. He couldn't watch the street. The other cars. Instead, he studied Brae's hands. Her fingers were wrapped around the wheel in a white-knuckle grip.

Was she scared?

Would she tell him if she was?

He raised his eyes to the rearview mirror and watched Ian for a moment. The boy looked frozen. Comatose.

Comatose.

Like Ashton.

Ashton had been in a coma for the first three days. *Three? Or five?* Mark groaned and turned his head to the passenger window. He didn't know. He didn't even know how long Ashton was in a coma. He had visited only once, and he had gotten sick in the tiny closet of a bathroom in her hospital room, and he vomited everything inside him, including some bones and maybe muscle and then he had dry-heaved, and then he just stood, head hung over the toilet and sobbed.

And Ashton had slept through it.

The doctors had told him that it was good. That the coma was Ashton's body's way of healing. She needed the rest. Her brain needed the rest.

Brae had visited her every day. She had gone by herself several times, and once, she took Ian, because he begged to go. Mark had been in the office when they came back home, and Ian had shot up the steps in a blur. Mark had known he was scared. But he hadn't gone to him.

Just how did you go about comforting your kid over losing his mom? When you were the one who took his mom in the first place.

"Slow down," Mark mumbled. He sat with his head against the seat, eyes closed. It felt like Brae was qualifying for the Brickyard, and she came up on the traffic lights like she was playing chicken, daring other drivers to get in her way.

"I'm not speeding," she snapped.

"Just slow down," he repeated.

"You wanna teach me how to drive, Dad?"

Mark opened his eyes and looked at her. His little girl was gone. He didn't recognize the ice-cold blue eyes, the ones that had always reminded him of Kamryn. Brae's face was twisted in a sneer. If looks could kill, he could just die and be with Kam. See if it was too late to apologize.

"Watch the road, Braelyn."

"You know what?" she asked softly.

Mark squirmed in his seat. She was paying too much attention to him and not enough to the road.

"I wish…"

"Watch the goddamned road, Braelyn."

Her eyes welled with tears. He saw them before she looked away, back to the road in front of her.

"I hate you."

The whispered words landed like slabs of stone on his chest. He sucked in a breath, but he couldn't push it back out. He heard Ian wiggling around in the back, but he didn't look at him. Not even in the rearview mirror.

"Shut up, Braelyn."

"You shut up, Ian," she snapped. "You don't even get it. You don't even know what's going on."

"I know Mom's dead!" Ian shouted. "I'm not stupid. I know what's going on."

"Just because you know she's dead, doesn't mean you know what's going on."

"Uh-huh."

"Enough." Mark spoke quietly. The ice pick felt like it was almost through his brain and out the other side of his head. Over his other ear.

He should have left them at home. He should have told them to wait, and he should have manned up and got in the damned car and driven to the hospital for Ashton.

"Just shut up, Ian," Braelyn repeated.

"Make me."

Mark wondered when Ian had learned the hateful words that were tumbling out of his mouth now. He had always adored his sisters, and he never backtalked Mark or Kamryn.

"I will, you little brat." Braelyn looked in the mirror this time. She started to reach over the seat, but Mark caught her hand.

She jumped and snatched her hand away from him. Like drunk-driving and killing someone and being a jerk was contagious.

"You are driving a car, Braelyn." He sounded preachy. Even he could hear it in his voice. But then, how was he supposed to sound? What was he supposed to do? Let Braelyn reach over the seat and smack Ian? And swerve into the other lane in the process?

He had had enough collisions to last him forever, and the kids were making his headache explode. Now the ice pick had gone to work over his eyes.

"Yeah, Dad, I'm driving," she snapped. "But it's okay. I haven't been drinking. All I had today was a glass of milk with a muffin. That okay?"

"Enough."

"Tell Ian—"

"I said enough."

The silence in the car was louder than the kids bickering back and forth, and his headache screamed on. When Brae parked in the hospital lot and cut the engine, another layer of silence sandwiched over the top of them, and Mark struggled again to breathe.

"You are so weird."

He watched Braelyn slide out of the SUV and slam the door shut. Ian got out next and went to stand by Brae. Mark gasped for air again when he saw Ian slide his hand into Brae's.

He had done this. He had made his kids orphans. Because he'd taken their mom, and he sure as shit wasn't dad material. Not now. Not without Kamryn.

Brae stared at him mercilessly through the windshield. She pointed at her watch. Mark took a deep breath and then unbuckled his safety belt and opened the door.

Kam! Kamryn? Kamryn?

She had hit the windshield first. He didn't really remember it. How exactly it had happened. It was a blur. Just the sound of metal on metal and the smell of blood. Kamryn had screamed, and Ashton had cried, and he sort of remembered Kamryn being thrown forward and smacking her head on the windshield and then falling sideways and smacking her head on the passenger window. The car had spun, somehow it had spun out of control, and a third car had hit her. A third car had hit Kamryn's side. The first blow had probably knocked her unconscious. The last had probably killed her.

"Dad!"

Mark swallowed hard and then pushed his door open further and got out. The walk across the lot to the doors was quiet and uncomfortable. The sun was out. In fact, Mark decided it was a little warm in his jeans. They were tight on his knee, too. He should've worn shorts.

He looked down at his shirt, not remembering what he put on before they left. What if looked mental? What if they tried to take him away and lock him up?

Who cared?

But he didn't look mental. He had on jeans and loafers and a Calvin Klein t-shirt and probably Brae was embarrassed to be seen with him. Because of the clothes. Because of the Scarlet D—drunk, dumbass, dickhead—on his head.

The medicinal smell that hung in all medical facilities, whether they were hospitals or nursing homes or even clinics, accosted him as they stepped inside. His breath caught, and he saw Brae glance at him. Probably wondering if he was going to stroke out or if he would need a psych consult before they got out of here.

Ashton was on the third floor. They crossed to the elevator bank, and Ian pushed the button, and they stood in silence. Ian used to count. When they were waiting for an elevator— no matter where they were—Ian would count to see how long it took a car to come. Now he stood silently, sullenly, fingers wrapped protectively in Brae's hand.

A lullaby played suddenly on the public address system. New baby. The nursery played a lullaby each time a baby was born. Mark had heard the same damned tune four times the night Kamryn died. He closed his eyes now, squeezed them shut tight because he was thinking about the day the girls were born. The way Kam had labored and pushed and blown his mind with her strength and then her tears of happiness when each of them held a baby girl.

"God, Dad," Brae groaned. "Could you at least act normal? You're such a freak."

The ding of the approaching elevator car saved him from a reply. They stepped onto the elevator, and three more people crowded in behind them, one of them carrying a big bouquet of balloons.

"Dad."

He looked at Ian and raised his eyebrows.

"We shoulda got balloons," he said quietly.

"What?"

"We shoulda got balloons," Ian repeated. "For Ash."

Mark took a deep breath and then deflated and fell back against the back wall of the elevator. They *should have* brought balloons or flowers or something.

Why the hell hadn't he thought of that? Why hadn't he brought something for Ashton? Or even done something at home? Decorated her room with flowers or balloons? Or posters or something?

He didn't even know what to say to Ashton when he saw her. He couldn't guess what she would say to him, and he was afraid. Afraid of walking into her room and talking to her. Of bringing her home.

Two of his children hated him. He couldn't bear the thought of another one hating him. He didn't know how to take care of her, either. What if he couldn't do it? What if he couldn't handle Ashton?

He was so completely out of his league. He wanted to punch the elevator button and go back down to the ground floor. And walk out.

He needed Kam. Just a few weeks into this single parenting thing, and he desperately needed Kamryn.

CHAPTER 31

ASHTON

Ashton watched as Dad and Brae struggled to put the middle seat back so that she could climb into the back and rest her leg on it. Dad couldn't do much with his arm in a sling, and though she had been fuzzy, at best, for the past several days—weeks?—she could see that he was getting pissed.

Ian waited slumped against the SUV, grumbling under his breath because they were messing with his, seat and why couldn't Ashton just sit on the other side?

Ashton leaned heavily on her crutches and squeezed her eyes shut. After such a long stay in the hospital—she had no idea just exactly how long, because she couldn't remember, and no one here was talking—being outside was giving her one hell of a headache. The sun was so bright, her eyes were watering. No one had thought to bring her any sunglasses. There was something in the air making her head hurt, too. She had never been bothered by allergies before, but something out here was killing her now.

Her leg throbbed, and she was beginning to feel weak. A little dizzy. Thank God the nurse was still here, even though the four of them had whisked out the doors like the hospital was on fire behind them. She didn't want to sit down in the wheelchair they brought her out in, but she was going to have to in a minute. Either that or go down and maybe splatter all over the sidewalk.

She wondered how they thought she was going to get in even if they did get the seat put down for her. If she had any upper body strength, maybe she could sit on that folded seat and pull herself up and back and keep her leg straight out. But her whole body felt like a limp noodle these days, and she figured there was no chance in hell she was going to make it into the back of the SUV.

Maybe if they'd brought their car.

Wait—What about her and Brae's car?

"Are you okay?" The nurse standing beside her laid a hand on her shoulder. Ashton tilted a bit to the side, but she recovered quickly and nodded. Sweat beaded on her upper lip, and she felt a drop roll down the small of her back. It wasn't hot out here. Not really. But standing here like this was killing her.

"Dad?"

Of course he didn't answer her. He was in some of kind of funk; there was something going on with him besides that broken arm. Ashton didn't have a clue what, or she didn't think she did, but she was kind of tired of him just giving her a blank stare when she spoke to him.

"Ian, ask Dad if I can just sit in the front."

Ian stood up straight and leaned into the SUV. Ashton didn't know if he really wanted to help her—if maybe she looked like she was going to pass out—or if he was just happy about the prospect of getting his own seat back. Ian was different now, too. No outward signs of something broken, like her and Dad, but he sure acted different lately.

She saw Dad jerk his head upright and look at her. Yep, apparently, she was looking sort of green, because Dad climbed back up through the SUV and then sort of jumped out and approached her.

"Are you okay?" He glanced at the nurse and looked away quickly. Ashton wondered what that was about. He almost looked embarrassed.

"I need to sit," Ashton told him. "I really need to sit down."

Dad nodded. He looked around again, past the nurse, and then back at Brae, now standing by the SUV.

"My wife drove this all the time," he explained to the nurse. "The rest of us never figured out how to do the seats."

Ashton frowned and closed her eyes. *His wife. Dad's wife.*

"Let's see if we can get the front seat moved back far enough that her leg's comfortable." Thank God, the nurse took charge and pulled the wheelchair out of the way and then hovered behind her as she used her crutches to move toward the front door.

Dad's wife.

The nurse yanked the door open, and Dad leaned down and hit a button. The seat moved back a bit. It was going to be tight, and Ashton dreaded the ride home. But she wanted to get the hell out of here. Days had gone by, and she had been laying and then sitting in this God-forsaken hospital, and she was desperate just to go home.

Her leg—the cast on her leg—fit in the front seat, but she couldn't elevate it. And it was already throbbing. The nurse studied her face for a minute, probably trying to decide if she was in enough pain to pass out and fall out the window or something, and then she stepped back out of the way and pushed the door closed.

Ashton leaned her head back and closed her eyes. Her stomach rolled, and the sweat continued to trickle down over the small of her back. Her whole damned body felt like someone had beaten the shit out of her with a baseball bat, and all she wanted was to go home. To go to her room and lie down on her bed and close her door and be alone.

"This sucks," Ian groaned from the back.

"What does?" Brae asked as she climbed into the driver's seat. Ashton turned her head and saw the nurse pushing the wheelchair back into the hospital. She turned to look over her shoulder and felt a flash of pain shoot up through her neck. Dad was sitting in the other backseat, beside Ian.

She squeezed her eyes shut again.

"Did you bring my sunglasses?" she asked Brae. "They were in the car. The sun is killing me."

The silence in the SUV dragged out for so long that Ashton finally opened her eyes. Braelyn was staring at her with wide eyes. She looked afraid. Geez, maybe Ashton really did look as bad as she felt.

Without answering her, Brae put the key in the ignition. Something clicked in Ashton as Brae turned the key and the engine caught.

Dad had said his wife always drove this car. Why was Braelyn driving?

"Dad?" Ashton blinked and tried to look at him again. The pain erupted in her neck and her left shoulder again. She could feel the blood thumping in the cut down the side of her face now. She had no idea how big it was, because she was too damned scared to look in a mirror. But judging from the way it was throbbing right now, she figured it must take up her whole left cheek.

"What?" Dad asked quietly.

"Where's Mom?"

Again, her words were met with silence. Stunned silence, charged with some kind of electricity, and Ashton felt like one wrong move might spark something and blow the car up.

The car.

Blow the car up.

She winced and ducked her head, as the pain flamed up from her neck and shoulder again. Her cuts and bruises all screamed right now, but mostly it was her head. Her head was going to explode. Right now. The noise. God, the noise was unbearable. That loud screech of metal on metal.

She balled her right hand into a fist. Her left fingers wouldn't quite squeeze like that. It took all she had to get them to curl around the crutch. She might be going home, but she wasn't going to be out and about for a damned long time.

"Ash," Dad whispered.

But now she didn't want him to answer her. In fact, she didn't want anyone to answer her. She didn't want to know.

She couldn't hear those words again. *Again...*oh God, hadn't they told her? Hadn't they already told her? Jesus, she was forgetting everything these days, right down to what day it was, to the name of the hospital she was in, to the accident that had put her there in the first place.

"She's dead, stupid."

Ian's cold voice did it. The tears slid slowly down her cheeks. She kept her eyes closed, praying that no one jumped on Ian's case about what he just said and *how* he said it. She couldn't deal with it. She couldn't deal with raised voices right now. Not in the car, in this tight little space.

"Nice, Ian," Brae mumbled. She checked the rearview mirror and then signaled and pulled out into the exit lane to leave the hospital parking lot.

"Well?" Ian snapped. "Isn't she? Because things wouldn't be so awful if she wasn't, would they?"

Point, Ian.

Ashton's leg hurt like hell, and her stomach lurched every time Brae put on the brakes. She wondered why Dad wasn't driving; he could drive with one arm in a sling. But she didn't ask. She was afraid to open her mouth. Afraid that she might vomit all the disgusting hospital food they had made her eat. Afraid that she might cry out loud. Afraid that she might never stop.

The drive seemed to take hours. Ashton's whole body was sticky with sweat by the time Brae pulled into the driveway.

"Just park it out here," Dad told her.

"So, you can go joyriding later?" Brae mumbled under her breath. Ashton opened her eyes, surprised at the sarcasm in her twin's voice. She wondered if Dad had heard her, but she wasn't going to risk another glance to the backseat. Her neck and shoulder hurt so damned bad, and now her head was pounding. Combination headache: a little bit of stress, some bright sunlight, some negative energy, some whiplash, a bruised collar bone, and a sprained wrist could work together to make a person wish for oblivion.

"So, I can help Ashton out of the car," her dad answered. Ashton waited for him. She hated to, because she hated to need help. From anyone. *God, what a summer this was going to be.* She'd probably pack on about twenty pounds since there would be no running. She would have a frigging cast on forever, so her leg would get all gross-looking. All pasty white and puny. Her muscles would atrophy; it would take forever for the rehabilitation to be done.

And then what the hell was she going to do about school? She still had the rest of April and most of May before summer. And she seemed to forget every third thing someone said to her.

Jesus, she had *forgotten* her mom was dead. If you forgot something like that, the rest of your junior year of high school didn't look too promising, did it?

She watched Brae disappear through the garage. Ian opened his door in the back of the SUV and slid out. He hurried around the front of the SUV and disappeared through the garage, too.

Finally, Dad opened her door. He stared at her for a moment, as if he expected her to snap at him.

"It hurts," she mumbled.

He nodded. "I know."

She waited again, while he opened Ian's door and fetched her crutches from the back. When he closed the door and put the crutches on the ground for her, she twisted around to slide out of the car.

Nausea threatened again. She took a deep breath and concentrated on calming her stomach. Dad must have understood how she felt, because he stepped back just a bit, in case she did get sick.

"I'm okay."

"Ash, look, I'm sorry." He sighed and then groaned, and she stared at him, wondering what he was apologizing for. "We should've brought you balloons or flowers or something. This was a big day for you."

She shook her head. "I don't need them." And she didn't. The only thing Dad hadn't brought with him that she wanted, that she really needed, was her mom. And she couldn't fault him for that, now, could she?

"This is hard, Ash," he said quietly. "It's really hard, and I'm so lost. I don't know what I'm doing. I don't know what I'm doing without her."

She nodded.

"Why can't I remember?" She swallowed hard, but the tightness in her throat remained. Her eyes filled again. "I mean, I remember…everything from before," she chewed on her lip as she spoke, "but I don't remember…"

Throat so tight now that she couldn't go on, she nodded to her leg. A few moments of silence passed. Ashton could hear the squeal of a swing from somewhere in the neighborhood. She listened to the voices of neighbor kids and felt a rush of emptiness. The kids made her think of her mom. She had loved this neighborhood. She had loved the safety and the sense of family their home had provided them. Mom had said that kind of stuff so much that Ashton and Brae had only rolled their eyes and left her to talk to herself whenever she got started.

Two story brick home. Suburbs. Security system.

None of that mattered.

What would her mom would say about it now?

"Why can't I remember?" she repeated.

"Honey, you had a serious brain…"

"Injury, I know." She nodded. She had been in a coma for days; they told her that. But she had forgotten that, too. She reached with her right hand to touch her face, the cut on the side of her face. Dad reached out to her and gently pulled her fingers away. Before she could touch her head, she knew. They had shaved that side of her head. That didn't bother her so much; maybe it would've if she was Braelyn and she had that long, thick hair. As it was, Ashton's would grow back to normal in time. Her hair would probably be back to normal before her leg was.

"Shouldn't I…shouldn't I remember Mom…what happened to Mom…here, though?" She squeezed Dad's hand and pushed their knotted fingers together to lay them against his chest.

Dad blinked, eyes bright with tears. "Doesn't work that way, Ash." His voice broke. He ducked his head and turned away from her.

Medical science didn't work that way. But life according to Kamryn McHale had worked that way.

Ashton cleared her throat. "I need to lie down."

He nodded. She slid out of the seat and took the crutches. For once, she was glad someone was walking with her, hovering over her as she walked. Her left arm hurt so badly, she could hardly hold the crutch. It took them a good ten minutes to make it up the curved front walk, but the front door meant navigating one big, flat step instead of the quick, shallow ones in the garage.

The sound of the swing had stopped, and suddenly the neighbor kids' voices were much closer. Ashton's breath caught in her throat when she saw a small group of them in the street, in front of the house next door to theirs.

"Just ignore them," Dad said quietly.

She refused to look at them again, but she felt the chill in the air as they watched her painstakingly slow progress up the walk. Some of the kids were little, Ian's age or younger, and she knew that to them she was some kind of monster or freak. Every kid had to do a double-take to check out someone walking with crutches. Every little kid thought crutches were a combination of cool and weird, and most every little kid wanted to try them. She and Brae had both felt that way when they were little.

But some of the kids she glimpsed in the street were older, maybe even as old as eighth graders. Ashton could feel the finger-pointing. She ducked her head and kept walking, but she heard little bits of their conversation, and she most definitely heard the hatred in their voices.

Drink and drive—

Mama dead, you're alive.

A bottle killed her—

Modern day thriller.

"God." Ashton groaned. It sounded like a song. Like, if she turned around right now, those kids would be jumping rope and chanting about their accident. Jesus, how nice to have your life, your loss translated into a jump rope chant.

"One more second," Dad said softly. He put the key in the lock, twisted the knob, and pushed the door open. Ashton was glad for her dad's hand at her elbow as she struggled to get inside.

"Who teaches kids to be so mean?" she mumbled. A new layer of sweat covered her body. "Why would you do that to somebody?"

Dad closed the door and locked it. He didn't answer Ashton, just shrugged.

She took a deep breath. *Drunk driving? What?*

"I just wanna lie down, Daddy," she said softly. "In my bed. Okay?"

"You bet. Do you want a pain pill?"

Drunk driving.

"No. Just let me lie down first. See if it quits throbbing."

"Okay."

Ashton opened her eyes and took a step. The house was eerily quiet. She had no idea where Brae or Ian was, but she desperately wished her mom was in the kitchen. That her mom would holler at them, tell them to come to the kitchen for a snack.

"What's wrong?" Mark asked. She took a few more steps and stopped at the foot of the stairs.

"Daddy."

Twelve stairs. *Twelve.* She would never make it. She would never make it to her room. All she wanted was to curl up in her own bed and bury her face in her pillow. And cry. And maybe eventually sleep.

"Daddy."

She glanced at Mark. He stared at her for a moment and then looked at the stairs. He deflated and sagged against the wall.

"Oh God, Ash, I'm so sorry." It sounded like he was crying. "I'm so sorry. I never even thought about this."

Mama dead, you're alive.

A bottle killed her—

CHAPTER 32

MARK

If he had thought that having Ashton home, eliminating the need to go to the hospital to visit her—and all that the visits entailed: asking Brae to drive him, the cold sweats as he stared at the SUV, the way watching her drive set his nerves on edge, the snide comments and the arguments between them, Ian's whining—would be easier, he was wrong. Nothing about having Ashton home was easy, and the difficulty had nothing to do with her injuries.

It wasn't that she needed a place to sleep, a place downstairs, that was hard. It was having to call someone for help. It was having your father-in-law look at you with hatred in his eyes. Having your deceased wife's friends shy away from you, like maybe drinking and driving is contagious and either they'll walk away dying for a drink or maybe that you'll just shove them out in front of a moving vehicle to see them dead. It was asking your deceased wife's friends to help put a twin bed in the office so your temporarily—you hoped—disabled daughter didn't have to wrestle the stairs. And then standing around in the home that Kamryn built and pretending like it was completely natural that Kam wasn't there.

The silence now, the silence of Kamryn's absence, hung low in the air and seemingly hummed each time it came in contact with any of them. It had been damned impossible to stand in the same room with Kam's dad. The hate had emanated from him like radiation. And it had been almost worse with her mom. He didn't feel hatred from her, just pity. Disappointment.

That was worse.

Adrie's husband, Darrick, had helped his father-in-law move a bed into the office. Nothing fancy, just serviceable. Just enough to get Ashton through the recovery period and back up to her own room. He had opted out of a professional delivery, not because of the fee, but because maybe it would make Ashton more comfortable with people she knew touching her stuff, being in her space.

Now he wished he would have just had the store deliver it and set it up. Ashton was parked in the living room, staring blankly at the T.V. Mark was in the office, staring at the floor, as if maybe he could find something there to say, other than the sentence fragments and empty sentiments that filled his mind.

Kam's dad put him out of his misery first. Or maybe he had left Mark to wallow in it. Mark stared at the front door that Kam's dad had closed behind him and wondered what the hell he was supposed to say to Darrick. Both men had talked to Ashton. Patted her hand and offered their sympathy for her loss and their support for her recovery. Ashton had barely glanced at either of them, but at least she remembered to thank them both. Kam's touch, of course. Her children were perfect and polite for the rest of the world.

It pained Mark to stand and look another man in the eye. He had killed his wife. He injured his daughter. And yet, it had been an accident. He would still swear he wasn't drunk when he got in the car. Not even buzzed, though maybe by legal standards. It could have happened to anyone else. It often *did* happen to other people. It could have been Darrick Fuller. He could have taken Adrie out for dinner and had a few drinks and had an accident on the way home. He could have killed Adrie. He could be the social pariah now, the man hated by his family. Whispered about by the world at large. Fired from his job. Floundering without his wife, his best friend.

Instead, it was Mark. And Kamryn. And now people pointed their fingers and called him a killer and whispered behind his back about his drinking problem.

The hell of it was that he could handle any of it. *Any* of it. With Kam there to support him. Mark had always felt like he could take on the world with Kam at his side.

"I was..." Mark swallowed hard, because he suddenly remembered a phone call just a while back when Kam told him Adrie's dad died. It seemed like just yesterday, but on the other hand, it felt like a hundred years ago when he had been gone, and Kam told him that. She was upset. Kamryn loved Adrie like a sister, and she had been upset, concerned for her friend. And what had Mark done? Offered banal words of comfort, just like anyone else would have done.

Why hadn't he stepped up? Why hadn't he wanted to take more time and talk to Kamryn and comfort her? Hold her while she cried? Reminded her that together they could do anything?

"Sorry...to hear that Adrie's dad passed away."

Darrick nodded. He shrugged and then shifted his weight from one leg to the other.

"Hard to let go," he mumbled. "But he had a good life."

Mark's brain filled in the blanks for him. Sure, it was hard to lose a parent. He had gone through it. Time sure as hell didn't make it better; it just sort of deadened the tissue around the loss and made it all feel sort of numb. Hell to lose a parent. But at least Adrie's dad was an old man. At least he had lived a long, full life.

Unlike Kamryn. Dead at 42.

With a whole hell of a lot of living left to do. She would never see her girls go to prom. To college. She would never see Ian confirmed or see Ian start high school. She would never see her children get married, never have grandchildren.

Mark nodded. Yeah, it sucked hearing that shit. It sucked to stand here in his home and listen to some guy imply to him how unfair it was that Kam was dead. And yeah, he kind of wanted to deck him. Just smash his fist in his face, maybe break his nose. Send his sorry ass on out the door.

But that would only stir up more shit. Give his daughters more reason to hate him, to think he was unstable. He had a feeling he needed to watch his p's and q's, or his in-laws might try to take the kids from him. The girls would be leaving in a year and a half for college, but Ian was still young.

Mark had no intention of letting anyone take his children from him. He fucked up once, and it had cost him his wife, but he would do anything, *anything he could*, to protect his kids.

What could he say to that? Of course Adrie's dad had a good life. Anger boiled in his gut, so he simply nodded and turned to the door, as if showing Darrick out. Thankfully, Darrick took the hint.

"Thanks for your help." The anger and the resentment and probably the shame, too, was stuck in Mark's throat. His voice was small and tight. He glanced at Darrick as he stepped out the front door, and he knew instantly what he would say in response. In fact, Mark could have said it with him, like a prayer or a chant.

"Anything for Ashton."

Mark might have hit Darrick in the ass with the door, so quick he was to close it. Arm still in the damned sling, he rested his left hand against the door and breathed.

The red door. It didn't work in here now. Kamryn had picked it out, and sure, it looked great with the house décor. Mark had to admit, their two-story home was probably the best-looking in the neighborhood. But it was empty now, and the small flashes of color that Kamryn had arranged just so—starting with the red front door—made his head hurt.

The colors weren't vibrant now. Everything in the house looked drab and gray. Like the house was twenty years old and in need of new paint and new carpet and maybe even new owners. That would probably do the trick quicker than anything else.

Hand still flat against the door, Mark remembered the day he and Kamryn had picked it out. They met for lunch, a sandwich for Mark and a salad for Kamryn. They sat opposite each other in a booth for two at Loafers, the café down the block from the building where Kamryn worked.

Kamryn was wearing red. He probably wouldn't remember that, if not for the fact that she picked out the red door. She wore a red button-down blouse, and the color made her eyes pop. Turned them up to a blue so intense that Mark had felt like they were touching him. They talked about the Cardinal baseball game on TV the night before, and there was a toddler wandering around the café. Kam had talked to the little boy. Cooed at him, the way Moms did, and Mark remembered thinking he wanted another baby. He wanted to share that bond with her again, and he wanted to see her belly and her breasts grow bigger with a baby. He wanted to see his wife rocking a newborn and hear her singing to a baby.

They left Loafers, hand in hand, and they laughed all the way to the old minivan they had before the SUV. Once at the home improvement store, where they shopped for doors, they got hung up on a line from a movie, and Kam had laughed so hard, she cried. He remembered shushing her and trying to smudge away the small marks of eye liner under her eyes.

And then the sales guy had asked if he could help and Mark had said no, he thought he got it all, and then Kam had come unglued and cracked up all over again.

They didn't buy the door there. Instead, they got the door and the windows from a locally owned place, and Mark had to admit once the house was done, that the red door with the gray exterior was perfect.

He had to admit that Kam was right.

He wished now that he had remembered that. Kamryn was usually right, especially about the kids.

"What's for supper?" Brae asked and startled him out of his thoughts.

Mark took a deep breath and turned to look at her. Her hair was down on her shoulders, kind of tousled and tangled-looking. She looked like a young Kamryn; he had to look away.

He cleared his throat.

"What do you want?"

Brae shrugged. "Just not pizza. Again."

He nodded. Of course he couldn't feed his kids pizza until they grew up and left home. He just didn't want to cook. And that had nothing at all to do with his broken arm. He didn't want to spend any more time than necessary in the kitchen. The kitchen was Kam's place.

The kitchen. The office. His bed.

Hell, the damned house was haunted, and he both loved it and hated it. He loved feeling Kam in every room of the house, and yet, he hurt to remember her fixing their dinner, at work on her computer in the office, playing Checkers with Ian sprawled on the living room floor. Making love to him, in their bed. Curled up beside him, with her head on his chest.

"Dad?"

Mark rolled his head on his shoulders, wishing he could work all the kinks out of his body.

"How about spaghetti?"

Braelyn rolled her eyes.

"Do you have a better idea?"

"How about Mom's lasagna?"

Mark's turn to roll his eyes. "That's gonna happen at six in the evening."

"I'm sick of eating crap, Dad," she groaned.

"Then cook dinner, Braelyn."

He followed her into the kitchen and started pulling out the pots and pans he would need for spaghetti. Brae stood there for a long moment, watching him. He wished he had something to say to her. But he knew whatever it might be, she would only answer with anger, and he couldn't bear it tonight.

Water on to boil, he slumped in relief when she left him alone. He hated the way she looked at him. But the kitchen was lonely, and a watched pot never boiled, and he thought of Kamryn. He missed Kamryn. He struggled with the jar of spaghetti sauce. After five minutes, he managed to get it open without dropping it. His arm throbbed so badly, he couldn't see straight. But damned if he was going to ask Brae to help him.

Ian shook his head when Mark tried to put sauce on his spaghetti. Brae rolled her eyes.

"Dad, he doesn't like sauce on it."

"Since when?" Mark asked. He looked from Ian to Brae and back to Ian again. "He used to."

"Yeah, well, now he doesn't," Brae snapped.

"Mom would know that," Ian mumbled.

"Well, I'm not Mom."

"No kidding."

"Braelyn."

Braelyn rolled her eyes again.

"Ash, you okay?" Mark asked. She stood at the counter, arms draped over her crutches, a far-away look on her face.

"I can't sit here," she said quietly.

Mark nodded. Of course she couldn't sit at the bar. Her leg would dangle, and it would hurt.

"That's not fair," Ian groaned. "Why does she get to sit in the living room?"

"She's not sitting in the living room, moron." Braelyn picked up Ashton's plate and her glass of milk and carried them to the dining room for her.

"I don't wanna sit in here by myself," Ashton said softly. She followed Brae slowly to the dining room.

"I'll sit with you."

Mark watched Brae take her own plate and drink to the dining room. He considered joining them, but the fact that Brae hadn't asked him to, that neither of the girls asked him to, hurt. Instead, he sat at the bar and stuck his fork in his spaghetti.

Moses, parked at Mark's feet, barked at him. Mark ignored him.

"He needs to go outside."

"It can wait," Mark answered.

"No, it can't," Ian told him as he slid off his barstool. "Mom always took him out just before we ate."

Mark sighed. Kamryn even knew best when it came to the dog. Ian scooped Moses up and carried him to the back door. The kitchen was too quiet. He strained to hear the broken conversation in the dining room, but he could only hear voices, not words.

He toyed with his spaghetti, not hungry enough to eat it and too lazy to get up and throw it away.

Ian's plate was still heaped with plain spaghetti noodles. One noodle was on the counter by his plate. There was a splash of chocolate milk on the counter, too. A jolt of pain spiked through Mark's chest. Hard and hot and quick.

Thank God Ian and Brae hadn't been with them. Thank God Ashton was okay. He might never get over losing Kamryn, but she would have wanted it this way. She couldn't have buried a child; she would never have forgiven him if she had lived, and they had lost Ashton.

CHAPTER 33

ASHTON

The first night home, she slept on the couch. No, she had *laid* on the couch, with a good inch to move either way. Her leg had ached, and she had listened to every frigging creak and settling noise in the house. She had believed that bullshit when she was a little kid, the standard parental line about the noises little kids hear in the night just being the house settling. Now, for the first time ever at sixteen—almost seventeen—Ashton knew houses could be haunted.

This house was haunted by memories, and lately, those memories weren't good or happy and they hadn't made her feel all warm and fuzzy through the night. In fact, she had heard the recent arguments over and over in her head, until it seemed like the voices were most definitely surrounding her. Like if she got up and walked into the kitchen, she would see her mom and dad fighting.

She got up once and hurried as much as she could with her crutches and got sick. Probably a combination of her dinner she hadn't wanted but had eaten anyway, the pain pill she taken after dinner, and the ever-so-comfortable couch. Her neck and shoulder were so stiff this morning, she could hardly move. Maybe that had been what had driven Dad to go out and get her a twin bed for the time-being.

Time-being. She hated that phrase. Time being what it was sucked. Time fucking crawled like a snail right now. Every minute in this house dragged by like an eon, and Ashton sat and felt like someone was picking her skin open with fingernails and reaching inside her and taking all of her out. Guts and blood and feelings.

"I can't," she mumbled.

"What?" Brae nearly bumped into her in the hall outside the office.

"I can't do this."

"What? Sleep in here? Why not?"

Ashton looked around the office. The new bed, minus a headboard, was pushed to the side of the room, close to the hallway wall. It didn't look like a hospital bed, but it made Ashton think of a sick bed, made up in a family living area, where old people or people with incurable illness slept. Where they waited to die.

"I can't." She shook her head. Dad meant well. No matter that she had been the one in the car with him, that it was her body that was broken to pieces and her memory with blips and gaps in it, she couldn't bring herself to hate him quite as much as Braelyn did. Maybe she hated him a little, but right now, she was just too damned confused to concentrate and put any of it together and truly *feel* anything. Other than the physical pain in her body.

"What's wrong, Ashton?" Dad asked. She turned to look at him, overcome with guilt. He had tried, and she still wasn't happy, and she was about to throw a fit. She felt it coming, but she knew there would be no stopping it.

"I can't sleep in here," she mumbled.

God, she couldn't be the freak of the family who had to sleep on a sick bed. She would probably have nightmares about dying if she slept in here.

Not to mention this was *Mom's* room. Mom spent a lot of time in here. There were framed posters in here, spouting encouragement and preaching confidence—all Mom's. A small bookcase in the corner held books that only Mom would read: stuff she read for work, but those God-awful true crime books, too.

At least there weren't any pictures of Mom in here. That would be terrible. Last night, in the dark, Ashton's eyes kept trekking back over the ceiling to the big family portrait on the wall. It was a few years old, yeah, and it was dark, but still. Ashton knew the picture well enough to see it in the dark: Ian, dressed in blue jeans and a white polo shirt, sitting in the crook of a tree branch, Mom, in blue jeans and a white blouse, leaning against the tree and Ian's hand on her shoulder. Mom's hand draped over Brae's shoulder. Dad, in the same blue jeans and white polo shirt, standing with his left hand on the tree and his other arm around Ashton.

Ashton had felt that smile, Mom's smile, all night last night. The hell of it was knowing Mom was gone, but not remembering it. Not remembering any of the accident or the funeral or where Mom's grave was or anything. It bothered her, not remembering any of that stuff.

"When was Mom's funeral?" she whispered. She looked around, needing Braelyn to answer her. But Brae had disappeared and left her with Dad.

"A few days after the accident." Dad's voice was gruff.

"Did I go?"

"No, Ash, you couldn't."

She squeezed her eyes shut, suddenly plagued with images of the funeral. The casket, the flowers, the people surrounding Dad and Brae and Ian. She saw it so clearly that for just a second, she wanted to argue with Dad and tell him that she had been there. That he was wrong.

Had she dreamed about the funeral? Had Brae talked about it when she was in the hospital? And now was she pulling those images into her mind and trying to convince herself that they were memories?

"Dad, I can't sleep here."

She was afraid to look at him. Really afraid. She hunched her shoulders over the crutches and waited for the anger. For that God-awful anger she'd heard him unleash on Mom so often lately. The night of the accident.

Wait. What? Ashton rolled her head on her shoulders. *The accident. Hadn't Mom and Dad been arguing? And Dad had been way pissed, blown everything out of proportion? He'd been mean. Flat out mean to Mom, and Ashton had cried.*

Right?

"Ash?"

Dad laid his hand on her shoulder, and she jumped. The crutch under that arm fell and clattered on the floor.

"You okay?"

She sniffled and nodded, still afraid to look at him.

"Does your head hurt?

"Everything hurts."

"Ash," Brae called. Ashton turned to her voice, relieved to turn her back to Dad. She watched Braelyn bound down the stairs, arms full of pillows and stuffed animals and even a book. "How about if we put some of your stuff in here with you?"

Ashton pressed her lips together and tried not to cry. Because her sister was trying. She was trying to help, and yes, it was nice, and it was really thoughtful, but Ashton still didn't want to sleep in the office.

"Thanks." She finally nodded. She watched Brae toss her stuff to the floor by the bed.

"Hang on, I'll get some sheets and make it up for you really quick."

Dad had picked up her crutch, and now he offered it to her. She took it, suddenly exhausted.

"What was the—what did the bouquet look like?"

"What?"

"On her casket. What did the flowers look like?"

"White roses."

"It's not fair," she whispered, "that I couldn't be there, Daddy."

"I know."

"I didn't get to say goodbye." She swiped at the tears on her face. "I don't even remember what we said to each other. Before. I don't remember that night. It's just...It's a black hole."

"Honey, none of us got to say goodbye. It was just...over. That quick."

"No, I know that," Ashton said quietly. She shook her head. "But I didn't get to say goodbye. At her funeral."

Brae hurried back down the steps and past them into the office. Ashton watched her make the bed for her and then place her pillow and stuffed animals at the head of the mattress.

"Be right back!" Brae ran out of the room. Ashton heard her thump back up the steps again.

"Would you..." Ashton took a deep breath and looked up at Dad. "Would you take me to her grave? Tomorrow?"

Dad winced, like she had hit him in the gut.

"I can't."

"What?"

"You'll have to ask Braelyn."

"Daddy?"

Ashton stared at him, trying to gauge the hard set of his jaw and the sorrow in his eyes. Did he just not want to see Mom's grave? Or did he not want to spend time with Ashton?

She flinched again when she heard the voices in her head. The harsh, loud tones. The angry words.

Mom and Dad had fought that night. In front of her. She had been caught in that damned booth with Dad, and he and Mom had started fighting, and she couldn't get away from it.

She had cried.

Dad turned and walked away from her as Brae flew down the stairs again. This time she was carrying a night shirt.

Ashton wondered where Dad went, but Brae took her hand and pulled her toward the office. Once Ashton stepped inside, Brae shut the door, closing them off from Dad and Ian, wherever they were.

"Want me to help?" Brae asked, offering the nightshirt to Ashton.

Ashton sighed. "Can you just get my shorts off me?"

"Sure. Hang on."

Ashton stood still as Brae gently pulled her shorts down over the cast on her leg.

"Brae?"

"Hmm?"

"Would you take me to see Mom's grave?"

Braelyn, on her knees in front of her, stopped moving and stared up at her. Ash felt a jolt of guilt slice through her when Braelyn's eyes filled with tears, and she looked away.

"Yeah. I will."

"Why can't Dad?" Ashton asked.

"What?"

"Dad said he can't."

Brae stood up in front of her. She took her crutches from her and waited while Ashton tugged her t-shirt off. She had never been particularly open, and she wasn't thrilled about undressing in front of her sister. But she didn't think she was up for any acrobatics either, so she quickly unhooked her bra, dropped it into Brae's hands, and yanked her nightshirt down over her head.

"Dad lost his license, Ash. He got a D.W.I."

"What?" Ashton blinked and then squeezed her eyes shut tight again.

"Yep. Dear old Dad. No wife. No license. No job."

"What?"

"D.W.I. Ashton. He's at rock bottom."

"But." Ashton frowned. She heard the voices again in her head, but she couldn't make out words. She couldn't make anything clear in her head, and suddenly she was thinking about how good it would feel to lay down. To take a pain pill and sleep.

"I hate him," Braelyn said quickly.

"It was an accident, Brae."

Braelyn shook her head. "I'd be fine with that, Ash, except that Mom's been on him about drinking too much for a long time now. Since before I got in trouble for coming home drunk that night. Didn't you hear them arguing then? Don't you remember? Dad's been hitting the bottle and hiding it from Mom."

Ashton tried to remember. She had to remember more than angry voices. But the memories wouldn't take shape in her head. There were flashes, and her head was pounding, and her heart was pounding suddenly, like she was going to have a heart attack.

"I got in trouble for that," Brae continued. "I got in trouble for calling for a ride home. Maybe if Dad had called for a ride home, or if Dad had let you drive, maybe we would still have Mom here."

Ashton ducked her head and rubbed at her neck.

"I need to go to bed," she mumbled. "I'm gonna be sick."

"Okay." Brae jumped out of the way and moved Ashton's crutches. "Want me to get you a pill?"

"Please."

Ashton perched on the edge of the bed and rested her leg out in front of her. She stared at her cast and wondered if she would ever run again. If she would be able to catch up in school, or if the holes in her memory were really holes in her brain. If she would have trouble in her classes now.

Brae came back with a pill and a glass of water. Ashton downed the pill like a pro, gulped the glass of water down, and then lay on the new bed—the time-being bed,—and turned her back to the room.

And prayed for sleep to take her.

CHAPTER 34

MARK

The dream again. The one with Kamryn walking away from him. With her back to him. He hadd decided, last night when he went to bed that he wouldn't call to her this time, if he dreamt about her. Instead, he would watch her, just stand and watch her and see where she went. See if she was leaving him or if she would finally turn and look at him.

If he would see her eyes and her smile.

And yet, who can control what he does in a dream? He called out to her, over and over again, and she kept walking awa,y and now here he was, awake in this damned bed he had shared with her, all alone.

He moved closer to her side of the bed, grateful that he could still smell her, even after the sheets had been laundered. He couldn't give her up; each tiny little bit of her that he had left was more precious than gold.

God, he missed her. He missed talking to her, coming home to her at night after work. Seeing her in the kitchen, making dinner and talking to the kids about school. He missed hearing her laugh, the way she brushed up against him when he was flipping through the mail, and she was cleaning the kitchen.

"Dad?"

Mark heard her. He had heard the four times she yelled at him earlier, too. It was Ashton, but each time she called for him and he didn't answer her or go downstairs, she sounded a little more agitated until just now, when she sounded more like Braelyn.

He closed his eyes, wishing there was a magical reset button somewhere. That he could turn back time and start this whole year over. He would listen to Kam. About the kids, about her worries. He hated that she had suddenly doubted him, the drinking, the questions about other women. Maybe that's why he got so angry and reacted so viciously. He still didn't believe he had a drinking problem, though maybe he could see why Kam wondered about that stuff. Every trip he took for business involved dinners and drinks with others in his field. Any time he called home in the evening to talk to her, he was out for dinner or drinks or both.

But Kam's doubts about his faithfulness had cut deep. He had never been interested in other women. He looked; hell yes, he had turned his head and checked out other women: blondes, brunettes, short or tall, big boobs, nice ass—whatever—he had looked. But he had never found himself in a situation where he had to choose between immediate gratification and hurting Kam or walking away.

It galled him that she might have believed him capable of hurting her that way. Maybe a tiny part of him could have understood her fears; after all, he traveled a lot. But on the other hand, he had made a vow of fidelity to Kamryn, and that vow meant everything to him.

Mark flopped over on his back again and stared at the ceiling. Had Kamryn just found herself alone once too often and let her fears take over? Was it natural for her to wonder from time to time if he had been with other women through the years? There had been times he had been distant with her over the phone, either because he was busy and distracted, or because he was frustrated or flat out angry with her. Had those times bred the uncertainty, or was it something else?

Had *Kamryn* fallen in love with someone else?

His mind flashed on the night of the accident; he and Kamryn looking at each other over the top of the girls' car. She'd said she couldn't do it anymore. Mark felt the words settle on his heart and push it into his gut. The thought made him sick. He had to believe she loved him right up until the end. He wanted, he needed, someone to tell him she loved him.

What? Because you deserve her love? Because you didn't jack with her the night of the accident? Because you didn't kill her?

Why should he permit himself the doubts about her, when he got so angry when she expressed her fear?

"Dad!"

"Goddammit, Ashton, what?" He climbed out of bed, forgetting about his swollen, sore knee, and hit the floor too hard. He grinded his teeth together to stop the flood of swear words he needed to say. His arm still lay in a sling, up against his chest. He hated it. Hated feeling like an invalid. Hated that he couldn't do what he wanted to do, be the man he used to be.

Hated even more that Kamryn would never be anything again.

He hurried, as much as he could, downstairs and turned to see Ashton sitting up in her bed in the office.

"What?" he snapped. "What do you want?"

He needed time to figure out all the stuff he and Kam had been fighting about. He didn't need his kids dragging his ass to the gallows every damned minute of the day.

"I need to go to the bathroom."

"And?" He shrugged and shook his head.

"My crutches," she whispered. Mark turned to follow her gaze. Her crutches were propped against the far wall. "I think Brae left them there last night. She forgot."

Mark's sigh turned into a groan. Ashton stared at him with big, innocent eyes. Eyes wet with tears. She hadn't told him she hated him, not once. *Yet.* But maybe he would deserve it if she did.

"I'm sorry," he mumbled. He grabbed the crutches and walked them closer to her bed. "How did you sleep?"

She lifted a shoulder, too lazy to answer him.

"I feel like a freak," she answered. "Mandy Roth's grandpa slept in a hospital bed like this in the living room until he died."

Mark had no idea who Mandy Roth was, but he figured he should, and he guessed she was a friend of some sort, so he didn't ask.

"Honey, this is just for the time—"

Ashton nodded. "Yeah, I know. Time-being. I hate that phrase."

"Was it at least better than the couch?"

She lifted her chin a notch and met his eyes. "Yeah."

"Good."

"When do you think I can go back to school?"

Mark raised his eyebrows, surprised by her question.

"Do you think you're ready for that?"

"Brae and Ian are back."

"Brae and Ian weren't in the crash."

"People use crutches at school all the time. Football players always have big casts on their legs."

"That's not what I meant." Mark perched on the edge of her bed.

Ashton nodded. She studied her hands, fingers trailing over the swelling in her left wrist.

"I don't like being here." She swallowed hard. "I don't like being here without her."

"I don't either, Ash." Mark winced and looked away when his voice broke. "I don't either. Your mom—she—"

He started to get up. It wasn't Kam's presence in the room this time that he needed to get away from. It was Ash. He didn't know if he couldn't handle her grief or if he was afraid her grief would merge into blame and hatred, the way Brae's had, but he needed to get away from her, out of the room.

"Daddy."

His hold on his emotions broke when Ashton laid her hand over his.

"Why's Brae so mad at you, Dad?"

"Because I took your mom away from you guys, Ashton," he cried.

"But it was an accident." Ashton's voice was thick with tears. Mark turned to her and leaned toward her. He put his good arm around her shoulders and drew her head to rest against him. He was thankful he could offer comfort to Ash, but he wished so badly that he could hold Brae and Ian, too.

"It was just an accident, Daddy," Ashton whispered. His own tears ran unchecked down his face when he felt Ashton's arm slide up over his back and her hand smooth the muscles in his shoulder.

"I know, baby, I know." He pressed a kiss on the top of her head. "I loved your mom so much."

"Did you?" she asked curiously.

"What?" He pushed her back enough to look her in the eye. "Why would you ask me that?"

She blinked. Her lashes were wet with tears. "Didn't you…" She frowned. Mark said a silent prayer that the confusion and the gaps in Ashton's memory were temporary. He hated to see her struggling just to remember the moments, the days before the accident. Although, if it were up to him, she would never recover the accident itself.

"Didn't I what?"

Ashton blinked again and then looked at him. "Were you and Mom fighting?"

Mark sucked in a breath sharp enough to cut his lungs. Did she remember? Was there any chance Ashton could piece together the sequence of events that led to her and Mark, alone, in Kam's office, sitting on this time-being bed?

"What?"

"I just…" She frowned and shook her head. "I feel like there was a lot of tension."

"When?"

"Just," she shrugged, "before-before everything. I feel like you guys were fighting a lot or something."

Mark sighed and hoped his relief wasn't too obvious. He hated waking each morning to the memory of the accident. Not just the way it had to all work its way back into his consciousness that Kam was gone, but the wreck itself. The sounds and the smells. The way Kamryn and Ashton had been thrown around the car, like dolls, their bodies breaking and bleeding. He would do anything he could to spare Ashton those particular memories.

"Were you?" Ashton asked him now.

"Yeah." He cleared his throat. "Things were kind of rough, but rough spots just make the smooth spots even better."

"Whatever." She rolled her eyes. Mark almost chuckled. That was the Ashton he knew and loved.

"Yeah, Ash, Mom and I were fighting a lot before. I think it was my fault. And I'm sorry everything happened the way it did. That I can't tell her that. Ya know?"

Ashton nodded.

"But I loved her so much," he continued. "You know that, right? Fighting doesn't mean anything. Not always."

"I know."

Mark took a deep breath and glanced at the clock on Kam's desk. It was after nine-thirty. Brae had been getting Ian up and ready for school since Kam had been gone. He had no idea how she was handling the loss, how she was doing in school. He hadn't talked to Braelyn, not in any way that mattered, since before that night.

"Are you hungry?" He turned to look at Ashton again.

She shrugged.

"I'm gonna go take a shower, and then I'll find something for us to eat."

He was almost to the door when she called to him again.

"Dad?"

"What?"

"I want to take a shower."

Mark swallowed hard. "Okay." He looked around, though he knew they were alone. "Do you want to call Grandma and ask her to come by and give you a hand?" He hated the thought of asking either his mom or Kamryn's mom to come by and help him. He hated to need help, and he hated to allow anyone other than himself and his kids into their private circle of hell here. But if Ashton needed one of them, he would understand. He couldn't afford to alienate her, too.

"No." She shook her head. "I can wait till Brae comes home from school. She'll help me."

"But what?"

She looked down at her casted leg and then looked back at him. "Do we have...like...a shower seat or something?"

He opened his mouth to answer her but found that he couldn't. Why hadn't he done this stuff before Ashton came home? Why hadn't he had a bed ready for her, completely ready, with fresh sheets and pillows and her own stuffed animals and balloons and a sign to welcome her home? Why hadn't he thought of all the little things she would need, for the time-being? Ashton hated that word, and yet, right now, they were in a stretch of *time-being*, and he was completely unprepared for it. *What an ass.* He had been wallowing in his grief and his guilt, and now Ashton had to sit around here and wait for him to catch up to reality.

Kamryn wouldn't have let her down.

"We don't," he finally answered. "But I'll get one."

"When?"

"Let me shower. And then I'll do it. Okay? Think about anything else you might need."

She nodded.

"Need anything right now?"

"Pain pill?"

"Okay."

He couldn't hurry. It might be a while before he could hurry anywhere, but he did the best he could to get her a pill and a glass of juice, and then he climbed the steps and found himself alone in the bedroom he had shared with Kamryn. The empty bed called to him. Kamryn's pillow lay sideways, from where he had laid earlier with his arms around it. It would smell like her, too. He could climb back into bed and close his eyes and pray for a better dream.

He took a step toward the bed, but stopped himself. Went to the dresser instead, pulled the last pair of clean underwear from the drawer, and limped into the bathroom so he could shower.

CHAPTER 35

ASHTON

The long day, the wait for Brae to come home from school and talk to her, help her shower, and take her to see Mom's grave, was made even longer by the fact that she couldn't do anything. She couldn't go anywhere, not that she wanted to, and there was no one to talk to because Dad left with Grandma to run errands, and she couldn't really move around the house too easily, either. Dad had helped her get comfortable on the couch before he left. He had plumped up some pillows for her, left a quilt within her reach, brought her a soda, a book to read, and the phone and TV remote.

Daytime TV sucked. Ashton hated talk shows and game shows. She had never been interested in soap operas, and though she often watched cartoons with Ian, right now the noise was giving her a headache. She hit the button on the remote to turn the TV off and picked up her book. She had started it before the accident.

Ashton smoothed her fingers over the cover of the trade paperback. *Eleven Days. Kallie Sanford.* She flipped through the pages, finding her bookmark on page 152. Not quite halfway through the book. The cover was intriguing: a desktop calendar with a big red X through the nineteenth day of June. The tips of a girl's fingers touched the calendar just under the box for 19. Her nails were chewed and ragged. Ashton kind of liked that the nails weren't perfectly manicured and polished. It hinted that there was something wrong and something big and bad coming on June 19, eleven days from the day the girl was living.

Ashton had no idea what the book was about. She couldn't remember ever seeing it before, much less reading to page 152. She turned it over so she could read the back cover blurb. Pretty much what she would have guessed. *Alyson Brody has eleven days to make her decision, a life-altering decision that might open a world of possibilities or tear apart the only world she's ever known.*

Ash sighed and laid her head back on the couch. She didn't want to read. First, her head hurt already, and reading didn't seem like a good idea. Second, at the moment, she could give a shit about Alyson Brody and her life-altering decision, because right now Ashton McHale had been through a life-altering event that had torn apart the only world she'd ever known. Who the hell needed fiction when life provided this kind of story?

Her stomach hurt, suddenly. Like a sharp pain. She felt pressure on her chest, like some invisible thing was sitting on her. *Life-altering.* She didn't like the sound of those words right now. Since the accident, since she had come out of the coma, she hadn't liked anything, least of all her situation. Her stomach had hurt often since the accident, and she kind of figured it wasn't a physical thing. It was fear. She was afraid of the future, of her own future, her own recovery.

Not the part where she got her cast off and had to learn to walk again. She knew she was in for a long road with her injuries; Brae had broken her arm when she was five. That had been hard on Brae. What would dealing with a broken leg be like?

But that's not what scared her. She was worried about her brain. Her mind. Her memory. She didn't get why she remembered some things and not others. She didn't get why she remembered something one day and completely forget the same thing the next day. Like Mom being gone. She knew that; she had known since she had awoke in the hospital. Dad hadn't wanted to tell her; she could read the reluctance as he tried to talk.

And yet, how many times had she forgotten? Since Dad had told her about the wreck, and about how she had been in a coma, and how Mom had had the brain injuries and the internal bleeding, and how it was for the best, and Mom was at peace now, that the doctors had assured him that Mom hadn't felt any pain, that it had been instant. How many times since then had she forgotten Mom was gone?

It wasn't fear now, though. It wasn't *fear* making her stomach hurt. She couldn't quite put her finger on it, on whatever it was that was making her feel sick. It wasn't physical, just some new emotion pushing around in her gut, trying to move the fear out of the way.

She closed her eyes. Thinking about it, trying to understand what she was feeling made her head hurt worse. She turned her head a bit to the back of the couch, but that only made her neck hurt.

Ashton wondered how long Dad and Grandma had been gone. The house was so quiet right now. It was quiet and still, the way the air felt charged and electric during a thunderstorm. She lay with her eyes closed, feeling like someone was watching her. Like if she opened her eyes, she would find Dad and Brae and Ian standing over her.

Would Mom be there, too? Was Mom in Heaven, watching her? She hadn't given too much thought to Heaven before. She had never given religion too much thought at all. It wasn't that she didn't believe anything; it was just more of the same school stuff poured in that she nodded about, learned, and filed away.

There was something called purgatory, she thought. Seemed like all souls went there first before they could go on to Heaven. Or Hell. Mom wouldn't go to Hell, though. She was certain of that. But it was hard to imagine Mom in purgatory or Heaven.

How did that work, anyway? *Surely Mom's body wasn't there. Only Mary and Jesus ascended into Heaven, right? With their bodies? So then Mom's* soul? *Mom's soul was somewhere out there?*

What did a soul look like? Ashton pursed her lips and considered the human soul. Maybe it looked like a heart. Except that the human heart didn't look like hearts that people drew to symbolize love. Why would a soul look like that? Maybe a butterfly. Maybe Mom's soul was up there, fluttering around and waiting, and looking soft and pretty like a butterfly?

"Jesus, Ashton." She groaned and reached for the TV remote. She didn't want the TV on, but she couldn't stand the silence. She couldn't lie here, waiting for Dad and Grandma to come back home or for Brae and Ian to get home, and think about

Mom's soul. That was just bizarre. *Shouldn't she just be thinking about Mom as she was? Remembering her?* What the hell was wrong with her? God, maybe her brain was more screwed up than any of them realized.

The Disney channel offered nothing good, not even any good background noise. She surfed until she found *Spongebob* and then struggled to get comfortable on the couch. She drew the blanket over her legs and closed her eyes, wishing for a pain pill. Her leg wasn't bothering her right now, but she craved the sleep, the escape, the pills brought.

Escape.

Interesting.

Life-altering. Escape. She had wanted out. Before the accident. She'd wanted out of something. But what?

DAD HAD BROUGHT HER LUNCH. She picked at the deli sandwich and ate less than half of it, not because she didn't appreciate it, but because her stomach still felt funny. Apparently, she drifted off, because she thought she was at the kitchen bar talking to Mom and Brae, and then suddenly she was hearing the back door open, and Dad was talking to someone, and she tried to sit up and see what was going on.

Mom wasn't in the kitchen. Dad had a grocery bag in his good hand, and he was looking back over his shoulder, talking to someone. Ash watched patiently, alternately excited about whom he was talking to—*was it Mom?*—and dreading the moment she would see the other face, because she knew without acknowledging it that it wasn't.

Grandma appeared behind Dad carrying more groceries. Ashton felt that huge bubble of anticipation in her chest pop. She turned back and sunk into her pillows, eyes closed. *Mom.* She had only been dreaming about Mom.

She had forgotten that Dad had called Grandma to drive him today. She'd forgotten that Dad couldn't drive.

God, she hated this. She hated how unreliable her freaking brain was right now. Would it ever heal? Would she be normal? How would she ever know if she truly remembered something or understood something? How could she trust herself?

"Hey, Ash."

Ashton had opened her eyes and tried to smile at her grandma. Grandma had kissed her cheek and then went back to the kitchen to help Dad put the groceries away. Ashton kept her eyes closed, pretending sleep so she wouldn't have to talk to them. That thing in her stomach hurt, and it made her feel weird, thinking about talking to them.

She hadn't opened her eyes again until she was sure Grandma left and Dad had offered her the sandwich. He sat at the kitchen bar and ate his own sandwich, and then he had left her alone again, and she had no idea what he was doing. He was in the house, though, and just knowing he was here and hearing him move around comforted her.

Brae and Ian came home just after three. The usual time Mom used to bring Ian home, after she left work to pick him up. Ian had climbed carefully up to sit on the end of the couch and watch cartoons with her. Brae sat down on the floor in front of the couch.

She picked up Ashton's book and read the back of it.

"Is this good?"

"I have no idea," Ashton mumbled. "I don't remember anything about it."

"Hmm."

"Anything happen today at school?"

Brae shrugged, but she didn't offer an answer.

"Do you have a lot of stuff to do tonight?"

"No more than usual. Why?" Braelyn asked.

"Can you help me take a shower?"

Brae looked back at Ashton over her shoulder. "Yeah. You sure you're up for that?"

"Mmm." Ashton blinked and sighed. *Not really. Not anymore.* But she wasn't going to admit that to anyone. She needed to see Mom's grave.

"Brae?"

"What?"

"Will you still take me?"

Brae looked at her sharply. Ashton raised her eyebrows.

"Yeah," Braelyn mumbled. "Yeah, I will. You wanna do the shower first?"

Ashton nodded.

"I wish we had a shower chair or something, so you could sit down."

"We do now," Ashton told her. She pulled herself to a sitting position and tossed the blanket off. Ian grabbed it and pulled it over his legs. Ashton noticed he was wearing school shorts.

"Is it warm out?"

"Not bad," Brae answered. "We have a shower chair?"

"Dad got one today."

"How did Dad do anything?" Brae asked quickly.

"Grandma came and got him."

Brae looked away without answering Ashton. Instead, she busied herself by moving things out of Ashton's way and getting her crutches for her.

"Ashton?"

Ash, leaning now on her crutches, looked down at Ian. "What, buddy?"

Moses was curled up by Ian now, though he had spent most of the day at Ashton's feet. Ian petted him gently as he talked. Moses cracked his eyes for a moment just to peek at all of them, but he stretched and closed them again, content to lie beside Ian.

"I don't wanna go, okay?"

"What?"

"I don't wanna go with you. When you go with Brae to see Mom. I don't wanna."

"That's fine."

"You sure?" Brae asked softly. They heard Dad's unsteady gait as he came down the stairs.

"I kind of just wanna be with Dad," Ian whispered. He looked away from the girls and down at Moses, like he was afraid to make Braelyn mad.

"That's okay, Ian," Ashton assured him. She noticed that his eyes were glassy with tears, but she said nothing. "We won't be gone long, okay?"

He nodded and turned back to the TV.

"Hey," Dad said as Ashton and Brae made their way to the first-floor bathroom. He was trying too hard to sound cheerful. Ashton knew Brae would whittle another piece of him away. "What do you girls want for supper tonight?"

"We just had lunch, like two hours ago," Brae snapped.

"What do you want? When you come home?"

"From Mom's grave?" Brae stopped walking. "What do we want to eat after we come home from Mom's grave? I don't think I'll be hungry, so don't worry about ordering pizza again."

Ashton sighed. The pain in her gut had turned to a continuous burn. Like she'd had acid with her breakfast this morning, and her stomach had been cooking all day.

"Dad went to the grocery store," Ashton said quietly.

"Wow."

"Braelyn." Ashton hunched her shoulders. She glanced at Dad. "Surprise us."

He tried to smile, but Ashton saw the sadness in his eyes. She wanted to say more, but her throat was too tight with tears. She hated that Mom was gone. She hated that she didn't remember the last conversation she had with her mom.

But she hated to see her dad so broken.

CHAPTER 36

ASHTON

"Why hasn't Garret called me?"

Brae glanced at her but looked quickly back to the road.

"What?"

Ashton hadn't bothered with styling her hair or putting on makeup, but the shower itself had taken awhile. Brae had helped her cover the cast with plastic so it wouldn't get wet, and she helped her strip down, and then she waited just on the other side of the shower door in case Ashton needed her.

Ashton had spent the first several minutes of her shower perched awkwardly on the shower chair, humiliated at having to have help undressing. She sat long enough for the steam to roll down over her, and then she moved slowly through the motions of the shower.

The hot water and the shampoo and the suds all felt good, but she was still weak, and she had known she needed to get moving so she didn't end up overdoing it and falling and hurting something else.

Braelyn had stood with her back to her while she dried herself as best she could, and then she'd helped her dress in a pair of cut-off sweats and an old Nike t-shirt. Ashton had studied the cut-off sweats for a minute, trying to remember if they were hers.

"They're mine," Brae told her finally. "I thought you might get pissed if I cut yours up."

Ashton felt a surge of gratitude, but Brae looked uncomfortable, so she let the moment go without comment.

"What did you say?" Brae asked now. It was almost five, but the days were longer now, and the cemetery gates would stay open later. Besides, Ashton didn't think she planned to stay at Mom's grave long. She just needed to see it. Not for *closure*. God, she hated that word. She just needed to know where her mom was, because her brain—being so screwed up at the moment—was having extra trouble putting Mom where she belonged. It wanted to tell Ashton to believe Mom was in the bedroom, or at work, or at the store, and the hell of it was, so often, Ashton *did* believe it.

"Why hasn't Garret called?"

Brae flipped the turn signal on and slowly turned right into the cemetery. She avoided Ashton's eyes as she maneuvered the SUV along the twisty, narrow roads.

"Was he there? At the hospital? Because I don't remember it."

"Ash." Brae turned the key in the ignition and then tugged it out. She turned sideways in the seat and looked at Ashton. "You guys broke up."

"We did?"

"Yeah. You broke up with him at a party."

Ashton frowned. "I broke up with him?"

"Yeah. You were—wait. You really don't remember this?"

"The last thing I remember, I think, is him giving me that stupid ring, when his mom took his class ring to the jeweler to fix something."

"Is it like this with everything?" Brae asked quietly.

"Is what like what?"

"Your memory. Is everything patchy?"

Ashton worked her mouth to answer Brae, but she didn't know what to say.

"Do you mean is my brain full of holes, and if it is, how am I going to graduate from school and go to college?"

Brae raised her eyebrows and tossed her hands, palms up. "Well, there's that, but I meant do you remember me? And Ian? Family stuff?"

Ashton stared at her sister, touched that Brae would be afraid she had lost memories of them.

"I remember everything, everybody, Braelyn," Ashton whispered. "But I can't keep all the dates and times and details in my head. It's like a leak springing up, and when I go to patch that leak, there's another one somewhere else."

"Do you remember how we used to sleep together when it stormed?"

Ashton smiled. "I do."

"So, is there something right now between you and me that you don't remember?"

"If I knew, I would remember, right?"

Brae laughed softly, but her eyes were sad.

"Do you remember telling me about Garret? Telling me you were tired of being with him? Tired of everything being about sex between you guys?"

Ashton stared at her in silence. "No. I don't."

"So, is it like a certain time period before the wreck is gone?"

Ashton looked around the cemetery, wondering which grave was Mom's.

"Yes. Sort of." She turned her eyes back to Brae. "Except later tonight, I might remember that and forget that Mom's...here."

"You're not sorry you broke up with Garret, are you?"

Ashton considered Brae's question for a moment before answering. Honestly, no, she wasn't. Sitting here in the SUV with Brae, thinking about not dating Garret anymore, not having to deal with all of that, brought her nothing but relief.

But it also felt like a cliffhanger ending. It seemed like there was so much more to the story.

Brae finally got out of the SUV on the driver's side and came around to help Ashton out. She placed Ashton's crutches in front of her and then waited for Ashton to start hobbling away from the car. They walked in silence; Brae led the way. Ashton's eyes took in the rows of gravestones and the bright flowers and the grave not far from them, with new spring grass and she knew that's where they were going.

"Was the sun out that day?"

Brae looked at her in askance.

"The day of her funeral?" Ashton's voice was gruff.

"It was sunny, but cold."

Ashton nodded. They stopped at the grave, the one with the fresh grass and no headstone. Ashton assumed it would take a bit for that to be ready.

"Did a lot of people come?"

"Yeah," Braelyn said quietly. "I didn't know most of them. It was hard, all these people getting in my face and saying they were sorry, and I didn't know half of them. So hard to stand there with Ian, wondering if he got what was going on. Ya know? I mean, he's old enough to get it. But." She shrugged. "With it being Mom, I didn't know if he really did. And then Dad was so messed up. He's such a train wreck. He should've just stayed home. Nobody wanted him there, anyway."

"Mom would have wanted him there."

"He killed her, Ashton. He had no right to be there. He has no right to be at home with us."

"It was an accident, Brae. It could've happened to anyone."

"But it didn't. It happened to Dad. Because he was drinking. And now you're messed up. I had nightmares the first week...that they would call from the hospital and say you... that you had..."

Ashton nodded and looked away.

"I don't think Dad was drunk that night."

"You remember it?"

Ashton shrugged and shook her head. "Bits and pieces. But I don't think he was drunk."

"He'd had enough. I heard him tell Grandma that the cops tested him, and he—"

"He wasn't drunk."

"Why are you defending him?" Braelyn lunged for Ashton and grabbed her arms. "Why would you defend him? It's his fault that Mom's gone."

"Because I know it was just an accident. He wasn't falling down drunk. It wasn't an intentional thing. It just happened."

Brae let go of Ashton's arms and turned her back to her. She squatted down to touch the grass over Mom's grave. Ashton pressed her lips together and hung her head. She couldn't even do that. She had missed the whole damned thing. She had forgotten whatever she had last said to her mom. She had missed the funeral, and now all she could do was stand and stare at the grave. From a distance.

"I think you're being too hard on Daddy."

"I hate him."

"What if he had died, too? What if they were both gone?"

Braelyn stood up and turned back to Ashton. "That might have been fair."

"You don't mean that."

"Maybe I do," Braelyn answered. "I'm not you, Ash. I don't think I can forgive him for this. Maybe if they hadn't spent the last couple of months all tangled up in a fight about the drinking, maybe then I could deal with it as an accident.

Maybe then I could feel sorry for him. Maybe I could see it as a symptom of his disease."

"Dad's not an alcoholic, Brae. You know that."

"Then what, Ash? Mom saw that someone was drinking and hiding it. Letting me take the blame for it. I've never seen them fight like they were just before the accident."

"It's not right for you to teach Ian to hate him either."

Brae wiped the back of her hand over her face, but it didn't stop the tears.

"I don't wanna be alone."

"You're not alone," Ashton whispered. "I'm here."

She reached for Brae's hand and squeezed as hard as she could.

"I'm here, Braelyn," she said softly. "But I don't hate him. I don't blame him."

Brae stepped away. Ashton watched her walk a few steps and then she turned back to Mom's grave. She didn't talk. Not just because Brae was wandering around, and it felt weird to say something to Mom that only Brae would hear. But because she felt so far away, standing there with her crutches, and because she didn't know what to say. She wished she could ask for Mom's help. For Dad. Ashton didn't know how she knew it, but she knew her dad wasn't drunk the night of the wreck.

They walked back to the SUV together, and Brae helped her ease back into the front seat. She stowed the crutches in the back and then hurried around to the driver's side and climbed in.

"So." Brae swallowed hard. Ashton wondered if she was swallowing more hate for Dad, since she knew Ash didn't want to hear it. "If you forget that Mom's gone, does it hurt every time you remember again?"

"Yeah." Ashton stared out at the unmarked grave as Brae drove slowly around the cemetery to the exit gate. "Braelyn, if Dad was an alcoholic, he would be drinking now. Again. Still." Ashton shrugged.

"Maybe he is."

"We've been home with him all the time. Nobody can hide it like that."

"Don't, okay?"

"Don't what?"

"Don't defend him to me."

"Don't blame him around me."

Brae shrugged. "Truce, I guess."

"Mom would hate this. She would hate what we've become."

"Starting with Dad."

Ashton ignored Brae and wondered what kind of anniversary Mom would celebrate tonight if she could. She wondered if the four of them left would ever sit at the table for a meal together again.

CHAPTER 37

MARK

It had been hell watching the three of them leave for school. Well, everything since the night of the wreck and losing Kam had been hell, and each new flame felt like it would be the one to finish him. But nothing put an end to it, and that was just a little bit more of hell.

It hurt him to see Ashton going back to school. No, actually, it worried him. He worried that she wasn't ready. Oh, sure, the physical injuries would hurt, but she could come home and take her pain meds and sleep, and that would all eventually fade away. He worried that she wasn't ready to face the world without her mom. What if her classmates swarmed her with questions? What if they wanted to know about the accident? How it happened? What if it all made Ash remember too much? What if none of her classmates knew what to say, about the accident or her injuries or her loss, so they all ignored her? Would that be worse?

He hated to see the girls leave so early with Ian, only to drop him off at the before-school daycare program. It was either that or put Ian on a school bus. Kamryn wouldn't hear of the kids riding the bus; she had always arranged her schedule to be able to drive the kids wherever they needed to be. Mark wouldn't do that to Ian now, anyway. Ian hadn't had much to say to him since the wreck, but things had never been easy for him at school before. Mark figured his classmates had probably all tagged him with questions. At that age, the curiosity outweighed the reluctance to ask personal questions.

At least he had never really had to ask Brae to take Ian to school; she had just assumed the responsibility.

Kam had been gone for several weeks now, but he was still having that damned dream, and Kam was still walking away from him. He still awoke, alone in bed, calling for her and reliving that whole damned night. His shrink told him it was natural; the dream was a manifestation of Kam's death, of her leaving him. Some crazy bullshit about how she never turned around because he could never see her face again now that she was gone.

Mark hated seeing Dr. Smith or Schmidt or whatever the hell his name was, and he never opened up too much. Never beyond the dream. He didn't bother telling the guy that the dream had nothing to do with the accident, and everything to do with the fear he had that Kam was planning to leave him anyway. That they had been having some problems in their marriage, and maybe sometimes love just wasn't enough to hold everything and everyone together.

The shrink had recommended that the whole family see someone. Mark would have shoveled buckets of gold into Smith or Schmidt's office if he could've talked his kids into seeing him. If talking to him would help. But the girls had been adamant the first time he mentioned it. Brae had mumbled something that sounded a lot like *fuck off*. He let it slide, though the words sliced right through him. Ashton had just said *no*, that she was fine. Which was a lie, and they both knew it, but he hadn't had the energy to argue with her. Ian, who had come around and let Mark watch cartoons with him a few times since the day Brae had taken Ash to the cemetery, had stared at him with huge, innocent eyes and said he only wanted to talk to Mom.

The house was way too big with Kam gone and the kids at school. Mark swallowed his self-pity and made the necessary phone calls regarding his sudden unemployment and insurance and banking and loans and all the cold, unemotional crap that comes in the aftermath of death. Once the calls were made, and he sat alone in the empty house, severed from his professional life—the very one that Kam had grown to resent—he hated himself for having the ability to turn off the heartache and talk with a strong, steely voice and do what had to be done.

He cried at night, mostly, when he was alone in his room. Other than the day Ashton had gone to Kam's grave, the day Ash had put her arms around him, and they had cried together, he had only been touched at the funeral. Friends and relatives. Some of them had simply shaken his hand, though his mom and Kam's parents had taken him in their arms and offered him their sympathy.

Ashton's arms had been a salve for the pain, whereas the touches at the funeral home had been almost mandatory and therefore, cold. Empty. He craved the closeness he once had with Kam. The way they used to curl up together on the couch to watch TV. The way they held hands everywhere they went.

He needed his kids to love him. He needed Brae to forgive him, but he was afraid that might never happen. It was okay. He wouldn't change it; he wouldn't change anything other than the accident itself. As hard as it was to hurt this way, he could never stand back and watch either of his girls live with this.

He finally got the cast off his arm, and he was doing physical therapy now. But not where Kam had worked. Mark couldn't stand the thought of seeing Adrie so often. Kam had loved Adrie like a sister, and not only did he fear the hatred Adrie probably felt for him, but he also just didn't want to be near someone else who had been so close to his wife. What if Kam had been planning to leave him? Or what if she had just been unhappy with him and she had confided that to Adrie? He couldn't stand the thought of Adrie knowing Kam's secrets, when maybe he didn't know them all himself.

Though his arm was still sore, and his knee was still touchy, too, he was glad to have the cast off. Mark figured he had to get off his ass and get a job. He couldn't care less about getting up in the mornings or fixing dinners or cleaning the house or submitting job applications or any of the other day-to-day shit that had to be done. But he knew he had to do it for the kids. Even if Brae gave him the impression she would have been happier to see him die, too, he still had to get himself together and bring life back into the house for the kids.

Kamryn would never forgive him if he let her death tear the rest of them apart.

He closed the photo album and rested his hands on the front cover. His eyes were drawn to the gold band on his finger. He would never take it off. He had no desire to find anyone new, and yes, he knew it was still early, still much too early to even think about. But he knew there had only been one woman for him, and why put another woman through the torture of never being enough simply because she wasn't Kamryn?

Since he still hadn't seen her face in his dreams, Mark looked for her smile in the framed portraits on the walls and the candid shots saved in their family albums. While the portraits on the walls showed Kamryn, glowing and beautiful and so happy, always so happy, the candids were his favorite. He loved the snapshots of her with the kids when they were little. A picture—crooked, almost completely sideways, actually—of a younger Kam, with two babies tucked in her arms. Kam's eyes were closed, but both babies were wide-eyed and looking at the camera. Kam with a two-year old Ian asleep on her shoulder and the twins huddled in close, needing to still be close to their mom, even at eleven. Kam with the girls at their First Communion.

He wanted to find their wedding album. Not the professional one. The pictures her parents and his parents had snapped with their cameras. Not the photos of the cake and the toast, but the shot of the quick kiss they shared after they had done all of that and thought no one was looking. The picture his mom had taken at the end of the night when he held Kam in his arms on the dance floor. Her hands locked behind his neck and her head on his shoulder and her eyes closed. A small, knowing smile on her face.

God, he loved her. What had she been trying to tell him? Why had the last few months of her life been so tense and hard? What had all the fighting been about? Had she honestly believed he had a drinking problem? The whole thing had been so out of the blue, it had blindsided him and knocked him for a loop, and he had reacted so stupidly. He had never been one to get up and have a Bloody Mary in the morning. He'd never been a man to knock back the whiskey or scotch at night. He had never been one to drink when he entertained doctors or medical staff at lunches. His poison had always been iced tea, sometimes with lemon and sometimes not.

How could she have seen his drinking a glass or two of wine at dinner a problem? Why had she seen it as a problem? It wasn't like Kam to get so upset about something without reason.

Mark sighed and dropped his head back on the sofa cushion. Well, she worried about Brae. Brae's phone call had been a little bit of a wake-up call for them. Or maybe just for him. Maybe she had suspected Brae was partying; maybe she had known it and was hoping to deal with it without having to drag him into it.

What about Ashton? If Brae had put herself in that situation, did that mean he should worry about Ashton, too? At least Ash and Garret weren't dating anymore. He didn't want to have that to worry about, too.

Mark stretched and then set the photo album aside. Kam had said someone had emptied almost a whole bottle of wine. He had said something asinine about maybe Ash and Garret had gotten into it. What did he think that would lead to? *Had Ash been involved with Garret? But they broke up. They broke up, no problem.*

But what about Brae? Brae was out with Andrew the night of the accident. What if? Did Kam know? Did she know how to deal with that stuff? Mark suddenly realized how unprepared he was to be a single parent to two teen-aged girls, one of whom hated his guts.

Okay, so Kam had mentioned the wine bottle. Had she said something else, too? The hard liquor maybe? They had quite a bit in the cabinet, though it was rare for either of them to touch the stuff. It was mostly there from parties, when someone might have left a bottle of vodka or gin.

He stood for a minute just to get his bearings. The dizziness and the weakness were all but gone. But the stiffness in his knee still made his movements slow and methodical. He hadn't eaten lunch today. His stomach reminded him of that now, but he didn't want to bother with fixing anything.

He would fix an early dinner for the kids. Something good. He glanced at the clock, without processing what it said, and raised his eyebrows. Maybe he should follow Kam's lead. Maybe he should fix a nice dinner and call this an anniversary. He wasn't sure what event he would be marking, but he could probably think of something. Could he do it? Could he pull it off? If the four of them could work together to get past the grief and the blame, maybe they could get to a good, safe place again, where at least Kam's spirit would be with them.

Mark rolled his eyes. Now he sounded like some new age spiritual advisor.

Kam was gone.

But still. He loved his kids, and he knew Kam would want him to try. To pull the family back together again.

He yanked the freezer door open and studied the frozen packages. He could grill chicken and make homemade fries for Ian. They could have a salad. Might be a little tough for him to do that, with his arm and hand still a little stiff. But maybe Brae would help him out.

Mark took a package of chicken breasts from the freezer and put them directly in the microwave to defrost them. While he waited, he leaned over and opened the cabinet below the kitchen sink. He couldn't squat down; his knee wouldn't permit that. As he leaned and looked at the bottles in the cabinet, he hoped the knee thing wouldn't be a problem now that only got worse as he got older. He knew guys who had wrecked their knees in college and still had problems now.

At first glance, the bottles seemed undisturbed. He even reached and tilted the front bottle, the tequila. The seal was cracked, and it looked like maybe a splash had been poured out of it. Probably at the last party they had. He almost stood up, but then he heard Kam's voice in his head. She had said vodka. He could hear her saying it.

He bent just a little and almost yelped at the pain in his knee. Finally found the vodka bottle in the back of the bunch. He pulled it out of the cabinet and looked at it in disbelief. It was bone dry. Completely empty.

He bent further, pain in the knee be damned, and fished around until he pulled out another bottle of vodka. This one was three quarters of the way gone.

So who was it? Who had Kam suspected? Besides himself? It hadn't been Kam, had it? She hadn't been hitting the bottle and then talking about it as a way of asking for help? No. That was ridiculous. She had been hell-bent on one of the kids sneaking the alcohol, and she'd accused him of setting a bad example.

Okay, so Brae. Right? Because Braelyn was the one who had been drunk and called for a ride home.

Not necessarily.

She had called for a ride home. What if Ashton had done the same thing? What if she had gone out with Garret and had too much to drink and hadn't called home? What if Ash was drinking and hiding it?

Mark's stomach clenched and squeezed painfully tight as he thought about it. He turned to the sink and poured the rest of the vodka down the drain. On autopilot now, he reached down to the open cabinet and took the bottle of tequila. Unscrewed the cap and started pouring.

Moments later the back door opened, and he heard the girls talking, and Ian rushed into the kitchen.

"Hey Dad," Ian called as he zipped through the kitchen, presumably to the living room to turn on the TV. Mark wondered if Kam let him watch that much TV, if he had to do homework first. He hated not knowing how his wife had handled everything while he was gone.

Gone on his job. Yes, it was his job. Travel was part of it. And Kam had known that, and she had never taken issue with it. Mark felt a jolt of regret in his gut. She had taken issue with the fact that he didn't see what she did; he had never given her enough credit for being the parent. For being the one at home, being the one to be here for the kids.

This time, his fingers grabbed a bottle of gin. He was pouring it out when the girls appeared in the kitchen.

Ash, still on crutches, was first, and then Brae, dropping first Ashton's backpack and then her own, on the floor.

"What're you doing?" Ashton asked quietly.

Brae took one look at him and rolled her eyes.

"Little early for a cocktail, isn't it, Dad?"

Mark glanced at both of them. Brae looked at Ashton, then.

"Told you we would have no idea if he was sitting at home all day drinking."

"I'm not drinking," he answered calmly. "Brae, I haven't had a drink since your mom…"

"That's big of you, Dad."

He had expected a smartass comment about closing the barn door after the cows got out.

"Why're you doing that?" Ashton asked him. She stared at the bottle in his hand. He watched her with interest.

"Because I don't want it in the house."

"Does that mean you're gonna start going to the corner bar every day?" Brae asked. "Oh, but, wait. We don't have a bar close enough to walk to. How will you get there, Dad?"

Mark set the gin bottle down and grabbed Brae's arm.

"Listen to me."

She yanked hard to pull her arm away from him, but he held on tight.

"Lemme alone."

"Listen to me."

"Dad, you're hurting me!"

"Yes, I was driving that car, and yes, we had a wreck, and yes, I'd had a few beers." His anger boiled to the surface. "I wasn't *drunk*, Braelyn. I wasn't drunk, but it doesn't matter. In the end, it doesn't matter, because no matter the circumstances, I was driving, and now she's gone."

"I know!" she yelled. Her face was suddenly as red as the front door on their two-story home. "I know that. She's gone, and it's your fault."

"I guess it was. Because I was driving. But it was an accident."

"That could have been avoided."

"I'm not an alcoholic. I wasn't drunk. I'm not drinking now. I'm sorry. I'm sorry your mother is gone, Braelyn. *God, I am sorry*. And if you need to hate me to deal with Mom being gone, then I get it. But I've had enough with the attitude."

"Enough?" she laughed. Tears streaked her face. "You've had enough? You've had enough?" She laughed again. "She's only been gone for a month. And you've had enough?"

"Your mom wouldn't want this. Your mom wouldn't want us living like this. Blame me, Brae, but keep it to yourself. Your sister and brother are trying to heal. Ash is trying to recover."

"It was me," Ashton whispered.

"What?" Mark glanced at Ashton. Brae tugged at her arm again, but Mark still wouldn't let her go.

"It was me."

"What was you?" He shook his head.

She licked her lips and shook her head. Her eyes were on the clear liquor bottle on the counter.

"It was me. I was drinking," she whispered. She looked up, eyes meeting Mark's. "I didn't think anyone would know."

"What are you talking about?" Brae snapped.

"It started almost a year ago." Ashton frowned. She swallowed hard and then squeezed her eyes shut. "Oh God. Oh God. It was me, Daddy."

Mark's whole body flushed with an ice-cold flash of heat. He hadn't meant for this to happen.

"Daddy? I did it."

Ashton's words broke what was left of him. He opened his mouth to answer her, but he couldn't speak. And he couldn't breathe. There was a knife in his throat. He curled his fingers around the edge of the countertop to hold himself up. His wrist throbbed, and his heart pounded painfully hard in his chest.

"Didn't I?"

CHAPTER 38

ASHTON

Ashton desperately wanted to go to her room, her real room —not this *time-being* shit in Mom's office. She wanted to hurry to her room, slam the door closed, and climb in bed. Bury her face in her pillows and block the rest out. Dad and Braelyn. Mom's death. The wreck. The fighting—God, that was making her nuts. First Mom and Dad and now Brae and Dad.

Dad was looking at her now like she had just struck out in the bottom of the ninth, with bases loaded and two outs. He looked like he felt sorry for her, like he was going to jump the island and grab her and hold her, like maybe if he didn't, she would shatter, and all of her pieces would fall on the floor.

Wouldn't Mom love that? Just something else to clean up.

Mom's gone.

Jesus. How could she have known for sure just five seconds ago and turn around and think about Mom like she's here? This was killing her. Absolutely killing her.

She wished it would have.

She wished she were dead.

Dad was still watching her, and Brae was staring at her like she just rattled off something in code. *What? What had she said?* Ashton racked her brain to remember the words that had just gushed out of her mouth, completely without her control.

A confession? Had she just confessed to something?

Wait. She'd confessed—ugh, God, she hated that word—she had *talked* to Mom about Garret. She'd told her mom that she and Garret had been having sex and that was why she broke up with him, because she was tired of that expectation in their relationship now.

Ashton felt a wave of dizziness engulf her. She reached for a barstool to steady herself. Her eyes wandered back to the empty liquor bottles by the kitchen sink.

Jesus. Had she really told Mom about her and Garret? She turned away from Dad and Brae and stumbled with her crutches to the office. To her *room*. For weeks she didn't remember breaking up with Garret ,and now suddenly she remembered breaking up with him and telling Mom about it? Telling Mom that she'd been sexually involved with Garret. But, Mom hadn't freaked out about it.

Ashton felt like she was going to be sick. Her stomach rolled and clenched, the way it did when she was sick with the flu and wishing she could just vomit and feel better. Her head felt like it was going to explode, like maybe suddenly her brain was remembering things, and it had to grow and grow to hold all those memories in, and there wasn't room for it anymore.

She moved to the side of the bed and perched there, still holding onto her crutches. Just in case.

"Ash?" Brae asked timidly.

Okay, so apparently, she *had* been the one to break up with Garret, and she'd talked to her mom about it, and it had gone okay enough. Either that or there had been a big blow out with her and her mom and she didn't remember it. She didn't think so, though. Because her mom had been worried about leaving her at home alone that day. The day of the accident. The day she had told her about Garret and the breakup. Dad had wanted to go for dinner, just him and Mom, but Mom had insisted she come with them.

Ashton looked up. Her eyes locked with Braelyn's, but she didn't see her. Instead, she saw the kitchen sink and the empty liquor bottles. All those empty bottles. *What the hell?* They had triggered something huge, so huge she didn't get it, and maybe she would never get it without someone's help. Except who the hell was going to help her, because no one could see inside her brain to know what the hell it was thinking.

"Ash? Are you okay?" Brae whispered.

"Braelyn, why don't you go check on Ian?" Dad came up behind Brae. He still had that look on his face. Panic. He looked like the house might come down around them at any minute.

Then again, maybe that had already happened. Maybe Mom was the backbone of the house, and now she was gone, and they were all stranded here in the ruins.

"Daddy, what's wrong with her?" Brae asked. Ashton blinked them into focus, wondering what she must look like for them to talk about her as if she wasn't there. Maybe she looked crazy. She sure as hell felt it.

"I don't know," Dad answered quietly. "Let me talk to her, Brae."

Reluctantly, Braelyn backed away from the door. Ashton felt like all the air in the room whooshed out of it when Dad came in and moved to sit on the bed.

"Talk to me, Ash."

She shook her head. "I don't know. I don't. I just keep having these flashes. All these crazy flashes, and I don't know if they're memories or what. I don't know what's real. There's something..." Ashton shook her head again and pressed her fingertips to her forehead. "There's something right there. Right there, that I need to remember, and I can't."

"It's okay."

"It's not okay!" she wailed. "I hate this! I hate how everything is all fractured and broken. Even my mind is broken, Dad, and I hate it. I need to pull it all together. I can't take this anymore."

"I think you're pushing yourself too hard."

"Have you ever remembered half of something and the other half of something else? After Grandpa died, did you forget every other day that he was dead? Because that's what I'm doing, Dad, and it's making me crazy."

"Ashton."

She took a deep breath and continued, "I was standing in the kitchen, and something hit me. Like right between the eyes. Something huge hit me, and then it was gone, just like that. And now I feel sick, and I keep thinking about Mom and wondering if I really talked to her that morning. If I told her about breaking up with Garret."

"You did."

"I did?" Ashton stood up. "Did she tell you? Did I tell her that Garret and I were too serious? That everything was about sex, and I had to get away from it?"

Dad didn't answer her. She turned to see him staring at her in shock. Apparently, if she had told Mom that, she'd kept that part to herself.

"You know what?" She pushed on, ignoring the fact that Dad was a lap behind, still shocked, probably hurt by the fact that she had confided something—*that*—to her mom. "This whole year has been awful. It's sucked. Garret and school and thinking that I need to get a job and quitting volleyball. And Garret. God, Dad, I hated this year. I hated him. I hated dating Garret. I hated that every time we were together, he wanted to do it, and there was never anything else anymore. I hated that. I hated the homework and the tests and the ACT and worrying about college. Dad, I was going nuts. I just wanted..."

"What?" Dad cleared his throat. "You just wanted what?"

"I just..." Ashton, balancing on her crutches in the middle of the room, hung her head. "I needed something to break. To give. I needed the room."

Dad sighed and raised his eyebrows.

"Everybody needs something to break now and then, Ashton. That's normal. You were under a lot of pressure."

"Yeah, but now look where we are. Something broke, Daddy. We all broke, and Mom's gone, and I feel like it's my fault."

"Why would it be your fault?"

"I don't know," Ashton sobbed. "I don't know, but I feel like it's my fault that this all happened. It's my fault that Mom's gone. That you and Mom were fighting all the time. That Brae hates you now. This is all my fault."

"None of this is your fault." Dad's voice was calm and soothing. Suddenly, he was there, standing in front of her. She slumped against him and buried her face in his chest. She breathed deeply, comforted by the scent of his soap and aftershave. "It's all gonna be okay," he whispered. Dad put his arms around her and kissed the top of her head.

"Nothing's ever gonna be okay," she answered. "I want Mom."

"I know, baby. I do, too."

"I have to remember." Ashton started to push him away, but both stopped and turned to look out the open office door when the doorbell rang.

Dad sighed, clearly frustrated.

"I'll be right back," he told her and then kissed her forehead. Ashton hobbled out to see who was there. Braelyn appeared down the hall as Dad opened the door.

"Hi, Mark." Adrie Fuller, still dressed for her workday, raised her eyebrows.

"Adrie." Dad leaned against the door and scrubbed his left hand over his face. He shook his head and then rubbed his neck.

"Can I come in?"

"Um." Dad frowned and looked over his shoulder at her and then Braelyn. "It's not really a good time."

"Ian called me, Mark," she said quietly.

"Ian? Called you? When?"

She shrugged. "Ten minutes ago?"

Ashton felt a pang of pity for Dad. He was trying. He was trying to put things back together, and he still missed Mom, and Brae hated him, and she had just dumped a load of shit on him. And now, here was her mom's best friend on the doorstep. What was she doing here? God, Ashton hoped she wasn't here to throw any more blame around.

"Can I come in?" Adrie asked again.

"It's just..."

Adrie laid her hand on Dad's chest and gently pushed him aside so she could come in. "Mark, let me help."

"You can't help," he mumbled. "There's no easy fix here, Adrie. I appreciate—"

"If it was easy, maybe it wouldn't be worth fixing."

CHAPTER 39

MARK

"Look, Adrie, I know you want to—"

"Daddy?"

Mark glanced at Ashton. She was pale. Pale like death, except her eyes. They burned bright and wild. Windows to the soul, blah blah blah. Cut to the chase, Ashton was having a breakdown, and he had two other kids to worry about. One of them was witnessing the breakdown—and hell, she was a twin. *What about that?* Was Brae feeling any of this? Was there anything to all that twin stuff? Did Brae's leg bother her because Ashton's was broken? Were Brae's mind and heart racing the way Ashton's were? And what about Ian? He had called Adrie; obviously he was upset. Mark hated that. He knew he should be sheltering him from all of this, but how? How was he supposed to protect Ian from Brae's bitterness? From her hatred? From Ashton's pain? He couldn't just banish him to his bedroom, although Mark wondered now if that's where he was. Probably curled up on his bed, snuggled up with Moses.

The thought made him hurt. Literally. He felt a rush of ice-cold heat moving up through his arms and his chest and wondered for a just a minute if this was a heart attack. His little boy was terrified right now, without his mother, with a loser for a dad, and with older sisters who were flipping out right in front of his eyes.

How in the hell was he supposed to do this? By himself? How did he handle all three of them at once? The hell of it was he knew that somehow Kamryn would have handled it. Mostly with grace, though now and then she had needed to lean. Now and then she had leaned on him, and now and then she had been angry or frustrated or—probably, Mark guessed now, out of her mind—and all she had needed was for him to listen.

All those times when he' call home to talk to her and she was distracted or worn out or snappy, all she had needed was for him to listen. To understand that as much as she loved their kids, *because* she loved their kids so much, being the one at home, in charge, took a toll.

He got it now.

"It's just not a good time," he mumbled, turning back to Adrie. He rubbed his hands over his face, exhausted.

"I'm not here for chit-chat, Mark," Adrie answered. "Let me help."

"It's not like I need someone to fix dinner or clean the house, Adrie." He stood up straight. "This is just something the girls and I need to work through."

Adrie looked over his shoulder to Brae, who was cowering further back down the hall, near the kitchen. She glanced at Ashton and then looked back at Mark.

"I don't think that's going very well."

"It's just family stuff."

Adrie nodded. "And Kam was my family, Mark. Let me—"

"Daddy?" The word exploded out of Ashton. He turned to look at her again. The panic was written in her eyes, in her mouth, twisted and turned down. In the fresh onslaught of tears that fell now. "Daddy? Was I driving?"

Mark felt that rush of icy heat again. This time he staggered backward and reached to rub his chest, just over his heart. He thought it might have stopped beating. He had been desperate to avoid this. The words stunned him, but he couldn't show it. He couldn't let Ashton see that. He couldn't let anyone see the way her words had affected him.

"Dad? Oh God." Ashton took a deep breath. She covered her face, sobbing again. Her crutches fell to the floor and clattered on the tile. "Oh my God. It was me. It was my fault."

"No!" Mark hurried to Ashton, forgetting that Adrie was standing there in his entrance hall. "No! It wasn't your fault."

"Daddy!" Ashton raised her face to look at him. Her skin was splotchy and red, and her eyes were swollen and red-rimmed. "I was driving. Mom didn't want you to drive. But. Oh my God."

Mark reached out, tried to take her in his arms, but she shook her head. She put her hands on his chest and held him back. "I had been drinking. I drank all day, Dad. I drank all day, before Mom made me go with you guys."

He felt himself deflate. Shrink. He had felt small since the accident, but he felt everything inside him drain away now. He had tried to fix this. He had tried to hide this, praying that Ashton had forgotten. That it would stay buried, and she would never have this guilt.

"You drank all day?" Brae spoke up from behind them. Slowly, she walked toward them, her face a mask of confusion. "What do you mean you drank all day? Ashton, what're you talking about?"

"It was me," Ashton whispered. "Oh my God, it was me."

Mark sighed.

Adrie moved up behind him and reached for Ashton's hand. "Ash, honey, let's go in the living room."

Ashton didn't move.

"C'mon. You need to sit down. You're exhausted. Your leg is going to be throbbing pretty soon, the way you've been on it here."

Mark stepped back and let Kam's friend slip her arm around his daughter. Braelyn picked the crutches up and handed them to Ashton. Both stepped out of the way as Adrie and Ashton moved slowly down the hall to the living room. Mark avoided Brae's eyes for as long as he could, but finally, there was nothing else to look at. Not the floor or the walls. He had to see her. To see her face. He had to know what she was thinking.

Still, when their eyes met, he felt a little jolt of fear. He didn't want Brae to hate him, but he couldn't stand the thought of Brae hating Ashton for what happened.

"Daddy?"

He didn't hear her so much as read her lips.

"Really?" she whispered. "Ashton?"

Mark stared for a moment longer, and then he dropped his gaze. He took two steps toward Brae, needing to know what she was thinking, what she was feeling. But Ashton was in the living room with Adrie, and he was worried about her. He needed to hold her, too.

"Why did you lie?" Brae's voice was still no more than a whisper.

Mark swallowed hard and then glanced toward the living room.

He didn't want to get into this. He didn't want to even admit to this. Not to Ashton. Not to Braelyn. Not to anyone. It had nothing to do with the police and the accident report or the fact that he had lied. He didn't want Ashton to grasp this memory fully. To know she had been the one driving the car.

He would never have guessed that she'd been drinking all day. She seemed fine when she took the keys from him and dropped into the driver's seat. And if she had been drinking all day and seemed fine, then apparently, she'd been drinking all day for a lot of days, and apparently, she was the one hitting the liquor and the wine and God knows what else in the house. Kamryn had been right, They'd had a hell of a serious problem on their hands.

And he hadn't listened. He hadn't believed Kamryn. He had accused her of overreacting. He'd been hurt by her hammering about the alcohol, and he had been hurt and angry that she hinted that he might want to be with other women when he was on the road, and he had been a complete ass.

He hadn't listened.

And now his wife was dead. And his daughter had figured out the truth.

This wasn't Ashton's fault. It wasn't Kamryn's fault. This was on him. He should've known what was going on, and he should've stayed on the same page with Kamryn instead of dragging his feet and dropping so far behind the rest of them.

Mark moved closer to Braelyn. His throat ached with emotion, so much that he couldn't speak. Instead, he reached out and touched her face. Skimmed the back of his fingers over her jaw and then cupped her chin in his hand.

Tears brimmed in her eyes, and a picture of a three-year old Braelyn flashed through his mind. She had tumbled off her tricycle and scraped her knees up. Mark had picked her up to take her inside. He used a cold, damp cloth on her knees and then dabbed a bit of Neosporin on the scrapes and bandaged them.

All the while, Brae had cried crocodile tears and held onto a handful of his shirt, scared to let go.

He had done that. Not Kamryn.

Brae ducked her chin into his hand and closed her eyes.

Mark dropped his hand and walked to the living room. Ashton sat on the couch, enveloped in Adrie's arms. Her whole body shook with her sobs. He felt his stomach fall as Adrie raised her eyes to his.

She mouthed the word *come*, and then she shifted Ashton in her arms and slid off the couch, making room for Mark. He sat down and drew Ashton against him.

"Gonna check on Ian," Adrie said so quietly he wondered if he imagined it.

Ashton cried long and hard, and at some point, Mark realized he was crying, too. For Kam. For Ashton. Brae and Ian, who had been scarred as deeply as he and Ashton, even though they hadn't been in the car that night.

When Ashton pulled back and rubbed her face, Mark realized Brae was sitting in the recliner. Knees drawn up against her chest, arms circled around them, she hunched over as if she was trying to make herself smaller. Tears and mascara streaked her face.

"Do you hate me?" Ashton whispered. Mark thought she was talking to Brae, but when he looked down at her, he saw that her eyes were trained on him.

"No."

Ashton shifted a bit in his arms, head against his chest, and looked at Brae. "Do you?"

Brae pressed her lips together and shook her head.

"You should. I killed Mom."

Brae shook her head again. "It was an accident."

"Why? Why is it an accident now? Now that you know it was me and not Dad?"

"Don't," Mark said quietly. "Don't do this to each other." He smoothed Ashton's hair and rested his chin on her head. "It was an accident. And if anyone's to blame, it's me."

"But I was driving."

"But I missed it," Mark said simply. "Your mom saw everything, and I missed it. And it's my fault."

"I did it…just to…get through. To get by."

Mark knew she meant the drinking. It crushed him, made him breathless to know that Ashton had been so lost, under so much pressure that she'd chosen to drink to get through it. To survive it. Why hadn't she talked to Kam? Why hadn't she come to him and Kam sooner and told them how she felt?

"It's not the answer, Ash."

"I liked the way…" She started, faltered, and then continued, "I liked the way it made me numb."

"You're sixteen," Mark said gruffly. "You shouldn't need to be numb."

"I'm sorry." She squeezed her eyes shut and tried to wipe the tears away.

"No, I'm sorry." Mark wished he could say it to Kamryn. He desperately wished he could say those two words to Kam. *I'm sorry.*

"You were dumping it. The stuff in the cabinet." Brae said it as a statement rather than a question.

He nodded. "I kept telling your mom she was…" Mark's throat ached again. He took a quick breath and then shook his head. "I didn't know. I just knew it wasn't me."

"Ashton, why didn't you just talk to me?" Brae wailed. "Instead of drinking, why didn't you talk to me? Or Mom?"

Ashton raised her eyebrows and took a deep breath. She was trying to control herself, to keep herself from crying again.

"Just wanted to be numb," she repeated in a tight voice.

Braelyn dragged her fingers back through her long, tangled hair. "God, I wish Mom was here."

Mark wished Kam was there, too. He could feel Ashton trembling against him. Brae rubbed her eyes for a minute and then like a flash, she jumped out of the recliner and hurried out of the room.

He was torn. Brae needed him. Ashton needed him. He needed them both, but he couldn't comfort them both. Not at the same time. Not right now.

"Just go." Ashton tried to scoot away.

"I can't."

"She needs you."

"You need me," he answered.

"Yeah, but I'm a killer, Daddy." She looked up at him with sad eyes. "You can't help me."

"Ashton McHale." He drew her close again and pressed her face to his chest. "I love you."

"Don't."

"It was an accident. It doesn't matter who was driving. It was an accident."

"It does matter. It's my fault that Mom's gone."

"No. No." He leaned his cheek on the top of her head. "It's not your fault, and I'm not going anywhere right now."

Adrie. God, Adrie, please check on Braelyn.

He knew he needed to go after Braelyn. But how could he possibly get up and walk away from Ashton right now? How could he leave her alone with her guilt? He had been fighting that demon since the wreck. Fighting and losing. How could he leave his broken sixteen-year-old alone to fight that battle? Guilt was a damned formidable enemy. He was afraid of what it might drive her to do.

CHAPTER 40

MARK

Mark held Ashton until shadows fell across the living room. She had cried, and then she had gone dry-eyed and quiet. Though the crying was hard, the quiet was worse. Mark could almost see through Ashton's huge, round eyes and into her mind, and he knew she was remembering. She was remembering the accident, and probably each time her mind went through it, another detail came back. Each time, the scene was probably clearer, and soon, Ashton would remember the whole thing. The sounds of the metal crashing against metal and the way Kam had hit her head and the blood and the eerie silence after the screech of metal on metal had stopped. That silence had snuck up on Mark more than once since that night. The silence. No crying. No talking. The way he'd been the only one in the car awake and the way the fear had jolted him and made him move. He had been so damned scared they were both gone.

She wouldn't remember that, Mark reminded himself. She was out. She couldn't remember that part of it, anyway. But still. It was against the law to do what he had done. To change the layout of the accident. It had been risky moving Ash to the backseat. Lying and saying he was driving. But there was blood everywhere, and he was relatively sure the police wouldn't test the blood in each cracked window. Not if everything looked as it should when they got there. Not if they thought he'd been driving, and they had given him a breathalyzer test.

He had known then that his actions would have dire consequences, but he hadn't cared. And he didn't care now. He wouldn't change anything. Nothing other than Kam dying and Ashton putting the pieces together now.

When the shadows had overtaken the living room, and he and Ash sat in darkness, Adrie walked Braelyn back into the room. Arms around each other, walking close together, they looked like Kamryn and Adrie, back in their college days. Kam wore her hair longer then. Mark's heart sort of twisted when he saw them. He just needed to talk to Kam. And yet, reality slammed into him. Kam was gone, and Adrie had come to help him with his children, with *Kam's* children. Braelyn looked lost and so small. He turned a bit on the couch, Ashton asleep now against his chest, and opened his other arm to Brae.

She was reluctant at first. He wondered what she was thinking. Did she hate him for lying? Would she always hate him, just a little bit, because of all the fighting before the wreck? Because if he had just listened to Kamryn, if he had listened and paid attention, maybe things would be different now.

He didn't blame her. Mark would never blame Braelyn for a second of her hatred for him. He would carry the guilt with him every day of his life, and his daughter's hatred was packed tight inside that guilt. But he loved her. He loved both girls desperately, and he loved Ian, and suddenly, he felt a gaping hole that had nothing to do with Kamryn and everything to do with his kids.

Who the hell was he kidding? Everything to do with Kamryn.

Everything.

Braelyn moved slowly at first, and then suddenly, she was there, sitting beside on him on the couch, her head against his chest.

"I'm sorry, Daddy," she whispered. Her tears wet his shirt. He closed his arm around her and sat in silence, with his girls in his arms. Grateful for that much but wishing for Ian.

Wishing for Kam.

"I guess I really fucked things up," he mumbled. His voice was gruff after hours of only whispered comfort for Ashton.

Adrie shook her head. "There's no right way to do this, Mark," she said quietly. "You were trying to protect them."

"If I'd have listened to Kam."

"Don't." Adrie, standing in front of him, reached out as if she was going to touch him. She let her hand drop to her side. "Just don't. You have to let that go. Love her." Adrie tapped her chest, above her heart. "Love her, Mark. But let go of the rest. Because you have to show them how to move on."

Mark kissed the top of Brae's head and then turned to Ashton. He turned his head and rubbed his cheek over Ashton's hair.

"She forgets things. She keeps forgetting that Kam's gone. And then when she remembers, she has to go through it all over again."

Mark saw Adrie wince.

"How many times will she have to relive tonight?"

"I know it's hard," Adrie answered. She squatted down in front of him and pressed a hand to his knee. "But secrets don't stay secrets. No matter how deep you bury them, they find a way out tear families apart. They both had to know."

Mark swallowed hard. "Where's Ian?"

"Upstairs. I found him in your bed, curled up with Kam's pillow."

"Dammit."

"We had a snack. Gave him some cookies and a glass of milk. He's asleep in his bed now."

"Moses?"

"Snuggled right up under Ian's arm. I think they might be out for the night."

Mark sighed. "I suck at this. I don't know how Kam did it."

Adrie shook her head. "Huh-uh. You don't get off that easy, Mark McHale. You buck up, and you do it. These kids need you to be their father."

"I don't…"

"Kam needs you to do it."

"I don't know how."

"You think Kam had a parenting manual?" Adrie's voice dripped with sarcasm. "You get up in the morning, and you put one foot in front of the other. You do it."

Mark dropped his head back on the couch and closed his eyes.

"You do it for Kamryn. That woman loved you and these kids more than life. Honor her memory, Mark."

He would rather have heard the words from Kamryn, but they still touched him. Maybe not really deeply inside his heart, the way Kam's voice would have made them. But they did touch him.

"And one more thing?"

He was so tired. God, he was tired. He opened his eyes and focused on Adrie, standing in front of him again.

"Ask for help."

"I'm the family pariah, Adrie. I killed my…"

"You're not a pariah, Mark. No one killed Kamryn. There was an accident." He saw her glance at Ashton. "There was a car accident. And it took her way too damned young. But the rest of you are here, and the rest *of us* are here, and we're waiting for you to reach out. Ask for help when you need it."

He started to argue but held his tongue. She was right. He hadn't killed Kamryn. *Ashton* hadn't killed Kamryn. It was an accident, and they were lucky to be alive, and he was lucky Brae and Ian hadn't been with them. It was an accident, and there had been enough blame and hatred. It was time to move forward. To take the next step.

Adrie disappeared into the shadows. Her shoes clicked on the tile floor and then the front door opened.

"Adrie?" he called softly, hoping he would catch her.

"Yeah?"

"Thank you."

He heard her clear her throat. Maybe she was hurting just like he was. Finally, she answered him.

"You're welcome, Mark."

He laid his head back on the couch again and closed his eyes.

You get up in the morning and put one foot in front of the other.

Helping his children grieve for their mother didn't mean he was putting her away. Forgetting her.

Honoring her? Is that what Adrie had said?

The worst of it was out in the open now. Probably Ashton would relive that moment of discovery over and over, and probably Mark needed to find someone for her to talk to. Hell, maybe they all needed therapy.

He would do it. He would make some calls and find someone. He would keep them all home from school tomorrow, and they would spend the day together. No detailed plans. No big dinner. Just the four of them, together. Alone.

Not an anniversary, but a goodbye.

And a beginning.

~

Thank you for reading Two Story Home. Please consider leaving a review on your favorite bookish site.

. . .

KEEP READING for a look at the women's fiction book, Just Like Them.

.

SNEAK PEEK AT JUST LIKE THEM

Prologue

October 2010

Teel

The blood had splashed over her arms and her shirt and even splattered her face, and she thought of the miscarriage. The second one, the way the blood had soaked through her shorts and then streaked her legs.

The girls didn't even know about the miscarriages, and so she found it funny that she would lie in bed and chase sleep and think about those babies. Keegan was not the middle child, no matter how you looked at it, and so it wasn't about birth order.

There had been three of them, one before Rachel and two between Rachel and Keegan. The first had been hard. So hard to be young...Well, they'd gotten married a little later and gotten pregnant a little later but still...In terms of pregnancies and motherhood, aren't you always young the first time? She and Bobby had wanted that baby so badly, and she'd ignored her mother's advice and purchased baby clothes and blankets and newborn diapers and then one day, just after the end of the school day, she'd sat at her desk grading English worksheets and felt a twinge in her belly.

The twinge hadn't bothered her. But by the time she left the school to go home to Bobby, she'd been in the grips of full-blown abdominal cramps, and she'd known that baby wasn't meant to be. Her second pregnancy had ended with beautiful Rachel, and she and Bobby had given her the moon anytime she'd reached a fat little hand for something and made a noise that resembled anything like *Daddy* or *Mommy*.

The miscarriage with the blood—the bad one—came when Rachel was just a year old. And though she'd told Bobby it was silly to blame himself, she often wondered if by making love too soon after Rachel and getting pregnant so quickly, if they'd done something to hurt her body or her chances of carrying a baby to term. Intellectually she knew that was ridiculous. Though doctors didn't advocate for women to get pregnant immediately after giving birth, it did happen, and most women and babies were fine.

She'd been further along than the first miscarriage, and she'd suffered through what seemed like hours of labor pain and Bobby had taken her to the hospital. Dr. Cash had said there was nothing he could do. The blood was so sticky and thick, and she remembered how it had seemed unfathomable that this blood had once been part of her baby.

The blood today had been warm like that, and a little sticky, but not thick. If she breathed too deeply, she could still smell the cloying scent, and she gagged, and then Bobby stirred in his sleep. She didn't want to wake Bobby. He had to be on site at six a.m. so he needed his sleep, and besides, what good would it do for Bobby to be awake? He'd held her earlier, until she'd finally drifted off to sleep, but dreams woke her, and she couldn't decide what was worse: the dreams or being awake and feeling the blood splash over her.

Funny that she would be thinking of those babies now. God knows there was so much she should be thinking about. And yet, no amount of thinking was going to change anything. Part of her thought she should get up and figure out how to help Keegan, but then part of her wondered just what the hell could be done to help Keegan. Exhausted, with her body aching from lying awake so long, she rolled to her back and turned her head on her pillow to look at Bobby.

He wore his age so well. Even now, after the blood—there had been buckets—and dealing with Keegan, and the looks her colleagues were sneaking in the hallways, she could look at him and see how attractive he was. She didn't quite feel the stirrings of desire she normally would, but that was okay. Not tonight.

Maybe it was just the blood. The sudden onslaught of warm, sticky blood would disturb anyone, and so maybe it was just the tactile memory of the miscarriage and maybe that's why she couldn't sleep for thinking of her babies.

The second one was a boy. She'd failed to give Bobby a son, though he'd never complained. He loved the girls just as much, if not more than she did. They'd have named him Robert Michael, after Bobby, if she could have carried him to term and given birth.

Maybe it was the pregnancy test stick she'd used just this morning, before the blood.

Maybe it was Keegan. Fear of losing her. Or maybe it was the fear that they already had lost her.

Want to keep reading Just Like Them?

Click here:

Just Like Them

ABOUT THE AUTHOR

Tracy Broemmer is the author of several contemporary romance novels including the 515 Whiskey Series, Shameless Santa, and the Mississippi Queen Trilogy. Tracy also writes women's fiction and is the author of the Williams Legacy series as well as several stand-alone titles.

Tracy's books have been called gripping, emotional, and timely, and readers describe her characters as real and relatable

Tracy lives in Midwestern Illinois with her husband of 30 years. Visit her on the web and sign up for her newsletter at www.broemmerbooks.com

ALSO BY TRACY BROEMMER

Women's Fiction Novels:

Luther's Cross (10th Anniversary Edition)

Fairytale (Writing as Therese Kinkaide)

Just Like Them

Small Hours

Picket Fences

Two Story Home

Green-Eyed Girl

Say Everything

Come Home for Christmas

Sketching Litchfield Lake

Ever, Again

Safe as Houses

Damsel

The Valentine Suite

Women's Fiction Series in Order

Lorelei Bluffs

Every Little Thing

Two A.M.

Blind

Leaving July

Hesitation Marks

Four Letter Words

See Kate

Loved You More

A Lorelei Ending

I Do

The Williams Legacy

Truth Is

Other People's Ugly

Omissions

Women's Fiction Short Stories

India Falls

Luther's Cross: 87,600

The Candy Cane Tree of Willow Lane

Delays

Same Time Next Year

Contemporary Romance Novels

Destiny's Calling: Your Future is Waiting

Wedding Day Shenanigans

Holiday Fling

The Kiss Off

Something Like Love

Plus One

End in Flames

Contemporary Romance Series In Order

The Mississippi Queen Trilogy

Love, Nashville

Forever, Duncan

Always, Jess

Truly, Dante (A Short Story)

The H Books

Gettin' Hitched

Hookin' Up'

Holdin' On (A Novella)

Timberton Hounds (Novellas)

Priceless Memory (A Short Story)

Endless Summer

Homeless Holiday

Restless Hearts (Currently included in Fall Into Love, an anthology
by Fluffy Fox Publishing)

515 Whiskey

Intoxicate Me (A Novella)

Taste Me

Rings on Wings

The Wine Tasting Series (Short Romantic Stories)
Perfect Pictures (Traminette)
Coming Home (Edelweiss)
Save Me Every Dance (Rosé)
Marry Me (Shiraz)
Birthday Wishes (Muscat)
Dad Jeans (Vignoles)

Contemporary Romance Novellas

Boone's Girl
Today, Again
Indian Summer
Dear Jaclyn Perris
Mistletoe Mishaps
Deadman's Hollow
French Stuff
Holdin' On
Toasted
End in Flames
Endless Summer
Homeless Holiday
Feels on Wheels
Rings on Wings
Intoxicate Me

Contemporary Romance Short Stories

Truest Love (Currently included in Show of Dreams anthology)

Swipe for Fangs (Currently included in the anthology Welcome to Whynot)

Mrs. Bennett

Peppermint Lane

The Principles of Accounting

Strawberry Wine

Love Letter

Sambuca Santa

Truly Dante

Leaving You

Priceless Memory

Perfect Pictures (Traminette)

Coming Home (Edelweiss)

Save Me Every Dance (Rosé)

Marry Me (Shiraz)

Birthday Wishes (Muscat)

Dad Jeans (Vignoles)

Other Novellas

The Devy Man, A Horror Novella
The Keeper's Heart, A Horror Novella

Anthologies

Just Coffee — French Stuff (2020)

Snowed Inn, Vol. 1 — Holdin' On (2020)

Aced, Back to School — Boone's Girl (2021)

Snowed Inn, Vol. 2 — Delays (2021)

Sweet Treats — Peppermint Lane (2021)

Sweet Sprinkles — Same Time Next Year (2022)

Rescue Me — End in Flames (2022)

Fall Into Love — Feels on Wheels (2022)

Cool Off — Endless Summer (2022)

Fall Back Into Love — Rings on Wings (2022)

Backing the Bluegrass — Leaving You (2022)

Kissing Santa Claus — Sambuca Santa (2022)

Let's Get Naughty — Homeless Holiday (2022)

XOXO — Trusting Cupid (2023)

Mrs. Right — Mrs. Bennett (2023)

Tease Me — Taste Me (2023)

Falling for the Boss — The Principles of Accounting (2023)

Ride a Cowboy — Seducing You (2023)

Love and Coffee — Makin' Whoopsie! (2023)

Fall Into Love — Restless Hearts (2023)

Welcome to Whynot — Swipe for Fangs (2023)

Let's Get Naughty, Volume 2 — Kissing You (2023)

Show of Dreams — Truest Love (2023)